A DEATH IN BERLIN

By Simon Scarrow

The *Eagles of the Empire* Series

The Britannia Campaign
Under the Eagle (AD 42–43, Britannia)
The Eagle's Conquest (AD 43, Britannia)
When the Eagle Hunts (AD 44, Britannia)
The Eagle and the Wolves (AD 44, Britannia)
The Eagle's Prey (AD 44, Britannia)

Rome and the Eastern Provinces
The Eagle's Prophecy (AD 45, Rome)
The Eagle in the Sand (AD 46, Judaea)
Centurion (AD 46, Syria)

The Mediterranean
The Gladiator (AD 48–49, Crete)
The Legion (AD 49, Egypt)
Praetorian (AD 51, Rome)

The Return to Britannia
The Blood Crows (AD 51, Britannia)
Brothers in Blood (AD 51, Britannia)
Britannia (AD 52, Britannia)

Hispania
Invictus (AD 54, Hispania)

The Return to Rome
Day of the Caesars (AD 54, Rome)

The Eastern Campaign
The Blood of Rome (AD 55, Armenia)
Traitors of Rome (AD 56, Syria)
The Emperor's Exile (AD 57, Sardinia)

Britannia: Troubled Province
The Honour of Rome (AD 59, Britannia)
Death to the Emperor (AD 60, Britannia)
Rebellion (AD 60, Britannia)
Revenge of Rome (AD 61, Britannia)

The *CI Schenke* Thrillers
Blackout
Dead of Night
A Death in Berlin

The *Wellington and Napoleon* Quartet
Young Bloods
The Generals
Fire and Sword
The Fields of Death

Sword and Scimitar (Great Siege of Malta)

Hearts of Stone (Second World War)

Writing with T. J. Andrews
Arena (AD 41, Rome)
Invader (AD 44, Britannia)
Pirata (AD 25, Rome)
Warrior (AD 18, Britannia)

Writing with Lee Francis
Playing With Death

The *Gladiator* Series
Gladiator: Fight for Freedom
Gladiator: Street Fighter
Gladiator: Son of Spartacus
Gladiator: Vengeance

SIMON SCARROW
A DEATH IN BERLIN

HEADLINE

First published in 2025 by
HEADLINE PUBLISHING GROUP LIMITED

1

Cataloguing in Publication Data is available from the British Library

Hardback ISBN 978 1 4722 8727 4
Waterstones exclusive ISBN 978 1 0354 3229 5
Trade paperback ISBN 978 1 4722 8728 1

Map and artwork by Tim Peters

Typeset in Garamond by CC Book Production

Printed and bound in Great Britain by Clays Ltd, Elcograf S.p.A.

HEADLINE PUBLISHING GROUP LIMITED
An Hachette UK Company
Carmelite House
50 Victoria Embankment
London EC4Y 0DZ

The authorised representative in the EEA is Hachette Ireland,
8 Castlecourt Centre, Dublin 15, D15 XTP3, Ireland
(email: info@hbgi.ie)

www.headline.co.uk
www.hachette.co.uk

For Luigi Bonomi,
'Fargli un'offerta irrifiutabile . . .'

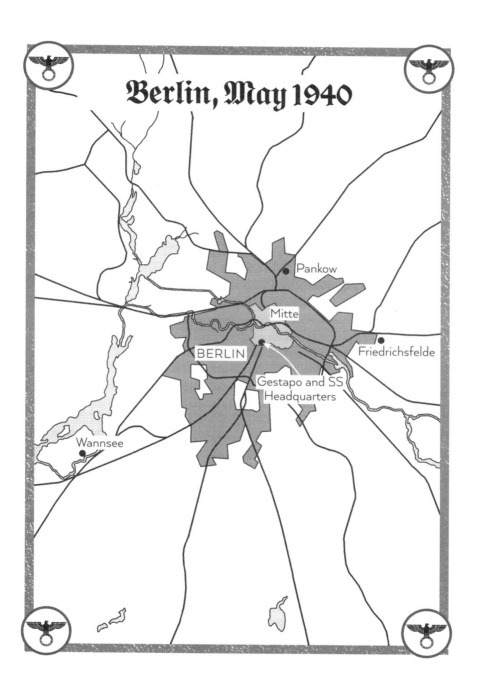

The Chain of Command

The Führer
Adolf Hitler

Reichsminister of
Food and Agriculture
Richard Darré

Reichsführer-SS
Heinrich Himmler

Reichsminister of
Public Enlightenment
and Propaganda
Joseph Goebbels

Chief of the Reich
Main Security Office
Reinhard Heydrich

Head of Abwehr
(Military Intelligence)
**Admiral
Wilhelm Canaris**

Head of
Kriminalpolizei
Arthur Nebe

Head of Gestapo
Heinrich Müller

Commander, Pankow Police Precinct
Oberführer Helmut Radinsky

Head of Pankow Kripo Section
Horst Schenke

Author note

Writing about life in Germany during the Third Reich inevitably brings an author face to face with some of the darkest aspects of human nature. It's impossible to write honestly about the time without referring to some of the attitudes of and terminology used by those in the regime. I hope that I have handled this aspect of the novel with sensitivity.

Chapter One

Berlin, 4 May 1940

Otto Bachmann took a sip from his beer glass as he surveyed the audience seated before him. The spotlight reduced them to dark shapes, to the extent that he could barely distinguish men from women, and even then some of them were probably cross-dressers, so who could tell them apart? Before the Nazis had seized power, such a thing would be common enough. The clubs and cabarets of the German capital were frequented by those who experimented with their couture and identity. But after seven years of iron rule by the Führer and his regime, there were few places where that was now possible.

The Ace of Hearts club was one of the handful remaining whose clients could dress and mingle freely. Amongst them were men in suits and Nazi Party uniforms, and the mistresses and girlfriends they brought with them to enjoy the forbidden shows and refreshments that were denied to the rest of Berlin's inhabitants. It was as if there were two worlds. The stern, stiff and, of course, patriotic reality of public life and the secret inner world into which most people silently retreated, from where they regarded the gaudy pageant of the Third Reich at a remove. The Ace of Hearts occupied a space

1

between the two. Those who entered the club understood and accepted that what happened within its walls remained there. The norms imposed on life outside were left at the door, and inside people could express themselves more freely. To a degree, at least.

That was understood by the club's owner, Max Remer, who had befriended influential members of the party for many years before they came to power. Back then he had mixed with politicians of all persuasions. After 1933, he ruthlessly cut ties with those declared *persona non grata* by the Nazis, even before they began to eliminate their rivals and banned political opposition. He cultivated his Nazi connections and his club was safe from the attentions of the police and the paramilitaries. He had been shrewd enough to join the party just before its leader had been appointed Chancellor of Germany, and thus escaped the contempt reserved for the opportunists who rushed to join once the Nazis had taken over.

Bachmann could see the club's owner sitting in a special booth close to one side of the modest stage, and noted the irritable flick of Remer's wrist as he indicated that he should get on with his act. Clearing his throat, he winked at the audience and prepared to deliver his finale. He had worked his way through a repertoire of jokes about the Jews, the soft, self-indulgent French and the insipidly effeminate British, and milked the audience's appetite for such low-hanging fruit. Now he needed to offer them something more daring than they were inclined to accept in the world outside the club. Something to make them laugh spontaneously before they took that self-conscious gasp of surprise and then laughed again at their timidity in such safe surroundings.

'You know, I sometimes wonder about some of the great men of state who are leading our glorious race of supermen to victory over our enemies . . .'

'To victory!' a voice slurred as a young officer punched a half-empty champagne bottle into the air and shot some of its contents over his female companion, who scowled and then snapped her expression into one of gleeful delight before he noticed her displeasure. 'Germany over all others!'

'Indeed, sir!' Bachmann grinned. 'With heroes like fat Hermann and tiny Joseph leading the way, how can we lose?'

There was laughter from the crowd. Bachmann had picked his targets wisely. A comedian he'd once known had been rash enough to have a crack at Himmler a year earlier and had disappeared shortly afterwards. Disappeared completely. The eyes and ears of Himmler's agents were everywhere, and while they might tolerate jokes made at the expense of others, mocking the Reichsführer SS and the Führer was suicidal.

'Speaking of Joseph,' Bachmann continued, 'have you ever wondered how a runt like him could have risen so high?' He pursed his lips. 'It's a good question and one I've heard many people ask. They say how is it possible for club-footed little Joseph to be one of those leading the way for the master race? Well, I'll let you into a secret, my friends. Our Joseph wasn't always a shrimp. Back in the old days, when he was sent to Berlin to lead the Nazi effort here, he was a tall, strapping fellow. What? You don't believe me? I can assure you it's true. I was there. I saw it with my own eyes. He was a head taller than our beloved Führer and the envy of almost every man.' He nodded and took another sip of beer. 'But our Joseph had a problem . . . A very small problem.' He leered as he raised his hand and wiggled his little finger.

There were sniggers from the audience and a few ribald comments.

'It seems that whenever he got it out, the women just laughed at him. If he got as far as the bed, they'd never know if he was inside them or not.'

A quick glance revealed Remer's cruel grin and Bachmann was relieved. Beside the club's owner sat his current mistress, a tall blonde who called herself Kitty rather than the more prosaic name she had been christened with. She took Remer's expression as a cue and chuckled dutifully as Bachmann went on.

'Anyway, a man's pride can only take so much, and Joseph, being the good Catholic boy he was back in those days, goes down on his knees one night and begins to pray.' Bachmann put his glass down and clasped his hands together as he stared up at the ceiling. '"Lord God almighty," he says. "Dear God, I have been a good man. A righteous man. A loyal servant of the party and our divinely anointed leader. Why have you cursed me with a dick the size of a peanut? I pray, I beg you to reward me for my years of sacrifice." At that moment, a thunderous voice fills Joseph's bedroom: "What is it you ask of me? Speak, and it shall be granted." Joseph replies in a flash. "I want the biggest dick that ever was! I want a dick so long that it touches the floor!" "Very well," says God. "Go to sleep, my son. In the morning you will wake up and it shall be so. Bless you."

'So Joseph dives under his covers and clamps his eyes shut and counts sheep until he passes out . . .' Bachmann chewed his lip for a moment. 'Well, when he wakes up, he leaps out of bed and drops to the floor – to find that his legs are a metre shorter!'

Most of the audience roared with laughter, though a handful

of the more inebriated or slow-witted looked around bemused. Bachmann saw that Remer was laughing, and he sighed with relief. As long as the club's owner was amused, he was safe. He beamed at his audience before raising his hands as the laughter subsided. 'Thanks, ladies and gentlemen! That's all from me tonight!'

There were hoots and clapping as Bachmann raised his glass and stepped off the stage. Remer, still smiling, beckoned to him and pointed to the red leather upholstery of the seating opposite. Bachmann felt his pulse quicken with anxiety. He'd hoped to beat a quick retreat to the bar, share a few laughs with the customers and cadge free drinks off them before he left. Instead he'd have to sit with the boss and warily tread whatever fine line Remer chose to torment him with, as he had done many times before.

The next act, a thin man wearing tails and burdened by a large accordion, was settling onto the stool that Bachmann had vacated. He tested a few keys as Bachmann slipped onto the seat and nodded a greeting.

'You've nearly finished your beer.' Remer gestured to the glass with a finger upon which a jewelled ring glinted. 'You must be thirsty. What'll you have?'

'I'm fine, boss.'

Remer glanced round and waved to a waiter, who scurried to him at once. 'A bottle of Dom Perignon. Make sure it's been chilled properly.'

The waiter bowed his head and disappeared into the gloom.

Bachmann forced himself to smile. 'Thanks. Throat's always a bit dry after a performance.'

'I would imagine so. I'd feel the same way if I had just told a joke about the Reichsminister of Propaganda. You never know who might be listening.' Remer stared at him, his dark eyes like polished ebony unblinking for a few long seconds before his lips lifted in the slightest of smiles. 'Take it easy, Otto. You're safe . . . Unless I decide you're not.'

Bachmann tried to hide the tremor in his voice as he laughed briefly and shook his head. 'You had me there, boss.'

Kitty exchanged a fleeting glance with him before she tapped Remer playfully on the sleeve. 'You big kidder!'

Remer's lips parted a little further to reveal large, neat teeth, white as piano keys. 'As I was saying, Otto, that's quite a joke. I'd be careful about telling it again.'

Bachmann indicated the customers at the other tables. 'Seemed to go down well enough, boss. The crowd liked it.'

'Yes, they did. But you see, Otto, that's the kind of joke people used to get away with. Now Germany is at war. And that means our political masters are going to be sensitive to any criticism, however innocent.' He suddenly reached over and took one of Bachmann's hands, closing his powerful fingers over it tightly. 'I'd hate for one of my customers to be indiscreet enough to repeat your joke outside the club. You know how it goes. Word gets round. Someone high up – someone who doesn't share our sense of humour – starts asking who is responsible for the joke. Before you know it, the boys in black leather coats beat down your door and make you disappear. More to the point, they might start taking a closer look at my club, my business, and that would never do. You understand?'

Bachmann nodded. 'Sure, boss.' He winced as Remer tightened his grip.

'You're hurting him,' Kitty said. 'Max . . . you're hurting him. Stop it.'

Remer flashed a steely look at her before he released Bachmann's hand and reached for a silver cigarette case inside his black velvet jacket. He helped himself to a cigarette before offering one to Kitty and then snapping the case shut. He struck a match from the bowl on the table, and a lurid red flare lit up his saturnine features before he inhaled, paused, and exhaled swirls of smoke in Bachmann's face.

The comedian fought back a cough and attempted to look composed. The glare of the spotlight had caused him to perspire, and now fresh sweat broke out on his brow. He was heavily built, with a round, boyish face that caused women to want to mother him – something he used to seduce them. But despite his heft, there was less muscle than fat on his frame. Unlike the lean-featured club owner opposite.

Bachmann had witnessed two drunks accost Remer and Kitty outside the club at New Year. Remer had floored the pair of them and then kicked them unconscious before straightening his tie and coat, putting his arm back around Kitty's shoulder and calmly entering the club as if nothing had happened. The drunks had been lucky. Men had died for less, according to word on the streets of Berlin. Bachmann had heard the details from someone who really knew where the bodies were buried. Some of them at least.

Remer aimed the glowing tip of his cigarette in Bachmann's direction. 'That was a good set tonight, Otto. The punters laughed. That pleases me. Just work on your material. Ease up on the powers-that-be and go for the obvious targets: the French, the British, communists, Jews – that sort of thing. My customers come here for cheap laughs and expensive drinks. Not to be provoked into second thoughts about Germany's leaders. It's too late for that. The Weimar days are long gone.

Dawn of a new age and all that. Those who don't adapt become extinct. Clear?'

'Blindingly so, boss.'

Remer chuckled. 'Very well. You can go.'

Bachmann hesitated. 'No champagne?'

'Don't push it, Otto. Use the side door in case one of Joseph's admirers decides to take exception to your quip.'

Bachmann rose to his feet as the first strains of a drinking song sounded from the accordion player. There was a rousing cheer from the crowd before they started to belt out the opening lines of the first verse. Keeping to the side of the room, he made for the door to backstage, closing it behind him with a sigh of relief.

Back in the booth, Kitty was still for a moment before Remer spoke in an undertone.

'You disapprove of the way I treated him.'

'I didn't say that.'

'Didn't have to. Your silence was thunderous.'

She turned towards him. 'All right, yes. I disapprove. Otto draws a good crowd. You wouldn't want to lose him.'

Remer gave a dry laugh. 'Not much chance of that. Where would he go? There aren't any other clubs that would tolerate his line of humour. No, he'll stay here and he'll be grateful for it. That's why he'll do as I tell him.'

'Someone else you can keep under your thumb, eh?' she remarked as she tapped the ash from her cigarette.

The waiter arrived with the champagne, uncorked and in an ice bucket, together with three flutes.

'The other gentleman will not be returning to the table,' Remer said. 'Take the spare glass away.'

The waiter nodded and filled the flutes, then strode off towards the bar. Kitty lifted her glass and took a belt.

'I needed that.'

'Enjoy it while you can. There's only a few dozen bottles left in the club's cellar. We're going to run short. Until France is defeated.'

Kitty arched an eyebrow. 'How likely is that? I thought the Führer was pushing for a peace deal.'

'Maybe not . . .'

'What have you heard from your party friends?'

'Enough. Let's just say things are about to get interesting, and if it works out, the Führer and his boys are going to be around for a long time. A very long time. So we have to stay on good terms with them, my dear. They're like any other criminal gang. They don't play by the book, so you keep them sweet.'

She nodded, then looked down into her near-empty glass. 'Are you afraid of them?'

'No sane man isn't. But right now, I have more pressing concerns. There are others I need to look out for.'

There was movement towards the rear of the club, near the main entrance, as four men entered. Three of them wore coats and hats. The fourth was pinned between two of his companions and was dressed in a suit, with cap pulled down over his eyes. One of the others indicated the direction of Remer's office and led his companions up the stairs beside the counter where the hat-check girl sat on a stool looking bored.

Remer set his glass down and rested his cigarette on the edge of the ashtray. 'I have some guests to attend to, Kitty. Enjoy the champagne.'

He slid out of the booth, put his hands in his jacket pockets and made his way around the tables to the stairs. Kitty watched him go, then leaned back and listened to the accordion player, though her mind was filled with dark thoughts about the future.

Remer closed the door to the office, cutting off the din from the drunken singing in the club. The room was carpeted, and oak-panelled around the bottom of the wall. There were framed posters and pictures of the stars who had graced the Ace of Hearts since he had taken over the club fifteen years earlier. A large leather-topped desk stood angled across one corner, close to the window that overlooked the interior of the club. Beside it stood a safe and some locked cabinets. The men who had preceded him up the stairs stood in the opposite corner, the dishevelled man held down by his shoulders on a plain wooden chair.

'So tell me, Wohler, where did you find our friend?' Remer asked.

The broad-shouldered man who had led the small party into the club took off his hat before he replied. 'He was at the Augsburgkeller. We waited until he came out and grabbed him in a nearby alley.'

'Did you make sure you weren't seen taking him?'

'Quite sure, boss. It was dark, no one else around. We bundled him straight into the back of the van.'

'Good work.' Remer turned to the man sitting in the chair. He was young, in his early twenties, his blonde hair shaved at the sides but left with a wave on top, as was the fashion. He reminded Remer of himself back in the day. Attractive and ambitious. But the man had been foolish enough to think he could cheat on his employer and get away with it. Remer had been loyal to his former crime boss until the day he had been gunned down by a rival gang outside the club. Since then he had demanded absolute loyalty from his own followers, just as he had given it before he took over the gang.

'Wilhelm Feldwitz,' he began in a weary tone, 'I am disappointed in you. How long have we known each other?'

'Listen, Max, it's not how it looks—'

'Five years.' Remer spoke over the top of him. 'Five years . . . You were a street boy at the time, living off pickpocketing, and I took you in and gave you a job managing the club. I saw you had potential and raised you up through the organisation. You've done well for yourself. Your own apartment, nice clothes and decent money. And blessed with a pretty face.'

Wohler gave a dry sniff of amusement.

'So, Wilhelm, you owe it all to me.'

'I've always been grateful . . .'

'So you should be.' Remer raised his hand and frowned as he recalled that he had left his cigarette resting on the ashtray at the booth. He glanced down through the window and saw that Kitty was still sat there, staring fixedly into the middle distance. He took out another cigarette from the case and used the heavy brass lighter on the desk. 'I don't like people who repay my kindness with disloyalty, Wilhelm. Not because I take such things personally, but because it's bad for business. It makes me look weak. It makes me look like a man who doesn't have control over those who work for him. That kind of thing can be dangerous in our line of work. So tell me, how long have you been selling my ration coupons to Paul Guttmann?'

The younger man affected a frown. 'I don't know what you're talking about . . .'

'Of course you do.' Remer smiled. 'Perhaps you need a little incentive to refresh your memory.'

He nodded, and Wohler opened his fist to deliver a hard slap across the younger man's face. Feldwitz blinked and rolled his head as a dribble of blood seeped down his chin and dropped between his feet.

'Not too hard, Wohler. I don't want to spoil the carpet. Work his ribs and gut next time.'

'Sorry, boss.'

'Now then, Wilhelm, I'll ask again. How long?'

'I swear I don't know—'

Wohler slammed his fist into the young man's stomach, causing him to fold forward with an explosive gasp before his minders wrenched him upright.

Remer took a steady drag on his cigarette. 'Don't insult my intelligence. I know exactly how many coupons have been printed and who we have sold them to. You were the one tasked with delivering them to our customers. No one else. So tell me, how else did Fat Paul get his hands on our product?'

The young man made no attempt to reply, and Remer clicked his tongue. 'You know, you might have got away with it if Guttmann hadn't recently started to sell coupons to our customers. And so word inevitably gets back to me. What was the plan, Wilhelm? Salt away a small fortune and then slink off to Hamburg or someplace and start over? Do you think I wouldn't have been able to track you down? You fool . . .'

He drew on his cigarette again and the tip flared bright red. 'Hold his head still.'

Wohler clamped an arm around the young man's neck and clenched his fist amid the fair hair. The other minders pinned his arms so that their prisoner could barely move, even as he strained with all his strength.

'You are out of the organisation, Wilhelm,' Remer said. 'You go back to the gutter where I found you. But I'll leave you a parting gift, something to remember me by. Something others will see and know that you betrayed me.'

'Please, Max . . . don't!' Feldwitz managed to grunt through clenched teeth.

Remer's lip lifted in a sneer as he eased the end of the cigarette towards the young man's face. Feldwitz clenched both eyes shut. Remer used his spare hand to force the lids of the left eye apart and pressed them back to expose the eyeball and iris. He thrust the cigarette home with a soft hiss and a wisp of acrid smoke. His victim let out a keening whine as every muscle in his body tensed.

Remer stubbed out the ruined cigarette on Feldwitz's cheek. 'Throw him out of the back of the club, once you've given him a beating. If he tries to show his face here again, make sure he disappears for good. Now get this piece of shit out of my office before he pisses on the carpet.'

Kitty looked up as Remer returned to the booth. She noted his sour expression.

'Trouble?'

'Not any longer. The matter has been sorted out.'

'What matter?'

'It doesn't concern you, Kitty. If it did, I'd say.' There was an edge to his voice. 'I've told you before – don't ask questions about my business.'

'You think I don't know what you do? Who you are? I've seen more than enough of what goes on. I'm no fool. I can use my eyes.'

'I know. That's one of the reasons I'm attracted to you.' Remer picked up his champagne glass and took a sip, then set it down with a look of distaste. The chill had gone off it. 'Kitty, I like you. I really do. But you need to understand something. Too much knowledge can be a dangerous thing. Best to ignore what goes on here. Whatever you see, you keep to yourself. Same goes for whatever you think you know about me and my business. For the good of those eyes of yours.'

She glanced at him, and then looked away with a shudder.

They stayed at the club for another hour, until the accordionist had been replaced by an exotic dancer clutching long fake feathers, with which she caressed her body, steadily revealing more of herself with a knowing look at her drunken, leering and cheering audience. Remer and Kitty barely exchanged another word, and drank little of the fresh bottle of champagne he'd called for. Just after midnight, he stirred.

'I've had enough. We're going back to the flat.'

He signalled to a waiter and instructed him to have the car brought to the front of the club. He helped Kitty out of the booth and they went to collect their coats and hats from the cubicle by the stairs. He left her waiting a moment while he went up to his office, coming back with a gleaming leather briefcase containing the club's takings for the previous month. A man at the entrance opened one of the double doors that gave onto the pavement, and they stepped out into the night.

The street, not far from the centre of the capital, was subject to the strict blackout conditions that had darkened every city and town in Germany. Windows were shrouded by thick material, street lights switched off, car headlamps masked, with only narrow slits to allow the merest beam of light to guide drivers. Even bicycle lamps were similarly concealed. The only concession to the safety of the people of Berlin was occasional strips of luminous paint on the kerb stones to differentiate road from pavement. Even so, the number of accidental deaths had soared since the imposition of the blackout. As had muggings, rapes, murders, prostitution and shady black-market dealing. The war had caused all manner of crimes to flourish, and Remer welcomed the conflict.

He stood with his arm around Kitty, holding her protectively. The night air was cool but not cold, and yet he sensed her trembling.

'The car will be here in a moment,' he muttered.

They heard the engine as it approached, a sleek, black four-door Daimler Double Six with a wide running-board and elegantly curved wings over the wheel arches. At a time when the party had ordered that all civilian cars be handed over for military use, there were still plenty on the streets of Berlin. Remer was permitted to keep his car so that he could carry out 'vital contributions to the war effort as a party member'. That permission had been approved by a senior official in the propaganda ministry who was a frequent recipient of a share of the proceeds and goods from Remer's black-market activities. Moreover, he had been gifted a Nazi stormtrooper to serve as his driver. The brown uniform was useful in discouraging any uniformed police from asking questions.

The vehicle pulled up outside the club with a ratcheted click of the handbrake. The driver darted round to open the rear door. Remer handed Kitty inside and glanced at the unfamiliar features of the driver, barely visible by the light of the dashboard dials.

'Who are you? Where's Kurtz?'

'He's been taken ill, sir. I've been assigned to you temporarily.'

'Your name?'

'Sturmmann Schlemminger, sir.'

'Schlemminger, eh?' Remer took in the man's solid build and the neat array of his webbing and lanyard beneath his cap. 'All right, we're heading to my flat on . . .' He hesitated.

'Kurtz told me the address, sir. Hangelstrasse in Pankow. I know the way, even in the dark.'

'Very well.' Remer climbed in beside Kitty. A moment later, the car pulled away, heading north towards Pankow.

Remer muttered in Kitty's ear. 'I'm not sure he is who he says he is.'

'Why wouldn't he be?'

'I've never known Kurtz take a night off since he started driving for me.'

He leaned forward to address the driver. 'Who ordered you to take Kurtz's place?'

Schlemminger kept his gaze fixed on the barely visible road ahead of the Daimler.

'Came from the top, sir. I work as a messenger at the ministry. Just happened to be there when Kurtz called in to say he was ill.'

'Called? He doesn't have a phone.'

'No, sir. He used the one in the block warden's apartment.'

'I see . . . Who gave you the order to replace Kurtz?'

'Schlacter, sir.'

Remer dimly recalled the name and put a face to it an instant later. A sallow, bald man who had been an academic until Goebbels had given him a job at the ministry. He eased himself back beside Kitty, reassured. She took his hand, squeezed it slightly and gave him a questioning look.

'We'll be fine. Besides . . .' He patted the bulge in his coat where he kept his leather cosh, a relic from his days as a street fighter for the party.

The Daimler made its way through the dark streets beneath a moonless sky. Only the brightest stars glinted through the thin smog hanging over Berlin. Some five minutes after leaving the club, halfway to the apartment as far as Remer could calculate it, the vehicle slowed and the driver muttered something to himself in an irritable tone.

'What is it?' asked Remer.

'Looks like a detour, sir.' Schlemminger indicated a figure in the street, just visible in the narrow beams of the headlights. He wore the coat and hat of one of the uniformed police, the Orpo, and he flicked on his torch and indicated a narrow alley to the right. The driver turned the wheel and drove the Daimler into the alley. The dark, tall bulk of factory warehouses and tenements loomed on either side. Then the headlights picked out a grimy stretch of wall at the end of the alley.

Remer leaned forward. 'What the hell is this? You bastards! Kitty, get down!'

The car drew up abruptly. Behind them the policeman approached the rear of the car.

All was quiet on the main street, then there was a series of dull flashes of light from the alley, and several loud reports crashed out, echoing off the walls on either side. Running footsteps sounded and then faded into the distance as a woman cried out in agony and screamed for help.

Chapter Two

Pankow Police Precinct, 5 May

'I am Oberführer Radinsky.' The precinct commander gazed down at his subordinates from the narrow platform. His men were gathered in the canteen for the monthly ideological education session. Their muted conversation died away abruptly as they turned their attention towards him. Radinsky had taken over from an acting commander at Pankow ten days earlier, following the suicide of his predecessor. This was his first opportunity to address all his men, aside from the handful patrolling the streets at this, the quietest time of day from a policing point of view.

He clasped his hands behind his back and lifted his chin slightly. He was a tall man, slender and in his mid thirties. Even though he had an alert expression and youthful features, his hair was already almost entirely grey, with only a darker patch on the crown of his head. He wore the uniform of the SS, which had raised a few eyebrows when he had first arrived at Pankow. Although a number of those at the precinct had accepted SS rank, in addition to that of the police, none had taken to wearing the uniform at work.

Radinsky cleared his throat and continued. 'Some of you

may be wondering why I was appointed to Pankow. The fact is that the precinct has achieved a certain reputation at the Reich Main Security Office. A reputation for being slack in enforcing the law. A reputation for being on the take. A reputation for having a significant number of those not in step with the ideology of the Reich. I have been sent here, on the direct order of Obergruppenführer Heydrich, to crack down on the lazy, the corrupt and the un-German alike. I have been sent to rebuild the reputation of the precinct and restore the honour of those who serve in the police. I will not tolerate any person who stands in the way of that. You will match the standards expected of you by the German people, or you will be kicked out of the precinct. Those found to be corrupt or harbouring un-German values will face the severest of punishments.' His cold grey eyes swept over those standing in the mess hall. 'I trust I have made myself clear.'

He turned to another man in SS uniform standing at the edge of the platform. The latter had been sent from the head-quarters at Wilhelmstrasse to deliver the lecture.

'Carry on.'

Radinsky stepped to the side as the junior officer carried a lectern to the centre of the platform and set it down, before taking the sheets of typescript from under his arm and arranging them before him. He swallowed nervously, then began in a loud, flat voice. 'Comrades! You are well aware of the challenges facing our sacred mission to win the necessary space for those of our blood to settle, tame and civilise for the benefit of mankind. You have read about the conditions encountered by our victorious soldiers in Poland and seen the newsreels depicting the barbarous nature of the Poles and the squalid, subhuman conditions in which they live. These are only exceeded in their repulsiveness by the character and manner of Poland's Jews.' He looked to the rear of the mess hall. 'Curtains, if you please, and ready the projector.'

While some men drew the blackout blinds across the windows, another turned on the projector, casting a bright shaft of light over the heads of the policemen. As soon as the last of the daylight was cut off, the projectionist started the propaganda reel. The clarion shrill of trumpets from the speaker attached to the projector filled the room as the familiar *Deutsche Wochenschau* newsreel titles flashed up on the screen. The narrator's breathless delivery recounted the glorious conquest of Poland over footage of Polish soldiers throwing down their rifles in front of grinning German soldiers and the unfurling of swastika banners from the balconies of public buildings while subdued civilians looked on.

At the rear of the mess hall, a small group stood slightly apart from their uniformed comrades. These were members of the precinct's Kripo section, the elite criminal investigation division of the police. Inspector Horst Schenke, a wiry figure, wore his wavy brown hair slightly longer than the austere cut sported by most men in Germany. In Berlin there was still something of an anti-authoritarian edge that characterised most of the capital's inhabitants, despite the best efforts of the regime. Schenke sat on the edge of a mess table, arms folded as he watched the newsreel.

'For God's sake, how many times have we seen this kind of thing?' the man at his side grumbled. 'You'd think Poland was only defeated yesterday . . . It's been six months.'

Schenke glanced at the thickset man with close-cropped hair. Sergeant Hauser was second in command of the ten men and two women of the section. A veteran police officer of twenty years, and before that a veteran of the imperial army who had served on the Western Front. He was a party member, but lax in his adhesion to its dogma.

'Just be thankful that the leadership are still rejoicing in this victory,' Schenke muttered. 'Rather than picking any fresh fights.'

'France and Britain are still in the game,' Hauser countered.

'True, but for how long? It's too late to save Poland and they're being given a good beating in Norway, so what is there to gain from continuing the war?' Schenke said in a dry, sardonic voice. 'As the Führer keeps pointing out.'

It was a line of argument Schenke had heard on many occasions and one that was often seen in newspaper articles presenting Hitler as a man of peace, striving to put an end to hostilities. However, there was a growing sense of anxiety in Berlin about the prospect of the war spiralling into a more dangerous conflagration. Schenke felt it keenly, though he shared such thoughts with only a handful of those he knew well enough to have trust in their discretion.

The newsreel moved on with a fresh title – *What is to be done with lesser races?* – accompanied by more trumpets, before the tone of the music shifted into a sinister register. There followed a montage of peasants standing beside their shacks, and then Jews in run-down suburbs. Schenke lowered his gaze and stared at the worn floorboards as his thoughts switched to a Jewish woman he knew, intimately and therefore illegally. Ruth had spent some weeks at his apartment until the bitter winter gave way to the first days of spring. She had had to live in silence while he was out, in case the neighbours detected her presence, and both of them were relieved when she found a room in a house close to the Siemens plant, where she now worked long hours for a pittance. He had not had a word from her in nearly a month and was anxious for news.

When he looked up again, the newsreel had moved on to a different topic and a new caption filled the screen: *Bringing law and civilisation to the east!* The narration extolled the courage and determination of the police battalions that were hunting down the remaining Polish partisans and clearing the farms and urban property of Jews to make way for German settlers. Schenke paid little attention to the details, and the newsreel soon came to an end with another flourish of trumpets.

'Open the blinds!' the Nazi education officer called out as the projector shut down. The curtain rails rasped and beams of light filled the mess hall. The officer glanced at his notes and addressed the audience.

'The last section was of particular relevance to police comrades. There are great challenges facing the Reich's mission to impose order on our new lands to the east. The police battalions already there are doing a fine job, but they are too few for the immensity of the challenge facing them. Therefore, new battalions are being formed to go to their aid. I am proud to announce that one is being raised here in Berlin and the call has gone out to experienced men to volunteer. We've already had a large number of volunteers amongst the young men of Berlin, eager to enlist . . .'

'No surprise there,' Hauser growled. 'Gutless creatures hoping to serve in a cushy, safe billet rather than wait to be drafted into the army and face an enemy that can fight back.'

It was a fair complaint, Schenke conceded. He had not heard of reports of casualties amongst the police battalions serving in Poland. Policing the conquered territory was surely a safer duty than being drawn into any wider conflict that might yet embroil Germany. He glanced over at the members of his section who were present. Persinger was in his forties and married. It was doubtful that he would volunteer for the new battalion. But Baumer, married the previous year, was younger and ambitious – he might well choose to serve and seek promotion to impress his wife. It was regrettable, since he showed some promise as a criminal investigator. Then there was Liebwitz, who had been transferred to the section from the Gestapo. Schenke had no clue what Liebwitz was thinking. The man's gaunt face gave nothing away as he watched the presentation. The others – Frieda Echs, a mature woman with close-cropped dark hair, and Rosa Mayer, tall, blonde and young – would not be eligible to serve in the field. In any case, given her expensive taste in clothes and perfumes, Rosa would not dream of leaving such luxuries behind. Working for the police was one of the few occupations that the Nazi Party exempted from its exhortations for women to perform the roles of wives and mothers. The remaining members of the section were off duty and fortunately spared from having to attend.

Schenke felt a familiar guilt and unconsciously reached down to his left leg. A motor-racing accident several years ago had left him with a limp and unfit for military service at a time when every man was needed to defend the Fatherland. Hopefully the conflict would end soon. The campaign in Norway was the only place the opposing armies were clashing. Elsewhere, the occasional naval and aerial skirmish aside, they stared at each other across the no-man's-land stretching along the heavily fortified French frontier while laughing at the crude propaganda leaflets dropped by the enemy. It was as if their respective governments were terrified of being drawn into repeating the horrors of the trench warfare of the previous conflict.

The education officer's tone became more sombre as he concluded his address. 'National Socialist comrades, those who volunteer for the police battalions will be making a vital contribution to the German people's mission to rid Europe of the Jews – the eternal enemy of our race. The Jews who cunningly seduce decent Aryan women, infiltrate our society, our professions, our businesses and our seats of learning to spread their poison against us. While at the same time closing ranks against us, absolutely refusing to mix with the hosts upon whom they prey like parasites, so that they might better plot in secret to bring down the Aryan race.'

Schenke saw Liebwitz raise his hand, an earnest frown on his bony face as the lenses of his round spectacles glinted in the light from the nearest window.

'Ah, Christ, there he goes again,' Hauser sighed. 'Might have guessed our former Gestapo boy might chip in.'

The education officer looked down the length of the mess hall at Liebwitz, momentarily unsure how to respond. 'Uh, it is customary to await the ending of the lecture before asking questions. I, er . . .'

He turned to Radinsky, who gave him a curt nod.

'Very well. What is it?'

Liebwitz spoke in his customary flat tone of voice. 'Sir, you say that Jews are seducing our women.'

'Yes. It is well known.'

He nodded. 'I have read some material on the subject in the *Black Corps* journal. However, surely they will find such a thing difficult to achieve if at the same time they are refusing to mix outside of their race. The two activities would seem to be mutually incompatible.'

The others in the audience turned to look at him, and some chuckled. Liebwitz had been seconded to Schenke's Kripo section from the Gestapo a few months earlier to observe an investigation into a politically sensitive murder. It quickly became clear that the real reason for the move was that the man's awkward manner and uncompromising intelligence was not appreciated by his Gestapo companions. He had since proved his worth as a diligent investigator, and Schenke had willingly accepted his request for a permanent transfer to the Kripo.

The education officer blinked, then checked his notes and coughed before he responded. 'Yes, that is typical of the cunning demonstrated by the Jews.'

Liebwitz frowned. 'That still doesn't account for—'

Radinsky stepped to the centre of the platform. 'The session is over. We have work to do and I am sure our comrade from the ideological education division has other pressing engagements he needs to attend to.'

The education officer nodded quickly as Radinsky took a deep breath and called out to his subordinates, 'Heil Hitler!'

The majority of the audience snapped out their arms and echoed the phrase. There were others, though, who looked surprised, as it had not been common practice under the previous precinct commander. They hesitated too long, Schenke and his section amongst them, and failed to join in before Radinsky and the others lowered their arms.

'Dismissed!'

The audience began to file out of the doorway behind the projectionist, who was already removing the spools and packing them away. As the Kripo section climbed the stairs to their office on the first floor, Hauser fell into step alongside Schenke.

'Bit of a starched collar, our new precinct commander.'

Schenke nodded. 'True, but not necessarily a bad thing. Particularly as far as Orpo are concerned. You know how it is. Some of them are on the gangs' payroll. We could do with having them weeded out of the precinct.'

'Maybe. Just as long as he leaves our lot alone and lets us get on with our work. This ain't the bloody army. We're professionals, we are. Not a bunch of monkeys in uniform.'

Schenke was accustomed to his subordinate's disdain for the uniformed police, and he smiled. 'Say that again, louder. I'm sure there's some in the basement who may have missed your assessment of their worth.'

'Ach, you start using long sentences like that and you'll confuse them.' Hauser turned and looked down at Liebwitz, who was a few steps behind them. 'Scharführer, why did you go and ask that question?'

Liebwitz shrugged his thin shoulders. 'He stated two apparently contrary propositions. I merely sought to direct his attention to that in order that he justify his comments. What is the purpose of an educational presentation if some of its premises are flawed?'

'Ah, but it wasn't flawed.'

Liebwitz raised an eyebrow. 'No?'

Hauser paused to let the younger man catch up, and then patted his shoulder. 'You'd better start getting used to holding two opposing ideas in your head if you're going to be a good party member and ever hope to be promoted beyond the rank of Scharführer.'

'That'll do, Sergeant,' Schenke interrupted. He was weary of Hauser's constant ribbing of the Gestapo man. Particularly as Liebwitz, through some flaw of character, was unable to judge whether the sergeant was mocking him or addressing him with candour, which resulted in a measure of distress. He needed more time to get used to his new Kripo comrades and their world-weary manner, which had been hardened by the harsher kinds of crime they had to deal with.

Back in the section office, the others returned to their desks and Schenke beckoned to Hauser. The sergeant followed him into the small cubicle in the far corner of the grey-painted room. Schenke took his seat and indicated the thick file on his desk. Hauser had no need to twist his head to read the label on the cover.

'That damned ration coupon forging case never goes away.' He grimaced.

Schenke nodded. 'Seems so. No one we've questioned on the streets or hauled in for interrogation will give up the names we need to track down the source of the coupons. We've nailed plenty of street dealers, but almost all of them prefer to do time in the Sachsenhausen camp rather than turn in their suppliers. The few who did crack merely got us one rung up the supply chain.'

'They're afraid. They're all afraid.'

'Quite. But I think we might have finally had some luck.' He flicked the file open and handed the top document to the sergeant. 'It's a copy of a report from the Kripo section in the Templehof precinct. They've got a lead on the fake coupons being traded. It points to a crime ring run by Paul Guttmann. Heard of him?'

Hauser nodded. 'He ran a protection racket in Mitte before

the party came to power. After that, he moved into clubs and brothels. Our Paul has a certain reputation for violence. More than a few bodies have been fished out of the Spree with his trademark left on their skin.'

'Trademark?'

Hauser nodded. 'His initials carved into their chests. Served as a warning to anyone thinking of crossing him. Most of that was before your time, though. Back in the days of the Weimar government. Before Adolf and his lads came in and drove many of the criminals underground, or at least off the front pages of the newspapers. You know how it goes: if it isn't reported, then the government gets to say it ain't a problem.'

Schenke made no comment. Even though he trusted Hauser, he still felt wary about openly criticising the party in front of one of its members.

He gestured towards the report. 'Seems like Guttmann has expanded into the black market since the war started, like most of his kind. Some of his men have been caught dealing the forged coupons, and more were discovered after their places were searched.'

Hauser smiled. 'Looks like we might have finally discovered the source.'

'Maybe . . . I don't know. The forgeries have been found right across Berlin. Do you think Guttmann's ring has developed that kind of reach so quickly?'

'It's possible,' Hauser countered. 'Since the war kicked off, hundreds of police have been transferred to the army and sent east. The blackout hasn't helped. Once it gets dark, we virtually lose control of the streets. It's feeding time for every petty crook, and especially the crime rings.'

'But they do like to protect their turf, and I find it difficult to believe that Guttmann is now one of the major players in Berlin.'

'Then it's possible that he wants to be, and is making his move by cornering the market for forged ration coupons. There's a fortune to be made out of that. High stakes. If Guttmann is behind it, there's going to be trouble with the other crime rings. They'll want a piece of the action, and if he refuses, there'll be blood on the streets and we'll be fishing bodies out of the Spree until it's over.'

'Or we get to the source of the coupons, smash the ring and destroy their printers.'

Hauser sat back and crossed his arms. 'What's to prevent some other ring starting up their own production of forged coupons?'

'They need the official ink if they want the coupons to pass muster. Someone is supplying them with that. Someone close to the official printing process in the food ministry.'

Hauser instinctively looked round before he lowered his voice. 'You need to be careful who you say that to, sir. You know that the powerful people have their fingers in every damned pie in the country. If it's one of their own, and they have the right connections, then you'd better have balls of steel if you want to take that on. And you'll have to go through Radinsky. The SS put party first, almost every time. You know it.'

Schenke could not help a dry chuckle. 'If that's what it takes . . . But if we're going to put an end to the forgeries, then our best chance is to tackle it from both ends. Find the ring that's turning them out and find out who's supplying them with the official ink.' He glanced through the glass partition into the section office and fixed his eyes on Liebwitz, who was ordering his desk with his usual serious expression. Files, notepad, pencils and his pen were arranged perpendicular to each other and the edges of the desk. He leaned back and regarded the arrangement, nodded in satisfaction and reached for the first document in his in-tray.

'I think it would be best to assign Liebwitz to tracking down the ink supplier. He knows his way around the Reich Main Security Office, and if there's any trouble with the party, he can fall back on his SS membership to offer him some protection.'

Hauser sucked a breath through his teeth. 'Not sure how much good that will do him. The only reason he's here is because Heinrich Müller wanted to get him out of the Gestapo and dump him on someone else.'

'He applied for the transfer,' Schenke reminded the sergeant.

'And you approved. Thanks to which we have one of Müller's boys in the office watching us like a hawk. I don't much care for it. Even if he's *persona non grata* at Prinz Albrechtstrasse, how do we know we can trust him?'

Schenke had dealt with his sergeant's suspicion of Liebwitz on several occasions and tried to keep the frustration from his voice as he responded. 'He's proved himself to be useful to us. He has the kind of mind we need in Kripo. He's methodical and will see a task through to the end.'

'He's like a machine, sir. Machines aren't perfect. Sometimes you have to act on gut instinct in our line of work. Look here, I'll admit he's good on details and he's smart, and he can handle himself well when the bullets fly.' Hauser paused.

'But?'

'He's just odd. He doesn't fit in. He doesn't have any friends. He's not one of us.'

'He is now, Sergeant. You'd better get used to him.'

Hauser was about to renew his protest when they were interrupted by a rap on the glass. Schenke looked up to see Rosa Mayer outside.

She opened the door enough to put her head round the frame. 'Sorry to interrupt, Inspector, but Oberführer Radinsky wants you up in his office.'

Hauser raised an eyebrow.

'Did he say why?' asked Schenke.

'No, sir.'

'Very well. Thank you.'

Mayer closed the door and returned to her desk.

'What do you think it's about?' asked Hauser.

Schenke smiled. 'I think it's about time to find out.'

'Ha ha.' Hauser left the office, leaving the door ajar.

Schenke examined his reflection in the glass, checked his tie and made sure his mid-brown hair was neat enough to avoid drawing attention to it. He had the kind of features that suited his profession – a certain blandness of appearance. His calm reserve contributed to that and had won the respect of those who served under him. But the same inscrutability often caused his superiors to regard him with caution, if not outright suspicion.

He cleared his throat and muttered, 'On my way, Oberführer . . .'

Chapter Three

The precinct commander's office on the top floor of head-quarters had changed considerably from the last time Schenke had been in the room. The previous incumbent had had family photos on the desk and mantelpiece, a bookcase laden with manuals and files, and a homely rug on the floor. There was no sign of any such personal touches, even though Radinsky had taken up the appointment nearly two weeks before. There was a replacement desk and chair, and the interior had been painted a uniform light grey. The only reminder of his predecessor was the small hole in the high ceiling where the bullet that had blown off the top of Oberst Kleist's skull had passed through and buried itself amid the rafters.

Oberführer Radinsky was standing at the window over-looking the courtyard at the rear of the building. The window was open and a cool early-spring breeze wafted into the office along with the sound of birdsong and the distant hubbub of the capital. His thumbs were resting inside his jacket pockets and his hands were loosely balled into fists.

Even though the door was open, Schenke paused on the

threshold and cleared his throat to announce his presence. 'You sent for me, sir.'

Radinsky turned to glance at him before he resumed staring out of the window.

'I noticed a certain reluctance from you and your Kripo companions to join in with the German greeting in the mess hall earlier. Care to explain the reason for that?'

The Oberführer's tone was mild, but his question sent a chill down Schenke's spine. He stepped into the room and stood erect as he responded. 'Sir, it has always been the custom for Kripo officers to operate in a more informal manner than our uniformed comrades.'

'Really? How quaint.'

Schenke could not help raising an eyebrow. 'It is the same across all Kripo sections, sir.'

'Not for much longer if I have anything to do with it. I will be reporting on the matter to Obergruppenführer Heydrich and recommending that all police officers, regardless of the branch they serve in, use the German greeting. No exceptions. And that will start here in Pankow. Kindly ensure that there is no repeat of this morning's omission.'

'Yes, sir.'

Radinsky turned away from the window, crossed to the desk and sat down, fixing his gaze on Schenke in a silence long enough to make him uncomfortable.

'I am taking a little time to get to know my subordinates at the precinct. Reading their service files, as well as those we keep at the Reich Main Security Office, before talking to them in person. You are the last on my list.' He smiled. 'No need to feel offended, Schenke. As a matter of fact, I was leaving the best until last. Your service record is exemplary. You were one of the most impressive in your intake and you have proven yourself to be a highly successful criminal investigator in the years since. Why, I have even heard Heydrich mention your name. What was it he said?' He closed his eyes as he recalled the words. 'Ah yes! "I have every confidence in Schenke's abilities. If only he had accepted the offer to come and work for me." He went on to say, "I wish I could be as confident in his loyalty to the regime."' Radinsky frowned. 'Why do you think he would say that?'

Schenke kept his expression fixed as he wondered about the context of such a comment. The thought of his being a part of any conversation involving Heydrich was unnerving. He cleared his throat and replied in as calm a tone as possible. 'I imagine the Obergruppenführer was pleased by the outcome of the recent cases I handled that came to his attention, sir.'

'Doubtless. But I am more interested in his final statement. Is there any reason for him, or myself, to doubt your loyalty, Inspector Schenke?'

Any trace of the earlier mildness of tone had gone, and there was an intensity to Radinsky's stare that tempted Schenke to look away, but he forced himself to return his superior's gaze as he replied.

'No, sir. No reason at all.'

'I am pleased to hear it. Good!' Radinsky relaxed his posture. 'I have no doubt that you will continue to serve under me with the same diligence as you served the late Oberst Kleist. Indeed, an opportunity has arisen for me to observe you in action. But we'll come to that in a moment. First, I'd like to get to know you a little better. It is important for a commander to understand the men he will depend on. You come from an aristocratic background, it seems. And yet you have chosen to drop reference to that in the name you now go by. Is that through some plebeian or socialistic aspiration, I wonder?'

'It was a bit of a mouthful, sir. I found it easier to do without. Besides, the Führer believes social class is an irrelevance.'

'Nevertheless, you are an aristocrat.'

'My family were very minor aristocrats, sir. In any case, they lost almost everything during the crash of '29. I did not see much point in clinging to a title with no land or wealth to back it up. I had to make my own way in life, like most people. I have no regrets.'

'I'm not surprised. You did well at university and you also achieved considerable fame as a driver for the Mercedes Silver Arrow team. Indeed, I saw you race on a number of occasions myself. Quite the dashing hero of the track.'

'Until the accident, sir.'

'Yes, until then. Still, the Silver Arrows' loss was Kripo's gain. How did you feel about that, I wonder? Do you miss the thrill of motor racing and the adulation of your fans?'

'I'd be a liar if I said I didn't, sir. But we must accept the hand that fate deals us.'

'Yes, we must,' Radinsky said with emphasis. 'The party is the future of Germany, whatever mistaken beliefs we may have had in the past.'

He paused long enough to make it clear a response was required.

'Yes, sir.' Schenke nodded. 'Absolutely.'

'I gather the accident left you with an infirmity in your left leg. That would be the slight limp I observed as you left the mess hall.'

Schenke was surprised by his superior's acute observation. He did his best to mask the limp from others. Then again,

Radinsky had read his files and knew enough to make it appear that no detail escaped his eye. It was of a part with the previous questions about his background. Schenke's surprise gave way to cynicism. His superior's approach was to uncover something of the character that Schenke revealed in his responses. He must continue to be guarded about what he said.

'Yes, I limp, and there are times when the knee joint is painful. I have learned to cope, and it rarely has an impact on me carrying out my duties, sir.'

'Judging by the results of your investigations, it seems that is true. All the same, it must frustrate you that the injury prevents you from enlisting in the armed forces. Particularly at a time when Germany's star is on the rise and her heroes are men in military uniform.'

'Germany needs criminal investigators as well as heroes, sir. We all have our part to play in the service of the Fatherland.'

'Spoken like a true National Socialist!' Radinsky offered a smile. 'And yet you are not a party member, nor have you applied for membership of the SS, something that has been extended to many of your peers. Why is that?'

Schenke had rehearsed the answer for such occasions and delivered his response in a steady voice. 'My work requires all my attention, sir. If I was to entertain ambitions to rise within the party, I fear that would be to the detriment of my duties here at the precinct. I best serve Germany, and therefore the party, if I concentrate on hunting down those criminals whose activities would undermine our country and our Führer. It is a question of efficiency.'

'Efficiency . . .' Radinsky repeated slowly. 'Very well. A fair response. Besides, there are many of us who were members before the Nazis came to power who tend to look down on those who joined afterwards, when it was convenient to do so with no risk. Although I would never accuse a man of your calibre of being such an opportunist.'

Schenke stood still, his expression giving nothing away.

'That still leaves the question of your not having a rank in the SS. Heydrich tells me he offered that to you at the end of last year. Yet you turned him down. Needless to say, the Obergruppenführer was somewhat surprised and a little offended by your rebuff.'

The icy sensation in Schenke's neck returned. Heydrich had seemed affable enough when the offer was refused, and yet here was Radinsky saying it had caused some ill feeling. Gratifying as it might be to think he had ruffled the feathers of Himmler's henchman, that was a luxury someone of Schenke's rank could not afford.

'I was deeply honoured by the offer, sir. But it came with the request to give up my police role and go to work for Heydrich. I had to turn it down for the same reason that I felt it a disservice to the Reich to join the party.'

'I appreciate that, but we are all servants of the state. If we are asked to do something, we do it. We don't refuse on the basis that we think we are of more use elsewhere. That is not for individuals of our rank to decide. You were very lucky that Heydrich was minded to tolerate your response. He must hold you in some regard. A lesser man he would have humiliated by demoting or sending to some backwater job. Very well, if he sees something in you, then I have to trust his judgement. However, it is my intention to have all officers and senior NCOs in the precinct hold SS rank, assuming they meet the race criteria, during my tenure as commanding officer. That includes you. Especially you, given your rating in Heydrich's eyes. It will please him to see you in SS uniform.'

And no doubt it won't do you any harm to be seen to be the one who persuaded me to accept, Schenke reflected.

'I will give it serious consideration, sir.'

'You'll do more than that,' Radinsky shot back. He hesitated, and then smiled. 'Come now, Inspector, I am only thinking about what is good for you, your career and therefore the Kripo division. I want my subordinates to succeed, win promotion and do Pankow credit. Besides, you have the kind of directness I like in a man. I feel that you have been viewing those of us in the party and the SS from the outside for too long. You need a different perspective. It would be good for you to get to know us socially. If for no better reason than to see for yourself that we are no different to any other German. We wear the party badge and the uniform, but we all want the same thing: to serve Germany loyally and put into practice the ideology that is going to make our nation the brightest beacon in the history of the world.

'So, I will invite you to one of our gatherings. There'll be a party at my house on Tuesday. I'll have a formal invitation sent to your office. You'll get to meet people. People of influence. Make a good impression and it will help your career immeasurably. Besides, I know my wife and her friends will be excited to meet Horst Schenke, the daredevil champion of the Silver Arrows, in the flesh. How does that sound?'

It sounded unbearable, thought Schenke. Denied his racing career, he had tried to move on, and found any reminder of the glamour and fame of his former career bittersweet. The idea of being fawned over by the wives of high-ranking Nazi officials added salt to the wound. He merely nodded, however. 'Very kind of you, sir. I look forward to it.'

'Good! Then it's settled.' Radinsky folded his hands together and recomposed his features into a formal expression. 'Now then, down to the first item of business.'

He reached for a folder on his desk, opening it and scanning the summary before looking up. 'Your section has been investigating the ration coupon forging that has been plaguing Berlin since last October. While you have been able to determine that the same ink is being used for the forgeries as for the official coupons, that does little to help move things along. The forgeries are wreaking havoc and causing all manner of shortages for certain items. It's stirring up unrest amongst Berliners. The Intelligence Service reports on popular attitudes have made uncomfortable reading for Heydrich, and he wants those responsible for the forgeries tracked down and eliminated.'

'Eliminated?'

'Not quite the sort of term you career policeman are used to, I suppose. All right then, brought in for questioning. After which the Gestapo will take them into protective custody, and that may well be the last anyone hears of them. And good riddance. The wheels of justice move more swiftly than they used to before the party took control, eh? That's the kind of progress we need more of.'

'Yes, sir.'

'In any case, Heydrich has tasked me with resolving the matter as swiftly as possible. Which means I am tasking you to do it even more swiftly.'

Schenke's brow creased and Radinsky laughed. 'Just my little joke. As long as you understand the urgency. Your last report details the arrests and interrogations of low-level members of the crime rings, without any result.'

'We have a name now, sir. The leader of a crime ring, Paul Guttmann. We'll be following up at once.'

'Do you think he's our man, this Guttmann?'

Schenke hesitated, recalling his earlier exchange with Hauser. 'He might well be, sir. We have information to link him to the source of the forgeries. If he is, then we can arrest him, locate the presses and close the operation down.'

'I sense you are not convinced.'

'Guttmann's operation seems too small to carry off something on this scale. He's either being very successful in keeping his activities hidden, or he's part of a larger ring. Or we're looking for someone else and Guttmann is merely selling on the forgeries.'

'Someone else? Who would that be? Do you have any ideas?'

'Not yet, sir. But it would have to be one of the bigger crime rings in Berlin. Someone we already know about. I can't see this being the work of a new organisation, given how quickly they have acted, and how well connected they are.'

Radinsky gave him a sharp look. 'Connected?'

'As you mentioned, they have access to supplies of the same ink used in the official coupons, sir. We had the dyes tested by the Kripo labs. The senior chemist confirmed that they come from the same source. Whoever is responsible may have someone on the inside at the food ministry. One of my men will be working that angle. If we can find the individual supplying the ink, we can lean on them to reveal who is behind the ring. If they refuse to spill their guts, or there's some kind of middleman cutting out the chain of command, then at least we shut off the supply and make it harder for them to keep forging coupons that pass for the real item.'

'But you have doubts about Guttmann?'

'Frankly, yes.'

'Ach! That's a pity. It would have been useful to both of us to hand Heydrich a quick result.' Radinsky closed the file and thought for a moment before he continued. 'Let's consider another name. What do you know about Max Remer?'

'He's a local boy, sir. Runs a club in Mitte.'

'Mitte? Then he's obviously done very well for himself.'

'Yes, sir. The word on the street is that he has been moving into the black market, along with vice and protection rackets. We've nothing firm on him as yet. That's mainly because my section is working on the forgeries. If I had officers to spare, we'd be giving Remer a closer look.'

'I cannot magic manpower out of the air, Inspector. Every officer I have spoken to at Pankow has asked for more staff. There's a war on, and we have to make do with what we have. In fact we'll soon have to make do with even less, once we lose men to the new police battalion that's being raised. Do you think Remer might be involved with the forgeries?'

Schenke considered the idea and shrugged. 'His name hasn't come up during our investigation.' He paused, and then asked, 'Why do you mention him, sir? Do you have any reason to think he might be implicated?'

'It might have been helpful to us if he had been. But if you have already dismissed him from your investigation, then it doesn't matter.'

'If you suspect him, I could have him brought in for interrogation, sir. At the very least he might have some information of use to us.'

'It's too late for that,' Radinsky replied. 'Which brings us to the second item of business. Max Remer is dead. He was shot after he left his club last night. Killed in his car. His mistress was with him. She was wounded. The driver has disappeared. More than likely he was the trigger man.'

'Where did this happen?' Schenke asked with a sinking feeling.

'On our patch, Inspector. Less than a kilometre from here. Orpo have cordoned off the scene of the crime. You'd better get over there. They'll be waiting for you.'

Chapter Four

An Orpo squad was guarding the entrance to the alley when Liebwitz parked the pool car nearby. Sergeant Hauser, sitting next to him in the front, let out a relieved sigh and waited a moment before speaking calmly.

'Apply the brake.'

The other man reached for the lever and pulled it with a sharp ratcheting clatter. He sat still for a moment and puffed his cheeks before he turned the engine off.

'That was . . . better,' Hauser remarked. 'We survived.'

He had been tasked by Schenke to teach the section's newest member how to drive. For a man with a powerfully analytical mind, and adept marksmanship, Liebwitz had proven to be a curiously inept student. At least now he knew the basics, Schenke mused from the back seat. There had been no fatalities in reaching the scene, and such small mercies were to be welcomed, even in time of war.

Liebwitz lifted the brim of his hat and mopped his brow as Schenke opened the rear door. 'Gentlemen, shall we?'

The three Kripo men climbed out and approached the small crowd gathered around the end of the alley. There were some children, two in the uniform of the Pimpf, the youngest branch of the Hitler Youth movement; several men in workers' clothes, a handful of housewives with shopping bags, and a press photographer and reporter. Schenke winced as he recognised the latter: Lustig, who wrote up – or rather sensationalised – crime stories for the *Völkischer Beobachter*, the Nazi Party newspaper. He lowered his head as he and the other two Kripo officers pushed through the crowd and made for the cordon.

'Hey! Schenke!' Lustig called out. 'Inspector Schenke, a word!'

Schenke ignored him and approached the sergeant in charge, a rotund man in his fifties with a sour expression. Even though they knew each other by sight at the precinct, he fished out his identity disc and held it up.

'Criminal Inspector Schenke.' He lowered his disc and indicated his companions. 'Sergeant Hauser, Scharführer Liebwitz.'

They exchanged nods before Schenke continued. 'Were you and your men the first on the scene?'

'Not me, sir. One of the patrol men, Huber. He was on his beat when he heard gunshots and shouting and came running. He found one passenger dead – Max Remer – and his female companion wounded. There was no sign of the driver. Huber called an ambulance for her, but there was nothing to be done for Remer. He's still in the car.'

'You're joking.'

'Do I look as if I am, sir? The ambulance crew took off with the woman and left the stiff. Never came back. Me and my lads were called in to guard the scene until you arrived.' The sergeant glanced at his watch. 'It's just gone eight thirty. I was expecting you hours ago, sir. We were supposed to go off shift at six.'

'The new precinct commander considerately laid on a party education event. We came as soon as we could, Sergeant.'

'An education event?' The man shook his head. 'So that's more important than dealing with a crime scene?'

'I don't know. You'd be better off asking Oberführer Radinsky. Frankly, I think you dodged a bullet on that one. Where was the woman taken?'

'Mittelstein hospital.' The sergeant pointed along the street. 'Five minutes in that direction.'

'I know it . . . Well then, you'd better take us to the scene.'

The sergeant led the way down the alley. There was a sharp tang of coal fires and boiled vegetables in the confined space. It was wide enough for a large vehicle to drive down, but there was not enough space to turn it round. On one side was a row of tenement blocks with a handful of small windows piercing the grimy brickwork. There were openings at ground level leading into the yards at the heart of each block. Faces were peering out of some of the windows, watching the four men make their way along the alley. On the other side stretched a long, low warehouse, equally grimy, with double gates halfway along. The alley was cobbled, and strewn with litter.

Fifty paces ahead, Schenke saw the rear of the car, a Daimler. It had stopped in the middle of the alley and all the doors were open. Two more Orpo men were standing beyond to keep anyone from approaching the car from the surrounding buildings. A short distance beyond them, a brick wall marked the end of the alley. Some three metres high and topped with iron spikes, it protected a yard backing onto the warehouse, Schenke assumed. The glass in the rear window of the Daimler had been pierced by what appeared to be a single bullet, and as they drew closer, they could make out flecks of dried blood on the inside of the glass that remained.

Hauser gave a low whistle. 'Daimler Double Six. Nice piece of engineering, even for a British car. What I wouldn't give for one. I'm in the wrong line of work. Should have joined a crime ring.'

Liebwitz looked at him sidelong, tempted to comment but wary of being subjected to the sergeant's sarcasm.

Halting the Orpo sergeant a few paces behind the car, Schenke looked over the rear, then extended his scrutiny to the ground on either side. There were some discarded wads of bloodied cloth and patches of dried blood on the cobbles to the left of the Daimler. He indicated them. 'Those left by the medics?'

The sergeant shrugged. 'I suppose so. They were there when my squad arrived. Huber would know.'

'We'll need to speak to him later. Is he still with the rest of your men?'

'Yes, sir.'

'Good. Apart from the medics, the scene hasn't been disturbed by anyone else?'

'That's right. We know our job, sir,' the sergeant said testily. 'How about you get on with yours so we can get the car and body taken away and me and my lot can go off duty, eh?'

He gestured to the two Orpo men beyond the car. 'The experts are here, boys, so we can leave it to them.'

As the three uniformed policemen strode back up the alley, their footfall echoing off the walls on either side, Hauser clicked his tongue. 'Touchy bastard.'

Schenke stepped up to the right-hand rear door and bent his head to look at the interior. There were more dressings in the footwell, and a small handbag, gleaming black with a gold fastener and a silver strip along the shoulder strap. Close by was a woman's shoe. On the far side of the rear seat sprawled a man in a fur-trimmed coat. His head was thrown back and tilted up as it rested against the parcel shelf. His mouth sagged and his eyes were fixed on the quilted roof of the Daimler. The entry wound in his forehead was off-centre. Blood and brain tissue were spattered across the parcel shelf and the broken glass of the rear window.

Hauser appeared at the rear door on the far side and also took in the details. 'Messy,' he muttered. 'Going to take some clearing up to get it back in a fit state to drive.'

'I suppose,' Schenke replied, and moved to examine the front seats. Although the engine had been switched off, the key was still in the ignition. An upturned Stormtrooper cap lay on the passenger seat, but otherwise there was nothing untoward to be seen here. Making his way round the front of the Daimler, he noted the small pennant on the bonnet that marked the car as an official vehicle. None of the tyres were flat and there was no sign of damage, or leaking engine fluids. He completed the circuit, then reached for the ignition key and turned it. The engine started at the first attempt and settled into a gentle mechanical purr. He turned it off and straightened up.

'That rules out breakdown as a reason for the car being off the road.'

Hauser glanced back up the alley. 'I'd say that was unlikely anyway, given the distance from the street. The driver must have been in on it. He either acted alone, or he had accomplices waiting in the alley. Whoever shot our friend drove him down here to do the job as far from any witnesses as possible.'

'Maybe. I can't see Remer not being aware of the danger,

though. If he was, the driver would have found it very difficult to drive and hold a gun on the pair in the rear at the same time.'

Schenke returned to the back of the Daimler for a closer examination of the body as Liebwitz climbed into the driver's seat and settled into position, hands on the wheel.

'A beauty, isn't she?' Hauser mused. 'If I served a hundred years, I could never afford one like this on a sergeant's salary. Be lucky if I even get the Strength Through Joy car I've been saving for.'

Liebwitz's forehead creased momentarily as he did the calculation and compared it against the probable value of the car. 'It should be affordable within that time. However, you will have retired long before then, Sergeant, so—'

'Thanks. I get the picture. A man can dream, can't he?'

Liebwitz blinked behind the round lenses of his glasses. 'Evidently.'

He turned his attention back to the wheel and reached inside his coat to where his pistol was holstered. Drawing his hand out as though holding a gun, he twisted towards the victim and froze as he considered the angle. 'It's not an easy shot to get right. Remer would have had time to respond once he realised he was in danger. He would have had a chance to attack the driver before he could fire.'

Schenke looked up the alley. 'Unless he took them by surprise and shot them both at the entrance to the alley, or even out on the street, before turning down here and abandoning the car.' He straightened up and scanned the cobbles until he saw the glint of shards of glass. 'No. They were shot here.'

He leaned in to examine the body again and pointed to the two small tears in the victim's coat, over the heart. 'Two to the chest and one to the head. Looks like the killer knew what he was doing.'

'What about the woman?' asked Hauser. 'There would have been at least four shots if she was wounded too.'

Schenke scanned the seat next to the body and pointed to a hole in the leather upholstery. 'There . . . Can't see any other injuries on our man here. Seems like four shots then.'

Liebwitz groped around the floor beneath the driver's seat. 'No shell cases. So the assailant used a revolver. Unless he used an automatic and retrieved the cases afterwards, though that would have delayed his escape from the scene.'

'Quite.' Schenke nodded. 'A revolver is the likely weapon.'

'There are far fewer revolvers in circulation these days,' Liebwitz observed. 'That may go some way towards tracking down the culprit.'

'Some small way,' said Hauser.

Schenke studied Remer's fixed, wide-eyed expression. It was hard to tell whether it was a look of surprise or whether he was reading that into the victim's face. It was difficult to work up any sympathy for a man who had run one of Berlin's biggest crime rings. From what Schenke knew, Remer's gang was believed to have been responsible for a number of murders and disappearances over the years. Besides assaults, protection rackets, brothels, illegal gambling premises and corruption of public officials. Although the latter had largely ceased to be a crime now that prosecutions were rarely brought against Nazis for fear of the consequences. Once in a while an example might be made of a particularly egregious individual, usually a person some way down the hierarchy who would not be missed by those at the top. Someone paraded before the public as proof of the party's incorruptibility before they were sent to serve a short sentence at one of the camps. Then the grift would carry on as before. Schenke had little doubt that Remer had had a number of senior Nazi officials in his pocket, and they had afforded him favours and protection from the attentions of the police. The Daimler itself was proof of that. However, he concluded, none of that had saved him from his assassin's bullets.

'Looks like a professional job,' said Hauser, miming the three shots that had killed Remer. 'But that begs the question, why spare the woman and leave a witness? That's poor tradecraft if our man is a pro.'

'We'll need to speak to her as soon as we can,' Schenke decided. 'And have her placed under protection. Word will get out that she survived, and the shooter will want to cover his tracks. That makes her a target.'

'I'll have some of the Orpo boys detailed for that,' said Hauser. 'They might as well do something useful.'

Schenke nodded. 'I want you to take charge here. Get some more of our people over from the precinct and go door-to-door in these tenement blocks. Find out if anyone saw or heard anything that might help us.'

'Slim chance of that.'

'Nevertheless . . .'

'I'll see to it, sir.'

'Take Huber's statement, and make sure no one gets close to the car before the body is removed. I want the Daimler taken to the precinct. Liebwitz, you're with me. We're going to speak to the woman.'

They made their way up the alley. Schenke paused to put on his gloves and try the double gates leading into the warehouse. They were unlocked, and he eased one of them open. Beyond lay a cavernous space, gloomily lit by skylights in the roof.

There was the unmistakable odour of coal dust, but no sign of any sacks or heaps. Berlin had run short of coal during the recent bitter winter, and the city was struggling to replenish its stocks.

'Either of you have a torch?'

Hauser shook his head, but Liebwitz slipped his hand into a deep pocket of his black leather coat and drew out an army-issue torch, which he handed over. Schenke thumbed the switch on and shone it around the interior. As he had hoped, there were footprints and marks in the dust spread across the concrete floor.

'We'll have this searched as well. Our man, or men, might have left the scene this way. See where the other exits to the warehouse are, Hauser, and if anyone saw anything. Get the gate handles dusted. The shooter might have left some prints.' He closed the door and returned the torch to Liebwitz.

Back at the entrance to the alley, there was a blinding flash and Lustig stepped into their path.

'That'll make a nice picture for the front page, Inspector. Along with the headline: "Kripo Inspector Horst Schenke races to the scene of the crime!"'

In Schenke's previous encounter with the reporter, Lustig had played up his motor-racing past, and that still rankled with him. He was a policeman now. 'Out of my way.'

Lustig did not move. 'I've been told the victim was the head of a crime ring and that a woman was involved. Was it a crime of passion?'

Schenke gritted his teeth before he raised his voice so that his words would be heard clearly by the Orpo men. 'Whoever gave you those details will also have told you the woman was injured and taken away for treatment. You will be provided with further details when Kripo shares them with you, not before. And if I discover that you have been given privileged information in exchange for cash, then the officer involved will face the consequences . . .' He glowered at the Orpo sergeant and his men.

'I have heard rumours that the killing was related to tensions between the crime rings,' Lustig pushed on. 'Well, Inspector?'

'No comment. Like I said, you'll be given further information when I decide to release it and not before. Now move.'

Lustig nodded and gave a smile. 'Just doing my job. The newspaper's readers have a right to know.'

'Newspaper?' Schenke sniffed. 'That's a tall story in itself.'

He brushed past the reporter and led his companions towards the pool car. Liebwitz hesitated on the kerb.

'You drive,' Schenke insisted.

'Yes, sir,' the Scharführer responded unhappily, and made his way to the driver's seat. As he started the engine, Schenke spoke to Hauser.

'Keep Lustig away from the car and any Orpo officers. I don't want details going out before we're ready.' He shook his head. 'Crime of passion or gang war . . . The press would like to jump in with both feet for either of those stories.'

'Sells copy,' Hauser mused.

'Yes, but doesn't help us much if we get inundated with bogus tip-offs from Lustig's readers. Make sure he doesn't get any other information to feed off.'

Hauser grinned. 'I can be very dissuasive.'

'I'll see you back at the precinct after we've spoken to the woman.' Schenke frowned. 'We don't even have her name . . .'

He cleared his throat and called out, 'Sergeant! Over here!'

The Orpo sergeant thrust his way through the gawkers. 'Sir?'

'The injured woman. What's her name?'

'Katharina Kunzler, she said.'

'Anything else?'

He shook his head. 'That's all Huber got out of her before she passed out.'

'Too bad.' Schenke exchanged a farewell nod with Hauser then slipped into the passenger seat. 'Let's go and see Fräulein Kunzler . . . And try not to drive too slowly this time.'

'Do you think her life is in imminent danger, sir?'

'She'll be safe once we have her under guard. *Her* life isn't in danger, but yours might be if you can't get the hang of driving rather more swiftly.'

'Sir?' Liebwitz looked at him with a concerned expression.

'It doesn't matter. Just get going, and keep your eyes on the road.'

Chapter Five

The Mittelstein hospital had been built at the end of the previous century, paid for by a wealthy Lutheran family to serve the needs of the workers living in Pankow. It had been an imposing building with a pillared entrance portico, high ceilings, and spotless, brightly lit corridors and wards that smelled of disinfectant. The founders' business had suffered badly, during the crash, and the depression that followed had made it difficult to find the funds to keep the hospital running. Appeals to government officials had resulted in warm words and empty promises, and the Mittelstein only kept going on the back of donations from the district's church congregations.

Liebwitz parked outside, and the two Kripo officers passed through the entrance and approached the porter at the well-worn reception counter.

'We're from Kripo. Investigating a shooting last night. I understand one of the victims was brought here. Fräulein Kunzler.'

'Katharina Kunzler?' The porter was silver-haired and wore an Iron Cross ribbon on his neat jacket, just above the empty sleeve pinned across his chest. 'She was taken to triage. Corridor to the right, follow the signs.'

Schenke led the way. The corridor was gloomy, as the windows had not been cleaned for a while. The paint on the walls was flaking in patches, and strands of cobwebs wafted delicately in the arches and the high doorways on either side. Thankfully the signage was clear, and after two turns they reached the triage hall. The duty doctor, a tired-looking young man with hollow eyes, glanced at Schenke's ID disc, then listened to him before he nodded.

'I dealt with her. First admission on my shift. Gunshot wound to the arm. No bone damage, but lost quite a bit of blood.'

Schenke looked past him. There were several nurses and orderlies dealing with other admissions – a young boy howling with pain as his burned arm was treated with a salve, his shrill cries echoing off the faded white walls, and some older men and women – but no sign of the young woman he was looking for.

The doctor noticed his gaze. 'She's not here. I had her sent up to the female ward once I had finished treating her.'

'How is she?' asked Schenke.

'She's stable and should recover well enough.' The doctor arched an eyebrow. 'Given that she has been shot and the man who was with her was killed, how do you imagine she would be, Inspector?'

'Traumatised and in some pain, I expect,' Liebwitz said with a mildly surprised expression. 'Given the circumstances.'

Schenke cleared his throat and responded in a firm voice. 'We need to speak to her as soon as possible if we are to find the people responsible. It would help our investigation. Is she in a fit state to talk?'

The doctor scratched his chin. 'Could you come back tomorrow? Or preferably the day after?'

'Now would be best,' Schenke said firmly.

The doctor gave a frustrated sigh. 'All right. I suppose so. Just don't agitate her. She needs to rest and keep still. The ward's up the stairs opposite the main entrance. Tell the ward sister that the duty doctor has approved you speaking to the patient.'

Schenke nodded curtly, and he and Liebwitz returned to the entrance hall and began to climb the stairs. Steps always tested his lame left leg, and he paused on the landing at the top to rub his knee and ease out some of the aching stiffness.

Liebwitz regarded him. 'Sir, are you able to proceed?'

'Just give me a moment . . .'

'Shall I fetch you a chair?'

'No, dammit! I'm not an invalid, Scharführer.' Schenke straightened and forced himself on, trying not to limp. Even after enduring the injury for several years, it still angered him when others commented on it. Particularly with any sympathy, which was always a very small distance from the pity he dreaded. Now that the Fatherland was at war once again, young men and even those of his age were donning uniforms to fight for Germany. Those who remained behind would be regarded with suspicion by the more enthusiastic patriots. That would become more pronounced the longer the conflict endured. Schenke fervently hoped that the warring parties would have the sense to end it soon. Any peace would be better than a repeat of the slaughter and chaos of the last war. Nothing could be worse than that.

The ward was a long room with tall windows overlooking the street. Rows of beds lined the sides; as many as forty, Schenke estimated. Most were occupied, and nurses ministered to the patients' needs. Curtains screened off a small number at the far end of the ward. As the two Kripo officers crossed the threshold, a nurse looked up from behind a desk to one side of the doorway.

'No visitors until the afternoon. Out you go.'

Schenke produced his badge again. 'Kripo. We need to question Katharina Kunzler.'

The nurse stood up, revealing an imposing physique. She squinted at the badge and scrutinised both men before she responded. 'Fräulein Kunzler is resting. You must come back later.'

'The duty doctor has approved it. Please take us to her.'

The nurse gave a shrug. 'If the doctor approves . . .' She set off down the wide aisle between the beds, and Schenke and Liebwitz followed. At the end of the ward she indicated the first of the curtained-off areas, and Schenke stopped at the end of the battered metal-framed bed.

Kunzler lay on her back under clean white sheets, head framed by shoulder-length blonde hair that gleamed in the light falling from the window. Her right arm was heavily bandaged and immobilised with splints. Her eyes were closed, and her chest rose and fell gently as she breathed in an easy rhythm.

'As you can see, she's asleep,' the nurse said softly. 'Leave the poor lamb alone for now. She's been through enough.'

She pointed to the coat and dress on hangers to one side of the bed. There were blots of blood spread across the material, looking like pressed flowers, brown and flat. Liebwitz walked up to the garments to inspect them. 'These should be taken in for evidence, sir. There are tears in the cloth. Most probably entry or exit points of the bullet that struck her.'

The nurse shook her head. 'Those are the only clothes she has with her.'

'What about her family?' Schenke asked. 'She can get some spare clothes from them. Have they been notified?'

'She said she doesn't have any family in Berlin. She's from Kiel.'

'Friends?'

'She didn't say. Just kept repeating, "Max is dead." I suppose that's the man the ambulance crew mentioned when they brought her in.'

The nurse waited for Schenke to say something, but he refused to respond and instead gestured to the coat and dress. 'We'll leave those here for now.'

He leaned closer to the patient and spoke gently. 'Fräulein Kunzler . . .'

She stirred and frowned, then ran her tongue over her dry lips. 'Hmm . . .'

'Kunzler,' Liebwitz repeated sharply. 'You must wake up.'

Schenke looked at him and shook his head.

'Sir?'

'We're here to get a statement, Scharführer, not to beat a confession out of her.'

'Yes, sir.'

There was a moan as the patient's eyelids flickered and opened. Then she started, eyes wide as she looked up at Liebwitz's austere features, and pressed herself back into the bolster, raising her uninjured arm as if to protect her face. 'No!'

The nurse hurried to her side and took her hand. 'There! It's all right, Katharina! These men are from the police. They just want to talk to you.' She shot a look at Liebwitz. 'Then they'll be gone, and you can rest again until the doctor comes to check on you.'

Katharina's features were taut before her expression eased and she slipped back against the bolster.

'Are you happy for them to speak to you?' asked the nurse. 'Or shall I tell them to come back another time?'

'Let them stay.'

'Are you certain?'

Katharina nodded, and the nurse released her hand and smiled. 'I'll be at my desk. Just tell them when you want them to go.'

The nurse glanced at Liebwitz with narrowed eyes. 'Briefly, remember.'

As her footsteps squeaked along the polished wooden floor, Schenke took off his hat and indicated to Liebwitz to station himself at the foot of the bed. 'Fräulein Kunzler, I am Inspector Schenke of Kripo. This is Scharführer Liebwitz. We're here to get a statement from you about last night's shooting. Are you able to do that?'

'Max . . .' She murmured and closed her eyes. When she opened them again, she sighed and nodded. 'What do you need from me?'

Liebwitz took out his notepad and pencil.

Schenke pulled the small side table round and sat on it to take the pressure off his left leg. 'It would help us to get as much detail as possible, Fräulein Kunzler.' He smiled encouragingly.

'Everyone calls me Kitty.'

'Kitty? Very well. How old are you?'

'Twenty-six.'

'I'm told you're from Kiel.'

'That's right. I came to Berlin two years ago. For work. I

had been studying medicine at the university in Kiel, until the party banned women.'

Schenke gave a sympathetic nod. It was one of the measures the Nazis had introduced in line with their views about the role of women in the new Reich.

'So, I needed work, or a husband. I had relatives in Berlin who worked in the film industry. I thought I might try and become an actress. I was introduced to some producers, but they wanted something for casting me in even the smallest parts. So I abandoned that ambition.'

'Something?' Liebwitz looked up from his notebook. 'Could you be specific?'

Kitty looked at Schenke. 'Favours, she means,' he said.

'Favours . . . Ah, sexual favours. I see.'

She winced, and Schenke spoke softly. 'Go on, Kitty. What happened then?'

'I went from one job to the next – waitressing, working in a haberdashery, cleaning – and then the job came up at the Ace of Hearts, as a hostess. Just talking to customers, making them feel comfortable, getting them to buy me drinks.' She gave him an anxious look. 'That's all. I swear it.'

'I'm not judging you, Kitty. Please continue.'

'It didn't take long for Max . . . for Herr Remer to take an interest in me. I was flattered. I knew he owned the club, and he had money, fine clothes, that car of his. People respected him.'

'Respected?' Schenke arched an eyebrow. 'Or feared him?'

'A bit of both, if I'm honest. Of course I knew there was another side to him. I overheard the conversations between Max and the men who worked for him, as well as the gossip from the people who came to the club. I wasn't blind to how he had made his fortune. Then he took me out for dinner one night. We spent the evening at the Adlon. Dancing once the meal was over. Max is . . . was a fine dancer. Then he took me back to his flat and . . . Anyway, that's how it began. I've been with him ever since. Since the start of last year.'

'Did he ever talk about his business with you?'

'Very, very rarely. Max may have been many things,' she smiled faintly, 'but he was no fool. Neither am I. I knew enough not to ask and where not to look. That's how it was between us.'

'Nevertheless, you knew that he ran one of Berlin's biggest crime rings.'

'I'd have to be an idiot not to know he was involved in something like that. Yes, I knew. I knew what I was getting into and I chose to accept it, Inspector. But I had no part in anything illegal.'

'But you were prepared to enjoy the proceeds of his illegal activities,' Liebwitz observed.

'What was I supposed to do? Do you have any idea how hard life can be for someone in my position? Besides, I came to like Max. He was kind to me. Looked after me and made sure I wanted for nothing. I knew it wouldn't last for ever. Sooner or later he was going to discard me, like he tired of the women who came before, but I was determined to make the most of it. We had a good thing . . . most of the time.'

'Most of the time?' Schenke probed.

'He had a temper. He was much better at keeping it under control than some, but it was there all the same. Although it had got the better of him recently.'

'Why was that?'

She thought a moment and shook her head. 'I don't really

know. There were some heated exchanges over the telephone back at his flat.'

'Who with?'

'I couldn't tell. I did ask, but he told me to mind my own business. Then there was a night at the club, perhaps two weeks ago. Max was quite agitated. He was expecting a very senior party member and some of his friends to come to the club, and he had gathered the staff to brief them and make sure they attended to the customers' every need, whatever they asked for. That included me,' she added in a hurt tone. 'He told me that the minister had a taste for women like me, blonde and thin. If he approached me, I was to do whatever he asked. It was the first time he'd ever required me to do anything like that. And the last.'

Schenke's mind was working swiftly, and anxiously. 'You said "the minister". Did Remer give a name?'

'No.'

'Did he say anything that might identify who he was talking about?'

She shook her head. 'Sorry . . . In any case, it was all for nothing. A man turned up to tell Max that the minister wasn't coming. I saw them speaking over by the coat check booth. When the man left, Max looked very worried. I'd never seen him that way before. I tried to talk to him when we got back to the flat, but he wouldn't tell me anything. He was gentle that night, though. It was the only occasion I ever sensed that he had feelings towards me. I wish I had seen that side to him before. He had a heart, Inspector.' She looked up at Schenke earnestly. 'I saw it.'

He nodded. 'Did you ever discover what it was that had made him worried?'

'No. After that night, he clammed up. Went back to being the hard man in control of himself. He was the same last night. I had hoped to encourage him to be more open with me. Now it's too late. He's gone, and I'll be on my own.'

Schenke felt a spark of sympathy at her plight, but it was swiftly extinguished by the knowledge of all those invisible others Remer had exploited and harmed in order to provide Kitty with the comfortable life she had enjoyed with the gangster.

'Tell me about last night.'

'It was like most nights. We went to the club, watched some of the acts. He had a word with Otto about one of his jokes.'

Liebwitz looked up, pencil poised. 'Otto?'

'Otto Bachmann, the club's comedian. It was only a brief discussion, then Otto left and Max told me he had to go and deal with something. He was gone for perhaps twenty or thirty minutes before he returned and said we were going back to the flat. We got our coats and went outside to wait for the car. It wasn't the usual driver. Kurtz was ill and a replacement was covering for him. A man called, ah . . . Schlemminger – yes, that was the name, I am sure of it.'

Schenke looked up to make sure Liebwitz had made a note. 'Did you get a good look at him?'

'No. It was too dark in the street and there wasn't enough light in the car.'

'Was there anything about him you remember?'

'He was taller than Max, well built. I got the impression from his voice that he was in his thirties or forties.'

'Any accent?'

'Definitely a Berliner. I've lived here long enough to know it.'

Schenke smiled. The clipped tones and speed of delivery of

the locals had taken some getting used to when he himself had first come to the capital.

'Is there anything else about him that you recall?'

'No. Like I said, it was too dark.'

'Did Remer recognise him?'

'Max was suspicious. But then he tended to be wary of anything he was not prepared for. He asked the man a few questions and seemed to be satisfied with his answers.'

'What questions?'

'He asked who had arranged for Kurtz's replacement, and maybe something else. I can't recall now.'

'And then?'

Kitty frowned as she recalled the details. 'We drove carefully through the blackout. The driver seemed to know his way well enough. He followed the usual route back to the flat as far as I could tell. Max seemed a bit preoccupied. I assumed it was something to do with the men who had come to the club earlier. That was when the car was stopped by a policeman.'

Schenke met Liebwitz's bespectacled gaze. 'What policeman?'

'An Orpo man. At least he had the coat and hat. He waved us into the alley. The driver said it must be a diversion and turned off the street. That was when Max knew something was wrong. He shouted something and made a move towards the driver. Then the car stopped and I was thrown forward, then back. I think Max was moving across in front of me to get at the driver when the shots were fired. I felt a blow on my arm.' Her face screwed up as the images of that moment overwhelmed her. 'I . . . I . . . couldn't move as Max was lying across me, so I kept still and pretended to be dead.' She closed her eyes. 'I heard the door open and the light came on in the back. Someone said, "They're done for", then there was shouting from above . . . another voice saying, "Run! Run for it!" I froze for a few seconds – maybe ten or so. Then I looked down and saw Max's head . . . Blood everywhere . . . blood and bone and . . . everywhere. I screamed and shouted, and then it all went black.' She gulped and licked her lips again.

'Do you need some water? Schenke asked.

She nodded, and he poured a glass from the jug on a shelf above the bed and handed it to her. Kitty's fingers trembled and he steadied her hand as she raised her head to take a few sips before slumping back. 'Thank you.'

He took the glass away and placed it on the shelf as she continued. 'I don't know how long it was before the ambulance men came for me. I remember them taking me out of the car and carrying me away on a stretcher, but I can't remember much else until I was here at the hospital and the doctor was dealing with the wound. There was so much blood I thought for a while that I must be dying. But he told me it was a flesh wound and I would be all right.' She looked down at her heavily bandaged and immobilised arm. 'Hurts like hell.'

'It will, I'm afraid,' said Schenke, recalling the time he himself had been treated in the emergency suite at Nürburgring after the crash that had ended his racing career. He turned to Liebwitz. 'Did you get all of that, Scharführer?'

'Yes, sir. Is there anything else you wish to add, Fräulein?' Liebwitz asked.

She shook her head. 'That's all. I'm feeling rather dizzy. I think I might be sick.' She closed her eyes again and breathed deeply until the nausea passed. 'Sorry.'

'No need for an apology.' Schenke rose from the side table and slid it back before replacing his hat. 'We'll let you rest. The Scharführer will type up his notes, and someone will come back to go over them with you, in case you remember anything else that may help us.'

As they made to leave, she raised her head. 'Will you find him? The man who shot us?'

'That's what the Reich pays us to do.' Schenke smiled. 'Rest and recover. No doubt we'll be speaking to you again.'

'I hope so.' She smiled back. 'Until then, Inspector.'

Outside the hospital, Schenke and Liebwitz returned to the pool car. Schenke sat in silence as he went over what Kitty had told them. His companion sat upright, one hand on the wheel and the other on the ignition key, waiting for instructions.

'Are you sure you got a full account in your notebook?' Schenke asked. One of the reasons he had come to value Liebwitz was his precise memory. The notes would provide a satisfactory summary of the interview, but Liebwitz would also have retained a wealth of other details that might prove useful later on.

'Yes, sir.' The Scharführer regarded him with what might have been a reproachful expression. 'My recollection of evidence has not failed me so far.'

'I'm sure.'

'Where do you wish me to drive you, sir?'

'We need to speak to the people at Remer's club, in case anyone noticed something of use to us. But first I need to eat. We'll pass close to the precinct on the way. There's a café on the next street. The Blue Rabbit? Do you know it?'

'I know of it, sir.'

Schenke shot him a glance. 'That doesn't sound like a recommendation . . .'

'To quote Sergeant Hauser, "the service is slow, the food is overpriced and tastes like shit and the staff are rude".'

Schenke laughed. Not only did the description sound like the kind of thing Hauser would say, it was delivered in an uncanny imitation of the sergeant's voice. 'You have him down perfectly . . . Scharführer, you have quite a talent for mimicry.'

'Do I?' Liebwitz raised an eyebrow. 'It had not occurred to me before, sir.'

'Well, I'm telling you now. Just don't try it in front of the sergeant, eh? He might not be such an appreciative audience.'

Chapter Six

There was an ulterior motive behind Schenke's decision to stop at the café. Two doors down was a closed-up shop he and Ruth had used for a simple communication system. If either needed to speak to the other face-to-face, a chalk mark was left on a brick low down in the doorway where it was not visible from the street, and they would meet at another café a few streets away. There was also a small slot between two bricks where messages could be hidden. It had been nearly six weeks since he had last heard from her, and Schenke was growing anxious.

He was playing a dangerous game by maintaining a relationship with a Jew, even if it only amounted to a fleeting meeting every so often to ensure that she was safe – or as safe as anyone of her race could be under the regulations imposed on Jews by the regime. They had slept together a handful of times at his flat before both agreed that it was too risky to continue. Nevertheless, he felt affection and an obligation to her as a result of their intimacy. An obligation for which he cursed his foolishness in allowing momentary pleasures to give rise to existential peril. He was in no doubt that the regime would delight in making an example of him if the relationship was discovered. He would be sent to one of the camps run by Himmler's SS, where the harshest treatment was meted out for 'race traitors' such as himself. The consequences for Ruth would be as bad, if not worse. Limiting their contact was the least risky strategy if they could not yet bring themselves to stop seeing each other.

Then there was the matter of Karin Canaris, the socialite Schenke had been dating before he encountered Ruth. They had intended to get engaged until the relationship had cooled. Karin had left Berlin – to visit friends in Bavaria for a few weeks, she had said. It had been three months since he had heard from her and he was resigning himself to the possibility that she had decided to break away from him, even if she had not yet told him so. He lived in anticipation of a letter or telephone call. He had tried to contact her in the second month, but her uncle – an admiral – had politely refused to divulge the details of where she could be reached.

It was a strain being emotionally bound to two women at the same time: Karin the physical epitome of the Nazi ideal of the German woman, though her political views ranged far from the party's ideology; and Ruth from a race the Nazis demanded all true Germans abhor. It was a situation he had found himself in even before he was fully aware of it. That was no excuse, he told himself. No matter what the circumstances, he had had the choice to act, or to choose differently, and that was his responsibility alone. His penance was to do what he could to help Ruth while hoping there was a way to save his relationship with Karin, even at this late date.

Liebwitz had tentatively turned into the Pankow street on which the Blue Rabbit café stood, and Schenke could already make out the sign hanging above the entrance. He indicated a spot by the kerb a short distance beyond, and turned to the Scharführer as the latter drew up.

'Want me to get you anything to eat?'

Liebwitz dabbed his brow with the back of his hand and then shook his head. 'No thank you, sir. I find that I have no appetite.'

Schenke patted him on the shoulder. 'Driving isn't always this traumatic. You'll get used to it.' He climbed out of the car and headed for the café.

It was not yet midday, and there were only two people ahead of him in the queue. He ordered sausage in rye bread and came out onto the street holding the paper bag. Liebwitz appeared to be staring straight ahead in the other direction, and Schenke stepped towards the boarded-up shop and kneeled down as if to tie one of his shoelaces. He glanced round to make sure that no one was paying him attention, then glanced at the brick beneath the sill of the shop's door. There was no mark, just the piece of chalk that he had left there before. He snatched it up and sketched a small swastika in the corner where it would be all but invisible to any passer-by, then picked up the paper bag again.

As he did so, he looked up and caught Liebwitz's eyes in the wing mirror of the car. He felt his heart quicken. The Scharführer stared back unblinking, and Schenke hoped that the stare was vacant and that his subordinate's thoughts were elsewhere, given that Liebwitz missed no details when his mind was focused. Rising to his feet as casually as he could, he winced as his left knee straightened with a soft crunch.

Back in the car, he eased the paper wrapper back and took a bite of his sandwich. He chewed and then mumbled, 'Let's get to the club.'

Liebwitz remained silent as he drove, keeping his attention on the road and gripping the wheel tightly, his knuckles white with tension. After a few minutes, Schenke's wariness eased off. If the Scharführer had noticed anything to arouse his suspicions, he would have said something by now. He was not the kind of man to keep his observations to himself – one of the reasons why he had been reassigned from Gestapo headquarters to the hinterland of the Pankow precinct. The Gestapo's loss was Kripo's gain, Schenke mused. Just as long as Liebwitz's attention remained focused on the section's investigations. Under the Nazi regime, fear of being found guilty of something weighed heavily on every German. More and more Schenke found himself thinking about his words before he uttered them to anyone he did not trust implicitly.

He finished the sausage and bread and brushed the crumbs from his coat.

'I wonder,' he began, 'were the killers after just Remer, or both of them?'

Liebwitz hesitated before responding, waiting until the road ahead was clear. 'Kunzler recalled the gunman saying they were both done for. There's also the matter of her describing Remer moving between her and the gunman before he was shot.'

'So?'

'There are some possible scenarios that occur to me, sir. Firstly, Remer might have been making a bid to tackle the gunman. Secondly, he could have been trying to shield the woman. Thirdly, there is the matter you raise of whether the gunman intended to kill Remer alone, or both of them. There is also the possibility, however unlikely, that Kunzler was the intended target and Remer's death was incidental.'

Schenke shook his head. 'I think we can discount that,

Scharführer. She was just his mistress. You heard her story: she came to Berlin to try to become a screen actress and ended up as a hostess in a club. I dare say there are hundreds like her in Berlin. Why would anyone want to kill her? Unless she was aware of something the killer did not want others to know about. Or even if it was suspected that she did.'

'I can't answer that without more information, sir. I was just pointing out some possibilities. There's something else to consider. She might have been shot at directly, or she might have been injured as a result of a bullet passing through Remer and striking her. In which case, three shots were fired, not four. We'd have a better idea if we had insisted on inspecting her clothing at the precinct, along with the car.'

Schenke wasn't sure if he detected a trace of criticism in his subordinate's tone.

'How does that have any bearing on the case, Scharführer?'

'I can't say, sir. Not until we've had a chance to consider the evidence. The available evidence, that is.'

Schenke briefly went over the information they had before he continued. 'As things stand, we'll proceed on the basis that Remer was the principal target. It makes most sense. He must have made many enemies over the years. It has the appearance of being a professional hit. He was set up. The diversion into the alley. The accomplice. The replacement driver. Somebody went to a lot of trouble to arrange the ambush. It points towards the Berlin underworld. We'll pursue that line for now.'

Liebwitz nodded slowly. 'As you wish, sir. It does appear to be the most likely explanation.'

There was a pause before Schenke responded. 'But?'

'Sir?'

'You have doubts?'

'I always have doubts, sir. Until the requisite evidence is obtained and criminality is proven. That is what I was taught at the Gestapo. Gruppenführer Müller was most insistent it was the procedure we should follow.'

'I've heard that the means of obtaining the requisite evidence is something of a grey area at the Gestapo.'

'Not at all, sir. We were empowered to use any means necessary.'

'Including forced confessions.'

'Yes, sir. A confession is usually the best evidence.'

'No matter how you achieve it, eh?'

Liebwitz risked a glance away from the road and stared at his superior for a beat before looking back. 'There are many methods of interrogation, sir. What matters is securing an honest confession to serve as credible evidence. If the known facts back up the confession, I see no problem in justifying the means to that end.'

'I imagine you wouldn't . . . It must be nice to have such clarity in your approach to your duties, Scharführer.'

'It is very helpful, sir.' Liebwitz nodded. 'And effective.'

Liebwitz pulled up in front of the club and the two men climbed out and briefly inspected the exterior. Before the war, and the blackout, the name of the club was highlighted by bulbs positioned behind the bold letters of 'The Ace of Hearts'. Now it only announced its presence during daylight. By night, any customers would have to know their way around the area if they were to have any hope of locating it. Apart from the black sheen of the double doors, there were no other entrances or even windows on the ground floor facing the street, and only two windows on the first floor, one either side of the sign. A smart-looking restaurant stood next to the club and a narrow alley ran down the side to the service entrance, passing between more buildings to the street beyond. Looking around, Schenke judged that it was a quiet middle-class residential area, with a few cafés, shops and restaurants on either side. Not unlike the district where he had his flat. Decent professional people going about their lives, mostly avoiding the club and not having anything to do with the man who owned it and the kind of business he was engaged in. If they had passed Remer in the street and recognised him, they'd have hurried by or offered an obsequious greeting if his gaze caught their eye.

He stepped up to the entrance and rapped on the right-hand door, just below the doorman's viewing slot. He waited a moment, then pounded on the door with the base of his fist. The slot snapped aside and a pair of eyes scrutinised him.

'We're closed until six.'

Schenke raised his badge. 'Kripo. Let us in. We want to speak to the manager.'

'Herr Remer's not here. Not yet.'

'I didn't ask to speak to the owner. It's the manager I'm after, or whoever runs the place for Remer.'

The eyes blinked and Schenke could almost hear the cogs in the man's brain grinding before he responded. 'That will be Feldwitz. But he's not here either. Not yet.'

Schenke forced himself to conceal his irritation. 'Is there anyone else in there besides you, friend?'

'Just two of the girls and Wohler, Herr Remer's business associate. Does the accounts for the boss. I can fetch him.'

'Open the door and take us to him. We need to have a look over the club in any case.'

The slot closed and they heard the rattle of bolts before the door opened and the doorman stood on the threshold, blocking the entrance.

'Who did you say you were?'

'I didn't. I'm Criminal Inspector Schenke and this is Scharführer Liebwitz.'

The man glanced at Schenke, taking longer to scrutinise the other figure, austere in his black hat and leather coat. 'Gestapo? Thought you said you were Kripo.' He regarded Liebwitz with wary respect.

'You'd better stop wasting our time and let us inside.'

The doorman was tall, with slick, dark curly hair and a moustache that was more full than was fashionable. He wore a velvet jacket that was tight over a large, muscular torso. He stepped aside to allow them in, then led them through a small panelled lobby to the club's interior. The coat-check counter was to their left, as well as a plain door. Before them the main area of the club opened up. Schenke estimated that there must be at least fifty tables as well as the booths on either side, all arranged around a stage some ten metres across. The chairs were stacked on the tables and there were cigarette stubs, napkins and fragments of snacks scattered across the dark wooden floor. Long black velvet curtains were drawn back on each side of the stage and looking over the interior the black and silver décor theme was clear to see. The bar counter was trimmed with polished steel, as were the mirrors behind the racks of glasses and bottles of spirits. There were more mirrors above that stretched along the wall beneath the coving, heavily designed in a swirling leaf pattern picked out in silver paint.

'Reichsführer Himmler would approve of the colour scheme,' Schenke muttered. Liebwitz glanced around and nodded. Two young women in work clothes and mob caps were sweeping around the tables. They barely acknowledged the two visitors before resuming their duties. The man who had let them in pointed to the door beside the coat-check counter.

'Through there and upstairs. The door to the office is straight ahead.'

'Fine.' Schenke indicated the women. 'Stay here with them. We will want to speak to you after we're done with Wohler.'

The doorman glanced at his watch. 'It's almost time for lunch break.'

'Then claim overtime if you have to. Just be here when we come back down.'

One of the women swore softly, but Schenke let it pass as he led Liebwitz to the door. It opened onto a narrow staircase with worn unvarnished steps. At the top was a short corridor. To their left a line of windows overlooked the interior of the club, and Schenke realised that these were what had appeared to be mirrors above the bar. A discreet means of keeping an eye on the customers. There were two open doors to their right, and as they passed them, he saw shelves laden with neatly folded napkins, boxes of glasses, cigarette cartons and several boxes of cigars as well as racks of spirit bottles.

The door at the end of the corridor was ajar, and a voice called out as they approached.

'Gunter? I told you not to bother me unless it was important!'

Schenke pushed it open and led the way inside the office, noting the varnished panelling and another window overlooking the interior of the club. The fine cream carpet was marked by some wear near the door and a few dark specks between the door and the desk in the far corner. The desk was large and topped with leather, and papers and folders were spread across the centre in front of the suited man sitting in the high-backed chair beyond. He was in his early forties, Schenke estimated. Closely cropped brown hair above a broad, flat forehead that reminded Schenke of a cliff. Deep-set grey eyes glinted like steel. His nose had been broken many times and was flattened and crooked. He revealed a bulky physique as he rose, and the overall impression was that of a boxer emerging from his corner to begin a bout. He was unlike any accountant Schenke had ever met.

'Who the hell are you?' he demanded.

'Inspector Schenke and Scharführer Liebwitz. Pankow precinct, Kripo.'

'Kripo, you say? Show me your badge.'

'I showed it to the heavy at the door. Sit down,' Schenke added firmly. His eyes scanned the office, noting the open drawers and cabinets along with the piles of papers on the desk. 'Doing some spring-cleaning, are we? Or lost something?'

Wohler regarded them with a hostile expression, and then his features relaxed slightly. 'What can I do for you, gentlemen? I imagine your visit has something to do with my late boss.'

Schenke's jaw twitched. The police had not yet released the name of the victim of the shooting.

Wohler chuckled. 'What? You think he didn't have a snout or two in the local police precinct? It's a mark to a pfennig that I knew about it before you did. Gunned down in some alley, along with that skirt he'd taken such a shine to.'

'You're well informed. I'll be sure to pass that on to the new precinct commander. Oberführer Radinsky doesn't look kindly on police officers who take bad money.'

'Money ain't good or bad, Inspector. It's just money. Some cops, on the other hand . . .'

'*Some* cops. They'll be weeded out.'

'Good luck with that.' Wohler reached for the small silver case resting on one of the open folders. He flipped it, extracted a cigarette and lit up as he eased himself into the chair.

'You seem to be making yourself at home,' said Schenke. 'And your boss isn't even at the morgue yet. Let alone buried.'

'He's dead.' Wohler shrugged. 'So his position falls to me.'

'Position? You mean head of the crime ring?'

Wohler placed his hand over his heart. 'Inspector, I'm mortified that you should make such an accusation. Herr Remer was an honest businessman who ran this club and a small import business. All perfectly legitimate, as any inspection of the records will prove.' He gestured towards the paperwork on the desk. 'You and the tax office are welcome to go over the accounts any time you like, once you produce the necessary authorisation. In the meantime . . .'

He slid some of the paperwork back into folders and closed them.

'You don't look like an accountant to me,' Schenke observed.

'Only a fool goes by appearances. It's been part of my work for years now. Speaking of appearances, it seems to me that your colleague doesn't look like a Kripo man. Is that how you operate these days? Bring a Gestapo thug along to intimidate the staff and the club's new boss?'

'Is that what you are? The name we were given was Feldwitz.'

'Feldwitz? He was sacked.'

'Sacked? Recently?'

'As recently as it gets, Inspector. Last night, in fact. Caught with his hand in the till.'

'So you go from accountant to owner and take over Remer's organisation. That's a pretty swift promotion.'

Wohler shrugged. 'True, but that's the way it is. Now I need to rise to the occasion, as the saying goes. My predecessor had no family to leave any of his property to. Everything of any value has been assigned to a trust, and I happen to be one of the trustees. So I am assuming control, pending all the relevant ownership documents and licences being put in my name. Nice and above board.'

Liebwitz coughed softly. 'Forgive me, Herr Wohler, but you seem very sanguine concerning the death of your boss.'

Wohler looked at Schenke with an amused smile. 'Is he for real? Listen, Scharführer, for the record, I am distraught over the violent and untimely death of Max Remer. All those who worked for him feel the same, and we mourn his passing.'

'And off the record?' Schenke pressed.

'One man's death is another man's opportunity. I can't bring Remer back to life, so what's the point in wasting breath over it? He was good at what he did and we all respected him for what he achieved. But success breeds enemies. There were plenty of people in Berlin who might have wanted him dead.'

'Such a heart-warming valediction,' Schenke responded flatly. 'I think I might cry.'

Liebwitz stirred and gave his superior a searching glance.

'Save your tears, Inspector. I doubt you'll ever find out who ordered the hit. And even if you dig up a suspect, you'll never have sufficient evidence to prove it in court.'

'Oh, we have a description of the gunman, and we know he had an accomplice. We'll find them. You and your underworld cronies are not quite the hard, silent types you think you are. There's always one who will break ranks and give us what we need. Once we have the shooter, we'll get the man who ordered the hit. You have any ideas about that?'

Wohler took a long drag on his cigarette and tilted his head back to exhale a swirling plume of smoke towards the ceiling. 'Like I said, Remer had enemies. If you want names, try the heads of the other crime rings.'

'Other crime rings?' Liebwitz interjected. 'So you admit Remer was a criminal.'

Wohler gave a dry laugh. 'Oops! You got me. I'm helpless before your razor-sharp line of questioning.' He raised his hands in mock surrender. 'Oh, I do like your Gestapo man, Inspector. Regular bloodhound he is. I'm sure you'll solve the case in a flash with him on your team.'

Schenke did not respond to the taunt and decided to shift tack. 'Where were you last night, between ten and two in the morning?'

'Let's see . . . I got to the club late, I'd say around eleven. I was with some friends, who will vouch for me. As will the man on the bar and the girls. The club closed around one, and once the last of the customers had gone, I sat with my boys and played cards until after three. Then we left and Gunter, the doorman, locked up. I made for home, stopping for a drink at the local beer cellar, where I chatted with the barman for an hour or so. I can give you his name and address if you need him to vouch for me.'

'So when did you find out about the shooting?'

'First thing this morning, when I got in. A friend at the precinct was kind enough to phone and leave a message.'

Liebwitz took out his notebook. 'What is the name of this friend?'

Wohler rolled his eyes. 'He's priceless, this one. His name, let me think . . . Ah yes, Michael Maus. His pals call him Mickey, I believe.'

Liebwitz started to note the detail down before Schenke could stop him.

'Who took the message?' asked Schenke.

'One of the girls.'

'And what exactly did she say the message was?'

'That Remer was shot dead on the way home to his flat. His woman, Kitty, was also shot but survived.'

'Did you believe it?'

'Why wouldn't I?'

'You didn't check with anyone else to confirm it?'

'I didn't have to. As soon as I got the message, I went to the alley to see for myself. I saw the Daimler. Then I came straight back here.'

'And carried on dealing with the accounts as if nothing had happened.' Schenke spoke drily. 'You have a funny way of showing grief for your former boss.'

'Would it help if I didn't get on with the job?'

Schenke turned towards the window and looked down at the stage and tables below. 'Did you speak with Remer last night?'

'Yes. Briefly. We had some business to sort out. We came up here to discuss it.'

'What exactly were you discussing?'

Wohler smiled thinly. 'Just business, like I said.'

'And then?'

'We went back downstairs and I went to the bar to join my friends while he went back to Kitty. They watched an act for a while, then got up to leave shortly after midnight. That's the last time I saw them.'

'I see . . .' Schenke responded. He was growing increasingly irritated by the way Wohler was fencing with him. 'Were you aware that his life might have been in danger?'

'Didn't you know? There's a war on. All our lives are in danger.'

'Just stop fucking around and answer the question.'

'Very well.' All trace of humour vanished from Wohler's face. 'The lives of such men are always in danger, Inspector. Same goes for me, and I'll not make the same mistake as my predecessor. Particularly when it comes to skirts. They're nearly always some kind of trouble. He went soft on Kitty. It was obvious he was smitten with her.' His lip curled with disgust. 'He let her get too close to him. Cared too much for her. He got distracted. I dare say if he hadn't been with her last night he'd have had his wits about him and would still be alive now. Remer used to be one of the best. He had a sixth sense as far as danger was concerned. Otherwise he wouldn't have got where he did. His falling for Kitty was what got him killed. That ain't going to happen to me.'

'Would that be because you're celibate?' Liebwitz queried. 'Or homosexual?'

Wohler froze. He glared at Liebwitz as his fists balled and he leaned his head forward in the way of a boxer preparing to exchange blows. 'Say that again . . .'

Schenke jumped in before his subordinate could respond. 'Do you know if Kunzler reciprocated his affection?'

Wohler breathed deeply and relaxed his fists, but his hostile stare was still fixed on Liebwitz as he spoke. 'You and your friend have outstayed your welcome, Inspector. It would be best for all three of us if you left right now, before your dim sidekick says anything else. Gestapo or no, I'll stuff his hat down his throat until he chokes on it and take my chances with Müller's lads at Gestapo HQ. Comes barging in here like I'm some cheap criminal and asks me if I'm a queer . . . If you want this fool to stay in one piece, I'd advise you to keep him out of my sight from now on. Get out, the pair of you.'

Schenke saw that there was little point in continuing to question Wohler for the present. He was typical of the Berlin underworld – a hard man who played for high stakes with little sense of remorse. He was not afraid of the police.

'We'll be back if we need to speak to you again. I take it you have no plans to leave Berlin.'

'Why would I? I ain't done anything wrong. Nothing to hide.'

'If you think of anything that might help our investigation, you can call the Kripo section at the precinct.'

'I've said everything I'm prepared to say. You won't be hearing from me. Now get out. I won't tell you again.'

Schenke refused to move just long enough to make it clear that he was choosing to leave rather than being told to. Then he tapped the brim of his hat in farewell and turned to leave the office, with Liebwitz falling into position at his shoulder.

Outside, as they made for the stairs, he addressed his companion in a low voice. 'Why did you ask him if he was homosexual?'

'I thought it was important to establish his sexuality, sir. That might be the reason why he rejects female companionship. It might have a bearing on the case.'

'It might also be because he is very particular about the female company he keeps. Did you notice the framed photographs on the shelf behind his desk? There were several face-down. Only one was still standing. The picture of Remer with Kitty on one side, and Wohler on the other.'

'I saw it, sir. What do you think it means?'

'I don't know. It's possible that Wohler isn't quite the

hard-faced criminal boss he makes himself out to be. Was he fond of Remer, or Kunzler, or perhaps both of them?' As they reached the top of the stairs, a further possibility occurred to him. 'Then again, maybe his fondness for them is now tempered by guilt.'

'Guilt? You think he may be behind the shootings?'

'Why not? Wohler wouldn't be the first gangster to climb over dead bodies to reach the top. However fond he might have been of those he killed to get his way.'

Chapter Seven

At the bottom of the stairs, Schenke paused and looked over the interior of the club. The women who had been sweeping the floor were taking the chairs down and arranging them about the small square tables. Behind the bar, the doorman was busy buffing the top of the counter with a chamois cloth. All three looked up as the two policemen made their way from the stairs towards the bar.

'Gunter. That's you, isn't it?' said Schenke.

The doorman nodded warily.

'Gunter what?'

'Breker.'

Schenke pulled out one of the stools and indicated to Liebwitz to do likewise. He glanced up at the mirrors above. It was almost certain that Wohler was watching them from his vantage point, unseen. Schenke gave a knowing smile in a bid to unsettle the man. Then he turned his attention to Breker.

'So you're the doorman, occasional barman and general dogsbody of the club.'

Breker stiffened as he stopped polishing the counter. 'I am

the deputy manager, as of this morning. Now that Wohler's the boss.'

'Then let me be the first to congratulate you on your promotion. How long have you been working at the club?'

'A while.'

'You can do better than that. It's not a trick question. How long?'

'Ten years.'

'Ten years,' Schenke repeated in a leaden tone. 'And all that time you've been the doorman. Hardly the stuff of dreams as far as careers go.'

'It pays well enough,' Breker said defensively. 'And there's food and drink thrown in. There are plenty of worse jobs in Berlin.'

'I'm sure. So you must have come to know Max Remer pretty well in all that time.'

Breker shrugged. 'As well as anyone does in my position. Which is to say that he was the boss and I worked for him and that's as far as it goes. He tells me, Gunter, do that, Gunter, do this, and I do it, and do it quick, and we got along fine on that basis. I run the bar, keep an eye on stock, and balance the takings against the cash held upstairs each month. But as for knowing him well, you've come to the wrong man, Inspector.'

'A pity . . . Sounds to me like you weren't particularly fond of your former boss.'

'I liked him well enough.' Breker returned to polishing the counter.

'Well someone didn't,' Schenke said, reaching across to grip the man's wrist. 'Someone disliked him enough to shoot him twice in the chest and in the head, and shoot Fräulein Kunzler while they were at it. So, Gunter, I'd greatly appreciate it if you chose to help us find those responsible. It's the least you can do for Max Remer, eh?'

Their eyes met and Schenke registered the hostile glint in Breker's gaze before he looked away and gave a sullen nod.

'That's better.' Schenke smiled, releasing his hold. 'Let's put the tough-guy act to one side now that you've done your best to impress me. I've seen it all before. Many times. So spare me the posturing and let's talk straight. The sooner we do, the sooner I'll be out of your hair and you can continue polishing the counter and trying to impress the ladies.'

Breker flushed slightly and folded his arms to emphasise the bulk of his shoulders. Schenke glanced over his shoulder at the two women and saw their amused expressions before they turned their attention back to sweeping up the litter between the tables.

'So,' he continued, 'Remer was a major criminal. One of the biggest in Berlin. You worked for him for ten years, so you cannot have avoided seeing and hearing many things about his business. I appreciate that there is a code of silence shared by such men and those who work for them. I admire loyalty. It's a good, solid German quality. But the man you were loyal to has been murdered, and I have been ordered to find his killers and bring them to justice. Reichsführer Himmler is determined that such matters are resolved swiftly to demonstrate to the German people that the party will not tolerate gangsters gunning each other down on the streets. There's a war on, and such things distract and unsettle the public. You, Gunter, are in the fortunate position of being able to do your patriotic duty in helping the investigation along. If you refuse to answer our questions, then regrettably, I will be obliged to have the Scharführer handcuff you and take you down to the precinct, and we will keep you there until I get the answers I need. Are we clear?'

'Yes, Inspector.'

'Good. Then let's try again in a moment. For now, the Scharführer and I would appreciate something to drink, since it is turning into a long morning. Two coffees.'

'Not for me, sir,' said Liebwitz. 'But a cup of tea would be welcome.'

'Tea?' Schenke repeated.

'Yes, sir. I find the taste of coffee undesirable. It also affects my thinking.'

'I should hope so. I can't think straight without it.'

'That's not the effect I was alluding to, sir. Coffee has an . . . uncomfortable influence. I don't like the smell either.'

Schenke shook his head in wonder. 'Very well then, no coffee for the Scharführer. Give him a cup of tea.'

'I doubt we have any,' Breker replied.

'I'd have a good look for it and find some,' said Schenke. 'Unless you want to be in the Gestapo's black books.'

Breker called to the nearest of the women cleaning the saloon area. 'Bertha! A coffee and a tea for our . . . guests.'

'Tea?'

'There'll be some in the storeroom. To the left of the stove.'

'Since you know where it is, it might be better if you make the drinks,' Schenke intervened.

Breker looked surprised, then angry. 'Now that Feldwitz is gone, I'm the acting manager. I say who does what in here.'

'We need to have a word with your staff. Preferably somewhere quiet.' Schenke pointed towards a booth to the right of the stage. 'That will do. You can bring the drinks over there.'

'That's the owner's seating,' Breker protested.

'He hasn't much use for it any more, if I am any judge of Herr Remer's condition.'

As Schenke strode across the floor of the club, he called back to Breker.

'Real coffee, mind. Not that ersatz shit.'

The barman scowled, threw down his cloth and stormed towards the swing door. As he disappeared, Schenke turned to the women.

'We have a few questions to ask about last night. We'll start with you.' He indicated the woman Breker had addressed. 'Bertha, right?'

She nodded and leaned the brush she had been using against the nearest table before self-consciously adjusting her cap and tucking her hair behind her ears.

'Why did you send the man to make the coffee?' Liebwitz asked quietly.

'He needed time to cool off. We'll deal with him later. Besides, I got the impression that he might be as unforthcoming as our friend in the office up there. Come.'

Schenke led the way to the booth and the two men slipped onto the padded leather-covered benches. A moment later, Bertha approached the booth as her companion ceased her labours and began to roll a cigarette.

'Sit down, Bertha.' Schenke nodded to the bench opposite. He noted that she hesitated before doing as she was told. 'I take it you don't get to sit there often.'

'Never.' She shook her head. 'It's against the rules. I'm not even allowed to touch it. Gunter is the only one who is allowed to clean this booth. Herr Remer was quite particular about it. There was a girl here, not long after I started, who sat here during her break. The boss was in his office up there and saw it. He came down in a rage. He didn't shout, or hit her or anything, but there was a look on his face. I was terrified. He glared at her for a moment and then told her to leave the club at once. And she wasn't to collect her wages owing, nor ever be seen here again.'

'Did he tell her what would happen if she did?' asked Liebwitz.

'He didn't have to. She almost ran out of the door and I haven't heard anything of her since. Herr Remer was not the kind of man who needed to say anything twice, if you know what I mean.'

'We've all met them,' Schenke said sympathetically. He looked the woman over. She had a rounded face with pronounced cheekbones and brown eyes. Her nose was slightly snubbed above full lips. Even without make-up she was pretty in a homely way, and looked innocent and vulnerable. That would appeal to some of the club's customers, he surmised. The kind of men looking for an idealised version of demure German maidenhood.

'Where are you from, Bertha?'

'Kreuzberg. I was born there. I live in an apartment nearby with some of the girls from the club now.'

'To get away from your family?'

'No, I have a good family. I just wanted to make something of myself and not go down the usual road taken by girls from the area: find a man, get married, have kids and wait for old age to come.'

'And working as a cleaner in the club is an aspiration?' Liebwitz observed as he made some notes.

'I can sing,' she shot back fiercely. 'I earn enough to pay for lessons. My tutor says I have a natural talent. He's going to help me break into the big time. I'm working towards getting on the programme here. Once I'm noticed, I'll get a chance to sing on the radio and be recorded.' Her eyes widened with excitement, but Schenke's heart had been sinking as she spoke. He was reminded of what Kitty had said about her own origins. There were many more girls like this, lured to Berlin by the prospect of stardom, or finding a rich husband, and escaping their drab lives and a future that promised more of the same. For every thousand who came seeking their fortune, only a handful realised their dreams. The rest were doomed to exploitation, frustration and despair as their hopes were ground to dust and blown into Berlin's gutters.

'How long have you been working at the club, Bertha?'

'Nearly a year now.'

'How old are you?' asked Liebwitz.

'Seventeen. I'll be eighteen in a month's time.'

'Seventeen . . .' He made a note.

'Long enough to get to know the people here well,' Schenke probed. 'And to be familiar with their comings and goings, right?'

'I suppose.'

'What did you think of Herr Remer? Besides being frightened of him.'

'Oh, that was only the once. The rest of the time he was good to me. And the rest of us.' She lowered her voice and glanced towards the mirrored windows above the bar. 'He kept his hands off the girls and made sure that his men knew not to touch us as well.'

'His men?'

'Gunter, Herr Wohler and the rest of the lads.'

'And do these lads work at the club too?'

'No. They work in Herr Remer's other businesses. They come here to drink and wait for orders. They never cause any trouble.'

Not in here maybe, thought Schenke. Doubtless they caused trouble to plenty of people who dealt with Remer's 'other businesses'.

'Did you notice anything different about Remer in recent days?'

She frowned. 'What do you mean?'

'Did he seem agitated or anxious, or even afraid?'

Bertha thought briefly. 'I wouldn't say I noticed that he was any of those things. Angry perhaps. He was short with all the staff for most of last week. Snapping at anyone who got in his way. I thought maybe he and Kitty had had a row over something.'

'A row? Did they often have such disagreements?'

'No more than most couples I know. But it can't have been easy for either of them.'

'Oh? Why is that?'

Bertha wrinkled her nose. 'He was a hard man and could be very cold at times. Kitty is outward-going and fun to be with. Even more so when he wasn't around. When he was, the light just seemed to go out of her and she had to behave like some ice-queen movie star for him.' She paused and lowered her voice. 'I guess that's why some people said she was a real bitch, pardon my language, Inspector.'

Schenke felt his senses quicken. 'Which people said that, Bertha?'

She nodded discreetly in the direction of the bar. 'Him for one.'

Liebwitz craned his neck. 'Breker?'

Schenke shot him a warning look. 'Keep it down, Scharführer. You want to wake the dead?'

The swing door beside the bar swung open and the barman reappeared carrying a small wooden tray bearing two steaming mugs. He crossed to the booth and set the tray down heavily so that the liquid in the cups spilled over the rims.

'Thank you, Gunter.' Schenke nodded before he turned to Bertha. 'While we're at it, do you want something to drink?'

'She doesn't get to drink on the club's time,' said Breker.

'But she's not on the club's time,' Schenke responded. 'She's on our time right now and doing her civic duty in helping the Kripo with their inquiries, like the good German she is. Show a little public spirit there, and some manners, and get the lady a drink, Gunter.'

He turned back to Bertha. 'Coffee?'

She looked down at the table, refusing to meet Breker's glare, and shook her head. Breker gave a cold smile and went back to the bar. There was a beat before Schenke continued.

'Let's talk about last night. Were you working here?'

Bertha nodded.

'Was it a typical night?'

'How do you mean?'

'The usual number of customers, the usual routine, the usual atmosphere, that sort of thing.'

'I'd say it was quieter than usual. It's been that way for a week or so, now that you mention it. That's not so good for me as it means fewer tips. I'd say we were less than half full when the acts started. The boss liked to begin the evening with the dancers and the other acts that catch the attention of the customers.'

'Oh?' Schenke arched an eyebrow.

'You know the sort of thing men like. The kind of acts that hold their attention while they get drinking. That's when the money rolls in.'

'Those would be sexually gratifying acts?' Liebwitz queried. 'Such as?'

Schenke coughed. 'Use your imagination, Scharführer, and save that for later. Just get the salient details down, eh?'

'Yes, sir.'

'So, Bertha, what then?'

'Once they're on the drink, the customers can get a bit rowdy with us girls. So that's when the comedian comes on, to distract them and keep them cheery. The final act is the accordion player. He gets them all singing, old-fashioned material mostly, and some party songs. Can go on for a couple of hours before he's done, then there's final drinks before the customers go and we close up.'

'Your boss and Kitty were there last night. How did they seem to you? Was there any sign of bad feeling between them?'

'No, not as I recall. At least not until Otto . . .' She paused. 'Herr Bachmann was called over to this booth to join the boss and Kitty. I was serving drinks on the other side of the club, but I could see that there was some trouble going on. After a few minutes, Herr Bachmann got up from the booth and went to the dressing room behind the stage.' She indicated a door half hidden by the folds of the curtain.

'Was there friction between Bachmann and Remer prior to last night?' Liebwitz asked.

'I don't know. The boss rarely talked to any of the acts. He left that sort of thing to Herr Wohler and Breker. I guess he had other things to deal with outside of the club and didn't have much spare time to run this place. If there was any bad blood between them, I didn't know about it. They just didn't seem to be on friendly terms last night, if that means anything.'

'What happened after the comedian left the booth?' Schenke pressed on.

'A little later I noticed that Herr Wohler and some other men had come in. They waited a moment and then went up the stairs. It struck me at the time because they didn't hand over their hats and coats to Magda.' She nodded towards the other woman, who had finished her cigarette and resumed her work. 'The boss left the booth and followed them. He wasn't gone for long. When he came back, he sat with Kitty until they left the club. That's the last time I saw them.' Bertha swallowed nervously. 'Then this morning, Herr Wohler said they'd been shot and he was now in charge.'

Schenke leaned forward. 'Do you recall what time he told you this?'

'First thing this morning.' She hesitated. 'At least that's when I heard it from Breker. He told me and Magda when we showed up at seven o'clock.'

Schenke turned to Liebwitz. 'News travels fast.'

'Gossip even faster, so it would appear, sir.'

'Quite.' Schenke was about to resume questioning Bertha when they heard voices and glanced towards the entrance. Three workmen in stained brown overalls entered. The last was carrying a metal container and a tool bag. The nearest approached the bar and rapped on the counter.

'Friend! We're here to see the manager. It's about the decorating job.'

'Decorating job? Who are you?' Breker's eyes narrowed before he relaxed. 'I'm the manager. You'd better explain what this is about.'

'You're in charge?' the workman asked doubtfully. 'Herr Wohler?'

Schenke saw Breker bristle before he replied testily, 'Like I said, I'm the manager.'

'All right then!' The workman raised his hand placatingly. 'Just needed to be sure.'

He reached into the bulging pocket at his side. There was something in his expression that instantly caused Schenke to tense up. The man pulled out a pistol and aimed it at Breker, who just had time to hold his hands up. 'No! Wait!'

There was a flash from the muzzle, and a shockingly loud crash that resonated off the walls of the club as the shot was fired.

Chapter Eight

Breker stumbled against the far end of the bar as the bullet struck him. Two more shots were fired and the glass of a framed picture several metres beyond him shattered. Schenke saw one of the other workmen draw a weapon as he took two steps in their direction.

'Down!' He leaned across the table and grabbed Bertha's arm, dragging her violently aside. She let out a gasp. Magda dropped her broom and screamed as she ran across the front of the stage towards the backstage door. Schenke fumbled for the Walther on his belt while Liebwitz came up with a service Luger and twisted round to crouch on the padded bench. Another shot crashed out, and Magda spun round and tumbled to the floor out of sight behind the tables. She let out a pained cry, and a moment later Schenke saw the backstage door ease open as she crawled through, trailing blood. He turned to Bertha, who was on her side on the far seat, knees drawn up and eyes wide with terror as she clutched her hands to her ears.

'There's two more of his men in the booth in the corner!' a voice called out. 'Work round to them! Vachek, get the place lit up!'

Two more shots were fired, and the bullets tore up the wood along the top of the booth, showering the two policemen and the woman with splinters. Bertha let out a sharp scream and closed her eyes tightly.

'We can't let them trap us here,' Schenke decided as he held his weapon up and thumbed off the safety catch. 'The man at the bar might still be there. I'll shoot it up. You get the girl and move behind the booth. Then cover me while I join you. That clear?'

Liebwitz had dislodged his wire-framed glasses as he ducked down, and was hastily readjusting them as he held the Luger ready.

'On two,' Schenke said through gritted teeth. 'One . . . two!'

He rose and took aim, cradling the butt of the Walther in his left palm as he pointed the weapon at the head and shoulders of the man who had shot Breker, now crouching behind the bar. To his right, he saw the top of another man's head bobbing up and down behind the tables on the far side of the club as he worked his way forward to get a better view of the booth. His trigger finger squeezed, and the Walther bucked in his grip as the first shot sounded deafeningly. A spirit bottle above and to the left of his target exploded, showering liquid and shards of glass over the man, who had ducked just in time. Schenke fired three more shots; one at the same place and one to each side, shattering more bottles and the patterned mirror behind. Then he turned sharply and fired at the tables where he estimated the second man was, splintering a chair leg stacked on top. He had no sight of the third man.

'Liebwitz, move!'

The Scharführer crouched as he exited the booth, grabbing Bertha's arm and hauling her off the bench. She yelped as she struck the floor and was thrust into cover. Liebwitz raised his weapon.

'Ready.'

'Moving!' Schenke called back as loudly as he dared. He clambered off the bench and landed awkwardly, sending a piercing pain up his bad leg. Grimacing, he half scurried, half stumbled around the booth as Liebwitz unleashed two shots at the bar and two more towards the second gunman before crouching again. An instant later, the second gunman bobbed up and fired wildly. Both bullets thudded through the leather covers of the booth.

Schenke crouched beside Bertha and took her hand.

'When I say, we go for the door.'

She nodded, and her eyes shifted towards the backstage door. It was still ajar, and there were streaks of blood on the floor where Magda had crawled to safety. Bertha's nose wrinkled. 'Can you smell that?'

Schenke tilted his head back slightly. 'Petrol . . . We have to get out of here. Liebwitz, I'll take her. You ready?'

The Scharführer nodded. Then he rose and fired again, emptying the remaining rounds of his clip at the two men. As the shots blasted out, Schenke gripped Bertha's hand tightly and scuttled towards the door. They rushed through and stumbled over Magda, lying at the end of a corridor. She screamed in pain and surprise and thrust Schenke away in panic. He staggered backwards, and grabbed the door frame to stop himself tumbling out into the open.

'Shit . . .' he muttered, heart racing, before his attention returned to Bertha. 'Get her out of the way!'

As Bertha bent to lift her companion to her feet and help

her along the corridor, Schenke pressed his back against the wall by the door frame.

'Liebwitz!'

'Sir?'

'Prepare to move.'

'A moment, reloading . . .'

Several more shots smashed into the booth as more splinters and puffs of stuffing burst into the air. The smell of petrol was stronger now, the intention of their attackers clear: to burn the club and kill anyone in it. Schenke recalled that Wohler was still in his office. There was nothing that could be done for him. He had to get Liebwitz and the others out, then deal with the gunmen.

There was a metallic snap as Liebwitz cocked his weapon. Schenke steadied his grip, and then quickly leaned round the door frame, his automatic levelled in the direction of the bar. He saw the man who had shot Breker edging along it, weapon raised. Their gazes locked, and they fired at the same instant. The other man's bullets struck the wall above the door, and plaster and dust exploded over Schenke's head. In return, he saw one of his own shots hit the gunman in the shoulder, punching him round as his weapon flew across the bar. Liebwitz ducked under Schenke's arm and hurried to the safety of the narrow corridor leading to the rear of the club.

Glancing to his right, Schenke saw a chair tumble off a table, nudged by the second gunman as he made his way back to the entrance. At that moment the remaining attacker emerged to help his wounded colleague behind the bar. He had a gun in his hand and loosed a series of shots in Schenke's direction, one of which struck the opposite side of the door frame and shattered the woodwork, causing Schenke to flinch back into cover. Glancing round, he saw Liebwitz standing two metres along the corridor.

'Winged one of them, but there's two left. Maybe a driver and more of them outside.'

'What are your orders, sir? What about Wohler?'

'We save the women first. Look for a service door. I'll stay here until you get them outside. Go.'

Liebwitz hurried down the corridor, which Schenke now saw stretched some twenty metres back, with a number of doors on both sides. To the rear, in the dim light of two bulbs, he saw Bertha with Magda's arm slung around her shoulder. He turned back to the interior of the club. No more shots had been fired and he could hear muted conversation above the ringing in his ears. The stench of petrol was heavy in the air, and suddenly there was a dull thud and a flare of light. Risking a quick glance, he saw flames leaping up around the tables and chairs, and through the wave of red and orange he made out the shapes of the three men covering the entrance. He closed the door, then changed the magazine before he holstered his Walther and followed Liebwitz and the two women.

They reached the service entrance just before him, and Bertha slid the bolts back, turned the handle and thrust at the door. It remained closed. She pushed again, to no effect, before Liebwitz stepped up beside her.

'Let me,' he ordered.

He grasped the handle and strained at the door. Then he braced his shoulder and tried again as Schenke caught up with him. The door opened a fraction and admitted a sliver of daylight but refused to move any further.

'They must have blocked it on the outside,' said Schenke.

He turned to the women. 'Is there another way out at the rear of the club. Another door? Window?'

Bertha shook her head.

'Keep trying, Liebwitz.' He hurried back to the door leading into the club and opened it fractionally to peer through. He was struck by a wave of heat that made him wince. The interior was ablaze from the counter to halfway across the floor. The bottles behind the counter and the mirrors were shattering in the intense heat. Flames raged around the stacked tables and chairs and consumed the fabrics draped along the walls. He looked up to the mirrored windows of the office. One had already burst, but there was no sign of Wohler, nor any prospect of saving him if he was trapped within. He closed the door and made his way back to the others, coughing to clear the hot air from his lungs.

Liebwitz made one last effort to shift the service door, his face contorted with effort, and then gave in.

'It's no good, sir.'

Schenke saw the frightened expressions of the two women and the blood dripping from the tips of Magda's fingers, which were clasped over the wound on her side. He turned to Bertha. 'Find something to press on the wound and stop the bleeding.'

'There'll be something in the dressing room,' she offered.

'Fine, take Magda with you and see to it while we try to get the door open.'

Once he was alone with Liebwitz, he spoke urgently. 'There's no way out through the club. The place is an inferno. If we can't get out of here in the next few minutes, we'll be roasted. One more go . . .'

They braced themselves against the solid wooden surface and

Schenke gave a nod. Both men heaved for several seconds, but the gap barely widened.

'It's no good, we need to find another way.'

'There isn't another way,' said Liebwitz. 'You heard her.'

'If that's the case, we'll have to try something else here. Search the storerooms. There may be something we can use.'

As Liebwitz moved along the corridor, glancing into each room, Schenke entered the dressing room. Magda was sitting on a stool, her apron and blouse lying in a bloodied heap beside her. Bertha had folded a cloth into a wad and was tying it over the wound with a bright red scarf. Crossing to the rails where dancers' frocks hung, Schenke snatched off the nearest three and hurried out of the room and back to the main door, beneath which smoke was already curling. He stuffed a frock into the gap at the bottom, and then did the same where he could along the sides. All the while he could feel the heat building up on the surface of the door. Even if he had managed to limit the smoke entering the corridor, there was nothing he could do to prevent the blaze breaking through and spreading to the rest of the building, incinerating himself and the others trapped inside.

Searching the nearest storeroom, he found a red bucket half filled with sand and a rusted stirrup-pump extinguisher. He hissed angrily at what appeared to be the club's firefighting provision and continued to work through the room without finding anything of use. There were several wooden crates on some sturdy shelving against the wall opposite the door, and he heaved one towards him in case it might contain something that would help them. Seeing that the top was screwed down, he let the crate fall onto its corner, and the wooden sides splintered, disgorging a bundle of coloured sheets of paper. When he picked one up and held it to the light coming in from the corridor, he saw neatly printed rows of ration coupons.

A shout from Liebwitz came from the corridor. Schenke pocketed one of the bundles and hurried out of the room to see the Scharführer holding up an axe.

'Well done!' He smiled grimly. 'Get to work on the door.'

Liebwitz took the axe in a double-handed grip and swung it. The blade struck the door with a loud bang and recoiled from the surface, leaving a deep dent but no further damage.

'You're obviously not a country boy. Give it to me.'

Schenke removed his coat and took the axe, adjusting his grip along the shaft to make sure he controlled the aim and force of each blow.

'Stand back.'

He did his best to get some power behind the strike in the confines of the corridor and targeted the area around the higher of the two heavy iron hinges. The first blow bit into the wood close to the frame and splintered some of the worn timber. He swung again and again, breaking up the wood and loosening the screws that held the hinge in place.

Liebwitz, watching from a safe distance, pointed towards the ceiling.

'Sir . . .'

Schenke looked up to see coils of smoke working their way overhead. He could hear the muffled roar of flames and saw the door at the end of the corridor begin to blister. He returned to his work, battering and smashing the gradually failing hinge until it began to come away from the jagged, splintered woodwork. There was a cry of alarm from the dressing room.

'See to them,' he ordered Liebwitz, and resumed hammering away at the hinge. Sparks flew with each strike. A final blow saw the hinge tear free and swing away fractionally, and Schenke lowered the axe and tested the door. There was more give, and the top of the door inclined away to reveal a strip of daylight a centimetre wide.

He turned to see the two women emerge from the dressing room coughing. Liebwitz came after them and closed the door behind them.

'Fire must have spread to the space behind the stage, sir. Where it backs onto the dressing room.'

Smoke was starting to fill the corridor as the door to the seating area smouldered and the first bright glint of flames showed through a split in the wood.

Hefting the axe again, Schenke attacked the lower hinge directly, carving up the wood above it as the edge bit into the iron. The door shuddered and rattled with every blow and the gaps around the edge became more pronounced. The smoke was thickening in the corridor, and it caught in the throats of those trapped inside. Schenke's arms trembled and the shaft twisted in his hands.

'Take over.' He handed the axe to Liebwitz and indicated the remaining hinge. 'Aim there.'

He stood aside as the Scharführer braced his legs and set to work. He had clearly learned from watching his superior and now handled the tool with skill. Several more blows were sufficient to batter the hinge free from the door, then he dropped the axe and both men heaved. To no avail. Whatever had been used to pin the door in place was more than a match for the two policemen.

'Let's try moving it to the side,' Schenke suggested, eyes streaming.

'Please hurry!' Bertha cried. 'Please!'

With muscles straining, Schenke and Liebwitz managed to ease the door a short distance along the wall, and were able to adjust their grip to the edge where the hinges had been fastened before. As the door grated along the outside brickwork and light poured into the smoke-filled corridor, they could see the first of the heavy wooden props angled across the alley. As soon as the door was far enough along, the end of the prop fell down across the threshold with a solid thud. The opening was large enough for them to get through, and Schenke nodded to Liebwitz.

'You first. I'll help the women out.'

Liebwitz squeezed his way into the alley and turned as Schenke beckoned to Magda.

'You next. Watch for splinters.'

He helped her negotiate the gap, and Liebwitz half carried her towards the street at the front of the club. Bertha slipped through easily, then Schenke snatched up his coat and worked his way between the door and the frame and out into the alley. The air outside was cool and clear, and he gulped down some breaths and coughed as he cleared the acrid smoke from his lungs. Pointing, he spluttered, 'That way! Run.'

As they set off, he saw smoke billowing into the clear spring sky and realised that the flames must already be burning through the roof of the club. There was a shuddering crash as masonry, timber and tiles collapsed somewhere within the building, and the cobbled ground seemed to tremble beneath their feet. The heat in the alley was intense, and he did his best to shield his face with his coat as he ran. He saw that Bertha's mob cap was smouldering and she was beating at it in a frenzy. Then they were out of the alley and in the street, rushing towards the gathering crowd.

A handful of Orpo men were doing their best to keep the

onlookers back. Magda was slumped against a lamp post a short distance along the street while Liebwitz waved down an approaching car. Bertha had torn the smoking cap from her head and hurled it aside, and Schenke guided her to join their companions as Liebwitz leaned towards the driver's window.

'This woman's injured. You must take her to the nearest hospital – the Mittelstein.'

The driver, a man in his fifties wearing an expensive suit, shook his head. 'I'll not have her bleed over the upholstery. Call an ambulance, young man. That's what they're there for.'

Schenke saw Liebwitz's eyes narrow behind his glasses as he tapped his leather coat. 'Who do you think I work for?'

The driver's haughty demeanour crumbled and he jerked his thumb over his shoulder. 'Put her in the back.'

Magda was helped into the vehicle and Schenke instructed Bertha to go with her to keep an eye on her, but also to make certain the driver did as he was told. As the car accelerated away, he could not help a wry chuckle. 'Nicely played, Scharführer.'

There was another crash of collapsing masonry. The club's façade was still intact even as flames raged behind it.

'God help Wohler if he's still in there,' Schenke muttered. In the distance, the clanging of the bell of an approaching fire engine sounded over the roar of the flames.

'He's safe, sir,' said Liebwitz and pointed to the far side of the crowd. 'Over there.'

Schenke saw the crime ring's new leader being held between two Orpo men. Even at a distance of fifty metres, he fancied he could hear Wohler's voice above the din shouting angrily at the policemen as he tried to break free.

'Come on, Scharführer. I'm keen to see what our friend has to say about this mayhem.'

Chapter Nine

'Idiot! You've got the wrong man!' Wohler bellowed into the face of the Orpo sergeant, who regarded him coolly.

'You can tell me all about it down at the precinct. Right now, I want you to be a good boy and stop giving my men an earful. I'll ask you nicely this once, and then I won't—'

Wohler's expression twisted furiously. 'What's your name, you jumped-up little prick? I have friends in the party. When they hear about what you clowns have subjected me to, you'll be lucky to have a job as a sewer attendant.'

'Friends in high places, eh?' The sergeant smiled. 'How many times have I heard that?'

'You fool . . . Do you know who I am?'

'Why? Have you forgotten? Lads, hold him nice and tight.'

The policemen on either side took Wohler firmly by the arms so that he could barely move. The sergeant bunched his gloved hands into fists and leaned forward as he spoke in a menacing undertone. 'This is what you get for calling us clowns.'

He slammed his fist into his captive's stomach, and Wohler lurched forward with a gasp before the follow-up blow struck him on the cheek, knocking his head to one side. The sergeant was about to strike again but was interrupted by a shout from Schenke as he came trotting up with Liebwitz at his shoulder.

'That's enough!'

The Orpo man turned to him, fists still raised. He gave Schenke a speculative glance before he took in Liebwitz's attire. He lowered his fists before stepping back a pace. 'Just teaching this one some manners. Who are you?'

'Criminal Inspector Schenke, Pankow precinct. Why are you holding this man?'

'Me and the lads had spotted the smoke and were driving up when we saw this lunatic standing in the street emptying his gun at a van. We stopped and arrested him. He was shouting some nonsense about men shooting the place up before they set it on fire.'

'He's telling the truth. This is Herr Wohler. He runs the club.'

Wohler looked up, gasping painfully. 'That's what I've been telling these numbskulls . . .'

'The Scharführer and I were in the club when the men began shooting,' Schenke added.

The sergeant looked at Wohler. 'You never mentioned that any police officers were attacked.'

'Didn't I? Must have slipped my mind. I was more worried about the bastards letting fly at my barman and the girls before they set fire to the place. Wasn't so worried about your Kripo friends.'

The sergeant's heavy jaw tensed as he made to deliver another punch, but Schenke stepped between him and Wohler. 'That will do, Sergeant. We'll take over from here. You and your men can help control the crowd when the fire brigade gets here.'

The sergeant hesitated, then nodded to the uniformed policemen. 'Release him, lads. We've got better things to do.'

Wohler shook his arms free and made to go after the officers, but Schenke caught him by the wrist. 'No.'

'I told those bloody fools to follow the van, but they let it get clean away while they arrested me. Idiots! Anyway, that fat bastard still has my gun.'

'And you won't be getting it back,' said Schenke.

'I need it. You saw what happened to Breker. I ain't going to be defenceless the next time I come up against them. I need a gun for my own safety.'

'Not for now you don't. I'm taking you into protective custody. You'll be safe enough at the precinct, and then we can have a nice cosy chat about what that was all about.' Schenke indicated the blazing building.

The first fire engine came roaring along the street and braked to a halt before it reached the crowd. The sergeant and his men were immediately occupied in driving the onlookers back. Schenke regarded the scene.

'Nothing more we can do here. Let's go.'

'I'm not going anywhere with you,' Wohler said defiantly. 'I've got a few places of my own where I can be safe. Places where I'll be protected by tougher men than you.'

'You think so?' Schenke gave a wry smile. 'The men who did this were after you. They asked for you by name before they started shooting. You're marked for death, just like Remer. They knew where to find both of you, and when you'd be at your most vulnerable. Do you think it was a coincidence that they struck when none of your thugs were with you? You were fortunate that Liebwitz and I were in the club at the time, otherwise they'd have searched the place and caught you in your office. You were lucky you managed to escape from the building in time. You were luckier still that those police officers were passing when you came out to shoot at your attackers, otherwise they might have come back to finish the job.' He paused. 'I'd say your guardian angel is on overtime today. Protective custody is merely the latest step in your run of luck. Cuff him, Scharführer, and let's get him out of here before that luck runs out.'

It was late afternoon by the time they reached the Pankow precinct and registered Wohler with the sergeant in charge of custody. Schenke had him entered under an assumed name to head off any lawyer Wohler might have on a retainer. It would also stop anyone else from tracking him down easily. As he was led off to the cells, Wohler shouted at them.

'You have me for the moment, Inspector, but I'll be out of here soon enough. You better watch your back! You and your Gestapo monkey!'

Liebwitz blinked. 'Monkey?'

'I wouldn't take too much offence at that. You'll hear worse while you serve with us.'

'I suppose so.' Liebwitz gave a shrug as he turned towards the stairs. 'Easy for you to say, sir. In any case, if I'm the monkey, that makes you the organ grinder.'

Schenke was caught by surprise. Was Liebwitz disrespecting his rank, or actually making an attempt at humour? 'Well I never . . .' he muttered as he caught up with his subordinate. He glanced at the Scharführer and saw the familiar deadpan expression, and wondered if he'd imagined the sardonic tone in the man's voice a moment earlier.

As they entered the Kripo office, Sergeant Hauser gave a low whistle. 'Look what the cat dragged in. You two been having a tussle in a coal bunker?'

Schenke realised that his face and clothing must be as streaked with grime as those of Liebwitz, and both of them reeked of smoke.

'What the hell happened to you?' Hauser continued.

'I'll tell you, but first I need a drink. Rosa! Some coffee, please.'

The young woman nodded and made off towards the canteen while Schenke led Liebwitz and Hauser into his office and hung his coat and hat on the peg beside the door. Once they were all seated, he told the sergeant about the interview with Katharina Kunzler at the hospital, and the others at the club before the shooting started. When he described the latter, and the blaze that followed, Hauser listened closely, shaking his head.

'You were both lucky to get out of there alive. Christ knows what we've walked into here. I thought it was just some mobster settling an old score with Remer. Now it seems we're looking at a full-on war between two of the crime rings. Just what Berlin needs with the real deal going on at the same time.'

'It may be as you say,' Liebwitz said. 'It's also possible that the murder of Remer and the attack on the club are not the work of the same people.'

'You think it's a coincidence?' Hauser asked drily. 'If it looks like a duck . . .'

'I don't understand the analogy, Sergeant . . .' Liebwitz's high forehead creased, then he shook his head and continued. 'In any case, it's possible that the attack on the club was opportunistic. Another crime ring taking advantage of Remer's death to make a move against his organisation. Remove his immediate replacement and destroy his base of operations before Wohler has time to cement his takeover. In either case, we can expect further violence.'

'I fear you are right,' said Schenke. 'And there's something else that concerns me. If the attack was opportunist, as you say, they must have found out about Remer's death very quickly. In which case Remer's ring is not the only crime gang with informants amongst those working out of the Pankow precinct.'

Hauser sighed. 'Shit, that's all we need. Some lowlifes in Orpo selling their souls to the gangsters.'

'It's not unheard of,' Liebwitz commented. 'It is possible that it's not only Orpo informants we have to worry about.'

Schenke saw the sergeant bridle. 'I have no reason to question the integrity of anyone in this section, Scharführer. Nor should you.'

Liebwitz stiffened slightly. 'I did not mean any offence, sir. I was just stating a factor we should not discount without consideration.'

'Well, I've considered it and now it is discounted. Is that clear?'

'Yes, sir.'

'Good.'

Rosa tapped on the glass and opened the door. Schenke smiled and thanked her as she set her tray down, and waited until she had withdrawn before continuing. 'There's something else.'

He reached into his jacket pocket and took out the coupons he had taken from the storeroom at the Ace of Hearts. 'These were in a crate at the club. There were several more crates on the shelves.' He paused to estimate the quantity. 'I'd say there was room for twenty such bundles in the case I opened. So . . . around a hundred and fifty more of these bundles.'

He untied the string and fanned out the printed sheets. 'Meat coupons . . . Must be at least two hundred of them, each one good for a month's rations for four people.'

Hauser whistled. 'That bundle alone would fetch a small fortune on the black market.'

'Quite. I wonder if the men who came to the club knew about these and intended to take them away after they'd dealt with Wohler. Only Liebwitz and I caused a change of plan.' Schenke tapped the pile of coupons. 'I'm certain these are the same forgeries we've been hunting down for months. Given the quantity I saw in the club, I'd say we're close to the source. I think Remer's ring was printing them. A pity we didn't have time to search the place before the fire.'

'I find it difficult to believe that he would have risked printing them at the club,' said Liebwitz.

'You may be right,' Schenke allowed. 'In any case, Wohler must know where they're being printed. He's a hard case. He won't be in any hurry to give us the location. But he will be keen to get himself released from protective custody. He needs to get a grip on the rest of his ring, make sure they understand he's the new boss and face down any rivals. Then he'll turn on those responsible for the attack on the club and the killing of Remer.'

'But he can't know who's behind it all,' said Hauser. 'Not yet.'

'I think he has a good enough idea. The fact that those forgeries were found on Guttmann's men means that Guttmann must know who supplied them. And that means he knows Remer was the source. What if Guttmann's got his eyes on the coupon racket? With that in his hands he could make a fortune. What if he's making a play to be the most powerful crime-ring leader in Berlin? But first he'd need to remove the leadership of Remer's outfit and help himself to their forged ration coupon set-up. Even if he wasn't responsible for killing Remer, it's possible he's behind the attack on the club. I dare say that if Wohler has reached a similar conclusion, he'll be taking the fight to Guttmann the moment he gets released.'

Schenke picked up the nearest mug and took a sip. The coffee had been oversweetened, as was Rosa's habit, but he was grateful for it nonetheless.

'You know,' Hauser said as he took his own mug, 'it's tempting to let Wohler go and leave him and Guttmann to shoot it out and save us a lot of trouble. We'll just pick off the survivors when the smoke clears and close down both rings. Job done.'

'I'll pretend I didn't hear that, Sergeant. Besides, I don't think Radinsky would be too impressed if any civilians got caught in the crossfire. We'd be lucky not to have the entire section transferred to that new police battalion that's being sent to the east.'

Hauser winced at the suggestion. 'I can't be having that, sir; I've served my time already. My wife wouldn't stand for it. We only heard yesterday that my oldest boy is being called up. He'll be starting training next week. With luck the war will be over before he gets involved in any fighting. If we go head-to-head with the French and British again, I pray to God that our boys are spared what I went through in the trenches the last time round . . .'

Schenke sipped his coffee thoughtfully. He'd often heard the accounts of those who had endured the misery and horrors of the previous war. This time the French were prepared. A vast system of fortifications had been constructed along the border with Germany, and the latter faced very heavy losses if the Führer gave the order to attack. Hauser was right to fear for his son. It would be best to change the subject.

'What happened after we left you at the scene of Remer's shooting?'

Hauser, ever methodical, took out his notebook and leafed through to the last few pages. 'The tow truck turned up not long after you left, but I had them wait until the lads from our section arrived to go over the scene. We got some prints off the steering wheel and door handles, and we'll check those against the body, Remer's girl, and the driver who should have been on duty last night.'

'We need to question him too,' Schenke intervened. 'I want to know who told him to take the night off.'

'Right.' Hauser nodded and continued. 'We got a partial print off the warehouse door, but nothing useful from the footprints left on the ground. But there were more than two sets, coming and going. Looks like someone had been there earlier to make sure the door was unlocked to provide an escape route. Seems the ambush was planned well in advance.'

'And by someone with enough clout to pull it all together,' Schenke added. 'What about witnesses?'

'Once we'd wrapped up the forensics and the car was brought back to the precinct, I had our lads go door-to-door in the tenement block beside the alley and those further along the street. Some of the residents were woken by the shots. There seemed to be a difference of opinion over how many were fired, but most people reckoned on three or four.' Hauser rolled his eyes. 'You'd think they'd know if they'd heard them.'

'Maybe not,' said Liebwitz. 'People being roused from sleep

have a tendency to imprecision in what they recall from that moment.'

Hauser gave him a look. 'Well, thank you, Sherlock. I'll bear that in mind.'

'Continue,' Schenke ordered.

Hauser glanced at his notebook. 'The last person I spoke to was the most interesting. A nightwatchman, he had come off his shift and was climbing the stairs when he heard the shots and went to a window overlooking the alley. He said there were four shots. He also reckons he saw two people beside the car. He called down to them. Wanted to know if they needed any help.'

Liebwitz's eyebrows rose. 'Help?'

'He said he thought it was a backfiring engine at first and says he knows his way around engines. Frankly, I'm not convinced that anyone who can't tell the difference is the kind of person whose recollections I would put much faith in.'

'Was he certain about seeing two people?' asked Schenke.

Hauser nodded. 'I pressed him on that. He was sure of it.'

'Two men?'

'That's what he said.'

'I doubt there would have been enough light in the alley to make anything out,' Liebwitz observed.

'The car's headlights were switched on. Even with the blackout masks, there would have been some light.'

'I think we may need to speak to him again at some point,' Schenke said.

Hauser nodded and made a note.

'All right then . . .' Schenke cradled his forehead as he collected his thoughts. Looking at the clock, he saw that it was nearly six o'clock. Outside his office he could see the rest of the section finishing their tasks and rising from their desks to go home. 'It's been a long day, and we aren't close to understanding what is going on. We'll pick it up in the morning when our minds are fresh. We'll start with Wohler first thing. He knows much more than he's told us so far. Let's leave him to sweat on it overnight. He'll be very keen to be released from the precinct. We can use that to put pressure on him. Meanwhile, Liebwitz, I want you to go over the notes covering all those we have questioned. Get the names of everyone we haven't yet talked to. Bertha mentioned that Remer spoke to the comic before he left the club. And there was that business with Wohler turning up with some men. I want you to speak to Bertha and Magda tomorrow. See if you can get an address for Otto . . . Otto . . .'

'Bachmann, sir.'

'Yes, Bachmann. Find him and get a statement.'

'Yes, sir.'

Schenke indicated the door to his office. 'It's getting late. You'd better get going, Liebwitz. I'd like a quick word with the sergeant.'

'Yes, sir.' Liebwitz left and closed the door behind him.

'Hauser, I know that your son going off to war will be a distraction.'

'I can still carry out my duties, sir,' the sergeant responded stiffly.

'I know you well enough to appreciate that. But your wife might not feel the same way about it. If you need to make the most of the days left before he goes to the army, then I'll not stand in your way if you apply for some leave. You've more than earned the right.'

'Thank you, sir. I'll see how it goes. Will that be all?'

'For today.'

Hauser hesitated. 'I've been meaning to ask something . . .'

'Go on.'

'It's a bit awkward. You haven't been quite yourself the last few months . . .'

Schenke felt uncomfortable. 'What do you mean?'

'I was just wondering. Is it something to do with Karin? You haven't mentioned her for a while now. She hasn't called you at the office. You've been on edge, too.'

Schenke cursed himself for having been so open about her previously with his subordinate. Particularly now that she had barely communicated with him since the start of the year, after their relationship had become strained and Karin had gone to stay with some friends in the mountains over the winter season. Now that spring was here, she would surely return to Berlin, if she had not already. There would have to be a reckoning. Both of them needed to know where they stood. He focused his gaze on Hauser and cleared his throat.

'The truth is, I don't know what the situation is.'

'She's a good woman, sir. You could do a lot worse.'

'Yes, indeed.' Schenke smiled, then felt a spasm of regret over the reason for the breakdown in his relationship with the woman he had intended to marry. Ruth's face formed in his mind's eye, and he felt the bitter taste of self-loathing over what he had allowed to happen between them. He had let his emotions get the better of his judgement and compromised his moral integrity as a result.

'I'll do my best to sort things out,' he continued stiffly. 'Anyway, you'd better get home, if you don't want to feel the sharp end of your wife's tongue.'

Hauser chuckled. 'You have no idea.'

Once Hauser had gone, Schenke let out a deep sigh. The shooting of a crime-ring leader, someone whose death most people would be hard-pressed to mourn, was in danger of escalating into a gang war. Already there had been another death, the wounding of a second woman and the immolation of the Ace of Hearts club. Much as he was privately tempted by Hauser's vision of the criminal underworld engaged in a mutually destructive conflict, he would do his best to keep Wohler off the streets to prevent that happening for as long as possible. The one thing all wars had in common was that innocent civilians always got caught in the crossfire. People like Kitty and Magda.

It seemed a little strange to be so preoccupied by such a conflict against the background of the wider war, which had already claimed vastly more lives. Schenke was powerless before such a catastrophe, but at least he could do his best to keep bloodshed off the streets of his patch of Berlin. He looked over to the file on his desk marked 'Wohler' and reached for it. It contained a few official documents listing his previous arrests, charges and a handful of petty convictions before he had risen far enough in the crime ring for others to do his dirty work. There were some notes about his army service and then one that made Schenke pause. 'Well, well. Small world.' There was not much else of interest, and he decided it was time to quit for the day.

Taking his coat and hat, he saw that he was not the last to leave the section office. Rosa was bent over some paperwork at the desk she occupied in the far corner.

'Go home,' he told her. 'Before the blackout starts.'

She looked up. 'As soon as I've finished this report, sir. I promise.'

'Report?'

'Domestic incident. The woman took quite a beating, sir.' She shook her head. 'There's been a big increase since the war began.'

'I know. It's keeping you and Frieda busy. Even so, don't work too late, Rosa.' He tapped the brim of his hat and left her to it.

Dusk was settling across the city as he emerged from the main entrance of the precinct. Pulling his collar up against a chilly breeze, he set off in the opposite direction to his usual route home. There was one final task he needed to undertake. Twice he paused as if looking in a shop window, and scanned the reflection to see if he was being tailed. When he was satisfied that he was not, he made for the street with the abandoned shop entrance. The area was busy at this time, which would help him to blend into the crowd, and he weaved his way along the pavement until he reached the shop, then slipped inside the opening and bent down as if he was retrieving something he had dropped.

Ruth's mark was there, and he felt his heart quicken with a mixture of eager anticipation and anxiety. The meeting was arranged, then. Tomorrow he would see her again. Even though they would have to be very careful, and their conversation would consist of snatched exchanges made in a whisper between banalities that might be heard by those passing or seated nearby, he yearned for it. At the same time, the more rational, calculating side of his mind warned him that this was dangerous, and that it would have been better if she had not responded to his request to meet. But in truth, he could not help himself, so great was his compulsion to see her again. He needed to be certain that she was not in immediate danger, and that she had a roof over her head and sufficient food to eat. There was also an element of dangerous delight in defying the party's rules against fraternisation between German citizens and Jews.

Caution was not just a watchword but the essence of their survival. It was a secret that neither could divulge to anyone else, no matter how close. Much as he trusted and liked Hauser, it was unimaginable that he would ever be able to tell his sergeant the truth.

He rubbed out the mark and pretended to put something in the pocket of his coat, then eased himself into the flow of pedestrians. At the corner, he crossed the road and started making his way back in the other direction, towards his apartment. His heart felt light and he wondered if it was mirrored in his expression to the extent that it might draw unwanted attention. He lowered his chin to better hide his face and walked steadily on.

Chapter Ten

6 May

'This was in the section's internal mailbox.' Rosa leafed through the documents she was holding and handed Schenke a white envelope with silver trim around the edges. It was addressed to *Criminal Inspector Horst von Schenke* in the ornate Gothic script that members of the party had adopted for formal documents. As he examined it, he became aware of a sweet, flowery scent and he looked up at Rosa. It was unlike her to wear perfume to work.

'Not me,' she protested, and indicated the envelope. 'That. An admirer, perhaps?'

Schenke raised it and sniffed. The odour was more pronounced. For an instant he wondered if it was a communication from Karin, finally. However, she was not one to be so ornate and formal. As he went to open the envelope, he saw that Rosa was hovering.

'Feel free to carry on with your job . . .'

She gave a slight huff and went off to distribute the rest of the documents still in her hands.

Schenke slipped his finger under the gummed wafer on the back and took out a card written in the same hand. He scanned the brief message.

> *Oberst Helmut Radinsky and his wife Marlene*
> *invite Horst von Schenke to a soirée at*
> *the Villa Edelweiss, Wannsee*
>
> *Tuesday 7 May, from 1 p.m.*
>
> *Formal dress*
>
> *Please confirm attendance directly*

He lowered the invitation with a sinking feeling. He had hoped the precinct's new commander was merely being polite in suggesting that they might socialise at some point, without it being a sincere and binding obligation. He read the card again and saw that there would be no way out of attending. The imperative tone of the last sentence was clear. It was an order rather than an invitation. The location suggested an opulence typical of those who had done well under the regime. In the years following the seizure of power, those party members with influence had helped themselves to the finest property across Germany. Much of it had come into their hands through coercing the Jewish owners to sell up for a pittance. Other properties had been confiscated from Jews, political opponents and those driven into exile and handed out to their followers by those at the very top of the party. Radinsky did not exude the refined veneer of someone who came from money, and it was likely that he had married into wealth, or acquired his villa through the largesse of a Nazi patron.

In which case he would be playing at being a member of the aristocracy, like most of the arrivistes of the Nazi Party, who revelled in the spoils of dictatorship. Schenke was sufficiently self-aware to check the impulse to denigrate the social aspirations of the kind of person he imagined Radinsky to be. After all, in some former age his own ancestors had won title and land by wresting them from the hands of previous holders. It was only the passage of generations that bred the sense of entitlement and social exclusivity that aristocrats mistook for intrinsic superiority.

All the same, the prospect of spending an afternoon with Radinsky, his friends in the party and their wealthy cronies did not appeal. He could guess at the Oberführer's reason for inviting him. Once again, the baggage of Schenke's former motor-racing fame would catch up with him, and he would be expected to regale others with tales of the track and play the role of the young hero he had never been comfortable with even when he had been a star of that most glamorous of sports. He could see himself being led amongst the guests by Radinsky or his wife and introduced as their friend so that they might bask in reflected glory. The truth of it was that Schenke would sooner forget his past. Forget the terrible crash at Nürburgring that had left him in hospital for months. He was still occasionally plagued by nightmares from which he woke sweating and trembling, in such a state of terror that he was too ashamed to mention it even to those closest to him.

He sat back and folded his arms with a sigh of frustration. If there was no avoiding Radinsky's party, then he would have to try and turn it to his advantage and create a favourable impression for his host and the other guests. It would do his career no harm and might result in some connections that might be useful if he needed to use influence to drive an investigation forward. The main thing that concerned him was the thought of having to rebuff any suggestion that he might join the party or accept membership of the SS. He would have to be careful not to cause offence or suggest that his beliefs did not run in parallel to the party's ideology.

'Tricky,' he muttered to himself. 'Very tricky.'

He retrieved his prized Montegrappa fountain pen from the drawer of his desk, took out a fresh sheet of paper and drafted his acceptance note. He let the ink dry, then placed the folded paper into an envelope, addressed it to Radinsky and placed it in his pocket just as Hauser arrived.

'Ready to tackle Wohler?' the sergeant asked.

'In a moment. Have you seen Liebwitz?'

'In the canteen, having breakfast.'

'Right, I need to speak to him. Wohler's file is on my desk. Have a read before you meet me down in the holding cells. You'll find something in the file that may be helpful.'

'Do you want me to have one of the interrogation rooms made ready?'

Schenke shook his head. 'Let's make this as uncomfortable for Wohler as we can. I want him to be as keen to be released from custody as possible. In fact, no need to rush. Make yourself a coffee and have a cigarette first.'

'My pleasure, sir.'

The canteen was bustling when Schenke entered the large hall. The aromas of porridge and frying filled the air, with the acrid addition of ersatz coffee. Liebwitz was sitting by himself at the end of a table close to the windows reading the latest edition of *The Black Corps*, the official newspaper of the SS. The sunlight caught his glasses before he lowered his head to take a bite from the rye bread sandwich he was eating. He made to rise as his superior approached, but Schenke waved him back onto his bench and sat opposite.

'Pardon me for interrupting your breakfast, Scharführer.'

Liebwitz's mouth was full and he could not immediately reply. He raised a finger, chewed furiously and then washed the dense bread down with a mouthful of coffee.

'Once you have spoken to the women we interviewed yesterday, see if you can find the nightwatchman Hauser spoke to. I want you to check his account against what Kunzler recalls. Get as much out of him as you can. I want to know if there are any contradictions. Anything we can pick apart if we're being sold a lie.'

Liebwitz hesitated. 'I thought you'd want me present when we questioned Wohler, sir.'

'I need your eye for detail elsewhere, Scharführer. If there are inconsistencies, you are the man to spot them and break down any attempt to mislead us. Hauser and I can handle Wohler. Turns out the sergeant and Wohler were in the same company of Steel Helmets back in '19 when they helped put down the Reds. That might prompt Wohler to be more cooperative. If nothing else, it will give him a chance to reminisce with an old comrade rather than heap abuse on us, like he did to me and you yesterday.'

'I don't much care for the man's manner in any case, sir,' Liebwitz replied.

'Nor do I. Once you're done with the nightwatchman, have a word with some of the people in the nearby buildings. Make a note of anyone else we might want to speak to as a result. I'll see you back here at noon. Enjoy the rest of your breakfast.'

'Yes, sir.'

After leaving the canteen, Schenke made his way up to the office of Oberführer Radinsky and left his acceptance note with the secretary. When he went back downstairs, Hauser was standing by the door leading to the cells, talking with the Orpo sergeant in charge of the prisoners. Both straightened up as they saw their superior approaching. The sergeant saluted and strode off towards the front desk as Hauser grinned.

'Our friend Wohler's been kicking up quite a fuss. Says you're going to be held accountable for letting the men who attacked the club get away. He's also been making a lot of noise about his political connections and how they're going to come down hard on you the moment they hear about his detention. Been at it all night apparently.'

'So he hasn't had any sleep? So much the better.' Schenke smiled. 'I think it's time we had a word with our guest.'

They made their way down the short flight of steps to the basement, where there was a long corridor lined with cells. Most were empty, but there were a handful of faces at the grilles set into the sturdy doors who stared at the two Kripo officers passing by. Some muttered insults until they were silenced by Hauser's glare. Wohler's cell was towards the end of the corridor, and the two men stopped outside and peered in. Wohler was standing on a narrow ledge at the far end, looking up through the barred window that provided illumination from an opening in the courtyard. As Hauser slid back the bolts and opened the door, he turned to face his visitors. Schenke saw that his suit was creased, his tie and belt had been removed and his jowls were stubbled. Weary eyes narrowed as he lowered himself from the window and took a pace towards them.

'I hope you have finally seen sense, Inspector. Not that it's going to help you when word of my treatment gets out.'

'I'll survive.' Schenke indicated the bed with its thin and threadbare mattress. 'Sit. We need to talk.'

'I've nothing more to say to you. Release me.'

'You'll be released when I think it's safe for you to go back on the streets.'

'I'll be perfectly safe,' Wohler snapped. 'Can't say the same for those who murdered the boss and attacked the club. Those bastards are going to pay for it.'

'That's our job, Wohler. Not yours. As things stand, I fear for your safety, and for that reason you will remain in protective custody until I deem there is no longer a threat to you or you can persuade me to release you.'

'And how would I persuade you?'

'Depends how far you cooperate with me. Now sit down.'

Wohler sat heavily on the bed as Schenke and Hauser perched on the edge of the table opposite. Schenke introduced his subordinate, and the sergeant took out his notebook and pencil and made ready.

'The bad news,' Schenke began, 'is that your man Gunter Breker is dead. One of your workers, Magda, was wounded and the Ace of Hearts is now a smoking ruin. Even worse, your stock of forged ration coupons has gone up in smoke.'

Wohler's jaw tightened, but he did not respond.

'I managed to save a sample from the flames. They're very good. Almost impossible to distinguish from the real thing. It must hurt to know they're all ashes now.'

'I wouldn't know anything about that.'

Schenke smiled. 'And yet there they were. In your club. Several big boxes of them. How do you imagine they came to be there, in your club?' he repeated with emphasis.

'I don't know, Inspector. Nothing to do with me. Maybe Breker was running a scam on the side.'

'Breker?' Schenke chuckled. 'I got the impression he was the kind of man who struggled to tie his shoes and say hello at the same time. I don't see him daring to operate any sideline under the same roof as you, or the late Herr Remer.'

'Really? It's a struggle to find good honest staff these days, I guess. I blame it on the war.'

'I hear that a lot,' Hauser commented. 'Come off it, friend. Let's not waste any more time on this charade. We know that you and Remer were up to your necks in the business of selling forged coupons on the black market.'

'But you *don't* know that. You can't know it because you can't prove it . . . And you're no friend of mine.'

'Is that any way to speak to a comrade from Richter's brigade of the Steel Helmets?'

Wohler did a double-take. 'You served under Richter? When?'

'Soon after I got back from the front in '18, served until late '20.'

'I joined in '19. But you already knew that, right?' Wohler responded cynically. 'It's on my record.'

'Of course. I have to say, I was pleasantly surprised to see it in the file. Means you were once on the side of right. You and I fought the Reds who were trying to take over Germany. We were comrades defending our country and what it stood for.'

In Schenke's view, the Steel Helmets were no better than the other murderous right-wing militia groups that had terrorised the streets in the chaos that followed the end of the previous war and the fall of the Kaiser. It was something of a stain on the integrity of the police that so many members of the militia groups were welcomed into the Orpo in the years that followed that period of strife.

'Yes.' Wohler nodded. 'Those were dangerous times. If the Reds had had their way, we'd be under Comrade Stalin's thumb today. And yet here we are, in alliance with them, thanks to the Führer. I wonder if the sacrifices we made for Germany during the war and afterwards in the fight against the Reds was worth it. What do you say, comrade?'

Hauser refused to rise to the bait. 'Hitler has his reasons. It must be a trap he's setting for the communists.'

'You really think so? I hope you're right.'

'We did our patriotic duty.' Hauser steered the conversation back towards safer ground. 'You and I fought to make Germany a better place. So I wonder how an old comrade from the Steel Helmets ended up as a common criminal?'

'There's nothing common about me, Sergeant. I've risen to the top in my line of business. I dare say I earn more in a month than you do in a year. Now that I'm taking over Remer's spot, I will earn far more. Oh, I've done very well out of the kind of place the party has made Germany into.' He snapped out his arm in the German salute. 'Heil Hitler! May God bless him for turning sacred Germany into a paradise fit for gangsters.'

There was an awkward silence before Schenke spoke. 'You know, I can have you charged for stating such sentiments. Quite aside from any involvement in criminal activities. Being responsible for printing and selling forged ration coupons on the black market could be the least of your problems.'

'Is that so? I've merely expressed my loyalty to the Führer. I have friends in the party, and more than a few good customers who are Nazis. Whose word do you think they will accept about anything we say in this cell? And let's cut the shit with your sergeant playing the old-comrade card. That was so long ago I can barely recall it. I've moved on from there. We are no more comrades in arms than the Führer is with that commie cunt Stalin. You are on one side of the law and I am on the

other. You haven't anything concrete to pin on me. You think
you can talk me into divulging anything I know about the
coupon racket? Think again. My crime ring might be behind
it, or it might not. But you will never know. I've no fears over
that. My only concern right now is getting back at the fat
fucker who killed my boss and destroyed the club and whatever
contents might have been stored there.'

'You think Guttmann is behind this?' Schenke hazarded a
guess.

'I don't think. I know. He wants to be top dog in Berlin.
He's made his play and now he's going to find out what a great
big fucking mistake that was.' Wohler's lip curled into a sneer.
'I'll see him on his knees slobbering for mercy before I put a
bullet through his fat head.'

'What makes you think we won't get to him first?'

'Because you fools are obliged to look for enough evidence
to take him in. By the time you have that, I'll have long since
dealt with him, and you won't even find his body.'

'You are right, of course. You do have an advantage in terms
of being able to act outside of the law, so perhaps I need to
even the odds for our side by keeping you in here while we go
after Guttmann.'

Schenke stood up abruptly. 'We're done with our friend for
the present, Sergeant. It's time we went about our business.'

'Yes, sir.' Hauser snapped his notebook shut.

'I thank you for your cooperation with our investigation,
Herr Wohler.' Schenke gave a polite bow of his head before
turning towards the cell door.

'What about me?' Wohler demanded.

'What about you?' Schenke glanced round.

'You can't keep me in here. Release me, now.'

'I can't do that. It would be irresponsible of me to let you go while your life is in danger. That's what I'll say to any of your party friends who come calling at the precinct. It's for your own safety. I'm sure they will understand and see it's for the best. In any case, I won't permit you and your men to be loose guns hunting for Guttmann and his gang. There's a war going on. I don't want to add to the body count if I can avoid it. Better make yourself comfortable; it may be a while before it's safe to release you from protective custody.'

'You bastard!' Wohler stood up and clenched his fists. 'I'll have you!'

Hauser stepped in between the two men, broad and built like an ox. 'No you won't. Sit down, before I knock you down.'

Wohler glared at him for a moment before backing off and lowering himself onto the corner of the bed.

'That's better.' Hauser followed Schenke out into the corridor and they re-bolted the cell door.

'You won't get anything out of Guttmann,' Wohler called after them. 'There's a code in our world. We keep our secrets and we settle things between us.'

'We'll see,' Schenke replied as he and the sergeant strode away.

'Who would have thought it?' Hauser chuckled. 'A sort of honour amongst thieves.'

'Honour?' Schenke sniffed dismissively. 'They're the scum of society. Every one of them. Thugs out for themselves, using violence and murder to get their way.'

As they climbed the steps out of the cells, he made the unspoken and unspeakable comparison in his thoughts. The words that few Germans were brave enough to utter to anyone but those they most trusted.

When it came down to it, such men were no worse than the gangsters running the Nazi Party. Remer, Wohler, Guttmann; Himmler, Heydrich, Goebbels . . . There was very little difference between any of them. And the Führer, Adolf Hitler, was the greatest criminal of them all.

Chapter Eleven

Schenke and Hauser drove to Guttmann's address in one of the pool cars, an Adler Trumpf Junior. Guttmann owned a large villa set back from a tree-lined boulevard in an affluent area of Mitte. An ornamental tower on one corner lent the place a passing resemblance to the fairy-tale castles beloved of German rulers in the previous century. The villa was on a slight rise overlooking a garden composed of neatly arranged flower beds that Schenke imagined would be a riot of colour when summer came. Surrounding the garden was a high wall with a spiked iron railing running along the top of the side that faced the boulevard.

'He's not taking any risks,' observed Hauser, slowing the car as they approached the gates. 'He already knows that Wohler and his gang are coming for him.'

'Indeed,' Schenke said. 'Seems like the crime rings have better intelligence networks than we do. And anything we do get is relayed back to them by the police on their payrolls. It's no wonder we rarely get the chance to lay a glove on them.'

A double gate opened onto a shingle drive that swept round to the front of the villa in a wide curve. Pairs of men in coats patrolled the grounds, while four others guarded the gate, where an Opel was drawn up, blocking the entrance.

Hauser drew up in the street beside the parked car and opened his window. 'Guttmann residence, right?' he called over to the men at the gate.

'Who wants to know?'

Hauser reached inside his jacket for his badge, and Schenke saw the men instinctively move their hands towards whatever weapons were concealed under their coats. Their tense expressions did not ease even as Hauser held out his identity disc.

'Sergeant Hauser and Inspector Schenke from Kripo. Pankow precinct. We want to speak to Guttmann.'

'He's not at home.'

'Really? Then why all the guards?'

'Herr Guttmann is not at home to visitors,' the guard clarified.

'We're not visitors, friend. We're Kripo, and we don't like to be fucked around with. You better let your boss know we mean to speak to him. If you try and give us the runaround, we'll be back with two trucks of Orpo lads and we'll take the lot of you into protective custody. Starting with your boss. I can only imagine how happy he's going to be with you when that happens.'

The man turned to one of his companions behind the gate. 'Go to the house and let the boss know.'

'That's better. Thank you,' Hauser said. 'Always pays to cooperate with those who answer to Reichsführer Himmler.'

He turned off the ignition and the two detectives climbed out of the car. Hauser took out a cigarette and lit it, blowing a plume of smoke in the direction of the man in charge of the gate party. He indicated the car parked across the entrance.

'What's the reason for your boss surrounding himself with so many of his heavies? Has someone had a crack at him?'

'Just a precaution,' the man replied curtly.

'Precaution against who? You'd need a small army to get through you and your pals.'

'The boss orders us to protect his home and we do as we're told. That's all we need to know.'

'My, what good little soldiers you are . . .'

The man shrugged and moved off to rejoin his colleagues.

Schenke had been quiet throughout the exchange, content to let Hauser try to provoke Guttmann's heavy into revealing some useful information. Now a different approach was required, and he made his way over and offered the man a cigarette.

The guard shook his head. 'Don't smoke. Boss doesn't allow it around him or his property.'

'Really?' Schenke didn't conceal his surprise. 'That can't be easy to enforce.'

'Easier than you think, if you want to keep working for him.'

'He'd need to pay well to make that rule stick.'

'He does.'

Schenke looked through the gate and counted another eight men visible in the grounds of the villa. 'So how long have you and the others been on guard duty?'

'Since first thing yesterday.'

They were interrupted by a voice calling out from the porch of the villa. 'Herr Guttmann says they can come in!'

The car was moved out of the way, and one of the gates was opened wide enough to admit a man. Hauser made to climb back into the pool car.

'Your car stays in the street,' the leader of the gate party instructed. 'You go the rest of the way on foot.'

The sergeant pocketed the keys and followed Schenke onto the drive. The moment they were through the gate, it was closed behind them and the Opel reversed back in front of it. They were watched closely by the men in the grounds as they made their way round the gravelled curve to the parking area at the front of the villa. Climbing the steps to the entrance, they were met by a well-built young man in a finely tailored suit. Even though he was no more than thirty by Schenke's estimate, he had already lost most of his hair, and only a fine band of brown stubble ringed his crown. He bowed politely and extended his hand.

'Eric Kolbenhoff. I am Herr Guttmann's secretary and lawyer.'

Schenke shook his hand. 'Criminal Inspector Schenke. This is my sergeant, Hauser. Pankow precinct.'

'Delighted to meet you.' Kolbenhoff offered a thin smile. 'Might I see proof of your identities, gentlemen? I don't doubt that you are policemen; your deportment and attire attest to that well enough. However, you might be French spies for all I know. We can't be too careful now that we are at war.'

'Spies?' Hauser frowned.

'Just my little joke, Sergeant. Your credentials?' Kolbenhoff prompted.

Schenke and Hauser's identity badges were examined, then Kolbenhoff led the detectives through the door into the hall of the villa, where another of Guttmann's men stood; an imposing figure, a shade taller than Schenke, with a broad chest, wide shoulders and a square jaw beneath a pair of deep-set dark brown eyes and closely cropped white hair.

'This is Reitz, Herr Guttmann's, ah . . . valet. If you would leave your sidearms with him, I am sure he will look after them well.'

Schenke exchanged a look with Hauser. Both were wary about being unarmed in the household of one of the leaders of a crime ring. But their whereabouts were known to the rest of the section at Pankow, and it would be foolhardy for Guttmann to risk harming them or holding them against their will. Schenke drew his Walther from its holster and handed it over. Hauser followed suit, and the servant placed the weapons on a table to one side of the door, then stood in front of it and folded his thick arms.

'There, no harm will come to them,' Kolbenhoff said, and gestured towards a corridor leading off the left side of the hall. 'Please follow me. Herr Guttmann is taking breakfast in the dining room.'

'Breakfast?' Hauser glanced at his watch. 'It's past ten.'

'My employer works late into the evening,' Kolbenhoff explained. 'He finds it easier to concentrate when there are fewer people to disturb him.'

The corridor was no more than ten metres long, with two doors on either side and two at the end, opening onto the villa's dining room. The latter was a high-ceilinged chamber with long windows on three sides that overlooked a terrace and the grounds to the rear of the villa. A dining table that could easily seat twenty ran down the centre of the room. The walls were panelled and hung with artworks, some of which, Schenke saw, were the kind of modern art deemed degenerate by the party. At the far end of the table sat a ponderous figure in a patterned silk dressing gown. Unruly grey hair topped fleshy features. A bulbous nose separated two stone-grey eyes. The table had been laid for one, and Guttmann was dabbing a napkin at his mouth as the two policemen and his secretary entered.

'Kolbenhoff tells me you are from Kripo. How can I assist you, gentlemen?'

'You are Herr Guttmann?' Schenke began formally.

'None other,' Guttmann replied in a soft voice. Schenke had noticed a slight lisp in the man's first words of greeting, and there was a dryness to his tone that put him in mind of a snake, despite Guttmann's bulk. He put the thought aside at once. He did not want such preconceptions to colour his view of whatever they gleaned from the interview.

Guttmann finished dabbing his mouth and laid down the napkin, easing himself back from the table. 'Would you be kind enough to complete the introductions, Kolbenhoff?'

'Yes, sir. May I present Inspector Schenke and Sergeant Hauser.'

'Very well.' Guttmann gestured towards the table. 'Please take a seat. Will you have some refreshment while we talk?' Before Schenke could respond, he continued, 'Of course you will. Kolbenhoff, have some coffee provided for these two fine men. And some of those chocolates that arrived yesterday.'

His lawyer dipped his head and left the room. Schenke put aside a moment's discomfort at having been ordered to take his host's hospitality rather than be offered it. He sat down at the end of the table next to Guttmann and indicated to Hauser to take the seat opposite.

Guttmann chuckled. 'Come now, Inspector. Is it necessary to accost me from both flanks? I shall get a stiff neck from having to face the two of you at once.'

Schenke doubted it, since Guttmann seemed to have little sign of a neck. His head appeared to merge with his shoulders via several layers of flesh. It was his eyes that seemed to do most of the work as he regarded the two policemen, tapping his fingers lightly on the table as he continued. 'Now, if you will do me the kindness of explaining why we are having this little chat?'

'We're here in relation to two investigations that we have reason to believe are connected. Your name has been linked to both.'

'Oh? And what would the nature of these investigations be?'

'We'll come to that in a moment. Meanwhile, my sergeant and I couldn't help noticing that you seem to be preparing for an invasion here. I counted at least ten men outside the house alone. Not to mention that mountain of muscle we encountered in the hall.'

Guttmann chuckled. 'You mean Reitz? He is built on an impressive scale, I agree. He used to be a professional heavy-weight boxer several years back, and could have made it to the top if Max Schmeling hadn't beaten him to a pulp. He might not have much in the way of polite conversation, but he's still good with his fists and scaring people to death.'

'I can imagine. Why do you need all this protection?'

'Don't we all? There's a war on,' Guttmann said glibly. Then he sighed and continued. 'Let's not play games, Inspector. You know why. Word travels fast on the streets of Berlin and it positively sprints through the underworld. I probably knew someone had killed Max Remer before you did. When the leader of a crime ring is gunned down, it tends to make people like me nervous.'

Hauser leaned forward. 'And precisely what kind of person are you, Herr Guttmann?'

'I like to think of myself as a respectable businessman.'

'I'm sure you do. But given your involvement in brothels, the black market and trading in forged ration coupons, to name just some of your lines of business . . .' Hauser shrugged. 'I may be going out on a limb here, but some people might not regard that as respectable.'

Guttmann showed no sign of being offended. 'Unfortunately, there are always those who will try to smear the good name of men more successful than themselves. I would merely point out that you have no evidence of my direct involvement in any of the nefarious activities you mention, my dear sergeant.'

'I'm not anyone's dear sergeant,' Hauser responded flatly.

'Who do you think might be a danger to you?' Schenke intervened. 'Such a danger that you need protection?'

'It might come as no surprise to you to know that the late Max Remer and I were not friends. Given the circumstances of his death, there are those who might assume I had something to do with it.'

'And did you?'

At that moment Kolbenhoff returned and took the seat next to Schenke.

Guttmann gave a dry chuckle. 'Now *you* know how it feels to be flanked, Inspector.'

He turned to Kolbenhoff. 'These policemen are implying that I have interests in certain criminal enterprises. As my legal adviser, what would you suggest I tell them?'

'To go to hell,' Kolbenhoff said amiably. 'Failing that, I would say that it is incumbent upon the police to provide evidence before making such accusations. I believe that is common practice amongst those working in law enforcement. Correct me if I am wrong, gentlemen.'

Schenke could see the angry flush in Hauser's face and

refused to rise to the bait himself. 'All right then. Let's not waste any more time on petty point-scoring. We are working on the assumption that Remer was killed by a rival criminal ring.'

'Based on what evidence?' asked Kolbenhoff.

'I am not here to answer your questions,' Schenke said tersely. 'It is possible that Remer's death is connected to the forged ration coupons that have come onto the black market in recent months. A significant quantity were discovered at the Ace of Hearts club before it was burned down. We also know that more forged coupons have been traded by a number of people, now in custody, connected to your businesses. How do you account for that?'

Guttmann puffed his flabby cheeks and shook his head. 'I'm shocked. Can this be true, Kolbenhoff? Have some of my employees been engaging in criminal activity? Do you know anything about it?'

'It's news to me, Herr Guttmann. But I will look into it, and if such allegations turn out to be true, I will ensure that the individuals concerned are sacked at once. We can't have anyone working for your businesses unless they are beyond reproach.'

'Quite so! Ah, here's the coffee.'

A maid entered with a tray bearing a coffee pot, cups and saucers and a plate of small but artfully made chocolates. She set the tray on the table beside Hauser and poured the coffee before leaving. Neither Guttmann nor his secretary said a word while she was in the room, Schenke noted. Clearly they were not prepared to create any hostages to fortune if they could avoid it.

'I'm sure you know the names of those I am referring to,' Schenke resumed. 'When we interrogate them, we shall see what they have to say about their connection to you and your businesses. I'm betting that they'll lead us to the source of the forged coupons.'

'Of course I hope these miscreants cooperate fully with the police.' Guttmann folded his pudgy fingers together. 'But I dare say you will find they say nothing to you that in any way incriminates me.'

'I wouldn't be so sure. They might be tight-lipped with the police, but they will be more forthcoming if we hand them over to the Gestapo for questioning.'

'No doubt they will endure considerable hardship at the hands of your colleagues, but I think you will find that the men I employ are discreet. They place a premium on their loyalty to their employer. They will reveal nothing of value to you or the Gestapo.'

'Loyalty?' Hauser scoffed. 'More like they're afraid of ending up floating face-down in the Spree if they spill the beans.'

Guttmann frowned. 'Spill the beans? You have been watching too many of those American gangster movies. I am just telling you that you are wasting your time if you think my men will tell you anything that threatens me or my business, however hard you try and beat it out of them.'

'Then they do possess incriminating information,' said Schenke.

Kolbenhoff spoke gently. 'Sir, might I suggest that we end this discussion. We have assisted the police as far as we are able or obliged to do, and—'

'Be quiet,' Guttmann snapped. 'There's no further need to pussyfoot around with these two.'

He gestured at Hauser but fixed his cold eyes on Schenke. 'I've humoured you long enough in order to glean what I need to know about how little progress you have made in your investigations, Inspector. It's clear that you have nothing to pin on me. And I have sufficient faith in my subordinates' fear of the consequences to be confident they will keep their mouths shut. In any case, they will be adequately compensated for any unpleasantness they suffer while in custody. I value those who serve me. I pay them well and they give me what I demand of them in return. I've lived long enough to know that everyone has their price, and their weakness. It's merely a matter of finding out what those are. That goes for you and your sergeant too. If, or when, the time comes when I might find it useful to buy your services, don't be naive enough to think that I won't find a way to do it.'

'Are you offering to bribe me?' Schenke asked in a deliberate tone.

Out of the corner of his eye he saw Kolbenhoff shift uncomfortably and make to intervene before thinking better of it and settling back into his chair.

'Oh, I'm aware that's an offence, Inspector. But do you really think that matters any more? Do you really think that someone in my position is without friends in the party who will protect me from the accusations of a mere criminal inspector from a precinct in the suburbs? You are of no more concern to me than any other microbe that impedes my ambitions. You might think I had a hand in Remer's death, but you can't prove it. As it happens, I didn't, but that doesn't mean I am going to forgo the opportunity that presents itself as a result. With Remer gone, along with his sidekick Wohler, his crime ring is ripe for taking over.'

Guttmann reached out and tapped Schenke's wrist. 'For your own sake, I suggest you confine yourself to taking down the small fry of Berlin's underworld. It's easy work and less dangerous than antagonising someone like me. Things are changing in this city. The party is focused on waging war. Fighting crime is no longer a priority. Indeed, thanks to the war, the luxuries the party's leadership has such a fondness for are no longer available through the usual channels. But there are alternative arrangements that can be made through businessmen like myself. As long as the Nazi hierarchy has a taste for the finer things in life, they will value those of us who can fulfil their needs.' He smiled. 'You might say that I play my part in Germany's war effort. Just as our armed forces need to be supplied, so does our leadership in order for them to function as best they can. I can assure you that if you try to interfere with my operations, you will draw down upon yourself not just my wrath, but also that of my friends in the party . . . I hope we understand each other now, Inspector.'

He glanced at the clock above the fireplace at the far end of the dining room. 'It's time for you to leave. I have more important matters to deal with. I trust that we will not meet again. However, if I ever have need of your services, or those of your sergeant, you will be contacted and offered the same terms as any other police official I have put on the payroll.'

'And if we should refuse your offer?' Schenke challenged him.

'Refuse?' Guttmann gave a dry laugh. 'None have so far. Don't make the mistake of thinking you will be the first to do so. Good day, gentlemen. Kolbenhoff, see them out. Heil Hitler.'

He raised his hand in mock salute, but Schenke merely nodded as he rose and followed Hauser and Kolbenhoff from the room.

Chapter Twelve

Neither man said anything for a few minutes after the car had pulled away from the gates of Guttmann's villa. Schenke was seething at their treatment, and he could tell from the tense lines of his companion that Hauser felt the same. At length he spoke.

'If Guttmann denies he had any involvement in Remer's death, then who does that leave, for the sake of argument? Could it have been another of the crime rings?'

'Fuck that. It was his doing,' Hauser growled. 'You heard his muscle on the gate. Those goons were in place before we even got to the crime scene. It's almost certain the fat bastard knew Remer was going to be killed and went to ground for fear of retaliation. That's why he tried to get Wohler too. I'd bet a mark to a pfennig that Guttmann was behind both attacks. He wants to take over Remer's crime ring. It's clear as day.'

'Yes . . . Interesting that he thinks Wohler is dead. Whoever was behind the attack on the club got the wrong man when they gunned down Breker.' It seemed clear that Guttmann's men were responsible, Schenke conceded, but certain details were niggling away at such an explanation. 'Maybe Guttmann first heard about the shooting from one of his informants at the precinct. He made it pretty clear that he has his hooks into one or more of the people at Pankow. It's a nasty thought, but what if he already has someone on the inside of our Kripo section?'

Hauser glanced at him and shook his head. 'Rubbish. I've served alongside most of them for years. Longer than you have, with respect. The only one I don't trust is Liebwitz.'

'You really think Liebwitz is capable of working for Guttmann?' Schenke challenged him. 'He's about the worst candidate for a criminal ring spy that I can think of. He stands out like a sore thumb and is as straight as they come. He'd probably have a stroke if he was called upon to pretend to be someone he isn't and lie into the bargain. No, I'd say Liebwitz is the least likely person in the section to be an informant.'

'Which is why he would be the perfect choice.'

'Ah, come on, you don't really believe that.'

'Perhaps not. In any case, I can't believe that of any of our lot, sir.'

'Me neither. But let's play our cards close to our chests for the present. We don't tell anyone in the section any more than they need to know about the investigations into Remer's killing and the attack on the Ace of Hearts.'

'I don't like it, but you're right to be cautious.'

'There's something I need you to do back at the precinct. Have a word with your contacts in the other precincts and see if any of them have noticed any similar reaction amongst the other crime rings. See if any of Guttmann's rivals have ducked into cover after Remer's death. If not, then his reaction looks more paranoid than reasonable. Unless, as seems likely, he was either forewarned or is behind the shooting.'

Hauser nodded. 'I'll see to it.'

'That brings me on to something else, to do with the forged coupons. Even if a few of Guttmann's foot soldiers have been caught dealing them, it doesn't mean he's the one responsible for printing them. Speak to the Kripo section that covers Guttmann's turf. Find out how many coupons they recovered from his men. I'd be surprised if they amounted to anything like the quantity I saw at the Ace of Hearts. It may be that Remer was behind the coupon printing. He could have thrown us off the scent by keeping his hands clean and selling them to middlemen to put on the streets. That's how they came into the possession of Guttmann's ring. It doesn't take too much imagination to see how attractive it might appear to Guttmann to gain control of the whole process. Kill Remer and his sidekick and anyone who kicks up a fuss before taking over the ring and the coupon forging business for himself.'

'Sure, but what about the risk? What goes for Remer goes for Guttmann. If he's behind it all, then he'll know we're on his tail. He'd be painting a target on his back as far as we're concerned.'

'That's true,' Schenke reflected. 'Maybe he likes taking risks, but he didn't seem that type to me. More the kind who likes to play cautious and be several steps ahead of everyone else . . . Shit, the whole thing is getting messier all the time. If Guttmann is behind it, then why not hit the club at the same time he hit Remer? Why give Wohler time to take over and prepare to fight back?'

'Are we certain it was Guttmann's lads at the club?'

'You heard Wohler. He was certain of it.'

'He could be mistaken,' Hauser cautioned.

'Then who else could it have been?' Schenke sighed. 'Let's

hope Liebwitz has better luck when he speaks to the women at the club.'

They were drawing close to the precinct and Schenke glanced at his watch. He was due to meet Ruth within the hour and needed to take some precautions before reaching the assigned meeting place.

'You can drop me here. I'm going to get a bite and think it through.'

'Want me to join you?'

'No. It's best you talk to the other Kripo sections as soon as possible. And find out about those forgeries as well. I'll speak to you when I get back to the precinct.'

Hauser pulled over to the side of the road and Schenke climbed out. He stood and watched as the sergeant drove away, turned the corner and disappeared from view. Pulling out a packet of cigarettes, he took his time to light up as he scanned the street for any sign that he was being watched. But there was nothing about the passers-by or those loitering outside shop windows to excite his suspicion. He turned and made his way to the next junction and took a left, increased his pace and then stepped into a shoe shop and watched those passing the window. Once again he saw nothing to concern him, and felt some relief. He spent a few more minutes inside the shop affecting interest in a pair of hiking boots, before leaving and making for the Café Labourdonnais.

The café had been chosen at their last meeting as it had a courtyard garden to the rear, rather than seating on the pavement or near a window that opened onto the street. Schenke reached the entrance with twenty minutes to spare and bought a copy of the *Frankfurter Zeitung* from the kiosk outside, then entered the café and passed through the crowded tables to the door at the rear.

There were twenty or so small tables in the courtyard, half of them already occupied, even though the spring temperature was chilly. He chose one in a corner, a little apart from the nearest of the other customers, and sat down, studying the front page of the newspaper while he waited for a waiter to come and take his order. The headline announced reverses for the British and French forces in Norway and was accompanied by images of smiling German soldiers celebrating their victories. The editorial asked the question 'What triumph is next for our Führer?' and suggested that the humiliations in Norway would soon prompt the Allied governments to bend the knee and beg for peace. After all, Prime Minister Chamberlain and President Reynaud were both in a weak position, unpopular at home and regarded with contempt abroad, according to the columnist. Schenke wondered how much of it was true and how much was made up by Goebbels' propaganda ministry.

The waiter came and Schenke ordered a schnapps to settle his nerves. As the man returned with a small tray, Ruth emerged from the interior of the café. She was wearing a navy-blue coat with a matching hat. They looked expensive, though Schenke was aware that they were dated as far as Berlin's fashions went. He stood up to greet her, and they exchanged a brief kiss on the cheeks and pleasantries as if they were old friends. He felt his heart quicken as he drank in her fine features and delicate complexion, and there was a familiar stirring at the pit of his stomach. An image of her beneath him on the bed back at his apartment filled his mind before he reluctantly banished it. That was something that should never have happened and must not happen again.

'What will you have?' he asked as they sat down.

She nodded towards his glass. 'I'll join you in one of those.'

As the waiter departed, they regarded each other awkwardly and then laughed simultaneously.

'You look thinner,' Ruth commented.

'Long hours will do that. You look well, though.' He indicated the coat and hat. 'I take it your position has improved. I'm glad. I've been worried about you. Very worried. It's good to see you again.'

She regarded him with her dark eyes, and the feeling in his stomach became more pronounced. The impossible longing for her strained his ability to keep up the cordial ambience.

'I've missed you, Horst . . . Now tell me why we are here.' An anxious expression flitted across her face as she lowered her voice. 'What's happened?'

'We haven't spoken for a while. I wanted to make sure you were all right.'

He saw her jaw twitch before she responded with a sharp edge to her voice. 'That's why you arranged this? For God's sake, what were you thinking? You're risking everything for both of us. We agreed not to meet unless it was urgent. What is wrong with you?' She closed her eyes and frowned for a moment before looking at him again with sad affection. 'Horst . . . you poor fool.'

He felt wounded and stupid and made a slight helpless gesture with his hand. 'I couldn't help it. I had to know how you were doing. I had to see you again.'

'You had to?' she repeated. 'You had to put us in danger?'

He swallowed. 'I'm sorry . . .'

She sighed softly and her posture relaxed. 'Well, we're here now and nothing can change that. So we might as well make the most of it. Anyway, if I left now, so soon after arriving, it would only draw attention to us.' Before she could continue, the waiter returned with her drink and she picked up the glass and made herself smile. 'To friendship, good fortune and better times.'

Schenke nodded, and they both sipped at the fiery liquid before setting their glasses down.

'How have you been?' he asked, quietly enough to be certain that they would not be overheard by the nearest of the customers, an elderly couple with an air of frayed gentility who were loudly discussing some film they had seen the previous evening.

'I'm fine,' she reassured him. 'I've been living in the spare room of a couple close to the Siemens plant.'

'You're still working there?'

'It's not easy finding anything else, Horst. Not for someone in my position. The shifts are long, the pay is pitiful and the foremen treat us with contempt when they are not groping us.'

He felt a surge of helpless anger at the thought of her suffering the lechery of some leering bully. But there was nothing he could do about it without his motives being questioned.

'Don't be too concerned. I've found ways of dealing with them. It isn't so bad when you know how to avoid them. Some are decent enough and look out for us. I've been very fortunate to have a room at the Doblins' house. The husband used to be a university professor. He's half Jewish and he lost his job back when they removed un-German academics. Since he's a war veteran and is married to an Aryan, the powers-that-be don't treat him as badly as they might. For now they make ends meet from their savings and the small amount I can contribute.'

'How did you find them?'

'His daughter works on the same shift as me. She introduced us. The only danger is if she and her husband are kicked out of their apartment to make way for an Aryan family. Then she'll be forced to move in with her parents and I'll have to leave. I'll miss these as well.' She indicated her hat and coat. 'Frau Doblin lent them to me.'

'Very nice.'

She laughed. 'No, they're not. But they are better than anything I have left. I have to be grateful for whatever small mercies come my way these days.'

Her words cut through to Schenke's heart and stirred a turmoil of emotions. Aching pity for her predicament, anger that she and her people should be subjected to the grinding oppression of the party, and frustration at the indifference of the wider public, which was almost as sickening as the bigotry of the converted. And then there was guilt that he worked for the very state that enabled all of it. He had rationalised his position by the narrow justification that someone had to enforce the law against the day-to-day evils that plagued the streets of Berlin, whatever the wider political context. But however he might defend his role, the truth was he was a cog in the same machine that had stripped Jews not only of their citizenship, but their humanity as well. Yet what could a single cog do to break the engine? The moment he was deemed defective, he would be stripped out and replaced by a more compliant part, and the machine would roll on, crushing all in its path and consigning his moment of rebellion to meaningless oblivion. He felt the crushing weight of it all at once, and the shameful horror of his impotence.

Impulsively he reached out and took her hand. 'What can I do?'

He meant it as an offer of help but, as was so often the case, an unintended inflection of tone caused it to be taken as an accusation. She withdrew her hand.

'Nothing. Like all good Germans. You did nothing when there was still a chance to prevent all of this.'

The truth of her words struck him like a blow, and he recoiled fractionally and caught his sleeve on his schnapps glass, knocking it over so the remains of the spirit were dashed across the table and onto the ground. He righted the empty glass and looked into her eyes as he spoke again. 'I mean it, Ruth. What can I do to help you? To protect you? Just say the word. I cannot fix what has already happened, much as I would give anything . . . everything for Germany to be a different place. Truly. All that is left in my power is to do what I can to help now. To help you.'

Her expression was rigid for a moment as she considered his words and the earnestness of his tone, and then she sighed deeply. 'I believe you. I believe in the feelings I know you have for me, and that I have for you, Horst. But we are playing with fire, you and I. In a different time, or a different country, who can say what might have been for us? But now? The only thing that matters is to survive. That is what we have been reduced to. The Nazis mean to kill us. Jews and those who oppose them. We cannot defeat them, so what is the point of standing up to them? And therefore we do the only thing we can and survive. That is my only ambition now and I do whatever it takes to achieve it. If I live long enough, maybe I will have the chance to bear witness against what has been done to those persecuted by the party. Maybe I will have the chance to make something of our relationship if we both outlive the Nazis.' She smiled sadly. 'I can see how that hurts you, but I will not risk all for the sake of love in a time of despair, nor would I ask it of you.'

Love. There, she had said it. It was the most bittersweet of moments. Almost unbearable. He tamed his seething emotions and forced himself to be calm before he replied.

'I understand. Even so, if you need help, tell me and I will do all that I can.'

'I know you will.'

The waiter came out of the café and loitered a moment before he saw Schenke's empty glass. 'Another, sir?'

'No . . . no thank you.'

'In any case, I'd better be going soon,' said Ruth.

Once the waiter had left, Schenke had an overwhelming urge to hold her and kiss her. He ached for the soft touch of her lips, to be close enough to catch the scent of her breath. But it was impossible in the courtyard of the café. He summoned his courage and asked her softly, 'Will you come to my flat?'

A mixture of longing, fear and dismay crossed her face before she shook her head. 'No. Not for a while. It's too dangerous.' She recomposed her features. 'In any case, what about Karin? Has she contacted you since we last talked?'

'No. I've heard nothing from her. She has left me for good.'

'You can't be sure of that. She may be waiting for you to make the first move. Horst, she could still want you. Even if she has given up, you have hurt her, and wounded women can be very dangerous.'

'Karin's not like that. If there is nothing left between us, she will move on and find another admirer. There will be no shortage of those.'

Ruth paused before she asked softly, 'Then why choose me over her?'

It was a difficult question to answer. For an instant he was reminded of those lists that some people drafted to set down the pros and cons of a choice, as if the desires of the heart ever deferred to reason. He smiled at that.

'What's so amusing?'

'I don't know . . . There are many reasons behind the choices we make. I suppose it's that I realise now that part of the reason I was with Karin was because she is the kind of woman most men think they should marry: beautiful, graceful, intelligent and wealthy. For her part, I sometimes got the feeling that she was playing that role too, to be desired.'

'I think you are being unfair to her, Horst. You can't know what she is feeling. All you can be sure of is that she chose to be with you.' Ruth lowered her eyes. 'I don't deny the truth of what we feel for each other, but that is a dangerous luxury we can't afford. If it's not too late, go back to Karin. If she will have you. If she does, that will be better for all of us. I would be happier knowing you were safe in her hands.'

He swallowed. 'Do you really mean that?'

'Yes.'

'I see.' He felt wounded, but also relieved and indebted. 'Whatever happens, I will do what I can for you. Promise me that you will come to me if you need help. And if, by some miracle, we both outlive the Nazis . . .'

'Let's not make any commitments we may not be able to keep. No plans but to survive. I should go now.'

'Must you?'

She nodded.

'Let me walk you out.'

'No. It's safer if you don't.'

She stood up, and he followed suit. Ruth hesitated, then

reached up to cup his face. Schenke lowered his head, and she turned her cheek to him. His lips grazed her skin, then he moved to kiss her on the lips, but she pulled away at the last moment.

'I will contact you only if I need to,' she said urgently. 'But don't arrange another meeting unless it is vital to do so. Promise me.'

'I promise.'

She turned away and walked off between the tables, dodging aside as two men rose from their seats. Schenke silently cursed them as they stepped in between himself and the entrance to the café, blocking Ruth from his sight. He felt an urge to go after her, to spend a last moment with her. Instead, he forced himself to sit back down. He saw that her glass was still half full, and picked it up. There was a smear on the rim where her lips had been, and he traced his finger over it. He turned the glass so that his lips would align with the mark and drank the rest.

He waited a few minutes longer before he left some money and a tip and passed back through the café, emerging into the street. The sun had come out through a gap in the clouds and bathed the street in a warm, bright light. Schenke looked right and left, but there was no sign of the blue coat and hat. For an instant something unsettling caught his eye and he turned to look across the street. He thought he had seen a man staring at him from amongst those waiting for a tram. He scanned the cluster of people, but there was no indication of anyone watching him. It might have been a trick of the light. That, or the paranoia of the hunted. He took a deep, calming breath, then turned in the direction of the precinct and strode away.

Chapter Thirteen

'You were right to check,' Hauser reported when Schenke returned to the office. 'No one I spoke to has seen any sign of the other crime rings gearing up for a fight. They're keeping their heads down for now, but I don't suppose it will last. Remer's murder and the attempt on Wohler is going to put the other criminal leaders on edge. Might be some who are tempted to act pre-emptively or settle old scores.'

'That's just perfect,' Schenke said as he sat heavily behind his desk. 'Gang wars on the streets of Berlin. You can imagine what fun Goebbels will have with that, asking what the Reich Main Security Office is going to do about it. Himmler won't be happy to have that dropped in his lap.'

'And when Himmler isn't happy, then Heydrich isn't happy either. And he'll put the pressure on our chief, Nebe, and Kripo right down the line until the hammer drops on us.'

It was charitable for the sergeant to say that, Schenke realised. In truth, it was he alone who would be held accountable for anything that required a scapegoat.

'Then we'll just have to hope that we find those behind the murder and the attack on the club as soon as possible. Before things get out of control and we have gunmen taking potshots at each other on the streets and burning their rivals' property to the ground.'

Hauser winced at the prospect.

'Any word from Liebwitz?'

'He called in while you were grabbing a bite. He's spoken to the woman who was shot at the club. She's actually on the same ward as Kunzler, and the other one, Bertha, was there with her. He got leads on two more of the people at the club the night Remer was killed.' Hauser thumbed through his notebook. 'The comic, Otto Bachmann, and a man who was with Wohler and his mates – Wilhelm Feldwitz. Bertha reckoned he wasn't accompanying Wohler's lot of his own free will. They took him up to the office, Remer joined them, and that was the last she saw of Feldwitz, she reckons.'

'What about Magda? Anything to add?'

'According to Liebwitz, she just agreed with everything her friend said.'

'That's not much use to us then,' Schenke observed. He noticed that Rosa had approached them and was standing on the threshold of his office. 'Yes?'

'Do you want anything to drink, sir?'

Schenke nodded, and Hauser continued talking as she turned away.

'Maybe our Scharführer is developing a soft spot for the ladies. Anyway, he got the addresses for Bachmann and Feldwitz out of them and he's gone to track them down, once he's had a chat with the nightwatchman from the apartment block overlooking the alley. I doubt he'll be back until late this afternoon. Particularly as he chose not to take a pool car and went out on foot. You can guess why.'

'He'll have to get over that. You know my rule. Everyone who joins the section needs to be able to drive.'

'Good luck with that one. I don't expect we'll be seeing him in pole position at Nürburgring any time soon.'

'Maybe not. I'll settle for him driving us around Berlin in one piece.' Schenke looked at the wall clock. It was past two already. He had intended to leave the precinct in time to hire a suit for Radinsky's party. If Liebwitz didn't report back to Pankow by five, he wouldn't be able to speak to him again until the next day. Not unless he left instructions for the Scharführer to pick him up at eleven and drive him to Wannsee. The thought of a nervy Liebwitz at the wheel for the length of the journey was not appetising. But it would be the best way of finding out what he had managed to get out of Bachmann and Feldwitz.

He scratched his jaw and made a mental note to have a good shave before attending the party. 'Let's hope he finds them quickly, gets the job done and is back here before I have to leave.'

A nearby church bell tolled the first quarter after two as Liebwitz found the apartment block where Bachmann was living. He stood back from the entrance and looked up. The building was typical of the tenements that lined the streets of this working-class neighbourhood. Six storeys high, built of bricks made drab and grimy with age and the smog that enfolded the city at certain times of the year. Most of the windows were streaked, but a few conscientious residents had endeavoured to keep theirs clean. Moving to the narrow alley to one side he made a circuit of the block in order to understand the layout of its entry points in case Bachmann was aware of his approach and intended to evade him for any reason. Satisfied that there was only one exit to the rear, he entered the yard in the centre of the block.

It was dimly lit from the square of open sky above. Two women were hanging laundry on lines stretched across one corner while several kids were playing with a battered football, trying to score against a goal chalked on one of the walls. All of them looked round as Liebwitz entered the yard. As soon as they saw his black leather coat and hat, the women froze momentarily, and then swiftly returned to their work, pretending to ignore him. Liebwitz approached the children, who stopped playing and stood in a half-circle around the visitor. He attempted a friendly smile to put them at their ease. Unfortunately, his bony face and pale skin, almost white, rendered any attempt to smile appear more like the grin of a bare skull. The youngest of the boys burst into tears and scurried off to bury his face in the skirt of one of the women.

'Children,' Liebwitz addressed them. 'I am looking for Herr Bachmann, of apartment 4b. Can one of you tell me if he is at home?'

The oldest, a boy of twelve or so, thin-faced, regarded Liebwitz shrewdly. 'Are you a policeman?'

'Yes.'

'Gestapo,' one of the women hissed audibly.

Liebwitz rounded on her. 'Kripo, actually.'

He turned back to the children. 'Herr Bachmann. Is he here?'

'Depends,' said the boy.

Liebwitz looked puzzled. 'Depends? On what?'

'On what you'll pay us for an answer.'

The other boys closed on their leader, emboldened. But the

Scharführer shook his head. 'I asked you a straightforward question. It is your duty to answer in kind. Assisting the police in their inquiries is not a mercenary matter. Members of the public are required to help the police at all times.'

The boy cocked his head to one side. 'Are you sure you're a policeman? You don't sound like any I have met before. You sound more like a schoolmaster.'

Liebwitz took out his identity disc and held it out to them with an impatient sigh. 'See? So, Bachmann, is he here?'

'Like I said, depends,' the boy smirked.

Liebwitz leaned forward and spoke in a low, flat tone. 'It depends if you want to spend the night in a cold police cell, young man. You and your friends.'

The boy swallowed and pointed up at one of the windows in the grim walls looming above the courtyard. 'I-I saw him go into his flat not long ago. He had a bag of groceries.'

Liebwitz leaned a little closer. 'If you are lying to me, I'll be back.'

He entered the common door at the side of the block the boy had indicated and climbed the narrow stairs. The enclosed space had the familiar odours of boiled vegetables, coal dust and sweat, and there was a dank, cheerless feel to it. On the fourth-floor landing were two dark doors, unvarnished and identified by stencilled letters and numbers in white. Liebwitz raised his gloved fist and pounded on the door of 4b.

He waited a moment, and when there was no response he tried again. 'Open up! Police. Open the door, Herr Bachmann!'

This time there was a muffled cough, and a chain rattled before a bolt slid back and the key turned in the lock. The door opened wide enough to reveal half the face of an unshaven man in his thirties. He scrutinised Liebwitz and the disc he held up.

'A moment.' The chain rattled again and the door opened fully. Bachmann was wearing a sweater, dark trousers and leather slippers. Smoke curled from a cigarette, barely more than a stub, in his hand. 'What do the police want with me? What have I done?'

'Done?' Liebwitz blinked. 'I am not here to accuse you of anything, Herr Bachmann. I have been sent to ask you for your account of what occurred the night before last at the Ace of Hearts club. I have been told that you work there as an entertainer.'

'I do a comedy turn, yes. Or I did, until the club caught fire. Now I'm out of work. I always told that fool Breker the place was a deathtrap. The wiring was dangerous and I'm sure there was a gas leak somewhere near the dressing room. Gas, or chemicals of some kind. I could smell it from time to time.'

Liebwitz nodded. 'That is an interesting observation. May I come in, Herr Bachmann? I would prefer that I took your statement in private.'

'Yes, yes of course.' Bachmann stepped to the side of the corridor that ran the length of the small apartment and gestured for Liebwitz to enter. Closing the door behind the policeman, he led the way past a tiny kitchen on one side and a toilet and a shower on the other. Beyond, a door to the right opened onto a bedroom with an unmade bed. A woman's shift lay over the back of a chair beside a dressing table upon which were arranged a few scent bottles and a brush. A pair of suitcases and a small briefcase stood beneath the window. Bachmann closed the door and indicated the living room opposite.

'In there. Please take a seat.'

Stepping over the threshold, Liebwitz saw two armchairs either side of a small table in front of a stove. There was a larger table with six chairs, and a bookcase filled with novels, plays, volumes of sheet music and a few histories. A dozen or so framed photographs hung on the walls. All featured a smartly dressed Bachmann with faces from the entertainment world that Liebwitz recognised, as well as a few party figures. A piano sat in the corner opposite the stove. The lid was raised, and the sheet music of a Mendelssohn aria was propped up on the stand. Two empty tumblers sat on the floor beside the instrument. Bachmann casually crossed to the piano, took down the music and placed it face-down on top of the piano before shutting the keyboard lid.

'You play Mendelssohn?' Liebwitz queried.

'I like to practise a range of pieces.'

'You must be aware that Mendelssohn is no longer approved by the party.'

'I know. But it is still legal to possess sheet music.'

'As long as you do not give public performances, or hand the music to a Jew.'

'Why would I do such an un-German thing . . .' Bachmann paused. 'I'm sorry, I did not get your name?'

'Scharführer Liebwitz, from the Pankow Kripo unit.'

'Please have a seat, Scharführer.'

They settled in the armchairs and Liebwitz took out his notebook and pencil. His ability to recall details was almost perfect, but the importance of taking notes had been drilled into him during his Gestapo training. Police officers were required to produce a contemporaneous record of the details of any suspect or witness questioned, for presentation in court if the need arose. He cleared his throat and began formally.

'You are Herr Otto Bachmann, is that correct?'

'I would hope so.'

Liebwitz glanced at him. 'Are you Otto Bachmann?'

'Yes.'

'This is your permanent address?'

'Sadly. I had hoped to aspire to better accommodation after ten years of working the clubs.'

Liebwitz stared at him, tapping the end of his pencil against the notepad. 'I do not understand why you cannot just answer yes or no to my questions. Do you have difficulty in understanding what I am asking you? Do you have defective hearing, for example? Or impaired cognitive processes arising from a head injury? Or hereditary lack of intelligence?'

Bachmann was taken aback. 'No.'

'Thank you. Then let's proceed . . . You are employed as a performer at the Ace of Hearts club, describing yourself as a comic?'

'That's what I am described as, yes,' Bachmann responded testily. 'A comic act. I've headlined in the best clubs of Berlin in my time, I'll have you know. Anyway, I am no longer employed at the Ace of Hearts because the Ace of Hearts no longer exists.'

'Have you been handed your notice, or otherwise been informed of the termination of your employment?'

'Not as such.'

'Then as the situation stands, you are still an employee of the club.' Liebwitz gave a brief sigh of frustration. 'Herr Bachmann, I would be grateful if you answered simple questions directly and did not digress. Other questions may well require such digressions. Please answer as appropriate.'

Bachmann frowned. 'Tell me, Scharführer, do you always talk to people in this fashion?'

Liebwitz thought a moment and nodded. 'I believe so. We

will continue . . . You were at the club the night Remer was killed.'

Bachmann's eyes widened. 'Remer is dead? How?'

'Were you not aware?'

'I . . . I . . . no, I hadn't heard. How dreadful. I just knew that the club had been burned down. Was he inside when it happened?'

'Who told you that the club had been burned down?'

'One of my neighbours. He saw the firefighters dealing with the last of the flames. Said the place was a shell.'

'Have you been to the scene?'

'No. I only heard about it last night. What about Remer? Did he die in the fire? Was anyone else harmed?'

'Herr Remer was shot dead in his car shortly after leaving the club the night you last performed there. The woman who was in the car with him, Katharina Kunzler, was also shot.'

'Kitty?' Bachmann swallowed. He was still for a beat before he continued. 'Was she badly hurt?'

'A flesh wound. She is expected to make a full recovery.'

'Thank God! What did that have to do with the fire?'

'That is what Kripo is trying to ascertain,' said Liebwitz. 'And why I need your statement.'

'Of course. I'll do whatever I can to help you catch those who shot my boss, and Kitty.'

'You said just now that the club had been burned down. Earlier you said it was a deathtrap.' Liebwitz was alive to the subtle inconsistency and decided to test Bachmann. 'Do you have any reason to believe the fire was started deliberately, as your statement implied?'

Bachmann shifted in his chair. 'I wouldn't know about that.

I imagine you have heard the rumours about Remer. That he wasn't exactly the straightest of businessmen.'

'No. He was a known gangster, and head of a crime ring. This is already known to the police.'

'And most of the rest of Berlin, I'll wager.' Bachmann smiled faintly. 'In which case you must know that he had many enemies.'

'Enemies? For example?'

'The leaders of rival crime rings would be at the top of the list. And there'll be plenty of others who crossed his path and came to regret it.'

'Do you have any of their names?'

'If I did, I wouldn't take the risk of sharing them with you.' Bachmann shook his head. 'Look, I'm just a comic, all right. I've been working for Remer for a few years now. I heard people talking about him from time to time. Talking about other aspects of his business. But I can't remember the details and that's the truth.'

'Then let's consider the night he was shot. Was it a typical evening, or did you notice anything out of the ordinary?'

Bachmann closed his eyes and concentrated for a moment. 'It was quieter than usual. Much quieter. The boss was in his booth with Kitty. I heard the other acts from the dressing room before it was my turn. I came on and did my routine. When it was over, I came back here.'

'What time did you get home?'

'Let me think . . . Would have been about midnight.'

'Did anyone see you come in?'

'At that time? No chance. I was already feeling unwell, and I went to bed and slept until mid morning the next day.'

'What about the lady you share the flat with?' Liebwitz gestured in the direction of the bedroom he had passed earlier.

'Oh . . . her. That's a woman I picked up a few weeks ago. She stayed here for a week or so, then disappeared. She hasn't come back for her stuff yet. I doubt I'll see her again. I'll get rid of it once you've left.'

'I see.' Liebwitz stared at him long enough for the other man to feel uncomfortable. 'You say you left the club after completing your routine.'

'That's right.'

'Did you speak to anyone before you left?'

'Ah, yes . . . The boss wanted a quick word with me. I joined him in the booth for a few minutes.'

'What did he have to say to you?'

'He praised my act before he told me that he wanted some small changes to the routine.'

Liebwitz saw the telltale twitch in the other man's expression. 'What kind of changes?'

'Have you spoken to Kitty yet?' asked Bachmann.

'Yes.'

'Then she'll have told you.'

'I want to hear it from you, Herr Bachmann.'

Bachmann could not hide his discomfort, and paused to weigh up what to say next. 'You have to understand, my routine is pitched at an audience who leave the world outside when they come into the club. That means things can be said inside that might not be wise to say anywhere else. That includes some of my jokes. I, er, poke fun at some of the figures in the party. Not the Führer. Never the Führer. I swear it.'

'Go on.'

'The boss said he wanted me to tone the material down. He

said it would be wise not to make fun of the party while there was a war on. Then he dismissed me, and I came back here.'

'Directly?'

'Yes, sure. Like I told you. Where else would I go at that time?'

Liebwitz considered what he had been told so far. There was something in the comic's demeanour when he had mentioned Remer that sounded false.

'How well did you know Remer?'

'As well as any man in my position can know his boss, I suppose. He paid well and on time. I never had to push for it. With some club owners it's like squeezing blood from a stone. He looked after those who worked for him. I respected him. We all did. Sometimes he placed extra demands on us – calling us in to work on our days off, buttering up some of his guests. That sort of thing. He could be short with us, but only if we had done something to deserve it. He didn't tolerate anyone stealing from the club, or taking too many days off, or answering back. They'd be gone just like that!' Bachmann snapped his fingers. 'He also had his favourites. Wohler, for example, and young Feldwitz. They could do little wrong in his eyes. Then there were the women. Kitty being the most recent. They rarely stuck around for more than a year or so before he dumped them and moved on to the next. He kept Kitty around for the longest. Guess he thought she was special in some way. God knows why.'

'How do you mean?'

Bachmann breathed deeply. 'Because she's a real bitch. A cold, calculating, heartless, greedy bitch. It's a shame she wasn't killed as well.' The words seemed to be out before he could stop himself. He watched Liebwitz nervously for a reaction before he spoke again. 'Can I get you a drink, Scharführer? Tea, coffee, or something stronger?'

Liebwitz shook his head and leaned forward fractionally. He was struck by the contrast between the timid-looking woman in the hospital bed and the version of her that Bachmann had conjured up. 'Why do you describe her in such pejorative terms?'

'Pejorative?' Bachmann repeated with a quick laugh. 'Are you really a police officer? You sound more like a lawyer.'

'I'll let that pass,' Liebwitz said. 'Just tell me what you have against Katharina Kunzler.'

'Me? Nothing. It's how she treats others. She never had any genuine affection for Remer, or anyone else. She sees men as a means to an end. Give them what they want and then claim her reward. Anyone who got between her and what she wanted found out the hard way what she was like. Take Bertha at the club. Remer had his eye on her before Kitty pitched up. Soon as she set her sights on him, Kitty went out of her way to sabotage Bertha's prospects. Bertha is a good singer. With the right backing and opportunities she could claim a spot on the programme of any of the top clubs in Berlin. But Kitty put a stop to that. Made sure that Remer never got to hear her sing and put her on cleaning duties instead. She was also playing a long game. She knew Remer would move on to someone else eventually, so she was already lining up another man for herself.'

'Who?'

'I'm not certain,' Bachmann admitted. 'I was behind her one night when we left the club around the same time. Remer had to go to some party function, the kind of invitation you don't turn down. Kitty walked for a hundred metres or so before she met a man waiting beside a kiosk. I was curious, so I stayed back and tailed them when they set off together. They went to the nearest U-Bahn station and then got on a train heading south, in the opposite direction to Remer's apartment.'

'Did you see his face?'

'No. Thanks to the blackout, I was barely even able to keep them in sight as I followed them.'

'And why were you following them?'

'Are you really as obtuse as you make out? I wanted Kitty for myself. She knew it. Just as she knew about every man who wanted her. And she played on that. Flirting with Feldwitz and Wohler at the club when the boss wasn't around.'

'Did she flirt with you?' asked Liebwitz.

'She did more than flirt . . . How do you think she got into the club in the first place? I met her at a party a while back. She seemed impressed that I had a regular spot at the club. One thing led to another and she asked if I would get her in one night so she could watch my act.' He gave a sniff of contempt. 'While I was on the stage, she was working her charms on Remer. He'd let her sit at his booth and bought her champagne even before I'd finished my routine.'

'So your hostility to her is motivated by envy. What about this other man? The one you think she was lining up in case Remer discarded her. Do you have any suspicions about who it might be?'

'I couldn't really say. I'd seen the way Wohler looked at her. And the way she'd looked at Feldwitz recently. Could be either of them, or maybe someone else. Someone from another crime ring. Or perhaps some party bigwig. It would have to be someone with money and influence. That's her type.'

Liebwitz considered this. 'That's not very helpful.'

'It's all I can tell you, Scharführer.'

'All right. What about Feldwitz? What was his relation to Remer? Did he work for him?'

'I imagine so. But it had nothing to do with the running of the club as far as I could see. Feldwitz was around the place a lot. Until a month or so ago, at any rate. Always had a lot of cash on him and some woman on his arm he was trying to impress. I never liked him. He tried to heckle me a few times, but I put him in his place and he gave up.'

'Could he have been the man you saw with Kitty?'

'It's possible. About the right build, but I couldn't see his face.'

'I understand Feldwitz was brought into the club on the night of the shooting. He was with Wohler and some other men, but he didn't seem to be a willing party. Did you see him?'

'No. I was in the dressing room before I went on stage. And when I'm on stage, I'm looking into the stage lights so it's almost impossible to pick out any faces. If he was there that night, I don't know anything about it.'

Liebwitz paused to mentally sketch out a scenario. 'If Feldwitz was having a secret relationship with Kitty and this was discovered by Remer, how do you think your former employer would have reacted?'

Bachmann gave a dry laugh. 'If Feldwitz was foolish enough to have anything to do with that bitch, he would be begging for trouble in any case. But if it had got back to Remer, the boss would be wearing his balls for cufflinks. He wasn't a forgiving type, no matter how fond he might have been of Feldwitz. You didn't humiliate Remer and live.'

'I see . . . I want to move on to another matter. You know the layout of the club, yes?'

'I suppose so. But there were parts of it that were restricted. I was only ever invited to enter the upstairs office once, for example. And some of the storerooms were kept locked – not even Breker had keys for those. Only the boss and Wohler.'

'Do you know what was kept in those rooms? Did you ever see what was inside?'

'Never. The doors were securely locked. I tried one once, to make sure. Breker caught me at it and reported it to Wohler. He said if I ever again showed any interest in those storerooms he'd break every bone in my body. He meant it, too. After that, I never went any closer to them than I had to.'

'Understandable,' said Liebwitz. 'Did either Remer or Wohler give any indication of what they might be concealing?'

'No, though I overheard Remer mention the delivery of a consignment of some kind a week or so ago. That's all.'

Liebwitz went over all that he had heard before he concluded that there was nothing more to be gained from further interrogation of the comic. Glancing at his watch, he saw that it was already mid afternoon. He needed to track down Feldwitz and get his statement before reporting back to the precinct. The inspector was not a man who tolerated delays easily. In any case, Liebwitz had developed an admiration for his superior and wanted to justify Schenke's accepting him into the Kripo section at Pankow. He was eager to appear as keen, efficient and punctual as possible.

He rose abruptly and pocketed his notebook and pencil. 'That's all I need for now. If there are further questions, you will be contacted. Do not leave Berlin without seeking our permission first.'

'Leave Berlin? Why would I? This is my home.'

'I saw the suitcases in the bedroom.'

'Those?' Bachmann chuckled. 'Spare clothes. I've run out of space in my wardrobe.'

Liebwitz gave a curt nod of farewell and left the apartment. Once he was back on the street, he strode at a quick pace. It took him no more than fifteen minutes to reach the more salubrious neighbourhood where Feldwitz lived. There were fewer men in work clothes on the streets here, and more of the formally clothed professionals. Most of the women were better turned out as well, he noticed. Clearly Feldwitz enjoyed a higher standard of living than Bachmann, although Liebwitz was no wiser about what he did for a living.

He reached the building given as the man's address and presented his badge to the concierge on duty at the entrance. A modest-sized marble hallway had mailboxes to one side and a leather couch to the other, next to a lift. Beyond, a flight of carpeted stairs climbed to the first floor. Liebwitz hesitated for a second, then chose the stairs out of an innate preference for simplicity. On the landing, he passed a man who had paused to adjust his pocket watch with gloved hands, and glanced at him briefly before dismissing any chance that he matched the description of the individual he sought – too old.

When he reached Feldwitz's apartment on the second floor, he saw that the door was slightly ajar. He rapped on the dark polished wood.

'Herr Feldwitz?'

There was no reply, and Liebwitz cautiously pushed the door open and stepped into a small but neatly decorated lobby with a carpeted floor. There was a door on either side, and before him lay a corridor with abstract paintings on the walls. He paused to listen, and heard light classical music playing softly, along with the slight crackle and hiss of a radio set. A hearty whistle joined in as he made his way along the corridor. Reaching the door at the end, he leaned round to look within. It was a large living space with two sofas either side of a marble fireplace, where a radio glowed above the mantelpiece. A desk sat against the window, opposite the doorway, and seated there was a man in a powder-blue suit. He had fair hair cropped at the sides and slicked back on top and was searching the open drawers as he whistled. Liebwitz took a step into the room and a floorboard creaked.

The man at the desk turned round, a wad of photographs in one hand as he began to speak. 'I have them, Hugo—'

He saw Liebwitz and gaped. One eye was covered by a dressing. His gaze shifted subtly, and too late, Liebwitz realised that the floorboard had creaked not under his own feet, but beneath those of the man behind him. Then there was a sharp blow on the back of his head accompanied by a blinding flash of white, and he slumped to the floor, unconscious.

Chapter Fourteen

Schenke stood in front of the wardrobe mirror and examined his reflection critically. The hired dinner suit fitted him well and had a neat satin gleam, and he had made a decent job of the bow tie. The only thing left to attend to now was his shoes. They needed a good polish before being presentable at a formal social event.

Liebwitz had not returned to Pankow by the time Schenke had had to leave to pick up the suit. Schenke had left a message at the precinct to notify the Scharführer to book out a pool car to drive him to Wannsee the next morning. That would provide an opportunity to go over any information Liebwitz had picked up from his interviews of the previous day. Besides, having a car and driver would confer a certain status when they arrived at Radinsky's villa.

He glanced at the invitation propped up on the dresser and felt a weight descend on his shoulders. He would rather not have to attend at all. Radinsky's social circle was almost certain to be packed with party members. Given his rank and long-standing association with the founding figures from the earliest years of the struggle, as they liked to call it, there were bound to be senior Nazis present. In which case there would be the inevitable and unedifying jockeying for favour. For many that would present a valuable opportunity to push for advancement, but Schenke himself was more concerned about the prospect of getting through the event without saying the wrong thing or giving any sign of his true feelings about the party. He would have to control himself carefully and play the part expected – demanded – by the Nazis.

Since coming to power, the party had made actors of the German people, he reflected. From the martinets at the top, performing the role of Teutonic overlords, the bit players of the party rank-and-file, and the wider public dutifully, or fearfully, playing along, right down to the victims of the Nazis, who had to pretend to recognise their own unworthiness, expected to step off the pavement if they passed an Aryan. The penalties for not performing the roles allotted by the Nazis ranged from social ostracisation to death, and it was possible to traverse this punitive spectrum on the flimsiest of failings. In a country where one could be sentenced to death for denouncing or merely mocking the party leadership, acting was the pre-eminent survival skill. Many, including Schenke, had no aptitude for it. He carried the burden of thinking that he lived under a placard that read: *This man is not a true German. He is a race traitor and has no place in the Third Reich!*

'Shit . . . it's shit, all of it,' he muttered, and then instinctively glanced round the empty room. Admonishing himself, he returned his gaze to the mirror and scrutinised his expression as he composed his features. There was nothing to read into that face, he told himself. No sign of his true beliefs and feelings. He could do this. He could get through Radinsky's party safely.

He would stay long enough to satisfy etiquette, then offer his thanks to his hosts and leave.

He took off the jacket and bow tie before removing the collar studs. Once the shirt, suit and tie were neatly arranged on a hanger, he put on work clothes and a jersey and took the shoes through to the small kitchen. Fetching a basket of polish, brushes and rags from the bottom of the cupboard, he sat on a stool and set to work, dabbing the rag into the polish before rubbing it steadily into the shoe leather. It was calming, satisfying work and the familiar aroma of the polish was somehow comforting as he concentrated on the task and pushed all other thoughts from his mind.

Abruptly the shrill ring of the telephone broke his reverie. He set the shoe down and wiped his fingers on a clean corner of the rag as he went to answer the device in the hallway.

'Schenke . . .'

'Sir, it's Baumer.'

'Ah, good. I assume Liebwitz has finally made an appearance.' Schenke glanced at his watch. It was quarter past eight. The Scharführer put in long hours.

There was a hesitation before Baumer responded. Long enough to unsettle Schenke.

'Liebwitz has been attacked, sir.'

'Attacked? Is he hurt?'

'He has a head injury, but he's back on his feet. There's more. The Scharführer was with a dead man, identified as Wilhelm Feldwitz. He came to and raised the alarm less than an hour ago. The block warden called the local Orpo station to send the police. I only just got the message, sir.'

'Damn.' Schenke sucked back his anger. The delay in calling the incident in to Kripo probably meant that the uniformed police were already trampling the crime scene with their heavy boots. 'Right . . . send a car to pick me up. Where is Liebwitz exactly?'

'At Feldwitz's apartment.'

'Is anyone else from our office still about? Sergeant Hauser?'

'He left at six. There's Rosa, sir. She was finishing up some work on a domestic case. She's down in the canteen at the moment.'

'Find her and send her over to the Feldwitz apartment with a forensic bag.'

'Yes, sir.'

Schenke hung up. He grabbed his hat and coat and put on the shoes he wore to work, then hurried from the apartment. Emerging onto the street, he waited for the car to arrive from the precinct. The blackout veiled his surroundings, and the few people abroad were only faintly visible in the dim illumination of masked torches and the luminous paint on the edge of the kerbstones. There was a tiny glow across the street that flared for a moment and then dimmed briefly before disappearing. For a moment Schenke was tempted to cross over and check on the smoker's identity, before his thoughts shifted back to his injured subordinate and the fresh murder clouding his section's investigations.

A few minutes later, there was still no sign of the car. Impulsively he darted across the street to the place where he had seen the glow of the cigarette. He was able to make out a delivery entrance between two shops. Taking out his torch, he shielded the beam as he scanned the space. No one was there, but there were several crushed butts on the ground. One of them was still emitting a fine curl of smoke. He picked it up and saw that some of the brand name was visible: 'Front'.

That could only be Neue Front, an expensive choice and hard to come by.

The slits of a pair of approaching headlights and the sound of an engine caused him to hurry back across the street. The pool car, driven by an Orpo sergeant, drew up, and Schenke climbed in and gave the address before ordering the man to get there as quickly as possible.

There were several uniformed police guarding the entrance of the apartment block when Schenke arrived. Two more were outside Feldwitz's flat, and they saluted as Schenke held out his identity disc and went inside. All the lights were on, and he made his way to the living room, where Liebwitz was sitting on a dining chair being questioned by an Orpo officer while a doctor put a dressing around his head. There was blood on the collar and shoulder of Liebwitz's shirt, and his leather coat was folded neatly on one of the armchairs with his crumpled black hat resting on top. A body in a light blue suit was slumped over the desk beneath the window. He had a dressing and eyepatch over one eye while the other eye bulged. That and the protruding tongue was enough to reveal to Schenke that he had been strangled.

Liebwitz made to rise from his chair, but Schenke indicated for him to remain seated before he turned to the Orpo officer.

'Is that Feldwitz?'

The officer nodded. 'And you are?'

'Criminal Inspector Schenke, Pankow precinct.'

'So Liebwitz *is* one of yours. I had him down as Gestapo. Either way, I want to know why he comes round in a room with a dead man in it and claims not to know the reason why.'

The doctor finished applying the bandage and tied it off.

'Have the stitches taken out in two weeks' time. Your head's going to hurt for a few days. If there is any dizziness, blurry vision or persistent headache, then get yourself to a doctor. Another doctor,' he added with emphasis as he began to pack up his bag.

Schenke faced the Orpo officer. 'We'll take over now.'

'Take over?'

'This is a murder scene.'

'I noticed.' The officer nodded towards the body. 'But thanks for explaining. Much as I would like to take on the investigation, I think it would be best to leave it in the safe hands of Berlin's best and brightest, eh?' He closed his notebook, then gave a crisp German salute and strode out of the room, calling on the men at the door to follow him downstairs.

The doctor picked up his bag. 'I'll be off too.'

'Wait,' said Schenke, indicating Feldwitz. 'I want you to take a look at him first.'

'Him? I'm a doctor, Herr Inspector, not a miracle worker.'

'I just want a professional opinion. It won't take up more than a few minutes of your time. The body will have a close examination at the morgue, but right now all I have is you.'

He was tired, and the words came out less politely than he'd intended.

'Since you put it so graciously . . .' The doctor crossed to the desk and leaned over the corpse. He scrutinised Feldwitz's contorted expression before he eased away the patch and winced at the ruined eye beneath. 'Something, or someone, burned out his eye . . .' Then he felt the victim's neck, and looked up. 'Give me a hand with his jacket.'

Schenke helped ease Feldwitz's arms out, and they placed the garment over one of the chairs. Liebwitz joined them as the doctor removed the collar and pulled back the shirt to reveal a livid red ring around Feldwitz's neck. He took a sharp breath.

'Nasty . . .' He probed the flesh. 'This was not a manual strangulation. The ligature used was somewhat more substantial than a cheese wire, but it was wire all the same, from the look of it.'

'You've experience of such things?'

'Yes, for my sins. I was a stormtrooper in the last war. It's what we used on French sentries during trench raids.'

'Useful to know,' Schenke commented.

The doctor continued his examination. 'You can see from the lesions and from the laceration cutting deep into the windpipe how much force was applied . . .' He tilted his head slightly. 'Whoever did this knew his business.'

He studied Feldwitz's fingers. 'See, just a couple of broken nails. Which means the lad here hardly had time to resist. It was all over quite quickly. I'd like to say he wouldn't have suffered too much, but that would be a lie.'

He stepped back. 'Anything else?'

Schenke shook his head and the doctor picked up his bag and left. Once they were alone, Schenke turned to Liebwitz. 'Stupid question, I know, but how are you feeling?'

'Like the doctor said, my head hurts.'

'But you're still in good enough shape for some work?'

Liebwitz closed his eyes momentarily and frowned, as if conducting an internal audit of his faculties before he made any pronouncement. Then he opened his eyes and adjusted his wire-framed spectacles so that the arms sat more comfortably over the bandage above his ears. 'I'm ready, sir.'

'Glad to hear it, Scharführer.' Schenke felt genuine relief. 'First, then, what happened?'

Liebwitz related what little he could about finding Feldwitz with the photos in his hand immediately before the attack. Then Schenke asked him about his earlier questioning of Bachmann. As Liebwitz was concluding, Rosa Mayer arrived with the forensic kit bag. She looked shaken by the grotesque expression on the corpse, and Schenke guided her to one side.

'See if you can get some prints off the doorknobs and any other surfaces the killer may have come into contact with.'

'Yes, sir.' She nodded.

'Most probably a waste of time,' Liebwitz intervened. 'If it was the man who I encountered on the stairs, he was wearing gloves.'

'Damn. Still, see what you can get, Rosa. We may strike lucky with someone else linked to the investigation.'

She carried the kit bag to the apartment door and set to work.

Schenke turned back to Liebwitz. 'This man Hugo, can you recall his face? Enough to give a description, or pick him out from the pictures we have on file?'

'No, sir. He was looking down at his watch as I passed him. I could only approximate his age.'

'A pity.' Schenke scrutinised the room and saw that one of the desk drawers was slightly open. Easing the body aside, he pulled the drawer out. There were a few scraps of paper – bills, receipts and some partial sheets of ration coupons – along with a pen and a deck of playing cards. Schenke examined the coupons but could not tell if they were real or fake. He dropped them back with the other papers and looked at Liebwitz.

'He had photos in his hand, you said.'

Liebwitz nodded.

'Could you make out any details?'

'I was struck down almost immediately, sir. I couldn't see what was depicted in the photos. I didn't even get any sense of who attacked me. He must have moved quickly and quietly.'

'Why do you think he didn't kill you, Scharführer?'

'I have considered that, sir, while giving my statement to Orpo. It seems to me that the assailant went to the apartment with Feldwitz to retrieve those photographs and intended to kill him once they were in his possession. There was no need to kill me. In fact, I would imagine doing so would have alarmed Feldwitz and made him more difficult to deal with when the time came. One does not murder a member of Kripo without drawing down the full weight of the police force.'

'Quite.'

'It was sufficient for him to incapacitate me. After all, I had seen almost nothing that might compromise his identity or the significance of the photographs he wanted.'

'For what it's worth, I'm pleased that he shared your measured view of what was at stake. Your death would have been a significant loss to my section.'

Liebwitz thought a moment and nodded. 'Yes, sir. I have no doubt about it.'

Schenke did his best not to betray his amusement while collecting his thoughts. 'Whoever was here knew what he was about. It takes a cool head to act as you suggest he did. An amateur might have panicked and killed you, even if he had been able to come up behind you without you knowing. He knocked you out, waited for Feldwitz to turn his back before he garrotted him, and departed with the photos without leaving any trace of a fingerprint, or letting you see his face if he was the man you recall passing on the stairs. He's a professional, and I doubt this was his first time.'

'I agree, sir.'

'A further thought occurs to me. I'm wondering if he might be the same person who killed Remer.'

'Sir?'

'He killed Feldwitz because he needed to, or was ordered to. You were spared because there was no need to kill you as well. If it is the same man, then perhaps he was only meant to shoot Remer, and Kunzler's wounding was incidental. He had no reason to kill her.'

'Except that she might be able to identify him, sir. In which case a professional would have shot her too.'

'Yes, that's true,' Schenke conceded. 'It's just that it took some planning to set Remer up and cool nerves to carry the deception through to the ambush in the alley. A rather uncommon set of characteristics as far as my experience goes of the rank-and-file of Berlin's underworld. He's dangerous. I wonder who he is really working for, if not Guttmann?'

'Sir, it's true he might be the same man, but we can't assume it.'

'No . . .' Schenke glanced towards the figure folded over the desk. 'Our dead friend there was an associate of the late Remer. We know that he managed the club, but I don't get the impression he was very high up the chain of command as far as Remer's criminal activities go. So if Guttmann is behind the killings, why bother with Feldwitz? And if Guttmann had nothing to do with this, then who else might want him dead?'

Liebwitz made no reply.

'What do you make of Bachmann's take on Fräulein Kunzler?' Schenke continued. 'Doesn't sound much like the woman we spoke to at the hospital.'

'Indeed, sir. I was surprised by the vehemence of his feelings regarding her. Either he is voicing the bitterness of a disappointed former lover, or she is a good actress.'

'That's possible. After all, that's why she came to Berlin in the first place. I think we need to speak to her again.'

Schenke picked up his hat, then spoke to Rosa. 'When you've finished looking over the place, you'd better call in the morgue boys to remove the body. The cause of death is clear, and I doubt the time was much after the Scharführer arrived at the apartment, so the coroner is unlikely to tell us anything we don't already know.'

'Yes, sir. If I find anything significant, shall I call you?'

Schenke nodded, taking a last look at the body before he addressed Liebwitz. 'I've got a car downstairs. I'll take you home first.'

'There's no need, sir. I—'

'Consider it an order, Scharführer Liebwitz. I don't want to risk you passing out on the street. You need to get home as quickly as possible to rest and recover. I have a job for you tomorrow.'

Liebwitz cocked an eyebrow enquiringly.

'You are driving me to Wannsee. You're to sign out the best of the precinct's cars and pick me up from my apartment at eleven.'

'Why are we going to Wannsee, sir?'

'It's nothing to do with the investigations,' Schenke explained. 'It's a professional engagement dressed up as a social gathering. Make sure that you get some rest, and wear your Gestapo coat and a hat large enough to cover the bandage comfortably. We'll need to look our best.'

The address Liebwitz directed him to turned out to be in an affluent part of Pankow. Not only was there a concierge behind

187

the counter in the lobby, but he was smartly dressed in a uniform dating back to the previous war. He stood and bowed his head in salute as Liebwitz and Schenke entered. The lobby was lined with marble, in addition to the marbled floor, and the brasswork on the lift was finely polished. Schenke could not help wondering how Liebwitz could afford accommodation that was better than his own, given the difference in their pay.

The apartment continued the display of opulence. Besides a spotlessly clean kitchen and bathroom, it had two bedrooms and a study, as well as a lounge, all carpeted. Liebwitz took off his coat and hung it, with his hat, on a stand in the corridor. He looked at Schenke awkwardly. 'Would you like something to drink, sir?'

Schenke had been tempted to politely refuse, but his curiosity was piqued and instead he nodded. 'Very kind of you. A coffee would be welcome.'

'There is no coffee, sir. I can offer you tea.'

'Tea it is then. Shall I help?'

'No, no. I can manage,' Liebwitz replied in a flustered tone, and disappeared into the kitchen. His head appeared round the door frame a moment later. 'You can, uh, make yourself comfortable in the living room while you wait, sir.'

As Liebwitz filled the kettle, Schenke made his way slowly past framed photographs depicting the unsmiling Scharführer at a graduation ceremony, in a fencing jacket holding a sabre, again unsmiling, and with several other men in SS uniform being handed their ceremonial daggers by Himmler. There was only one armchair in the living room. A crammed bookcase filled one wall, while at the far end, under the window, was a large table covered with a thick board upon which a partially constructed model of a sailing ship rested on a stand.

Surrounding it were pots of paint, varnish and glue, modelling knives and reels of fine white cotton. Schenke marvelled at the detail of the model: the tiny brass cannon on gun carriages lining each side of the deck, the neat coils of rope beside the guns, and the fine tracery of rigging and intricately carved blocks suspended from the mainmast. The foremast and the mizzen lay to one side, ready to be added to the model in due course. There were other model ships lined up on top of the bookcase, each finished with the same attention to detail.

'Your tea, sir.'

Liebwitz entered the room, a steaming mug in either hand. He set one down on a small side table next to the armchair, then crossed to the table and pulled out a stool from beneath it.

'Your ships are fascinating,' said Schenke as he lowered himself into the armchair. The models had reawakened the passion he had once had for such things as a child, like almost every other boy. It seemed incongruous that Liebwitz, a grown man, should pursue such a hobby. But then, Schenke realised, it was totally within his character: meticulous, patient and careful.

'Yes, they are,' Liebwitz said proudly, and smiled with satisfaction as he looked over his creations. For an instant, Schenke had a glimpse of the boy the Scharführer had once been, and his heart warmed towards his subordinate. Liebwitz's gaze shifted back to Schenke, and the smile vanished beneath his habitual deadpan expression. 'I imagine you find this rather an odd pastime for an adult, sir.'

'It's . . . surprising, I suppose, but they are works of art in their way. I just never thought of you having such an interest outside of police work.'

'As it happens, I find it helps me to think about such matters. It's a form of meditation.'

'I see.'

'Do you?' Liebwitz looked at him curiously.

'For me, it's music. Listening to my gramophone helps me to think.'

Liebwitz nodded. 'Then we have something in common. I'm not sure the same could be said of Sergeant Hauser.'

The comment immediately put Schenke on his guard. He had served with Hauser for some years now and had developed considerable respect for him. 'Don't ever underestimate Hauser. He's a damn fine cop and has a good record. I appreciate that he is inclined to make fun of you. He's the same with anyone new in the section. He's testing you to see how you respond. I wouldn't take offence. He's intelligent and experienced enough to know a good criminal investigator when he sees one. At the moment he is just trying to work out what kind of person you are.'

'I expect he would be most amused if he knew of my hobby.'

'I imagine so. But he won't hear about it from me.'

Liebwitz nodded and Schenke continued.

'May I ask why the interest in sailing ships?'

'There's something inspiring about such craft. Something elegant. Intricate vessels operated by skilled hands in order to harness the elements. They are also things of beauty, of grace. When I was a child . . .' Liebwitz paused and stared at Schenke. 'You will recall I told you about what I endured in the homes where I was raised.'

Schenke thought back to the night they had been held in a dark, freezing cellar while they had been investigating the murder of disabled children some months earlier. That was when Liebwitz had spoken of his early years, of being sent to a home for children deemed mentally defective due to his peculiar manner. Of the long years of suffering and abuse before he was adopted. 'I remember.'

'At those times when my life was hardest, I used to dream of running away and going to sea. Sailing to the far side of the world. I imagined myself on ships such as this.'

'Do you still dream of it?'

Liebwitz lifted his mug and took a sip. 'No. It was a form of escapism. Nothing more. Now it is merely a means of relaxation.'

'I used to make models of cars when I was a kid,' said Schenke. 'Racing cars mostly. I was fascinated by their speed, their sleekness. The power of their engines. It's what led me into motor racing, before I joined Kripo.'

'Cars . . .' Liebwitz mused. 'I've never understood the attraction. Loud machines. Grease . . . oil . . . fumes. Sailing ships, on the other hand, are things of grace and beauty, driven across the boundless oceans by the elements.'

'Why, Liebwitz, if I did not know you better, I'd say you have the soul of a poet.'

The Scharführer looked at him blankly, then winced and reached up to touch his bandage.

Schenke stood. 'You need to rest. I'd better go. Make sure you look every inch a Gestapo man when you pick me up tomorrow.'

Chapter Fifteen

7 May

Schenke smiled as he saw the Horch limousine turn the corner onto the street where he was waiting. Like many of the police pool cars, it had been appropriated from a wealthy Berlin family on the outbreak of war, and he looked forward to arriving at the Radinsky villa in style. He had long since learned that the Nazi Party measured a man by the trappings of material success, and being chauffeured to the party would confer some status on him. A driver in the garb of the Gestapo would no doubt improve that status still further. As the car drew closer, he could see Liebwitz through the windscreen, hunched forward in anxious concentration as he steered the car towards the kerb and pulled up sharply enough to lurch forward.

Schenke climbed into the passenger seat. 'Good morning, Liebwitz. How is your head feeling?'

The Scharführer, still gripping the wheel tightly in his left hand, while the right was closed about the handbrake, looked at him with a strained expression. 'I was feeling fine until I started driving, sir.'

'Look, you got here in one piece. Have some confidence in yourself.'

The words were spoken in an encouraging tone, but Schenke was struggling to maintain his composure as he regarded the other man's appearance. The Scharführer's wide-brimmed black hat had been pulled down over the bandage as far as it would go, with the result that his ears had been pushed out slightly and his head looked like a wingnut. A trickle of sweat was running down his cheek, and he removed his hand from the wheel long enough to cuff it away. Schenke's sense of amusement gave way to sympathy for his subordinate.

'You'll do fine. The more practice you get, the easier it becomes, as with all things.'

'Yes, sir.'

'Then let's be on our way.'

Liebwitz released the handbrake and reached for the gearstick, engaged first and lifted the clutch. The Horch moved smoothly away from the kerb.

'Very good,' said Schenke, then grabbed the side strap as the car gave a sharp jolt. The Scharführer muttered something to himself and resumed his earlier hunched posture as he concentrated on the route ahead, only changing gears when the revs built up to a loud volume. As they navigated their way out of the city, Schenke grasped the strap firmly in one hand and the edge of the seat with the other, and tried to look nonchalantly out of the window to distract himself. Poor Liebwitz, he thought. If only they could have sailed to Wannsee instead.

Emerging from the suburbs of Charlottenburg, they passed into open country before the road entered the Grunewald and the trees of the ancient forest closed in on either side. Glancing at his watch, Schenke saw that they were already running late, and ordered the Scharführer to increase his speed. At length they emerged from the trees into a smart residential area with large houses lining the road. Liebwitz slowed as they crossed the bridge onto the island where Berlin's wealthiest had built substantial houses and villas on the shoreline. They turned right towards the Heckeshorn, and Schenke looked for Radinsky's villa. Ahead he saw a line of cars parked either side of a pillared gateway. The drivers were leaning against the cars in small groups and smoking while a squad of SS troopers in their wartime grey uniform were guarding the gate.

'Pull over,' Schenke said, and Liebwitz came to a stop. At once an Oberscharführer approached, and Schenke lowered the window and held up his invitation. It was glanced at quickly before he was asked for his identity card. The guard compared the photo on it with Schenke's face, then nodded before returning it and opening the door. Once Schenke had stepped out, the Oberscharführer ducked his head to address Liebwitz.

'Park along the road there.'

The car pulled away, and Schenke was directed towards the gate. There was a light drizzle, and a footman in smart white livery emerged from a guard hut and opened an umbrella to cover him as they walked down the drive towards the villa. The route curved slightly so that it was not possible to see the building directly from the road. Schenke glimpsed more armed SS men patrolling the wall that appeared to surround the house as far as the waterfront. He had assumed that Radinsky's villa would be one of the more modest abodes along the Wannsee shore, but it was clear that it was more substantial than he had anticipated.

'Why all the security?' he asked, nodding towards the men pacing along the wall.

'There's quite a few senior members of the party present,

sir. As you might expect, given that many of them have places on the island.'

'Anyone I've heard of?' Schenke probed.

The footman gave him an amused glance. 'Heydrich, Darré and Goebbels for a start. There will be others arriving. And some leading figures from the film world. Quite a gathering.'

The drive straightened out, and ahead of them Schenke could see the villa. Built on two floors, it had a pillared portico and looked more like a small palace than a lakeside home. Several large cars were parked to one side, with triangular official pennants on the bonnets. He let out a low whistle.

'I had no idea Oberführer Radinsky came from money.'

'He doesn't. It belongs to his wife,' the footman explained. 'Frau Radinsky is from the Krupp family. You can imagine how loaded that makes her.'

'I don't have to imagine. I can see it.'

There were four more SS men at the door, and Schenke's invitation and identity card were examined again before he was allowed to enter. The footman collapsed the umbrella and trotted back down the drive, while another took Schenke's coat. The entrance gave onto a large ochre-painted hall with paintings hanging on the walls. At the far end a gleaming oak staircase rose to a landing before ascending again to the upper floor, where a gallery ran around both sides and over Schenke's head. Although he had been to many country houses and a few castles when he was a child in Prussia, and later when he had enjoyed fame as a racing driver, he was still impressed by the grandeur of the villa, and especially some of the artwork adorning the walls.

He could hear music and the hubbub of conversation to his left, and another footman indicated a corridor leading off the hall.

'You'll find the other guests in the ballroom, sir. At the end of the corridor and turn right.'

'Thank you.'

Schenke experienced a growing sense of discomfort as he left the hall. He had thought this might be a small social gathering with a few mid-ranking Nazi members. Instead he was going to be mixing with the elite of the regime and their friends. It was obvious why Radinsky had invited him. It had nothing to do with getting to know his subordinate socially and everything to do with Schenke's reputation from his racing days. He sighed as he realised he would be performing the role again.

Towards the end of the corridor there were double doors, one of which was open, and Schenke glanced in on a fine library where a fire burned in a huge ornamental grate. Dark bookcases ran along both sides and a bow window looked over the garden at the front of the villa. Leather couches and side tables were distributed around the carpeted room, as well as some potted tropical plants. He gave a last wistful look at the extensive collection of books before he continued to the corner, and there ahead of him was the large arched doorway of the ballroom.

The room was a good thirty metres in length and perhaps twenty metres wide. A string quartet in red jackets were playing on the stage at the far end. Before them were more than a hundred men and women, formally dressed and gathered in loose groups as they chatted and laughed. Some of the men were wearing military or party uniforms, but most, Schenke was relieved to see, were dressed as he was in smart civilian suits.

Radinsky was standing just inside the ballroom, and he smiled as soon as he caught sight of his guest. Taking the elbow of a large, broad woman with round cheeks and brown hair neatly pinned up, he steered her towards Schenke.

'My dear, let me introduce you to one of my colleagues at the precinct. This is Criminal Inspector Horst Schenke.'

Frau Radinsky looked Schenke up and down with a cool expression, as if she was calculating his pedigree, then her eyes widened fractionally and she smiled. 'Ah! Horst *von* Schenke, you mean. *The* Horst von Schenke. I am delighted to meet you.'

She held out her gloved hand, and Schenke bowed his head and momentarily made a show of kissing it. 'Enchanted . . .'

Radinsky put his hand on Schenke's shoulder. 'Let's get you a drink and introduce you to some people.'

As they made their way through the throng, the Oberführer continued, 'Treat this as an opportunity to make some useful connections in the party. I know you aren't a member yet. That might be tricky to arrange, but a position in the SS should be well within the bounds of possibility. Especially given your background. Himmler has a particular liking for aristocratic blood. It adds lustre to the organisation.'

A footman appeared with a tray of champagne flutes, and Radinsky took one and handed it to Schenke. 'There. Enjoy yourself. I apologise, but as the host, I have to attend to my guests, you understand.' He gave a sly wink. 'One in particular. You'll see.' Then he was gone, making his way back towards the ballroom entrance.

Schenke self-consciously took a sip of champagne as he scanned his surroundings and the other guests. There was a high ceiling from which two large chandeliers were suspended, and tall windows overlooking the lawn that stretched out to the shoreline, where there was a boathouse and a small pier. The drizzle was accompanied by a light mist into which the water merged seamlessly. A melancholy prospect that contrasted with the gaiety inside the villa, thought Schenke.

He moved to one side of the room, from where he could look over the other guests. There were some familiar faces. Himmler, in his black uniform with silver insignia, was listening to the diminutive Goebbels as he talked animatedly. Every so often the little group around them, men and women alike, would laugh at some comment and Himmler would affect a chuckle or a smile. The two men might be party comrades, Schenke reflected, but there seemed to be some tension between them, like rival hyenas circling a carcass.

He caught sight of an austere grey-haired man with deep-set eyes and felt a lurch of apprehension. It was Admiral Canaris, Karin's uncle. He was tempted to approach and ask after her, if only to know how he stood with her. However, if Karin had told Canaris about his neglect and coolness, he doubted he would be regarded with much favour by the admiral. A pity, since he admired and liked the man.

'Inspector Schenke!' A high-pitched voice cut across his thoughts. Schenke turned and saw Heydrich approaching with a companion at his shoulder, a pale man with a high forehead, tired-looking eyes and a sour expression. 'I thought it was you.' Heydrich smiled and drew up without offering his hand. 'Radinsky mentioned you would be here. What a delightful surprise.'

In Schenke's experience, it was better not to be talked about by those who ran the state's security services. He bowed his head politely. 'I have to admit, I am rather surprised to be here myself, sir. It's a far cry from the Kripo section at the Pankow precinct.'

'Nonsense. With your past I am sure you attended many such gatherings. I can assure you that Radinsky didn't just invite you out of consideration for your fine police record. He likes to rub shoulders with the glitterati, like most arrivistes.' Heydrich half turned to his companion, who was regarding Schenke with a neutral expression.

'May I introduce Reichsminister of Food and Agriculture Richard Darré. Richard, this is Criminal Inspector Schenke.'

'Inspector.' Darré dipped his head and spoke in a flat tone. 'A pleasure.'

'Besides being one of our finest police officers,' Heydrich continued, 'Horst von Schenke achieved considerable success in another field.'

'Indeed?'

There was a pause before Heydrich shook his head. 'Surely you have heard of him?'

Darré's brow creased slightly. 'No. I can't recall the name.'

'Horst von Schenke of the Silver Arrows racing team?' Heydrich prompted.

Darré shook his head. 'I have never been a follower of motor racing. Frankly, I do not have the time to devote to such matters, what with my important work for the party.'

Heydrich looked disappointed. 'Come now, Richard. All work and no play . . . I have been reliably informed that you do like to play. It seems you were a regular at a certain club that sadly burned down a couple of days ago.'

Schenke saw the icy glint in Darré's eyes as he replied. 'As it happens, I had already decided to withdraw my custom from that club weeks ago. Your information is out of date, my dear Heydrich. I have no more interest in the club than I do in this man's past driving career.'

'It was a long time ago, sir,' said Schenke. 'I would imagine very few people remember that part of my life any more.'

'Well I remember,' Heydrich said coolly. 'I am somewhat cursed by having a fine memory. There is very little I forget. Your achievements as a star of the track being an example. Not to mention your tracking down that fiend who was murdering women last year. That was a fine achievement. One that went some way towards making up for your interference in the matter of the SS doctor who was murdered shortly afterwards.'

Schenke fought to hide his anxiety. 'I was doing my duty, sir.'

'Yes.' Heydrich's eyes bored into his before he turned to Darré with a smile. 'Do you know, I offered this fellow a position in my office and he turned me down flat. Because of his devotion to his duty as a police officer. I am still not sure if I should be impressed by that or insulted. Anyway, this is the man who is in charge of hunting down the scoundrels responsible for flooding the black market with forged ration coupons. That's why I brought you over here to meet him, Richard.'

There was something in his tone that implied a dig at his companion, thought Schenke as he saw Darré's expression darken.

Darré edged closer and spoke in an undertone. 'How near are you to putting an end to the forgeries?'

'The investigation is at an advanced stage, Reichsminister. I hope to discover the identity of those responsible soon.'

'Soon?' Darré scoffed. 'How much more time do you need? The damned things have been in circulation for six months now. Do you have any idea how destabilising that is to the home front in Berlin? All sorts of shortages are occurring as a result.'

'I understand that, sir,' Schenke replied calmly. 'That is why my Kripo officers and I have been devoting our attention to this matter.'

'Not good enough. I demand progress, Inspector. I want regular updates on the progress you are making.' Darré turned to Heydrich. 'He's one of yours, isn't he?'

Heydrich's thin lips lifted in amusement. 'Technically, the chain of command goes through Nebe as Kripo's chief and then via myself to Himmler.'

'I don't give a damn about technicalities. He's one of yours. You need to order him to report to me on this matter.'

'Of course, Richard. I'll speak to my boss as soon as possible.'

'Do so. In the meantime, Inspector, I'll have one of my officials, Stoffler, contact you directly to confer on this matter. You may expect a call from him first thing tomorrow.'

Schenke bit back on his anger at being addressed in such a manner. He had no desire for the hunt for the source of the forgeries to be hampered by one of Darré's underlings, and to have the man interfere with the parallel murder investigation.

'Naturally, Kripo would welcome any assistance we can get, sir.'

Darré glared at him before he muttered, 'Do your damn job, man, so that I can do mine.' Then he turned and veered away through the other guests and out of sight.

Schenke gave a relieved sigh.

'Our Reichsminister for Food and Agriculture is quite the little martinet, isn't he?' Heydrich mused.

Schenke gave a non-committal shrug, not keen to pass judgement on Darré in front of his superior.

'Your thoughts are safe with me, Schenke. But I appreciate your caution. It's one of the reasons I offered you a position on my staff. Unfortunately for both of us, that boat has sailed.

I only make such an offer once. I hope you can find another potential patron. In today's Germany a man can only get so far without powerful connections. Even a man as talented as yourself.'

Schenke was unsure of how to respond to the compliment, but before he was put on the spot, Heydrich glanced over his shoulder and continued, 'And speaking of such patrons . . . Good evening, Admiral! How are you?'

Schenke saw Canaris approaching and felt his heart sink a little. The admiral smiled and shook hands with Heydrich before he directed his piercing gaze at Schenke.

'Horst, what a pleasant surprise. I had no idea you were part of Radinsky's social circle.'

'It's good to see you too, sir. And I had no idea that I was either.'

All three shared a brief chuckle before Canaris spoke again. 'I was sorry that things didn't work out for you and Karin. You were well suited, I thought. Which goes to show you that even the senior officer at the Abwehr makes bad calls from time to time.'

'As the saying goes,' Heydrich chipped in, 'military intelligence is an oxymoron.'

Canaris's eyes glinted before he affected an amused look. 'In any case, Horst, I thought it a pity that the two of you had broken off your relationship.'

Throughout the exchange Schenke was trying not to reveal his feelings. So Karin had decided to end things. He felt a mixture of sorrow and hurt. She had not even tried to contact him to discuss it. But then, he chided himself, it was not as if he had made the effort either. For an instant he was tempted to consider the if-only scenarios that began to suggest themselves.

Then he thrust such thoughts aside. It was over. At least there was relief in the certainty of knowing that, even as he felt a surge of affection for the memory of her. He cleared his throat to reply to the admiral in a steady voice. 'Yes, sir. A great pity.'

'She's here today, you know. She spotted you the moment you entered the room.'

Schenke's pulse quickened with anxiety. Karin here? He resisted the urge to scan the crowd. 'Then it would be nice to say hello to her, sir. I hope we can remain friends at least.'

'You can put that to the test yourself. Here she comes.'

Schenke almost sensed her presence in the air and picked up a waft of her favourite perfume – Vol de Nuit – then she was standing at her uncle's side. Her hair had been dyed black when he had last seen her, but now she had reverted to her natural blonde, and he felt something stir in the pit of his stomach as he returned her gaze.

'Karin . . . how are you?'

'Very well, Horst. Very well indeed. You look tired, but then you always did. It must have been hard for you to balance your professional obligations with life outside of Kripo. I understand that now.'

'Karin, I never meant—'

She raised a hand to stop him. 'It's all right. I don't blame you. I know how important your work is to you. In fact I am grateful we didn't pursue the relationship any further. It was best that it ended when it did, before we came to regret it.'

He was dumbfounded by her directness. Heydrich and Canaris made their excuses and filtered away through the crowd in search of another drink.

'If that's how it is, then I wish you well, Karin. Truly.'

'That's kind of you. As it happens, I have met someone else.

A young Luftwaffe officer. Quite dashing, and he adores me. It's early days, but we'll see how it goes. That's him, over there by the pillar.'

Schenke saw a slim figure with wavy brown hair and sensitive features looking in their direction. The officer raised his glass in salute as he returned their gaze. Schenke gave a nod in return as he suppressed an urge to dislike the man out of envy.

'I hope he treats you well.'

'He does, and he is very attentive. How about you? Is there anyone else in your life?'

Schenke thought of Ruth and almost smiled, but caught himself in time. Whatever there was between them must remain a closely guarded secret.

'No. Like you said, there is not enough spare time outside of work.'

She gave him a sad look. 'You should make time. You can't solve all the world's crimes. One day you'll understand, and when you do, I hope there is someone there for you.'

'I hope so too.'

'Good.' She nodded. 'I should get back to Kurt. You take care of yourself, do you hear?'

'I will.'

She touched his cheek, then turned away and crossed the ballroom to rejoin her airman. Schenke watched as Kurt put his arm around her waist and kissed her before resuming his conversation with the other young officers and their partners gathered around him.

Unsure of how he should respond to Karin's dismissal, he drained his glass and went in search of a footman to give him a refill. As he passed the other guests, he realised how few faces he recognised, and those he did were people he would rather not socialise with. Despite having arrived less than half an hour earlier, he was keen to get away as soon as possible. With Radinsky and his wife still hovering around the entrance to the ballroom, however, that would not be possible without looking unconscionably rude. Instead, he decided to temporise. He finished his second glass of champagne and made for the doorway.

'Excuse me, sir,' he said quietly. 'Where can I find the toilet?'

'To the left of the staircase in the lobby.'

Nodding his thanks, he made his way back along the corridor, pausing outside the library door. He waited until no one was in sight, then ducked within and eased the door shut. Looking around, he examined his surroundings. It was a fine private library. There were rows of leather-bound volumes, together with more recently published books, periodicals and bundles of newspapers and magazines. A large landscape painting in the manner of Caspar Friedrich hung above the marble mantelpiece. It depicted a man climbing a mountain path above a misty landscape. The kind of nostalgic appeal to mythical manhood that was a popular motif amongst Nazi art collectors, Schenke reflected. A life-size bust of the Führer rested on a small table to one side of the fireplace, together with a copy of his great work. Schenke opened the cover and saw a dedication scrawled on the first page – *To my former comrade in arms, Helmut Radinsky* – with the signature below it: *Adolf Hitler*.

'That explains a lot,' Schenke muttered.

He looked up at the painting and realised that it was a Friedrich original after all. Moving across to sit on one of the couches between two profuse ferned planters beside the door, he leaned back and stared at the ceiling. He decided that he would not be missed for a while. When he did return to the ballroom, he would endure no more than an hour of the party before he made some excuse about needing to return to read through some files in readiness to push the investigation forward. He closed his eyes and tried not to think about Karin, or Ruth. Instead he tried to fit the pieces of the investigation together into meaningful patterns. He was certain that Guttmann was pulling a number of strings, but to what precise end? And if he was, then there were some apparent wildcards that Schenke could not make sense of yet. There was clearly more to Kitty Kunzler than he had initially thought. Bachmann's view of her did not square with Schenke's original impression of the woman.

He heard a number of cars approaching the villa and then someone shouting orders. Almost certainly another party bigwig making their entrance, he surmised, and mentally returned to retracing his steps. He had barely begun to reconsider Kunzler's account of Remer's murder when the door to the library swung open and a tall figure in a black uniform, gleaming jackboots and helmet entered the room and looked round, before pointing to Schenke with a white-gloved hand.

'You, outside. Now.'

Schenke froze, his first thought being terror that he had been found out for some crime, even though that could not be the case. The soldier stepped up to the couch and was about to address him again when someone else interrupted him.

'That's not necessary. Let him be. Close the door behind you.'

The soldier snapped his chin down and clicked his heels before marching from the room and quietly pulling the door to.

Schenke had recognised the voice at once, the familiar

Austrian accent, and he was already on his feet as Hitler appeared beyond the edge of the fern. The Führer was wearing his formal grey military jacket, as he had promised the people he would until Germany had vanquished its enemies. He reached up to shift a loose strand of his brown hair, and Schenke saw that he looked weary and slightly anxious, perspiration pricking out on his forehead. He was used to seeing newsreels and press pictures of the Führer in which he was depicted as the tireless father of the nation. This more vulnerable and careworn individual seemed almost like another man. It was a shocking revelation. And yet for Schenke, the awe of being in his presence somehow became yet more overwhelming and poignant as he saw something of the man behind the public mask.

'I apologise, my Führer, I will leave at once.'

'No.' Hitler gave a flap of his hand. 'That's not necessary. I just need a quiet moment.' He frowned. 'I know your face . . . We've met before.'

Schenke was not sure how to respond. He did not dare to correct the Führer, but at the same time could not mislead him with a dishonest affirmation of his assertion. He was saved by the other man's question.

'What is your name?'

'Horst von Schenke, my Führer.'

'Von Schenke . . . von Schenke . . .' Hitler's eyes suddenly gleamed and he snapped his fingers. 'Yes, I recognise you now, young man. Horst von Schenke of the Mercedes Silver Arrows team, yes?'

Schenke was taken by surprise that the Führer recalled him. He nodded, seeing at once a lively animation in the other man's expression as he stepped closer and grasped Schenke's hand with both of his and shook it warmly. 'I used to follow you and the team before I became chancellor. Mercedes make the best cars. Sadly, the affairs of state leave little time for such enthusiasms. Although I was delighted to see one of my SS men win an event in Italy recently.' Hitler chuckled. 'Mussolini and his Italians like to brag about their cars and their drivers, but they'll never match German technology and German guts, eh?'

Schenke gave a slight smile as he nodded.

Hitler released Schenke's hand and folded his arms. 'Let me see, you used to drive a W23, I recall.'

'That's right.'

'A fine car. One of the best. We make good machines here in Germany. Racing cars, planes, tanks, guns. It is a reflection of our racial genius and the envy of the world. At the time you were racing I used to drive a Mercedes also. A Tourer. Lovely car. Fast and sleek. Like a wolf chasing down its prey.' He smiled at the memory. 'Happy times . . .'

The smile faded and his face resolved into the earlier expression of weariness as he sat on the couch that Schenke had vacated. His stare intensified as he looked past Schenke towards the bay window overlooking the front lawn of the villa. 'Alas, those pleasures are far behind me. Far behind all of us. Germany faces her greatest test, and we must all dedicate ourselves to her triumph. We must triumph. We will triumph. That is our destiny.'

Schenke had the feeling that Hitler was no longer speaking to him and was barely aware of his presence. But then he blinked and turned his intense gaze back to the inspector. 'In another life, I would have preferred to be someone like you. Free to pursue what I enjoyed doing most. But fate chose otherwise. And we are all servants of fate. So tell me, my boy, are you still involved in racing?'

'No longer, my Führer. I was forced to leave the team after a crash several years ago.'

'A crash?' Hitler looked him up and down. 'But you recovered fully, it would seem.'

Schenke patted his thigh. 'My left leg was crushed and I was in hospital for months. Afterwards, there was no going back to a racing career.'

'I see. It is a sad thing to see a young German, a hero of the circuit, crippled and of no further use to his calling. But we must honour our heroes. They have given so much for our people.'

Schenke bridled but did not respond. He was hardly a cripple. To be sure, he had a limp, which he did his best to hide, and there were times when he experienced shooting pains, but it was not as if he was one of the amputees from the first war that one still saw on the streets of Berlin.

'We need our young men, our heroes, now more than ever.' There was a more distant look in Hitler's eyes as he continued. 'This is their hour. This is their time to honour the sacrifices made by their fathers in the last war and win back the destiny that was betrayed by the cowards and traitors who led Germany to humiliation. I dare say you wish you could join your brothers in the great adventure to come, eh?' He offered Schenke an encouraging smile. 'The great Horst von Schenke racing his tank to be the first to reach the coast of France!'

Schenke made himself smile back. 'France, my Führer?'

Hitler's expression became serious. 'And beyond ... far beyond. To the west and to the east. There is nothing Germany cannot achieve with men of your calibre. If only my generals shared the nerve you displayed on the racing track. But for the most part they are timid old fools, tied to tradition. I have spent too much time in their company, listening to their excuses about what can and cannot be done. As if I know nothing about waging war. You and I, Horst, we know what it is to take risks to win the great prizes in life. We know what courage is and what it can achieve. Isn't that so?'

Schenke tried not to recall the blind terror he had felt at that moment when he had pushed his luck beyond the limit in the race that ended his career amid tearing metal, flames and agony. He swallowed before he could reply. 'As you say, my Führer.'

'Good man! I spend too much time with generals and politicians and too little with men like you. You have refreshed my spirit and now I am ready to face the others.'

When Hitler stood again, the tiredness of earlier was gone and there was a gleam in his eyes. He gave a cheerful grin as he patted Schenke on the shoulder. 'Come with me. I have something to announce. Something you will want to hear, so that you are able to say to your children and your grandchildren, "I was there the day the Führer announced . . ." Well, you'll see. Come, Horst. Be at my side when I speak.'

He put his arm across Schenke's shoulders and they left the library. Outside in the corridor, more of the black-uniformed soldiers stood to attention at regular intervals on either side as the pair made their way to the ballroom. Ahead, Radinsky looked stunned as he saw Schenke approaching in the avuncular embrace of the Führer, then he stiffened and thrust his arm out.

'Heil Hitler!'

At once the other guests fell silent and turned to welcome

the Führer with raised arms and a loud chorus of the German greeting. Schenke's right arm was trapped between himself and the Führer's jacket, and he made to raise his left before realising that it would throw off Hitler's hand on his shoulder, so he stood mute at the great man's side. Hitler seemed not to notice as he beamed at the crowd and then responded by bringing his own right hand up at the elbow and tilting his wrist back in his characteristic acknowledgement. He seemed to clutch Schenke closer to him as the salutes were exchanged. Then he lowered his hand and Radinsky and his guests followed suit, standing in silence as they waited for him to speak.

Hitler raised a hand to his mouth and cleared his throat.

'Party comrades . . . fellow Germans, our kind hosts . . .' He nodded gratefully, and Schenke saw Radinsky and his wife beam with proud delight. 'It is a pleasure to be with you today. To be amongst those who always believed in the truth of our great cause. I won't speak for long. Trust me, I know how important it is to enjoy these precious moments together on the eve of our greatest days. So, my dear Heinrich, you can finish that glass shortly and start another!'

Himmler glanced down bashfully and then smiled as polite laughter rippled across the ballroom. Hitler waited for it to subside.

'Some months ago, Germany embarked on the first step to greatness. First Poland, then Denmark and Norway fell into our hands. The French and the British will be thrown back into the seas off Norway and now their leaders wait anxiously to see where we will strike next. Over the last few weeks I have been working alongside my generals to prepare for the greatest offensive in history. A vast army is massing to strike at our enemies. The largest and best-equipped army that Germany has ever fielded, and, I might say, the most powerful army the world has ever seen. Our panzers, our aircraft, our soldiers and airmen are the finest and as well prepared as they can be for the forthcoming campaign. Indeed, I have just come from a meeting with their commanders in Berlin. It has been exhausting work dealing with every obstacle they have placed in our way. At first the generals said it could not be done. Should not be done. You all know how cautious our senior military ranks can be,' he added in a jovial tone, and once more there was some laughter, though Schenke saw the stern expression on Canaris's face.

A bead of sweat gently eased down Hitler's temple as he continued with passion in the warm room.

'But they have listened to reason. They now understand the great destiny that providence has laid before me to realise the dream of making Germany the most powerful state in the world!'

There was a fanatical glint in his eyes now. For a moment his expression was one of unhinged ambition, and Schenke felt himself in the icy grip of terror. Then Hitler's features softened as he continued in a more moderate tone. 'It has been a tiring business talking them round ... I was in two minds about whether I should join you at this gathering. I was exhausted and wanted to rest, but I wanted the most loyal of my comrades and followers to be amongst the first to know that the decisive hour approaches. So I paused in Radinsky's marvellous library to draw breath, and there I met this fine young man.' He removed his arm and half turned towards Schenke, who was too astonished to react other than to stay still and keep his expression neutral.

'Horst von Schenke, a hero of the racetrack. A man who

reminded me of the raw courage it takes to risk all and win through. A man whose split-second judgement made the difference between winning a race and losing it. This is the spirit of the generation that is going to carry the banner of Nazi Germany forward and plant it in the capitals of our enemies. These are the kind of men who will march in the victory parades through Paris, London and beyond. We old soldiers of the last war look upon them with pride as they forever remove the shame that was imposed on Germany by our old enemies. Horst von Schenke, you were an inspiration on the racetrack; may you and your generation inspire us anew as you inspired me earlier and rekindled my hope and fervour for our success. I thank you.'

He took Schenke's hand and shook it warmly. As he released his grip, there was a slight pause as he stared at Schenke, and it took the briefest of moments for him to grasp what was expected of him. He raised his right arm steadily, even as his stomach churned in nervous apprehension and self-loathing, and spoke the German greeting clearly. 'Heil Hitler.'

Hitler gave a nod and turned to the crowd. 'And now, comrades, please, enjoy the party.'

Abruptly he turned away from Schenke and stepped over to Radinsky to exchange greetings. Schenke lowered his arm, feeling foolish and uncertain what to do next. A gap opened up in the crowd as Hitler made his way through, shaking hands, patting arms and smiling. With all the attention focused on the Führer, Schenke slipped around the crowd, avoiding the curious and envious gazes of those who glanced at him in passing. His heart was beating quickly and his throat felt tight and dry. Helping himself to a fresh glass of champagne, he took a generous gulp and breathed deeply.

* * *

213

An hour later, Schenke emerged from the villa gates to find Liebwitz leaning against the door of the car, arms folded as he stared into the middle distance. The other drivers had gathered in small groups to smoke and chat and share flasks of spirits, careful not to drink too much. Some sixth sense alerted the Scharführer to his approach, and he glanced round, eased himself away from the car and hurriedly opened the door for his superior. Schenke climbed in and Liebwitz got into the driver's seat and started the motor.

'How did it go, sir?'

'Go?'

'I saw the motorcade enter the gate. Some of the drivers said it was Hitler.'

Schenke nodded and could not help a tremble as he recalled the way he had been held up as an example, to be used to feed the Führer's rhetoric. He was aware that Liebwitz was waiting for him to speak.

'Get me away from this place. Take me back to Berlin.'

Chapter Sixteen

8 May

Sergeant Hauser looked on in awe as Schenke finished relating what had occurred at Radinsky's villa, and the events of the evening before that. They were sitting at Hauser's desk in the middle of the section's office. The sergeant had arrived at first light and had been going through the paperwork delivered that morning. It was not yet eight o'clock, and only a handful of others had arrived. Liebwitz was at the next desk, listening intently.

'Sweet Jesus, the moment I leave the precinct it all goes to shit.' Hauser rubbed the back of his head. 'It's lucky the Scharführer has such a thick skull, otherwise we'd be looking into another murder.'

'Robust rather than thick,' Liebwitz observed. He was wearing a fresh bandage, which Rosa had insisted on applying when he entered the office. She had made a good job of it, ensuring that it cleared his ears and would not be obvious under his hat. Once the old dressing had been removed and the puckered skin and black thread of the stitches exposed, Schenke could see the injury for the first time. It was worse than he had thought when he had gone to Feldwitz's flat, and he felt guilty at ordering the Scharführer to drive him to the party the following day.

'So this Feldwitz was strangled?'

'Garrotted,' said Liebwitz.

'Dead at any rate. That's three people associated with the Ace of Hearts who have ended up at the morgue, and two more wounded. Not to mention the place being burned to the ground. The Berlin guidebook entry for the club is going to need an addendum.'

'A deletion would be more appropriate,' Liebwitz responded thoughtfully.

'Thank you for the correction.' Hauser shook his head. 'Anyway, I've got some interesting news for you about the place. But first, I have to ask, I really do . . . What's he like? The Führer? I've only ever seen him a few times, and always in a crowd at a distance. You've only gone and shaken the man's hand and had a quiet head-to-head. So? Tell us all.'

Schenke tried to recall what had stood out most about his encounter with Hitler. 'He was sweaty.'

Hauser stared at him for a moment before he repeated, 'Sweaty . . . That's it?'

'And he likes fast cars.'

The sergeant let out an exasperated sigh. 'For fuck's sake . . . Many Germans would give their right hand to have been in your shoes.'

Many Germans had already given a lot more than that for the Führer, thought Schenke, and many more would in the months and years to come, unless the war ended quickly.

'What would you have said to him, Sergeant? What would you have asked him if you had been in my place?'

Hauser puffed his cheeks as he was put on the spot. 'I'd . . .

I'd ask him where he gets the strength to serve as our leader all these years. I'd ask him when he thinks the war will end. And I'd like to thank him for making Germany strong and respected again and for taking back control of the Reich from those who betrayed it. And . . . and . . . Well, anyway, that's what I'd have said if I'd been in your shoes.'

'I wish I'd asked him when the war will end,' Schenke conceded. Then, sensing the awkward tension that pricked between them whenever the topic of the party and its leader became too pronounced, he changed the subject.

'What about the club? What have you got for us?'

'This.' Hauser reached over to his in-tray and picked up a document. 'It's the Orpo report on the fire. There were witnesses who confirmed a van stopping outside the club and three men entering the Ace of Hearts while a fourth, the driver, remained in the van with the engine running. The witnesses confirm the sound of shots from inside and seeing smoke coming from the roof after the fire was lit.'

'We know all of this,' Schenke interrupted.

'All right, for the impatient listeners I'll skip to the really interesting item, in the third paragraph on the second page: "In what was left of a large storeroom at the rear of the club, the remains of a Vogler printing press was discovered under the rubble, identifiable from the manufacturer's plate bearing model and serial numbers."' Hauser looked up triumphantly. 'How's that for good news? We've found the source of the forged coupons. Remer's ring was behind it – there's our proof. Now the printing press has gone and the fire has consumed the stock of coupons you discovered there. All that remains is for the coupons still in circulation to be used up and the case is closed.'

'Just leaves us the small matter of the bodies that are stacking up,' Schenke pointed out.

'Every cloud has a shitty lining, eh?' Hauser rolled his eyes. 'Can't we at least celebrate putting a lid on the forgery case?'

'You're assuming that the Vogler press was the one used to forge the coupons,' said Liebwitz.

Hauser rounded on him. 'Well, what else do you think it was used for, my little Gestapo genius? Printing raffle tickets for the annual crime rings' Christmas ball? Besides, where do you think the boxes of coupons the inspector found came from?'

They were interrupted by the phone, which Rosa answered. A moment later she called to Schenke, 'Sir, there's a man on his way up. The sergeant on the front desk said he's from the Reich Ministry of Food and Agriculture. Herr Stoffler.'

'Stoffler?' Hauser frowned. 'Who the hell is he and what does he want with Kripo?'

'Our liaison man from the ministry,' Schenke explained. 'The forgeries have been causing trouble for Reichsminister Darré. He's not been happy to be shown up in front of his friends amongst the senior Nazis – he made that clear to me at Radinsky's do. He threatened to send me someone to oversee how we deal with the case. Looks like he's making good on that threat.'

'Only he's arriving just in time to be told that we've found out who was responsible for the forgeries and that the operation has been burned down. A wasted trip for Herr Stoffler,' Hauser declared.

The door to the office was opened by a uniformed officer, who stepped aside and waved a slender man in a brown coat through the door. When he removed his hat, Schenke saw a middle-aged individual with a nervous expression and watery eyes that the thick lenses of his glasses made appear bulging. He looked round the office quickly before his gaze fixed on Schenke and the others.

'I'm looking for Criminal Inspector Schenke.' His voice had a Low German burr as he turned his hat around in front of him. 'I'm Stoffler, from the Reich Ministry of Food and Agriculture.'

'You've found him.' Schenke stood and Stoffler approached and shook his hand. Once the introductions had been made, Schenke pulled up a spare chair and they all sat down. 'How can I help you, Herr Stoffler?'

'I understand you met with Reichsminister Darré yesterday.'

'That's right. At a party. In passing. It was not a formal meeting of any kind. He was keen to discover how far Kripo had got with its investigation into the ration coupon forgeries. He mentioned that he might send you over to Pankow to follow it up.'

Stoffler looked uncomfortable. 'The Reichsminister put it in rather more direct terms when he called me. I am not so much here to follow up as to observe and direct you until the investigation has been resolved and the forgers brought to justice. I was ordered to stick close to you until then and report back to the Reichsminister on a daily basis.'

'Understand this.' Schenke spoke with quiet authority. 'No outsider directs Kripo investigations.'

'I'm only repeating what I was instructed to do,' Stoffler replied. He half reached for his breast pocket. 'I have my orders in writing if you wish to see them?'

'Not necessary. Whatever your orders, I am in charge. You are here to help us with the investigation. Clear? Outsiders interfering with our work only get in the way.'

'Amen to that,' muttered Hauser with a nod in Liebwitz's direction. 'The powers-that-be seem to have a disappointing lack of faith in Kripo's ability to do its job these days.'

'Oh . . .' Stoffler was taken aback. 'I don't mean to interfere. I'll do my best to be of assistance while I am with you.'

'In any case, it appears that there may be no call for you to work with us at all,' said Schenke. He indicated the Orpo report on Hauser's desk. 'We found the remains of a printing press and the presence of a large number of recently forged ration coupons on the premises of a nightclub that burned down. The owner was the leader of a crime ring. He's dead, the coupons were burned and the press destroyed. In which case it's all over and you can go back to the Reichsminister and tell him the good news.'

Stoffler did not react. He leaned forward. 'Do you mind if I read that for myself?'

'Be my guest.' Schenke replied. He felt a twinge in his leg and stood up to work the thigh muscle with his fingers to relieve the pain. 'Once you have finished it, you can go. As I said, there's no need for you to be here any longer.'

'Thank you, Inspector, but I'll read this first and then decide what I will do.'

'Suit yourself. I'll be in my office. Hauser, let me know when our guest has finished with the report.'

'Yes, sir.'

Making for his sectioned-off cubicle, Schenke sat at his desk. He hoped his attempt to brush off Darré's man would work. Even if Remer had been using the club as a front for the forgery racket, as the presence of the printer and the stash of coupons indicated, there was still the matter of the murders. They were connected to the forgeries in some way, he was sure of it.

In which case there was some way to go before the case was concluded. In the meantime, he was not keen to have Stoffler tagging along and getting in the way of the investigation. If he could ditch him, he would.

Hauser rapped on the door frame. 'He's done.'

Stoffler had removed his glasses and was rubbing the lenses with a small cloth. Without them he looked much younger, and there was a fussy refinement in his cleaning movements, as if he was determined to achieve a perfect result. He squinted at Schenke as he drew close, then slipped the glasses back on.

'So?' Schenke queried.

'The Orpo report makes for interesting reading, I agree. However, there is no certainty that the Vogler printing press was the one used to produce the forgeries. In fact, I would venture to say that I do not believe a Vogler press would be capable of being set up in such a way as to do the job. I know this model well. I used it when I was working on the student newspaper in Heidelberg. It's only good for small-scale printing. It outputs individual sheets no bigger than a handbill. The genuine coupons are printed on a bigger press using large spools of paper. The quality is higher than the Vogler can achieve. If the Vogler press had been used, you would have spotted the difference between the genuine coupons and the forgeries in an instant, I am certain of it.'

Schenke felt deflated. 'Is that so?'

Stoffler nodded and responded in a deliberate manner. 'I would stake my reputation on it.'

'And what exactly are your credentials in this regard? What makes you such an expert?'

Stoffler gave a slight smile for the first time. 'I am manager of the official ration coupon printing plant here in Berlin. That's why the Reichsminister chose me to assist your investigation. If anyone knows the ins and outs of the matter, it's me.'

'Ah . . .' Schenke was caught off guard. He had thought the man was some political flunkey. Instead it seemed he might be of some use to the investigation. 'I see. And you're quite certain about this? There's no way the Vogler press could have been used?'

'Believe me, Inspector, I cannot see any way in which such a limited device could have been used to print the number of coupons that are in circulation. Nor could it have produced forgeries good enough to withstand a moment's close scrutiny.'

The three Kripo officers exchanged a look before Hauser let out a bitter sigh. 'Fuck . . . Just when I thought we'd nailed it. What now?'

Schenke was turning over the situation in his mind. Stoffler stirred uncomfortably. 'I'm not trying to cause problems. I'm just telling you the truth about that press. Anyone who knows anything about printing would have told you same thing.'

Schenke looked up. 'In which case it's very helpful that you have been sent to assist us.'

'It is?' Stoffler looked surprised.

'Indeed. I think it's time we found out more about precisely how the coupons are produced and distributed. Maybe we've been looking at this from the wrong end of the problem.'

'How do you mean?'

'We've been focusing our attention on the criminals selling the forgeries on the black market. I want to know more about the genuine article. I want to see how it works and what's involved at each stage. You're going to take us on a tour of the printworks you manage.'

Stoffler opened and closed his mouth quickly before he blurted out, 'I-I'll have to refer the matter to the Reichsminister first.'

'No you don't. Your orders are to assist the investigation. You're the manager of the printing plant, the one in charge, and you're going to show us over the site. So let's go and see how the process works.'

'I can't. Not just like that. There's a protocol to follow. The site is one of the most secure installations in Berlin. For good reason.'

Hauser reached over and slapped him on the shoulder. 'Then aren't we lucky to have you on board, Herr Stoffler? Besides, we're Kripo. We're the good guys. Your precious printing plant has nothing to fear from us.'

Stoffler looked at the uncompromising expressions on the faces of the policemen. 'Well, I shall have to mention this to the Reichsminister when I report to him this evening.'

'You do that.' Schenke nodded and made a show of glancing at his watch. 'No time to waste. Hauser, Liebwitz, you're coming too.'

The ministry had handed the printing contract to a company that had once produced a liberal Berlin newspaper. The party had closed it down and sold its assets to cronies of the Nazis shortly after seizing power. The printworks were situated in Friedrichsfelde, to the south-east of the city. The offices and factory floor were contained in a sprawling building set within a compound surrounded by high walls topped with rolls of barbed wire that gave the impression of being a prison camp rather than a place of work. Storage sheds and piles of discarded equipment lined the walls. The printworks sat amid several other companies in an industrial zone, surrounded by grim workers' apartment buildings.

Schenke was driving, as he did not want the already nervous Stoffler to be made more nervous with Liebwitz at the wheel. Above the capital the sky was a ragged patchwork of scudding clouds, and light rain came in fleeting downpours before the sun emerged again, accompanied by iridescent rainbows. They had passed most of the drive from the precinct in silence, the presence of Darré's man inhibiting conversation. That was how it was these days, Schenke reflected. People exercised caution before speaking with any candour in front of a stranger. Stoffler had stared out of the rear window, not volunteering small talk or further details about the printing plant or his role there. He seemed anxious, thought Schenke.

The main gate, comprised of solid iron bars with spikes on top, was closed and a guardhouse stood a short distance behind in the yard, where the watchmen would have a clear view of any vehicles that approached. Schenke drew up and sounded the horn. A moment later, a man in trench coat, peaked cap and army boots emerged and stood behind the gate without making any attempt to open it.

'I'll deal with him,' said Stoffler, opening the rear door and climbing out. 'I'll have to sign us in.'

He approached the gate and spoke to the guard before producing his identity card. The guard inspected it and nodded, then hauled the gate aside, and Stoffler entered the guardhouse. He reappeared shortly afterwards and climbed back into the car.

'Drive round to the right. That's where the vehicles park.'

Schenke eased the car through the gate and past the guard-house. The yard was paved and neatly kept. The storage sheds were labelled according to their contents, and their small windows were barred. The main façade of the printworks was pierced by high windows, grimy on the outside and covered within due to the blackout regulations. To the side where Stoffler had directed them lay a glassed-in entrance lobby and loading ramps some distance beyond. There was only one other car parked there, a cream-coloured Opel that Schenke thought he recognised as he drew up and turned the engine off.

'What is it you want to see here exactly?' asked Stoffler.

'We need the complete tour,' Schenke replied. 'Let's start in your office and go from there.'

Stoffler led them through the lobby to a reception desk manned by another burly-looking watchman. He presented a log book for the manager to sign in his Kripo guests. Before Stoffler could slide it back to the man, Schenke intervened.

'Wait.'

He scanned the most recent page and then flipped through a few earlier ones, but there were no names he recognised. He closed the book and returned it to the watchman as he addressed Stoffler.

'What hours does the plant operate?'

'The first workers arrive at six to set up the machines for the day's output. The main workforce arrives at eight. We work through to five and then the maintenance crew check the machinery and clean up before leaving an hour later. After that the night security shift takes over.'

'How many people work on the site?'

'Varies, depending on demand. Most days I'd say we have fifteen or so in the offices and another fifty in the factory and stores.'

'What about the security staff? How many of them are there?'

'Two on the main gate. Two on the service gate at the rear of the site, one man here on the desk and four patrolling inside the yard.'

'Are they armed?'

'The day shift have truncheons. The night watch have pistols. We had a few attempts to steal from the coal bunkers during the winter. It was an inside job. Neger, our head of security, dismissed the previous security staff and brought in a team of men he recruited from the Steel Helmets. They're tough and reliable. Some men tried to get over the wall by the storage sheds a week or so ago. A warning shot was enough to make the thieves take to their heels. We've had no trouble since then.'

'Was there any attempt to steal anything else? To break into the main building or the stores?'

'None that I recall. We take security very seriously, Inspector. We have to, given what we do here. But you can ask Neger all about that. That's his car outside. He should be on site somewhere.'

'He has a permit to drive a car?' asked Schenke, surprised.

'He needs one. He's in charge of the security for a number of sites. He's only here two or three times a week.'

'Then it seems we're in luck. I'll have a word with him later.'

He gestured to Stoffler to lead on, and they followed him up a staircase to the first floor, where a corridor ran the breadth of the building, with offices to the left and large windows opposite overlooking the floor of the printing plant. Even through the glass, the whir and clatter of the machinery assaulted their ears. Men in overalls were tending to the large presses. Others took the printed and cut sheets and placed them in small crates under the watchful eye of a foreman.

They reached an open door, and Stoffler stopped and rapped on it. An older man with a pinched face and fine grey hair looked up.

'All running smoothly, Hemmrich?'

The man nodded and tilted his head to look past Stoffler at the men in the corridor.

'These gentlemen are from Kripo. They wanted to see what we do here.' Stoffler turned to address Schenke. 'This is Klaus Hemmrich, my deputy manager. He's running the show while I assist you.'

'There is one thing, sir.' Hemmrich shuffled through the paperwork on his desk. 'Came through from the ministry first thing . . . Here.' He pulled out a document with the ministry's letterhead and tapped it. 'We're to stop printing meat and coffee coupons for Jews.'

'Good thing too.' Stoffler nodded. 'That'll save us ink and time. Those rascals can do without.'

Schenke's thoughts turned to Ruth and her people, incrementally being stripped of their rights, their property, their livelihoods, their access to theatres, cinemas, restaurants and parks, and now even their choice of what to eat and drink. Soon they would be ghosts that no Germans openly associated with, haunting the streets until they faded out of existence while their former compatriots lived on unwilling to admit they had ever existed. Surely they could not endure for much longer under such intolerable circumstances. What then?

Stoffler was about to close the door when he remembered something. 'Hemmrich, have you seen Neger this morning?'

'Yes, sir.'

227

'Good. These policemen want a word with him. If you see him again, tell him to come and find us. Carry on.'

He halted outside the next door, upon which was mounted a brass plate bearing his own name under the bold title of *Manager*. He waved the three Kripo officers inside. With the door shut, the clamour of the machines was muted enough to carry out a normal conversation. Besides the chair behind his desk there were two others opposite, so Liebwitz stood by the window overlooking the yard. The only other furniture consisted of a pair of filing cupboards and a small shelving unit bearing a handful of framed photos. The obligatory one of the Führer, and another of Darré shaking Stoffler's hand. The Reichsminister was unsmiling, as he had been at the party. There was no sign of any family photographs.

'I apologise for the noise,' said Stoffler. 'The presses run most of the time.'

'Just for ration coupons?' asked Hauser.

'Oh, that's not all we do. There's all manner of official print jobs. ID cards, pay books for the Wehrmacht, official forms for the other ministries.'

'Let's stick to the ration coupons,' said Schenke. 'How often are they printed?'

'As you can imagine, there's a constant demand for those. They're our main output. We supply most of the main cities in this part of Germany. There are other printing facilities in Hamburg and Munich, but we're the biggest by far,' Stoffler concluded proudly.

'The coupons are printed using specific types of ink, I understand.'

'That's right. How did you know about that?'

'We've been on the case for months, Herr Stoffler. I take it the inks are stored on site?'

'Yes.'

'And they are kept secure?'

'Of course. And fully accounted for in terms of what is used and reordered. I oversee that personally.'

'There's no way anyone could take any supplies off site without you knowing about it?'

'That's right.' Stoffler looked indignant.

Hauser interjected. 'There's always some bastard who finds a way.'

'Not here,' Stoffler insisted. 'We keep all the materials used for the coupons under lock and key. You have my word for it.'

'How reassuring . . .'

'We'll need to inspect the site,' said Schenke. 'And speak to your head of security, Herr Neger. You'd better get him up here. Now.'

'Very well.' Stoffler picked up the telephone. 'Hello, Frau Schneider? Put me through to Herr Neger . . . When? Where did he go? . . . I see. When will he back?'

He replaced the handset with an apologetic shrug. 'Neger's gone. He was called to another site shortly before we arrived.'

'But his car's still outside,' Liebwitz pointed out.

'There are other places he has responsibility for nearby. He must have walked.'

'That's too bad,' Schenke mused. 'If he comes back before we leave, we'll have a word with him then. Otherwise have him call us at the precinct. No doubt we'll have some questions for him once you've shown us over the place.' He stood up and gestured towards the door. 'After you.'

* * *

Stoffler walked them round the factory floor, shouting to be heard over the noise of the machinery, explaining each stage of the production process. When he had finished, he took them outside into the yard that surrounded the main building and closed the heavy sliding door. Schenke found that his ears were still ringing as they followed the manager towards the nearest of the store sheds.

Jerking his thumb over his shoulder, Hauser observed, 'Given that lot back there, I can't see any way that the Vogler job at the club could do anything on that scale. Looks like Darré's boy is on the money.'

Schenke nodded. 'In which case, the source of the forgeries can't have been the club. The boxes of coupons I saw came from somewhere else. Maybe Remer had another place we don't yet know about. Somewhere big enough to contain a larger printing press.'

'That's possible. But you saw how big the presses were in there and how much noise they make. How could he keep such a thing secret? It'd deafen anyone within a hundred metres.'

'Then perhaps we should take a closer look at Guttmann and his ring. What if we got it the wrong way round? Perhaps he's the one behind the forgeries and Remer was one of his customers? They fell out over something and that's why he got the chop.'

As they reached the nearest of the store sheds, Stoffler indicated the small shuttered and barred windows and the sturdy metal door. 'This is where the inks and paper for the coupons are stored. As you can see, we keep things securely under lock and key here.'

'Who is responsible for the keys?' asked Liebwitz.

'I have them locked in my desk. If access is required, I

log the name of the key-bearer and the time it goes out and comes back. The inventory is checked at the end of each day. If anything went missing I'd know about it at once, and know who was responsible.'

Liebwitz went to the door and tested it. The metal surface did not budge. He turned to Stoffler. 'What happens at night if there is an emergency? Such as a fire. Does anyone else have access to the keys if you aren't here?'

'Neger has a spare set. But he's never had to use them yet.'

They made a circuit of the long, low building and Schenke was satisfied that there was no other means of gaining entry. The roof was comprised of heavy sheets of corrugated iron bolted securely to the trusses beneath. If what Stoffler said was true, it would be impossible for the forgers to steal the materials to print the coupons.

'Who supplies you?' he asked Stoffler. 'Where does the ink and paper come from?'

'That's the clever part. Darré has arranged things so that the manufacturers don't know what their product is used for and where it is destined when it leaves their factories, and the printers don't know where it comes from when it is delivered.'

'Do *you* know?' asked Liebwitz.

'No. It's a closely kept secret and I'm not senior enough to be let in on it. Darré likes to keep such things confidential.'

Schenke looked round, noting once again the high walls and barbed wire. 'I've seen enough. We're due to interview some witnesses at the hospital. You needn't come with us, Herr Stoffler. There's nothing there to concern you or the Reichsminister.'

'I have my instructions, Inspector. Herr Darré is not the kind of man who would respond favourably if he discovered I was not carrying them out to the letter. Hemmrich will keep things going in my absence.'

'Very well. Back to the car then.'

With Schenke at the wheel once again, they made their way to the gate, and the watchman emerged from the guardhouse to let them out. Schenke drove into the street beyond, then drew up sharply and stopped.

'Back in a moment.'

Climbing out, he strode swiftly to the gate just as the watchman slid it back into place and locked down the bolt. The man was about to turn away when Schenke called to him.

'Wait!'

He approached the heavy iron bars and looked through them. 'Herr Neger left the site not long ago, right?'

'Yes, sir.'

'And you'd have logged him out?'

The watchman nodded.

'Did he happen to say where he was going?'

'No, sir. I'm not paid to ask that. I just sign people in and out. That's it.'

'When did he leave? Can you check the time in the log book for me?'

'Don't have to. I can recall it well enough. It was ten thirty-eight. Five minutes after you arrived with Herr Stoffler. In fact I saw him come out of the far side of the building just as you entered the lobby.'

'Is that so?' Schenke mused.

'Sure. It's not like I have much else to do in this job except note timings.'

'Do you have a phone in the guardhouse?'

'Yes, sir.'

'Connected to the offices?'

'That's right.'

Schenke nodded his thanks and returned to the car. As he slid back behind the wheel, Stoffler leaned forward. 'Is there a problem, Inspector?'

Schenke shifted the car into gear. 'Just needed to clarify something. That's all.'

He said no more, and Stoffler eased himself back onto the rear seat as the car accelerated away from the gate.

Chapter Seventeen

Bertha heard the approaching footsteps and looked up as Schenke and the others approached, then smiled as she stood to greet them politely. The sun was out again and streaming through the long windows along the ward, filling the space with a honeyed light and burnishing her hair with a golden glow. It was the first time Schenke had seen her without a head covering, and it suited her. She had looked dowdy the last time he saw her, but now he saw that she was striking in the way that the party propaganda depicted German women – blonde, sturdy and demure. She could have modelled for Goebbels' publicity posters.

'Good to see you again,' Schenke greeted her. 'Though it's almost like you have nowhere else to be.'

'The club has gone, Inspector,' she shrugged and indicated Magda who was lying propped up on the bed. She looked pale, and glanced at the four men without offering any comment.

'So I'm looking after my friend,' Bertha continued before she turned shyly towards Liebwitz. 'Scharführer. Thank you again for saving me . . . I mean us. Magda and me.'

'It was a lucky escape for all of us, Bertha,' Schenke replied before he introduced his companions. 'Liebwitz you already know, of course. The others are Sergeant Hauser from my section, and Herr Stoffler, who is assisting our investigation.'

As Liebwitz removed his hat, there was a sharp intake of breath from Bertha. 'Goodness, what happened to you?'

'I was hit with some form of blunt instrument from behind and rendered unconscious,' Liebwitz explained in his usual monotone.

'Oh . . . That must have hurt.'

'Only on regaining consciousness. I thank you for your concern.'

Hauser huffed impatiently. 'If you two lovebirds don't mind, can we move on?' Bertha looked down to hide her blush.

There were no spare chairs in the ward, so Schenke and the others stood at the foot of the bed while he gestured to Bertha to resume her seat.

'How are you feeling?' he began, taking off his hat.

'Still shaken,' Bertha replied. 'I don't think I'll ever forget seeing Gunter being shot dead . . . And what happened afterwards.'

'That's to be expected. In time the memories will fade. How about you, Magda?'

She stared back with a sullen expression. 'How do you think? I've been shot and I'm in constant pain and they won't give me any more opiates because they are needed for the army. So I'm not happy, Inspector.'

'Fair enough. I'll have a word with the doctors when we're finished here and see if there's anything that can be done for you.'

'If I'm a good girl and help you, right?'

'In any case. You have my word I'll try to do what I can.'

235

'Good luck with that.'

'How can we help?' asked Bertha.

'We won't be long. I need to ask you a few more questions concerning Kitty.' Schenke used her informal name to encourage the two women to talk more openly.

'Is she all right? I tried to go and see her earlier, but the matron said she can't have any visitors.'

'It's to protect her. She might be in danger, so I've requested a police guard.'

'Oh . . . How frightening for her. Poor Kitty.'

Schenke felt a stab of pity for the young woman. Given what Bachmann had told Liebwitz, Bertha might not be so sympathetic if she knew the truth about Kitty. If that really was the truth.

'As for her health,' he went on, 'I'm told that she is stable and should make a good recovery.'

Magda sniffed. 'Lucky her.'

'I'm not sure that being shot is lucky,' Schenke responded. 'As you would know. Now let's get to our business here. Kitty was Remer's girlfriend. When we last spoke, you gave me the impression that their relationship had been steady until recently. I need you to give me some more detail about that.'

'How do you mean?' asked Bertha.

'Would you say that they were still happy together?'

'I suppose so. Well, they seemed to be until recently.'

'How recently?' asked Hauser.

'They'd seemed a bit distant from each other for the last month or so. Wouldn't you say, Magda?'

'Sure. Maybe Remer was getting tired of her. And why not? She was only in it for the money he spent on her. He was bound to move on to someone else at some point. I'd say her time was up.'

Bertha shook her head. 'She's not like that. Kitty's a good person.'

'For God's sake, Bertha! She's not some bloody fairy-tale princess, so stop behaving as if she is. She was after his money and it's obvious what he wanted in return. That's how Remer has always treated his women.'

Bertha looked down at her lap, and her jaw trembled.

'Is that how he treated you, Bertha?' asked Liebwitz.

There was an uncomfortable pause before Magda sighed. 'Obviously, and she knows it. She knows that Kitty was on her way out, too, and she's just young enough and innocent enough to think she had a chance of replacing her when the time came. I've been trying to tell her that's a bad idea. But she's seen Kitty's furs and jewels and wants to be like her. Don't you, girl? That ship has sailed, though . . .'

Bertha shuddered and sobbed as she tried to fight back the tears. Magda reached out and took one of her hands, giving it a squeeze.

Schenke waited a moment before he continued. 'So the relationship was close to ending?'

Magda nodded.

'Was there anyone else Remer showed interest in?'

'Not that I noticed.'

'What about Kitty? Was she looking for someone else?'

Magda gave a cynical smile. 'Now there's a thing . . . There was someone she spent quite a lot of time with when the boss wasn't around. When the cat's away . . .'

'Who was that?'

'Our good-looking manager at the club. Blonde, slender,

well-dressed, charming and amusing. Wilhelm Feldwitz. He wasn't much of a manager. Left most of the work to Breker. When he deigned to turn up, he sometimes came on his own, but often with others. Friends of his, I suppose. But he started to spend a lot of time with Kitty. From the way the two of them flirted in the club, I'd say there was something going on behind Remer's back.'

'Do you think Remer suspected anything?'

'I don't know. He was a difficult man to read. I never got close enough to really know him. Besides, Feldwitz was one of his favourites. He could charm everyone, women and men alike. I think even Remer fell for it sometimes, even if Wohler tried to warn him. You should speak to Feldwitz if you want to find out what was going on.'

'Bit late for that,' said Hauser. 'Feldwitz is dead. Someone strangled him. Same person who did that to the Scharführer.' He indicated Liebwitz's bandage.

'Another murder,' said Schenke. 'All of them related to the club.'

The two women exchanged a look, and he watched their reaction closely.

Bertha swallowed nervously. 'Are we in danger?'

'Is there any reason why you think you might be?'

'I don't know! I don't know! Who would do all this?'

'Does the name Guttmann mean anything to either of you? Did anyone mention it at the club? You might have overheard something said by Remer, Wohler or Feldwitz. Or perhaps by a customer?'

Both women shook their heads, and Schenke hid his disappointment. He decided to try another name and shifted round slightly so he could catch any response on Stoffler's face. 'What about a man called Neger?'

'No,' Magda replied. 'Never heard of him.'

'He might have gone by the name Hugo. How about you, Bertha?'

'No, sorry.'

'Never mind,' said Schenke. 'That's all I wanted to ask.' He turned to his subordinates. 'Any further questions?'

'Just one,' said Liebwitz. 'Did you ever see Fräulein Kunzler talking with Otto Bachmann?'

'The comic?' Bertha raised her plucked eyebrows. 'Hardly at all lately . . . Not for the last few weeks. Before that, I saw them at the bar together quite a few times. He cheered her up, made her laugh. But then he made us all laugh. On and off the stage. We liked having him around. But he hasn't talked to Kitty for a while.'

'Do you know why?' Liebwitz asked.

'It might have been something to do with Herr Wohler. I remember he came in one night and stood watching them for a while before he went over and spoke to Otto. They went upstairs, and when Otto came back down, he didn't rejoin Kitty. Just stood by the entrance for a moment looking at her, then left the club. I'm pretty sure that's the last time I saw them together, until the night the boss and Kitty were shot . . . I thought it was a pity.' She paused and smiled shyly at Liebwitz. 'That's all I can remember. I hope it helps.'

'It might be of assistance,' Liebwitz replied.

There was a brief silence as Schenke looked to Hauser, who shrugged.

'All right then, we'll leave you for now. I don't think either of you are in any danger. If there's anything else you remember that might help us, you can call the Kripo office at the Pankow precinct.'

The men turned away and left. Schenke replaced his hat as they emerged from the ward and climbed the stairs to reach the top floor, where Kitty Kunzler was recovering in a isolation room. As they made their way up, Stoffler gave him a sidelong look. 'Why did you ask them about Neger?'

'Just a hunch.'

'A hunch? What kind of a hunch, Inspector?'

'It doesn't matter. Turned out neither of the women knew the name.'

Schenke was interested in Stoffler's reaction to his mention of Neger. He had seemed more anxious than surprised, and he had made no comment about Schenke's suggestion of Hugo as a first name. Why not?

There was a uniformed policeman sitting on a chair outside the door to Kitty's room, and he stood as he saw Schenke and the others approach.

'We're from Kripo.' Schenke held up his badge. 'How is the patient?'

'Unhappy about being in isolation and not having any visitors. She gave me an earful about it when she called me into the room.'

'That's too bad. Has anybody come up and asked to see her?'

'No, sir.'

Schenke entered a cell-like space, just big enough for a bed, side table, chair and hanging rail. There was a small window above the bed with blackout curtains on either side. Some flowers stood in a jar of water with an envelope beside them. Kitty lowered the magazine she had been reading. Her wounded arm, still heavily bandaged, lay at her side. For a fleeting instant her brow creased with anger before she offered a gentle smile to her visitors.

'Inspector Schenke, it's good to see you again, but can you tell me why I have been transferred to this room and have a policeman standing watch outside the door? I feel as if I am being treated like a suspect of some kind.'

Schenke returned the smile as he replied. 'It's for your safety. You were a witness to a murder. Until we find the killer, you are at risk.'

Her eyes widened. 'Are you saying he might try and come for me? Here?'

'Not now you are under our protection.'

'I hope so,' she responded doubtfully, and glanced past him. 'I recognise your Scharführer, but who are these other gentlemen?'

'That's my sergeant, Hauser, and Herr Stoffler, who is helping in our investigation. We're here to follow up on your earlier statement. We have some more questions to ask you.'

'Not too many, I hope. I am rather tired.'

'Very well. I'll be direct. We have witnesses who say that you were having an affair with someone else while you were Remer's girlfriend. Is that true, Fräulein Kunzler?'

She stared at him with a hurt expression for a moment before she replied. 'Someone at the club telling tales again? That place is – was – a hotbed of back-stabbing intrigue. Let me guess, was it Magda?'

When Schenke didn't reply, she looked away. 'Who else would it be? She never got over seeing her little friend Bertha being pushed aside by Max when he took up with me. The woman has been drip-feeding her poison into the ear of anyone who would listen.'

'Is it true?' Schenke asked again.

Kitty hesitated. 'What difference does it make? Max is dead. It hardly matters any more if I was seeing someone else.'

'Just answer the question.'

'Much as it may frustrate the prurient appetite of the police, the answer is no. I was not seeing anyone else. To be clear, I wasn't seeing anyone else in all the time I was with Max. I'm not that stupid. I knew what kind of man he was and what he might do if he found out I was cheating on him. Besides, I did love him . . . I really did. And he loved me. He didn't show it much, but I believe he did, as surely as I am lying here now. There's your answer, Inspector. Is there anything else?'

It seemed to Schenke that there was a sincerity to her tone, but – he reminded himself – she had once had ambitions to be a professional actress. If she was good at her craft, she could fake her sincerity. Not just with regard to her words now, but perhaps in the way she had behaved towards Remer. Had he fallen for the oldest of all con tricks? It was hard to believe that a man as hard-bitten and wary as the leader of a crime ring had to be would fall for such a ploy. How good an actress was she? he wondered.

'Our witnesses came up with the name Feldwitz as the man you were seeing behind Remer's back.'

'Feldwitz? Wilhelm . . . We were friends, but that was all. Anyone who says otherwise is not telling the truth, Inspector. What evidence do they have to prove their claim?'

'What evidence? That's a strange way of putting it . . .'

For the first time he saw something that looked like a genuine reaction in her eyes; a glint of fear. Then it was gone.

'I was not having a relationship with Wilhelm Feldwitz. I would swear that under oath, because it is the truth. As I say, we were friends, and only casual friends at that. Those who accuse me of anything else are malicious liars.'

'I see. Given that that is the case, I imagine you would not grieve too much to know that Feldwitz is dead.'

Schenke watched her reaction. Her jaw sagged slightly as she let out a soft gasp and instinctively raised her uninjured hand towards her mouth, before stopping and composing herself.

'He's dead . . .' she repeated softly. 'How did it happen?'

'Garrotted in his flat the day before yesterday.'

'Murdered . . .'

'That's usually the case with garrotting,' said Hauser. 'Not come across any suicides by that means in my time. Would you know anything about it?'

Kitty shifted her gaze to the sergeant. 'Why would I? Are you saying I had something to do with it?' She gestured to her bandages by way of exculpation. 'I haven't even seen him for over a month now.'

'Really? He was there at the club the night Remer was murdered.'

'If he was, I didn't see him.'

'So you say,' Hauser responded.

'We're asking if you know anything that might shed some light on his murder,' said Schenke. 'Why would anyone kill him?'

'How should I know?'

'You say he was your friend. Then maybe you might know something about who his enemies were. He might have been worried enough to tell you something. He might have mentioned some names. Try and remember.'

She was quiet for a few seconds before shaking her head. 'No names. But he did seem on edge the last time I saw him.

Excited about something, but anxious. He'd had a drink and said he was going to strike it rich some day soon.' There was that brief flash of fear again.

'Did he ever tell you about some photographs that had special value to him? He appeared to be searching for them just before he was murdered.'

'I don't know anything about any photographs. He never mentioned them.'

'Do you think there was any connection between the photos and his plan to get rich?'

'How would I know? I told you, he never said anything about photographs to me. All I know is that he claimed he was going to come into money.' She closed her eyes and grimaced. 'I'm tired, and I'm in pain. I've told you all I know. Now let me rest. I'm not answering any more questions.'

'You damn well will, my girl,' Hauser said. 'You'll up and answer the inspector until he says otherwise. Understand?'

She turned away, and Schenke waited a moment before he sighed. 'All right then, you can't help us with Feldwitz. What about Bachmann? What was your relationship with him?'

'Otto? What have they been saying about that down at the club, I wonder?'

Schenke nodded to Liebwitz, who took a half-step towards the side of the bed. 'I questioned Herr Bachmann the same afternoon Feldwitz was murdered. He said you two had had a relationship before you moved on to Remer.'

'Relationship? No, we had sex. Once. It was a mistake. I was feeling lonely and anxious and turned to him for comfort. It was over before there was any question of any relationship. Like I said, it was a mistake, for both of us.'

'What happened afterwards? Did you remain friends?'

'Yes . . . At least I did. I think Otto was after something more and resented me for not giving him that.'

'How do you know?' asked Schenke.

'Oh, there were occasional pointed comments, that kind of thing. Especially after I had taken up with Max. I did my best to ignore them, but sometimes it was too much and I had to put him in his place, then we wouldn't speak for days. But he would always come round and apologise, and on we'd go. He's good company.'

'What did Remer think of him? I wouldn't imagine he'd tolerate Bachmann upsetting you.'

'Otto never did anything like that in front of Max. But Max knew something had happened. He had a sixth sense for what people were thinking. I guess that's what kept him alive for so long.'

'Until it didn't,' said Hauser.

Kitty shot him a hostile look before she relaxed again and continued. 'Max knew there were tensions between us, but as long as he didn't have to deal with them, he was content not to say or do anything.'

'Why?' asked Schenke. 'He could easily have sacked Otto and found a new act if he knew he was upsetting you.'

'Otto was good at his job. He pushed his humour to the limit and was known for it. That's what drew so many customers to the club. Or at least it did until they began to stay away recently. But I don't think that was anything to do with his act. There was something else going on.'

'What was that?'

'I don't really know. Max was a bit distant. Spent a lot more time talking to Wohler. There was one time I overheard a telephone conversation. Only one end of it, of course. But

Max was furious with someone. He called them a turncoat and a double-crosser. He said they needed to be taught a lesson. Something they'd never be able to forget.'

'Was it Feldwitz?'

'I couldn't say. He never mentioned a name. In any case, it wouldn't have been Otto. He was never a part of Max's other business dealings. In the end, Max's sidekick, Wohler, warned Otto to keep his distance. I don't know if that was on Max's orders or whether Wohler himself thought something might be going on between us. Whatever the reason and whoever gave the order, it worked, and he stayed away from me.'

'Until Remer's last night.'

'Yes. Until then. But I've told you about that already.' She grimaced. 'I really am in pain, Inspector. I've told you all I know. I need to rest. I'm not going anywhere. If you have any more questions, you know where to find me.'

There was a pleading look in her expression that cut no ice with Schenke. His initial impression of her had given way to a realisation that she was as much a hard-edged opportunist as any in Remer's circle of associates and could not be trusted.

'All right, Fräulein Kunzler,' he concluded formally. 'You will remain under our protection for now. I trust that if you recall any further information that may be of interest to us you will immediately pass it on, via the man outside your room.'

'Of course.' She smiled sweetly, but her eyes were stone cold as Schenke led the other men from the room.

Chapter Eighteen

'What now?' asked Stoffler as the four men sat around a table in the precinct canteen. They were nursing mugs of ersatz coffee and smoking as they reviewed what they had learned that day. Liebwitz sat slightly back from the table to try and keep clear of the smoke as he sipped his tea.

Stoffler continued. 'I still don't see much of a connection between the murders you are investigating and the coupon forgeries. I know Remer was in possession of a quantity of the forgeries, but I've heard nothing to indicate that was anything to do with his murder, or with any of the other deaths. Looks to me like score-settling between the crime gangs.'

Schenke tapped his cigarette against the edge of a steel ashtray. 'Is that what you'll tell Darré when you report to him this evening?'

'What else can I say? Despite having the ten-pfennig tour of the printworks, you've come up with nothing concrete to advance the hunt for the forgers. If anything, you're further wide of the mark than ever since I explained the limitations of the Vogler printer at the club. Where does that leave you, Inspector?'

'That's right, just rub Kripo's nose in it, why don't you?' said Hauser. 'You've been with us less than one day. How long do you think we've been after the forgers? We've been on the case since before Christmas. You think you can just march in here and demand that we solve it before you get home for dinner and a cosy wrap-up with the Reichsminister to put the whole thing to bed . . . Bloody civilians. Five-day fucking policemen, the lot of them.'

Stoffler flushed and stabbed a finger at the sergeant. 'Now just you look here. I am the manager of the printworks. I am the man Darré personally chose to assist with your investigation. I demand you show me a little more respect. I will not be spoken to like some damned apprentice. Inspector Schenke, I'm disappointed in you. Why don't you discipline your subordinates for addressing their superiors in such a manner? I dare say the Reichsminister will have something to say about it when I tell him.'

Schenke looked at Darré's man with a weary expression. 'You won't tell him, though, will you? Your master wants results. If you're the one telling him there aren't any, then he's not going to be pleased, and who do you think will be the first in line when he expresses that displeasure? Not Mrs Darré, not his mistress. Not his rivals in the top echelon of the party, who will be looking for any opportunity to undermine him. It's going to be you, Stoffler. Now why do you think he picked you for this task? Because he thought you were one of his best men? No, he picked you because he wanted a messenger boy to report back. It's not as if he thought you were indispensable. Your assistant manager at the printworks is on the ball. If you dropped dead tomorrow, he'd fill your shoes without breaking stride.'

He paused to let his words sink in, and then indicated Hauser and Liebwitz. 'These men, on the other hand, *are* indispensable. If we are going to track down the forgers and break the case, it will be because of men like them. You?' He pointed the dull glow of his cigarette at Stoffler. 'You're not even a first-day probationer in Kripo. So while we greatly appreciated the guided tour of your printworks, beyond that you are little more than dead weight to us at the moment. If you want respect, you're going to have to earn it by helping us get closer to solving the case, rather than by acting like some regimental runner who thinks he's a field marshal. Do you understand?'

Stoffler swallowed, set down his cigarette. 'I . . . I need to go to the toilet.'

'Do you understand?' Schenke said with a little more emphasis.

Stoffler hesitated, and then replied quietly, 'Yes.'

'Good. Go right out of the canteen. Door on the left. You can't miss it.'

The three Kripo men watched him depart before Hauser fixed Schenke with a concerned look. 'A regimental runner who thinks he's a field marshal . . . Do you think it's wise to say such things, sir? I'd really rather you didn't.'

Liebwitz slowly swirled the dregs of his tea. 'Why not? I think it was an apposite comparison.'

'You do? Have I really got to spell it out to you, Scharführer?'

Liebwitz frowned. 'Spell what out?'

'Sweet Jesus . . .' The sergeant rolled his eyes. 'What was the Führer's role in the last war?'

Liebwitz looked surprised. 'He was a private. A messenger. Everyone knows that.'

'And?' Hauser motioned joining the dots with his forefinger on the top of the table.

Liebwitz's eyes widened, and he nodded. 'Ah, I see. An implied criticism of the Führer. But I don't believe that was the purpose of your comment, was it, sir?'

'No,' Schenke replied. 'Of course it wasn't.'

Hauser was not amused. 'Just be careful what you say, sir. For the love of God.'

Schenke gave a vague nod before he took another pull on his cigarette. 'What do you make of our friend Stoffler?'

'You heard what I think of him.'

'What about you, Liebwitz?'

The Scharführer reflected for a moment. 'He appears unremarkable, sir. He has cooperated well enough with us and provided some useful background information about the coupons. However, it's likely that we would have discovered the irrelevance of the Vogler printer soon enough.'

'He might still be wrong about the printer,' Hauser responded. 'It's our strongest lead in finding the source of the forgeries.'

'I'm not sure I agree. The man knows what he's talking about with regard to printers . . . All the same, there's something about Stoffler that doesn't feel right. I don't think he has been playing completely straight with us. I've been thinking about it ever since we left the printworks. There's something off about him, and that security manager of his, Neger.'

'Is that why you mentioned Neger at the hospital?' asked Liebwitz.

Schenke nodded. 'Something tells me the two of them are more deeply involved than just happening to work in the same place. Look, I haven't time to go into details before Stoffler returns. I want to have another crack at Wohler before we end the day. Hauser, I want you with me when we go back to his cell. Let's see if he reacts to what we have uncovered so far.'

'You seriously think he'll have anything more to say than last time? Aside from some fresh choice insults to throw our way. A few days in the cells can do wonders for a man's breadth of invective.'

'Oh, he'll be steaming all right. But we might get something out of him, you never know. In any case, I want him stirred up. I want him ready to be caught off-guard.'

'And how do you expect to do that?'

Schenke looked at the clock on the wall before turning to Liebwitz. 'Scharführer, it's just gone four now. In ten minutes the sergeant and I will make our way down to the cells. I want you to take Stoffler back to the section office and ask him to help you draft a report of today's visit to the printworks.'

'For what purpose, sir?'

'Just tell him we need it for our files, and that you want him to confirm the details to ensure the report is accurate. Before you start, have a quiet word with Rosa and ask her to come to you at half past four and say that I want you and Stoffler to join the interrogation. You should be down here no more than ten minutes after that.'

Liebwitz nodded before Hauser shook his head in bewilderment. 'Mind telling us what this little charade is all about?'

'You'll see. If I'm right. If I'm not, then at worst we'll pick up a few more colourful phrases from our guest in protective custody. Right, Stoffler's coming back. Just do as I say and let's see what happens.'

Wohler started up as they entered the cell. His time in custody had not improved his demeanour, nor his appearance. His cheeks and jaw were covered in bristles and his hair was uncombed and untidy. His expensive suit was creased and had lost some of its shape. The tie had been discarded in a small heap at the foot of the bed. He stood up, nose flaring with impatience and indignation.

'So, you have come to your senses at last?'

Schenke raised an eyebrow enquiringly as Hauser pulled the cell door to. 'I'm sorry, I don't understand.'

'Don't fuck about with me, Inspector, or you'll regret it. Release me.'

'Sounds to me like he's making a threat to a police officer, sir,' said Hauser. 'Not the sort of thing we like.'

'No. We don't,' Schenke responded.

Wohler took a step towards the door. 'Just let me out of here.'

Schenke shook his head. 'Not yet. We've come to have another chat with you. Cooperate and I'll see what can be done about getting you released.'

'It's in your power to do that right now, so stop playing games.'

'I have to get the order counter-signed by the commander of the precinct. I'll put the release form in front of him the moment I am satisfied you have told us all we need to know. Now sit down. Or stand. Your call.'

Schenke and Hauser took their places either side of the cell door and stood waiting. Wohler took a calming breath and leaned against the wall beneath the barred window. There was a tense moment before Hauser nodded towards the tie on the floor. 'Think we need to remove that, sir? And his belt. Might be a suicide risk.'

'Sergeant,' Wohler began, 'I am very fucking far from being

a suicide risk. I'm more likely to use that tie on you and your inspector.'

'Feel free to try it,' Hauser goaded him.

Wohler gave a dry laugh. 'You think you can frighten me? I'm telling you, once I get out and have dealt with Guttmann, I'll find out where you both live and then me and some of the boys will pay a visit to your homes. You have family, Inspector? Wife? Kids, maybe?'

When Schenke didn't reply, Wohler turned to Hauser. 'Perhaps not. But you're a family man, Sergeant. The ring gives it away. So, married. At your age that means a few children. Three or four. Could be there's a girl amongst them, eh?' He winked.

Hauser tensed up and Schenke saw his fist clench. 'If you even think about it, I'll beat you and your men to a pulp . . .'

'That'll do,' Schenke intervened. 'Help us and I'll do what I can to get you out of here. If you want to play games with the sergeant, I can assure you that when it's over he'll be the only one capable of walking out of this cell.'

Wohler relaxed his posture, and a few beats later Hauser followed suit.

'Let's start with the club,' said Schenke. 'There was an interesting find in the ruins. The remains of a printer. Given that we're looking for the source of forged ration coupons, what do you make of that?'

'Not much. The printer was a relic of a small business that occupied the premises before Remer took it over. They used to print handbills, political pamphlets, that sort of thing. Hasn't been in use since. You're barking up the wrong tree, Schenke.'

'Is that so? A printer on the same premises as a stock of forged ration coupons? What a coincidence.'

'If you think that antique at the club was up to the job, then you don't know much about printers.'

'I know enough to link the two. I wonder if a Reich prosecutor will agree with me?'

'If they did, they'd be making themselves into as big a fool as you. Anyone who knows anything about printing will tell you the same.'

'How would you know?'

Wohler gave a sardonic grin. 'Maybe someone tried to use the printer to forge some coupons and realised it wasn't suitable for the job.'

'Would that someone have been Remer? Or you?'

'I'm merely offering a suggestion.'

'I see . . .' Schenke glanced at his watch and saw that he had less than ten minutes before Liebwitz arrived with Stoffler. He needed to move on. He needed to start getting under Wohler's skin.

'Let's say you're right about the printer, for now. There's another matter we're trying to clear up. We've spoken to some people at the club who say that all was not rosy between Remer and Fräulein Kunzler.'

'Club tittle-tattle, Inspector. I knew Remer well. Hate to say it, but Kitty had got to him. Turned out the boss had a heart after all. I warned him it wasn't a good idea to get too close to her, but he wouldn't listen to me. I told him you can play around with skirts but you never let them inside the business, or under your skin. If they get too close, you have to move on and put that behind you. That's how it is if you want to stay alive in our line of work.'

'We've heard that he was cooling off. Getting ready to dump her.'

'If only. What he was doing was getting suspicious. It didn't take a genius to work out that Kitty was playing around and someone else was on the scene.'

'Who would that have been?'

'Could have been Feldwitz, or Bachmann. I had to warn both of them off. They were the ones playing up to her. But it could have been someone else entirely. Why don't you ask her? Or put the screws on Bachmann or Feldwitz? Either of those yellow bastards will cough up the answers willingly enough.'

'Feldwitz is dead,' said Schenke.

Wohler looked surprised, and then sneered. 'Good riddance. What happened to him?'

'Strangled in his flat. Know anyone who uses that method of killing?'

'A few. But none who would want Feldwitz dead.' He shook his head. 'It doesn't make much sense. He'd been taught a lesson. There was no need to go any further.'

Schenke's mind went back to the doctor's comments when he had examined Feldwitz's body at the latter's flat.

'By taught a lesson, do you mean having an eye put out?' Schenke suggested. 'Isn't that what happened to Feldwitz?'

'He had behaved in a way that needed to be punished.'

Schenke felt his stomach turn as he imagined the scene. 'Did you do it?'

'Not me. I can say that with a clear enough conscience, Inspector.'

'But you know who did. Remer?'

Wohler did not answer at once. He considered the matter for a moment and then nodded. 'Remer's dead, so what difference does it make? Yes, it was him. He did that and then had

Feldwitz cut loose. Whoever killed him was nothing to do with our boys.'

'Then who was responsible?' Hauser demanded. 'Guttmann?'

'Maybe. But I can't think of a good enough reason for him to do it either.'

The hinges on the cell door gave a squeal as it swung open and Liebwitz entered.

'Just a couple of my colleagues joining the interrogation,' Schenke explained.

Behind Liebwitz came Stoffler. Stepping aside, Schenke watched closely for any reaction from either Wohler or the printworks manager. He was rewarded at once. Wohler's lip curled in a sneer and Stoffler flinched.

'You two already seem to be acquainted,' said Hauser. 'I wonder how?'

Wohler leaned back against the wall and chuckled. 'So you've turned police informer then, Stoffler?'

Stoffler recoiled as if he had been struck. 'I don't know what you are talking about. Inspector, I have never met this man before!'

'Odd that he knows your name then,' Schenke observed. 'How do you explain that?'

Stoffler's eyes darted from man to man as he stammered, 'Must be to do with the club. Yes! I-I went there a couple of times. I remember his face. We might have talked.'

'Oh, I'd say it was more than a couple of times,' Wohler smirked. 'Quite a few more. You spent a lot of time there with your pal. Your good friend, who turned out not to be such a good friend after all, eh?'

The blood seemed to drain from Stoffler's face as he edged back. Liebwitz slid between him and the door to block the exit.

'I've just been told that your friend's dead,' said Wohler. 'I wonder how you feel about that? Relieved, I should imagine. Or perhaps not.'

'Shut up!' Stoffler shouted shrilly. 'Shut up!' He suddenly snarled and hurled himself at Wohler. The gangster braced himself and caught the other man's wrist, wrenching his arm down and striking him hard across the cheek with the other hand. Stoffler's glasses went flying as he collapsed to his knees. Wohler made to strike again, but Hauser moved between them, fists raised.

'I wouldn't . . .'

Wohler's nostrils flared, and then he spat at Stoffler. 'You're right, he isn't worth it, the cowardly streak of piss . . .'

Schenke intervened. 'Liebwitz! Get Stoffler out of here. I want him in another cell. But don't sign him in under his own name. Use another . . . Sauckel will do.'

'Yes, sir.'

Liebwitz grasped the collar of Stoffler's coat and hauled him up, then scooped up the glasses. One lens was cracked. He manhandled his charge out of the cell.

'You're wasting your time with me, Inspector,' Wohler said. 'You'd be better off with Stoffler. That one will be only too willing to spill his guts with the right prompting.'

'I imagine so. But don't sell yourself short. You've been more help than you know in clearing things up. We'll speak again soon. Come, Hauser.'

The two Kripo men made to leave the cell and Wohler called after them. 'Wait! What about me?'

'What about you?' Schenke responded.

'When am I getting out of this hole?'

'I'll let you know when I'm good and ready.'

He strode out into the corridor, and Hauser closed the door behind him and slid the bolts into place.

'You can't keep me here!' Wohler protested. Then his face was pressed against the small viewing grille. 'Let me out! Or so help me, I'll gut you like a fish!'

'Charming,' said Hauser.

Liebwitz emerged from the neighbouring cell and secured it before Schenke led the way to the stairs at the far end. Wohler's cries followed them all the way. As their footsteps echoed off the grey walls, Hauser spoke.

'Mind explaining what the hell happened back there? Why have you put Stoffler in a cell?'

'Because he's in on the forgery business, I'm sure of it. You saw how they reacted to each other.'

'Sure, but a few harsh words and a slap on the chops doesn't prove much.'

'It proves enough. I think we have things the wrong way round. Maybe Remer wasn't the key figure behind the ration coupon forgeries. It may have been his bird at the start, but not recently.'

'Are you saying it's Guttmann?'

'Seems likely. It's possible he's been planning to take over the whole forgery business from the outset and wipe out Remer and his ring at the same time. If so, he's been playing a deep game and we haven't uncovered more than a fraction of it. There are still things that I can't make much sense of.'

'Such as?'

'Why the elaborate set-up for the ambush on Remer? Why not just gun him down outside the club? Or at his apartment?'

'Sir,' Liebwitz intervened, 'aren't you forgetting something?

Stoffler is supposed to report to Reichsminister Darré this evening. What happens when he fails to do that?'

'We've bought ourselves a little time on that front. There's not much Darré can do until the morning. He'll be waiting to tear a strip off Stoffler when he appears at the ministry. When he doesn't, he'll call me and I'll say Stoffler left the precinct earlier. Meanwhile he's entered into the log as Sauckel, so if Darré speaks to anyone else here, then that's covered.'

'You're playing a dangerous game, sir,' Hauser cautioned. 'Darré's going to hit the roof when he discovers you lied to him.'

'Not if I can prove Stoffler's complicity in the forgeries.'

'Let's hope we do, then.'

Schenke glanced at his sergeant, touched by Hauser's implicit offer to share the responsibility. He shook his head. 'If this goes the wrong way, it's my head that rolls. The rest of the section were just obeying my orders, understand?'

They had emerged from the stairs and started across the precinct's entrance hall when Schenke saw Radinsky coming down the building's main staircase. The Oberführer was wearing his cap and was buttoning up his greatcoat as he approached them. When he saw Schenke and his companions, he paused.

'Inspector.' He nodded. The three men returned the nod deferentially before Radinsky continued. 'I understand you are still holding Remer's lieutenant in our cells.'

'Yes, sir.'

'I trust that means you are making progress in tracking down Remer's killers, as well as that business with the forgeries.'

'Yes, sir.'

'Yes, you are? Or simply yes, sir?'

'I believe we are closing in on the perpetrators in regard to both matters, sir.'

'Good. I look forward to the resolution of the investigations as soon as possible.' Radinsky pulled on his gloves. 'By the way, Schenke, you were quite a sensation at the party. It's a shame you left as early as you did. Everyone was discussing the Führer's new favourite. Many of my guests had not heard your name before. Now they have. Such enduring fame brings its rewards and preferment, as long as you are touched by success. However, in the event of failure . . . Anyway, I am late for an appointment. I wish you and your men well in your endeavours.'

They exchanged another nod and Radinsky strode towards the main entrance of the building.

'In the event of failure . . .' Hauser repeated.

'Quite, so let's make sure there is no failure.'

Back in the section office, Schenke returned to his desk to write up an outline of the day's events and sketched out some lines of inquiry to take the investigations forward. Meanwhile Liebwitz assigned Persinger to keep watch on the two men in the cells overnight, to be relieved by Baumer in the morning. By the time Schenke had finished setting his words down and locked the file away in his desk drawer, it was dusk and most of the members of his section had gone home. Only Hauser and Rosa remained. The latter was drawing the blackout curtains and looked round as Schenke emerged from his cubicle.

'Do you want me to type up today's reports, sir?'

'No need, thank you. It's late. You should get home, Rosa. I'll see you tomorrow.'

'Yes, sir.'

They exchanged a smile before Schenke put on his coat and hat and left the section office. It was not quite dark outside, and it was still possible to make out the forms of people on the street. Some of the vehicles and bicycles passing by had already switched on their lights, casting narrow beams through the slits masking the headlamps. Schenke turned in the direction of his apartment as he made plans for the next day. A short distance further along the street, a car was parked by the kerb. A man was talking to a woman, who abruptly turned away and disappeared into an alley. Schenke registered the moment in passing – a couple's squabble, or a disagreement over price between a prostitute and a potential client, perhaps.

The man opened the car door and stood by it as Schenke approached. Then, at the last moment, he moved quickly to step in front of him.

'Inspector, get in the car.'

Schenke stopped abruptly, no more than a pace away from the man he now recognised from his earlier visit to Guttmann's villa.

'Reitz.'

'Well remembered.' The thinnest of smiles flickered across the larger man's face before he nodded to the open door. Schenke made to back off, heart beating fast, but Reitz stepped forward swiftly, a pistol in his hand. He jabbed the barrel into Schenke's midriff and spoke in a menacing tone. 'In the car, now.'

Glancing towards the open door, Schenke saw a man at the wheel, a hat pulled low enough to hide most of his features. Reitz gave him a shove, pushing him down into the passenger seat before closing the door. A moment later, the car drew away from the kerb.

'What the hell is this about?' Schenke demanded.

'Quiet!' Reitz ordered from the rear seat. 'Keep your mouth shut and stay still.'

Schenke was over the initial shock now, and anger flowed through him. 'Stop the car!'

He began to turn to face Reitz. 'You tell Guttmann—'

There was the briefest of blurring motions in the dark interior, and then a fierce white explosion inside Schenke's skull before he blacked out.

Reitz put his pistol away and reached over the seat to prop up the unconscious policeman. 'Don't say I didn't warn you . . .'

Chapter Nineteen

The first thing Schenke was aware of was a savage pounding inside his skull. Then came the nausea, and as his eyes opened, he lurched forward and retched. He clenched his eyes shut again and tried his best to focus his thoughts.

'Easy does it, Inspector . . .' A hand closed on his shoulder and drew him firmly back against the car seat. 'Can't have you knocking your head against the dashboard. The boss needs you to have a clear mind when he sees you.'

'The boss . . .' Schenke muttered, struggling to think straight as he dealt with the pain and the urge to vomit. Gradually the nausea faded as the car jolted and the sound of its engine filled his ears. He recalled being held up in the street, being pushed into the car – and then nothing. He eased his eyes open and took in his surroundings. Next to him, the driver had his attention fixed on the road ahead. On either side were trees interspersed with the looming dark masses of urban villas.

'You're taking me to see Guttmann.'

'That's right. Almost there, so be a good policeman and don't give me any trouble. Don't want to have to tap you on the head again if I can avoid it.'

'Tap?' Schenke said incredulously. 'Feels like you belted me with a sledgehammer.'

Reitz chuckled. 'You think so? Then you'd better pray I never have any reason to hit you harder.'

'I think you're already in enough trouble for assaulting a Kripo officer without making it worse for yourself by making further threats.'

'I'm not the one in trouble, Schenke. You're wasting your breath.'

The car slowed to make a turn into another street. Schenke slowly reached under his coat, fingers groping for the butt of his pistol, but the holster was empty. He considered his options before slipping his hand towards the door.

'I wouldn't do that,' Reitz warned him. 'You'll just hurt yourself and look a mess when you're in front of the boss. You'll get the Walther back when I drop you off afterwards.'

Schenke was silent, relieved to hear that this wasn't a one-way trip. Then again, that might be a trick to encourage him not to resist or escape. Not that there was much chance of either when dealing with Reitz. 'Why does Guttmann want to see me? Why now, at this hour?'

'Who knows? I just carry out his orders. You'll find out soon enough. Ah, we've arrived.'

The car slowed and turned towards the gateway that Schenke had seen a couple of days earlier in daylight. There was no longer a vehicle parked in front of it. Instead, two figures stepped forward and a torch flashed through the driver's-side window, causing the car's occupants to flinch. An order was called out as the beam of light snapped off, and a moment later the gates lurched inwards, accompanied by a grinding squeak of protest from the iron hinges. The car passed between the pillars and made its way up the drive, drawing up outside the entrance. The door behind Schenke opened and then his own swung out to reveal the hulking outline of Reitz.

'In you go, Inspector. Best not keep the boss waiting.'

Nursing the bump on the side of his head, Schenke got out of the car and was steered up the steps towards the entrance. Once through the blackout curtains hanging across the doors, the light from the chandelier in the hall was dazzling, and he squinted as he was turned towards the corridor. This time they stopped short of the dining room where he had interviewed Guttmann earlier. Reitz rapped on a door to one side.

'Come in,' came the muffled reply.

Reitz eased the door open and stepped forward. 'I have the inspector, Herr Guttmann.'

'You took your time.'

'He works late hours, boss.'

'How commendable. Bring him in.'

As Schenke entered, he glanced around the room. It was clearly the crime ring leader's study. Heavy velvet curtains covered a bow window that faced the grounds at the front of the house. A bookcase ran along one wall opposite a large fireplace above which hung a portrait of an elegant-looking woman in a plain black gown. The style of her dress indicated an earlier epoch. Not a wife then, Schenke guessed. The mother, perhaps. He felt a brief amusement as he recalled an American gangster movie he had seen some years earlier. Gangsters, their molls and their mothers were the same the world over. Jung would have had a thing or two to say about that.

Guttmann was sitting behind a gleaming oak desk in a large leather chair. There was no other seating in the room. He was dressed for a formal dinner, and his heavy jowls and a roll of flesh on his neck overhung the spotless white collar of his shirt. He had a small volume of poetry open in front of him, which he closed before he fixed Schenke with his steely eyes.

'Thank you for coming to see me, Inspector,' he began with studied politeness.

'I didn't have a choice.'

'I find that is often the way with people I have dealings with. Reitz, stay here and close the door.'

Reitz did as he was ordered, then stood in front of the door, hands folded together, feet braced apart. Any hope of overpowering Guttmann and fleeing via the window had gone. Schenke forced himself to stand tall and conceal the anxiety that gripped him.

'So, you have my attention, Guttmann. What do you have to say to me that's so pressing you drag me here at this hour and delay your going out for the evening?'

'The party . . .' Guttmann paused and smiled. 'The party, in both senses, can wait. Pressing the flesh of those amateur crooks is demeaning.'

'Amateur?' Schenke arched an eyebrow. 'They're running the country.'

'Pfft. An easy achievement when all you have to do is confect lies to dupe the gullible into voting for you and then change the rules so that you never have to face them at the ballot box again. The only ability that takes is lying convincingly to fools. Operating outside of the law while appearing to live within it and getting away with that year after year takes true intelligence, Inspector. If it didn't, you'd have had me behind bars long ago. Instead,' he wafted a hand at his comfortable surroundings, 'I live a life of luxury, beyond the reach of the law.'

'For now. There's plenty of time to take you down. You and the others like you.'

'Not as far as you're concerned, Schenke. That possibility no longer exists. From now on you will do my bidding, serve my interest, take my coin and resign yourself to being the kind of policeman you despise.'

Schenke took a breath. 'What on earth makes you think I would ever do that? Sounds to me more like I'm getting close enough to bringing you down to make you afraid.'

'Afraid?' Guttmann chuckled. 'The very idea is laughable. Honestly, Inspector, I had hoped you were smart enough to understand our relative positions. I would hate to be mistaken about that, given that I am on the verge of making a considerable investment in you and your career.'

'You can fuck your money. I have no plans to soil myself with it.'

Reitz took a half-pace forward. 'Want me to teach him some manners, boss?'

'No. Not yet. Despite his crude language, the inspector is a man of reason. Very well, it is time to reason with him. If that fails, that will be the time for you to step in with your own particular brand of pedagogic pugilism.'

'Er . . . yes, boss.'

'Now then, Inspector, it's true that you have been probing into aspects of my business that I would really rather shield from the gaze of Kripo's finest.'

'You're talking about the printworks.'

'Precisely. Your visit did not go unnoticed by those who work for me.' Guttmann's gaze shifted briefly to look over Schenke's shoulder before he continued. 'I would really appreciate the opportunity for my faith in your intelligence to be restored.

Tell me what conclusions you have drawn from your visit there . . . Come now, you can be honest with me. After all, you won't be revealing anything I don't already know.'

Schenke considered the situation before risking any reply. There were two intertwined lines of investigation – the source of the forged coupons and the murders of those who were somehow tied into the forgeries. There was very little he might give away with regard to the former, while there was a chance that he might glean some useful information about the latter if he played his cards carefully.

'There are no forged ration coupons,' he began. 'That's why Kripo has been chasing criminals down a blind alley these last months. The coupons are the real thing. They just happen to be unauthorised. They're being printed at night after the day shift has left the site. We were looking for forgeries and hidden printing presses when all the time you were operating in plain sight, or rather, under cover of darkness, at the same works where the official coupons were being printed.'

Guttmann smiled. 'Very good, Inspector. Go on.'

'The team working during the night were the same people brought in to guard the place recently. Brought in by the man tasked with the site's security. The man called Neger, although that's not his real name, is it, Reitz?'

'He's good, boss. I'll give him that,' said Reitz from the door.

'Yes. You should be impressed that the inspector considers you competent enough for such a role.' Guttmann chuckled. 'Carry on. This is all very reassuring insofar as it confirms my faith in your detection skills.'

Schenke collected his thoughts. 'Obviously Neger – Reitz – couldn't get away with it unless he had help from official quarters. After all, he needed to be appointed head of security and then be given the nod to recruit his own team to man the night shift and, presumably, replace those working the system before then. You needed someone on the inside. Someone with the authority to see it through. That would be Stoffler.'

Guttmann nodded. 'The man is a pathetic weasel. He took the first bribe I offered, spiced with a little blackmail, without any attempt to negotiate a better sum. Rather typical of the lesser breed of venal officials that the party has chosen to put into positions of power. I sometimes wonder how they can hope to keep their tawdry show on the road for much longer. Despite the gorgeous costumes, rhetorical posturing and preening self-regard, they are little better than street thugs. Why, I could scrape up dozens of such petty criminals from the back alleys of Pankow and have the makings of a more effective government than that of the Nazis.'

'You would be wise to keep such views to yourself, Herr Guttmann.'

'Do you think I am mistaken, Inspector? Do you really think we are being ruled by the best that Germany has to offer? If that Austrian vagrant and his cronies are the acme of political talent, then I fear for our fortunes in the present war. What do you think?'

'I am not paid to consider such matters. I'm paid to put an end to people like you.'

'People like me are running Germany. The only difference is that I am smart enough to keep the profits and maintain a low profile. If the war ends badly for Germany, I'll still be in business, while they will be climbing the steps to the scaffold. If we win the war, then I make more profit. Either way, I win. People like you, Schenke, need to decide if they are on the side of people like me, rather than phoneys like Hitler and his crew. Why, even Stoffler has enough brains to understand that.'

'Then maybe I am not as smart as Stoffler.'

'Neither of us believes that, so let's not pretend otherwise.'

'Fair enough.'

'Please continue, Inspector.'

'It seems to me that you weren't the first gangster Stoffler sold out to. After all, Reitz only brought in his night shift recently, some time after the coupons appeared on the streets. Someone else set it all up. Remer. I saw some of his stock of coupons at the club during the fire.' Schenke paused. 'That blaze was the work of your ring, wasn't it?'

'Of course. As soon as I heard that Remer was dead, I saw the opportunity to set the seal on the destruction of his gang. Wohler has a reputation for being headstrong. I've met him a few times. He's a dangerous man. He needed to go. With both men out of the way, there was no chance of anyone throwing a spanner in my printworks, if you'll pardon the quip. Reitz and his lads carried out the job. It's a damn shame you and your Gestapo friend were there, as I'd hoped to get my hands on Remer's remaining coupons before the place was torched. A sad loss, but one I can make good easily enough.'

'I can imagine. Anyway, Stoffler was in Remer's pocket before he was in yours. Which begs the question, how exactly did you manage to get him to switch his loyalty? Although loyalty is hardly the word for his motivation. You had to find a weakness that ensured he came over to your side. As you mentioned, bribes work well enough with someone like that. But I dare say Remer was just as capable of bribing or frightening him into staying on his payroll. So it had to be something else. Some other means of persuasion. Something more effective, more frightening. Blackmail, like you said.'

Guttmann leaned back and pressed his hands together in an arch. 'And what kind of blackmail do you think that might be?'

'I am on more uncertain ground here, but I can guess. As you almost certainly know, one of Remer's associates, name of Feldwitz, was murdered in his flat a couple of days ago. One of my men was assaulted and knocked out at the same time. Just before he was attacked, he saw that Feldwitz was holding some photographs.'

'So?'

'At the moment my man encountered him, Feldwitz was expecting to see someone else in his flat. Someone he addressed as Hugo. Someone who was powerful enough to garrotte him with ease. Someone who has made something of a habit of knocking out Kripo officers.' Schenke turned and nodded at Reitz. 'Hugo Reitz . . . You've sunk a long way since the days when you were a rising star on the boxing circuit. A fair fight is one thing, but cold-blooded murder . . .'

'His facility with the latter is precisely the reason why I employ him,' said Guttmann. 'He's been pretty reliable in that regard so far.'

'So I've seen. And you've been keeping him busy these last few days. But getting back to the photographs . . . They were obviously important enough to kill for. That points to blackmail. And Stoffler is the most likely target for such a thing, given what I know so far. I doubt he would be so concerned about being caught with a woman that he would buckle to Remer's will, and then yours. But being caught with a man, now that would be a very dangerous revelation these days. The

Nazis are not known for their toleration of such a thing. I dare say the other man in the photos was Feldwitz.'

'Spot on!' Guttmann clasped his hands together and dipped his head in a mock salute. 'Bravo, Schenke. I knew you were a man of sound professional judgement, but you have surpassed yourself.'

'I'm not finished yet. There are still a few details I need to clear up. I can see that Feldwitz had outlived his usefulness, and I understand why you sent your men for Wohler at the club, but why go to all the effort of setting up the elaborate ambush of Remer? It was Reitz who replaced the usual driver that night, wasn't it? Reitz who shot him dead and wounded Kitty Kunzler.'

Guttmann frowned and shook his head. 'I'm disappointed. You were doing so well for a while there. As it happens, I had nothing to do with Remer's killing. That was just a fortunate coincidence. I admit, I fully intended to have him removed after I had turned Stoffler. There was every danger that might have provoked Remer into some unfortunate act of violence. The last thing any criminal underworld needs is a war between gangs. Too many bullets flying and too many bodies stacking up tends to draw the attention of you and your superiors. Remer had to go. But I had nothing to do with it. Nor did Reitz. He's not your trigger man. At least on that occasion.'

Schenke shook his head. 'I don't believe you. Who else could it have been?'

'I honestly don't know. And I honestly don't care. Whoever killed him did me a favour and that's all that matters. Of course, if you ever discover who was responsible, I'd be curious to know. Someone close to him did approach my lawyer, Kolbenhoff, with an offer to help have him removed. That was a month or so ago. I saw no point in it at the time and told Kolbenhoff to ignore the message. Maybe that's your culprit.'

'Who was it who made the approach?'

'It wasn't in person. Just an anonymous note with details on where to leave a reply. It went into the fireplace, where such crank letters belong. Maybe the person who sent the message went ahead without my help. Maybe not. Makes no difference any more.'

Schenke was caught between surprise and disbelief. But what reason could Guttmann have for lying about Remer's killing? It made no sense for him to deny it if he had been responsible for setting the trap. But then who else could have been behind the shooting?

'Nobody's perfect,' Guttmann continued. 'Your deductions were impressive up until that point and fully justify my confidence in your abilities. You'll make a fine addition to the payroll. I may even offer a bonus payment, enough to sweeten the pill. I know how hard it is for honourable men to get over their professional distaste for the work they do for me.'

'You're wasting your time, Guttmann. I have no intention of betraying my position. Save your money for the mole you have already bribed at the precinct.'

'Oh, they're well taken care of. It's you I want. Having a criminal inspector under my thumb will be very useful indeed. Especially if you get promoted, as you deserve to be. Given the shortage of manpower, the situation is ripe for rapid advancement. I'll have eyes and ears in the heart of the capital's policing establishment.'

'No you won't,' Schenke said defiantly. 'I told you. I can't be bought.'

'Really?' Guttmann looked amused. 'Well, let's see . . . As

a policeman, I am sure you are aware of the terms of the Nuremberg decrees. In particular, the banning of sexual relationships between Aryans and Jews. The punishments for those who break the laws are quite harsh, I believe.'

Schenke felt his guts clench as an icy ripple of fear traced its way down his spine. For a moment the room seemed to sway, and he felt almost as dizzy as he had been back in the car.

'I see that you know where this is headed, Schenke. You've laid your cards on the table and now it's my turn. After your first visit here, it was clear that I needed to know more about you. Find out if you had any weaknesses I could exploit. You know the sort of thing – family, children, gambling debts, drug use. Instead, I discovered that you had some kind of relationship with a Jewess. You were with her at the Café Labourdonnais. She was followed back to an apartment in Mitte, and it was easy enough for my man to discover her name. Ruth Frankel . . . Now, you can imagine how your superiors would react if they were to discover what you and Fräulein Frankel have been up to.'

'She is a police informer,' Schenke countered, desperation surging through his veins. 'She helped with one of our cases at the end of last year. You are barking up the wrong tree.'

'Am I, though? Maybe she was an informer to start with. But now? I think there's rather more to it than that.'

'You can't prove anything,' Schenke responded, desperately trying to control his expression. 'Do you seriously think that anyone would take the word of a known criminal over that of a Kripo officer?'

'Sadly not. Which is why I always take the measures necessary to offset that deficit of trustworthiness. You see, the photographs of Stoffler are not the only ones in my possession.'

Guttmann reached for the drawer to his right and pulled it open. He took out a file and set it down on the desk in front of him, then turned it round and opened the cover to reveal several photographs inside. The top one showed Schenke standing to greet Ruth at the café. He fanned them out, revealing more shots of the two of them sitting and talking. There was no hiding the obvious intensity of the looks being exchanged between them.

'This one I like especially,' he said, drawing out the one at the bottom of the thin pile. Schenke stared at it in horror, feeling his heart racing as his stomach lurched. He saw himself frozen in the act of kissing Ruth. There was the evidence that would destroy his career and see them both sent to one of Himmler's camps. It would mean months of brutal treatment for him until the SS deemed that he had been 're-educated'. Once he was released, he would never be permitted to rejoin the police. He would be a social pariah – a 'race traitor', as the party termed it – for the rest of his days. For Ruth, the consequences would be worse. She would be sent to a camp and would die there.

Guttmann swept the photos back into the file and closed it before he regarded Schenke with a superior smile. 'You see, Inspector, my cards trump yours. As they always will. The choice before you is bleak, is it not? You can serve me and be rewarded handsomely for it and I will leave you and your Jewess to conduct your relationship as you wish – though I would urge more caution than you have shown so far. Or you can stick by your principles and suffer the consequences. As we both know, they will be rather more dire for Fräulein Frankel.'

Schenke swallowed. 'You bastard . . .' he hissed.

There was a movement behind him, but Guttmann gave a

slight shake of his head and Reitz shifted back to his position covering the door.

'Let's not pretend that I am offering you a choice. I understand that this is hard enough for you as it is. It would be demeaning for you to have to accept any offer I made to you in any case, so I'll spare you that humiliation. You are my man now and there is nothing you can do about that. It will take you a little time to accept it and learn to live with it. Better men than you have had to do the same. It will hurt like hell to begin with, but you will find that you can carry on chasing other criminals and doing your job as before, with my blessing. And you will have a useful extra income and from time to time any black-market luxuries that I pass on to you. In exchange, I will ask favours of you. Information. Advance warning of any police activity that may affect my business. That sort of thing.'

'You make it sound so easy . . .'

'It's nothing of the sort. It's a dirty thing for a man like you to be involved in my business, but that's the hand you have been dealt. If it hadn't been Frankel, I would have found some other line of attack. Everyone has their secrets, and secrets are weaknesses. Weakness is what men like me prey on. You may think the law is the supreme achievement of mankind, Inspector, and so it is – the law of the jungle. The strong will always be the masters. The Führer is right in that much at least. He might want to dress it up in terms of race and fate, but the unadorned truth of the ages is that might prevails. Those who refuse to accept that will be crushed under the boots of their masters.' Guttmann paused. 'Reitz will take you back to Pankow. You'll want some time to adjust to the way things will be from now on. In the morning, I want you to make sure that Kripo turns its attention away from the printworks. You've got the remains of a printer at the Ace of Hearts, and the coupons you saw there. I want you to push that line of inquiry for now.'

'That won't work.'

'Make it work,' Guttmann replied coldly. 'Now it's time for you to go. I'm running late as it is. Reitz, take him back and have another car brought to the front of the house.'

'Yes, sir.' Reitz tapped Schenke on the shoulder. 'You heard the boss.'

They left the study as Guttmann put the folder away in the desk drawer and locked it. Outside in the cold night air, Schenke shivered, not because of the temperature but at the horror of the situation he had been thrust into. The world, already a dark and uncertain place, now felt like a steel trap tightening around him, crushing the very light and air and filling him with hopelessness.

Chapter Twenty

As soon as Reitz had dropped him close to the precinct, the car pulled away into the darkness. Schenke waited until it was almost out of sight before he turned and strode quickly towards the derelict shop used as the drop for the messages passed between himself and Ruth. This time there was no question of merely giving the sign that he wished to meet. It was vital that he see her as soon as possible to warn her of the terrible danger to them both. A short distance from the shop, he stepped into a side alley and took out his notebook and torch. Shielding as much light as possible, he wrote a brief note telling her to meet him at the fallback rendezvous – a workmen's bar in Mitte. He told her that if he was not there she must wait until he arrived, for the sake of them both. He hoped the note would convey the urgency he intended it to.

Turning off the torch, he tore out the sheet and folded it carefully until it was little bigger than a postage stamp. Making his way to the drop, he glanced both ways along the street, and only when he was certain that he was not being observed did he slide the message between two bricks and use the chalk to make the mark. Then he made his way back to his apartment at a brisk pace. His mind was a raging torrent of bitter self-recrimination for his foolishness in getting involved with Ruth. At the same time there was a growing despair about his betrayal of his principles, his career and his comrades. The thought of Hauser, Liebwitz and the others ever discovering the arrangement with Guttmann appalled him. That he had been blackmailed into it would not be accepted as an excuse by anyone. Just as he himself would feel no pity for an officer in his position if their places were switched.

When he reached his apartment block, he gave the doorman the barest of nods and refused to meet his gaze, as if his guilt and shame was there for all to see. He hurried up the steps, heedless of the pain in his bad leg, and fumbled with his keys outside his door. They fell from his grip, and he stooped to pick them up with a curse.

'Herr Schenke?'

He looked round and saw that the door on the far side of the landing was half open. The block warden regarded him curiously.

'Is anything the matter?'

'No. I'm fine.' Schenke fitted the key and hurriedly turned it. He entered, closing the door behind him firmly before slipping the security bolt and hanging up his hat. He saw that his hands were trembling, and he clenched his fists so that his nails bit into his palms.

'Shit . . .' he hissed. 'Shit, oh shit . . . What have I got myself into?'

He paced down the hallway and into his living room. The blackout blinds were still drawn from the night before, and he turned on the reading lamp and slumped into one of the armchairs at the side of the stove. He sat still for a moment, slowly recovering his breath and his nerves. His mind was in torment and nausea twisted in his guts. He wished that there was someone he could confide in and ask for advice. Advice and reassurance that, bad as his predicament was, he was blameless because he had acted with the best of intentions. His desire to do what he could to protect Ruth had led him to this. What was that saying? He smiled grimly: *No good turn goes unpunished.* Now the fates, or whatever malignant synchronicity had chosen to make an example of him, had found the most agonising manner in which to punish him.

He found himself longing for the time before he had met Ruth, when his life was more settled and his future more certain. When he had been with Karin he had looked forward to his marriage and ongoing career. If there had been any issues, any reflections on his job or concerns about the direction Germany was headed, he had been able to discuss them openly with her. He had let that relationship end. Worse, he had sabotaged it by allowing himself to develop feelings for Ruth – as reckless an affection as anyone could choose in Nazi Germany.

As he let himself sink into introspection, he began to understand the lure of the tales of knightly deeds that had enthralled him as a youth. Such moral values had been driven home by his aristocratic father, who had ensured that he was familiar with his lineage and the honour that his forebears had bestowed on the family name. Schenke had always set much store in being seen as a gentleman, because he believed in the values that went with the role. Since the Nazis had taken power, those values had come to seem more pertinent than ever against the backdrop of the brutal kleptocracy practised by the regime. It was one of the reasons why Schenke had resisted the pressure to accept membership of the SS on every occasion it had been suggested or offered to him. Himmler liked to portray his black-uniformed corps as being a new form of chivalry. To Schenke it seemed like the antithesis of the tradition, and Ruth's fate had been the wedge that had been driven between Schenke's values and those espoused by the Nazis.

He recalled how Karin had urged him again and again to make a stand against Hitler and his followers. To join with those who were working in secret to undermine the Nazis. At the time he had been aware of the dangers of the path she had urged him to take. He had tried to explain to her that his first duty was to uphold the law, no matter who was in power. Even as he had offered the argument, he had known how hollow and redundant it seemed when men little better than gangsters ruled Germany. She had barely hidden her disdain for the position he had advanced. It was ironic that Ruth – the catalyst that had caused him to defy the Nazis and what they stood for – had caused his engagement to Karin to come to an end amid the shameful guilt of a secret parallel relationship. If only he had let his head rule his heart when it most mattered, he would have still been with Karin, and Ruth would not have been drawn into the peril that he had brought about.

The thought that Karin at least would be spared whatever fate befell Schenke and Ruth was some small comfort. In any case, she had moved on and found herself a new partner. A safer partner. All the same, Schenke missed the reassurance of freely discussing matters with her at that moment. He hoped that Ruth would check the message drop as soon as possible. She had to be warned. If there was any means to spirit her away to another city far from Berlin, to hide her identity, then he might be able to fight back against Guttmann secure in the knowledge that she was safe. It would be too late to save himself, however. Guttmann had the photos of them together, and that, with proof of Ruth's race, would be enough to destroy Schenke.

He suddenly realised how exhausted he felt. The long hours, danger and complications of the investigations into the forgeries and the murders were taking their toll. He needed rest but knew that it would not come easily. Not that night. He rose from the chair and crossed to the drinks cabinet beside his bookcase, where he poured himself a large brandy. Then he returned to his chair and savoured the settling effect the spirit had on his stomach and mind.

He turned his thoughts to the difficulties of steering attention away from the printworks. Even though he had only divulged the full scale of his deliberations to Guttmann, he feared that Hauser and Liebwitz were reaching the same conclusions, especially after the day's bit of theatre in the cells. He had one card up his sleeve as far as the crime ring leader was concerned. Guttmann was not yet aware that Wohler was still alive. That might yet prove to be of value as the desperate situation played out.

There was another, more pressing reason for keeping Wohler hidden under an assumed name – the presence of Guttmann's existing informant at the precinct. If it was someone in the Kripo section, it was imperative that as few of Schenke's comrades as possible knew about Wohler. And Stoffler, for that matter. That would be tricky, given that Darré would soon be asking why his subordinate had failed to report in. Questions would be directed at Schenke, and there was only so long he would be able to fend them off. He must find a way out of this trap within days or else he would be snared by

Guttmann for ever. With Stoffler in the cell, the only other people aware of the true identities of the two prisoners were Hauser and Liebwitz. He would have to ensure that they understood the importance of not letting anyone else know. And then he would have another crack at Stoffler, alone. Now that the source of the forgeries had been uncovered, there was still the matter of the shooting of Remer and Kitty to be resolved. It was possible that Stoffler knew something about that. Something that would help Schenke finally fit the last pieces of the blood-soaked puzzle together.

Then there was Ruth. Unwittingly caught up in the web of Guttmann's machinations. If she didn't respond to his message the next day, he resolved to track her down to her new address and warn her face-to-face. That entailed an unnerving degree of risk. Even if Schenke managed to throw off any tail that Guttmann had tasked to spy on him, there was the danger that he was also having Ruth watched, or that some nosy neighbour might take an unhealthy interest in visitors to a Jewish household and denounce them all to the local police. Despite such risks, she had to be made aware of the new threat and consider what she chose to do about it.

Schenke drained his glass. The alcohol was having its effect, and he had to brace his feet to stop himself swaying. Making his way to the bedroom, he took off his coat and lay on the bed fully clothed. Before he closed his eyes, he made sure that he set the alarm, not trusting himself to rise with the daylight. Then, thoughts slowly swirling down into oblivion, he finally fell into a dreamless sleep.

In the early hours, a distant air-raid siren sounded as a small number of enemy aircraft carried out a harassing raid and dropped propaganda pamphlets across the capital. Schenke, like many other Berliners, had long since grown used to the false alarms, and barely registered the siren as he, and most of the rest of the city, slept through it.

He reached the precinct before anyone else from his section and went to the cells. Persinger was sitting on a canteen chair, his head leaned back against the wall between the two cells he was guarding. Schenke could hear his snoring even before he reached the bottom of the stairs. Striding forward, he gave the leg of the chair a savage kick and nearly toppled Persinger onto the floor.

'What the hell are you doing? You're on bloody duty, man. Stand up!'

Persinger scrambled to his feet and stood to attention. Schenke glared at him for a beat before he sighed. 'Anything to report?'

'Not much, sir. A few drunks and prostitutes were put in some of the other cells to sleep it off. There's been some banter from one of the prisoners.' He nodded at Wohler's cell. 'Mostly threats to the other one. I told him to shut his mouth if he didn't want me to douse him with a fire hose. Did the job. Been as quiet as a lamb ever since. That's why I nodded off, sir.'

'That's no excuse and you know it. If I catch you asleep on the job again, I'll break you back down to a rookie. I'll take over here until Baumer arrives. One more thing.' Schenke paused to make sure the other man was paying full attention. 'You are not to mention anything about these prisoners to anyone else. Not even to anyone else in our office. Understand?'

'Yes, sir.'

'Go home now, and when you come back on duty you are to be fully awake and alert. I won't warn you again.' Schenke jerked his thumb in the direction of the stairs and Persinger hurried away, anxious to escape the ire of his superior.

Turning to the cells, Schenke checked on Wohler first. The man was lying on his bed, back to the door, apparently asleep. Schenke hesitated. He must speak with Wohler, but only when the time was ripe for what he had in mind. Instead he made for the cell with the name 'Sauckel' chalked on the board outside. Looking through the grille, he saw Stoffler sitting on the edge of his bed, his spectacles eased up onto the top of his head while his face rested in his hands, a picture of misery.

He looked up in alarm as the bolts of the cell door slid back with a loud rattle. Schenke swung the door inwards and stepped inside.

'You don't look like you've had much sleep,' he observed mildly. 'I'm afraid the accommodation provided to our prisoners is on the basic side. I'll have some food brought to you after we've talked.'

Stoffler slid his glasses back onto the bridge of his nose and looked at Schenke warily. 'I'm not a prisoner. I haven't done anything wrong. No one has charged me with a crime. I demand that you release me at once. When Reichsminister Darré discovers how you have treated me—'

'I doubt he'll be that concerned when he finds out that you are in the pay of Herr Guttmann.'

'That's a lie!'

Schenke was still suffering from anxiety and lack of sleep, and suddenly his professional calm shattered. He strode over to Stoffler, grabbed him by the lapels and hauled him to his feet so that their faces were so close he could almost smell the other man's fear.

'Listen, you little weasel, people have died because of your fucking forgeries. I know exactly how it all works. I know you were stupid enough to get blackmailed by Feldwitz and you sold yourself to first Remer and now Guttmann. I know that Guttmann's thug Reitz, or Neger as you called him, has put in his own gang of men to work the coupon printers at night. I know you were seen with Feldwitz at the Ace of Hearts club on many occasions . . . For God's sake, man, you're up to your neck in this mess, and the moment Guttmann knows that you've been held and questioned by Kripo, you're as good as dead. The same goes for Darré when he discovers your involvement. If you're lucky there will be a show trial, public humiliation, and you'll hang, or be guillotined. Otherwise you'll just disappear into the night, another body in an unmarked grave somewhere in the woods. You're finished. Do you understand?'

Stoffler's jaw quivered and Schenke shook him viciously.

'I said, do you understand?'

'Y-yes!'

He thrust him away so that Stoffler fell onto the bed. He shuffled back into the corner, as far from the policeman as he could get.

'Listen,' Schenke continued. 'I'm the only hope you have left. I can offer you protection from Guttmann, and if you cooperate with the investigation, I will do what I can to mitigate the punishment you'll get from the court. It may save your neck, but you will be sent to a camp. That's for certain. It's what happens to anyone who betrays the trust of the party and abuses their position as grievously as you have.'

Even as he said the words, he felt like a hypocrite. There but for the grace of God, he thought, bitterly anticipating the same fate as Stoffler when his own involvement with Guttmann was inevitably discovered. Perhaps the difference would be that he would have the integrity and strength to turn himself in when the time came. But only after he had made sure that Ruth was safe.

'Stoffler, I know you were tricked into all of this. Feldwitz was a professional seducer. He did it for the money. Blackmailed men and women alike. You were used by him. Used by Remer and Guttmann. Remer is dead, but you can still get back at Guttmann. If you want my help, though, I'll need a full confession from you, detailing everything you know about the forgeries, every name you can recall. Most of all I need you to tie Reitz and Guttmann into this.'

'But I never had any dealings with Guttmann. It was always Reitz, or Guttmann's lawyer.'

'Kolbenhoff?'

Stoffler nodded.

'You never met Guttmann? Never spoke to him on the phone or had any written communication from him?'

'No.'

'That's a pity . . . Guttmann has friends in the party. Unless I can find some evidence damning enough, they'll protect him. I need something that will persuade them to throw him to the dogs.'

'I don't know anything that would incriminate him.' Stoffler shook his head. 'I really don't.'

'I know that Reitz killed Feldwitz. Was he also involved in the shooting of Remer and his girlfriend?'

Stoffler was silent for a moment before he shook his head.

'Think, man!' Schenke urged him. 'You dealt with Reitz. Did he ever say anything to tie him to the shooting?'

'No . . .'

'That's no good to me. I can't help you if won't give me

something I can use.' He began to turn back towards the door in frustration.

'Wait!' Stoffler leaned forward, eyes gleaming hopefully. 'There was something. At the club. It was crowded that night and I was with Feldwitz. This was after Remer had got his hooks into me. I had to go to the toilet. When I went back to the bar, Feldwitz wasn't there. I looked round for him in the crowd and saw him talking to someone close to the entrance. As I went over to them, neither of them saw me until the last moment. I heard Feldwitz say, "What about them?" and the other man said, "Reitz will take care of it when the time comes." Then Feldwitz saw me and introduced me to the man. A business acquaintance, he said. I didn't know him at the time, but I did later on. It was Kolbenhoff. He made no attempt to introduce himself and left. I thought he was just someone trying to pick Feldwitz up.'

'"Reitz will take care of it when the time comes." You're sure he said that?'

'Yes.'

'Not take care of *them*?'

'I-I can't quite recall. What difference does it make?'

'It probably makes no difference,' Schenke conceded. 'But you didn't overhear anything else? No names? What about afterwards? Did you ask Feldwitz what they had been talking about?'

'Of course. He said it was just business and nothing to do with me. I tried to push him for more details, but he got angry and told me to drop it.'

Schenke tried to work out what the significance of the encounter with Kolbenhoff might be. It was a troubling new aspect to the case. It might be something quite innocent, or sinister. He did not know enough to decide. He focused his attention back on his prisoner. 'You'll be staying here for a few days. It's the safest place for you. One of my men will be outside. Don't make any fuss, and whatever you do, don't tell anyone your name. You've been logged in under the name of Sauckel. Understand?'

'What happens now?' Stoffler pressed him.

'You sit and wait. And pray that I find some way of getting to Guttmann before he gets to you.'

'You said I'd be safe.'

'No one is safe from Guttmann right now,' Schenke replied with a weary sigh. 'No one.'

Chapter Twenty-One

9 May

Baumer turned up just as Schenke had slid the bolts back into place. He listened carefully to the inspector's instructions, then took his place on the chair between the cells. As Schenke climbed the stairs to the Kripo section office, he went over what he had learned from Stoffler. The man had been no help in finding a way to get at Guttmann directly, and now there was the matter of what Kolbenhoff had been doing at the club and the meaning of the brief exchange that Stoffler had overheard. It might be wishful thinking to assume it had something to do with the shooting of Remer and Kitty. Even if it did, how did that help Schenke in his present predicament? He had a limited time to find a way to defeat Guttmann before the crime boss began to use him as an informer and dragged him into his clutches, along with the person at the precinct he had already snared.

Aside from Persinger, the rest of the section was in the office. As Schenke entered, Hauser and Liebwitz looked up expectantly from their desks. He felt a stab of guilt at their eager expressions. He nodded to his cubicle, and they rose and followed him inside. He sat, and indicated the two chairs on the other side of his desk.

When all three men were seated, Hauser began. 'So we've got Stoffler in the bag and we know Guttmann is behind the forgeries.'

'Do we?'

'Of course he is, sir. I went over everything when I got home last night. Stoffler was Remer's man first, then betrayed him and switched to Guttmann. He's using the printworks to print extra coupons while Guttmann's thugs provide the night watch. That man he called Neger, I'd bet that was one of Guttmann's boys. Reitz most likely. That's why we couldn't track down the source of the forgeries, because they were never fake in the first place. Now we've got Guttmann!' Hauser slapped his thigh. 'We've got him!'

Liebwitz nodded.

'What's the next move, sir?' Hauser continued. 'When do we arrest the fat bastard?'

'Not yet. We still need more. The last thing we want is to bring him in only for one of his party friends to call Radinsky and get him released.'

Hauser snorted. 'Once they know he's behind the forged ration coupons, they'll cut ties quicker than shit through a goose. You'll see.'

Liebwitz's high forehead creased as he considered the analogy, then he pursed his lips and nodded again.

'I agree,' said Schenke. 'But we can't give them any excuse to haul his arse out of the fire. When we bring him in, I want every single charge to stick. The forgeries, the murders of Feldwitz, Remer and Breker, everything.'

'There is a high degree of likelihood that his arrest and interrogation will provide the basis for further charges to be brought against him,' Liebwitz observed. 'I agree with the sergeant. We already have enough evidence to persuade his party contacts to disavow him. We have enough to prosecute him, bring down his crime ring and put an end to the forgeries. The most reasonable course of action is to arrest him as soon as possible, sir.'

Hauser nodded vigorously and jerked a thumb at Liebwitz. 'What he said . . . sir?'

Schenke regarded them calmly even as his mind was in turmoil and his heart heavy with guilt.

'Look here, I am as keen as you two to break this case right now, but we've spent months working our way up to this point. It's been hard graft all the way. It would be a kick in the balls if we threw away our chance to nail Guttmann and his cronies because we overlooked some detail that allowed him to get away with it. No. We'll take him when the time is right, and not before.'

Hauser shook his head. 'Sir, the time is right now. If he remains at large, that only gives him the chance to worm his way out of trouble. If he doesn't already know we were at the printworks yesterday, he soon will. When Stoffler fails to turn up, it won't take long for Guttmann to guess we have him, and that the little weasel will spill his guts the moment we interrogate him.'

'I'm sure Stoffler will talk, and when he does, I want him to tell us everything we need to close the case on the forgeries and the murders. But first we let him stew a little longer in his cell. That way he'll be easier to break down.'

'He's ready for it right now, sir. You saw him. The man has a spine of watery jelly. He'd piss himself if I went in there right now and said "Boo!" too loudly. Just give me the word.'

Schenke shook his head. 'No. I want him left alone for

another twenty-four hours. No one is to speak to him. The grille on his door is to remain closed. By tomorrow morning I guarantee he will tell us all we need to know.'

Hauser gave an exasperated sigh. 'By tomorrow it may be too late. Guttmann will have cleaned house and there'll be next to nothing we can stick on him.'

'I agree, sir,' Liebwitz intervened. 'There is no good reason to delay.'

'This is not a debate, gentlemen,' Schenke responded formally. 'I've made my decision.'

'What are we supposed to do in the meantime?' Hauser's impatience was causing him to raise his voice. Through the glass Schenke could see other members of the section looking in their direction. 'Are we just supposed to sit here counting fucking paper clips?'

'Sergeant Hauser, you forget yourself!' Schenke slammed his palm down on the desk. 'How dare you address a superior in that manner? I have given my instructions and you will obey them and not question my authority. If there is any repetition of your insubordination, I will have you removed from this section. Do you understand?'

All three men in the cubicle froze, while those outside exchanged surprised glances. Hauser's mouth opened as he made to retort, but Schenke raised a warning finger.

'Don't . . .'

Hauser forced himself to speak calmly and respectfully. 'Sir, we've worked together for some years now. We've broken some good cases. Tough cases. Because we understood how the other was thinking. But this? I just don't understand it. Tell me why you're doing it? It makes no sense to me.'

'It doesn't have to make sense to you, Hauser. I know

what I'm doing and why I'm doing it. If you don't trust my judgement, that's a matter for you to think about in private. You do not get to question it in public. You are dismissed. You too, Liebwitz.'

The Scharführer's expression, usually deadpan, registered surprise and confusion before he gave a curt nod and stood up. Hauser followed him out of the cubicle.

Schenke took a long, slow breath, forcing himself to keep his expression neutral. Inside he felt the raw pain of the bitterest shame for having given a fine man like Hauser such a humiliating dressing-down. His sense of disgrace was only matched by the seething hatred and contempt he felt for Guttmann and his kind – death-dealing parasites who did not care in the least about the misery they inflicted on their victims. That they thrived under the Nazis was further proof, if it was needed, of the dark symbiosis between the party and the crime rings; between the monsters who led the party and men like Guttmann, the gross kingpin, Reitz, the violent brute, and Kolbenhoff, the silky manipulator of the law. The crime empire they ruled was no more than a microcosm of the Nazis' Reich, and now Schenke was sinking into their moral mire. He could almost smell the foul stench of their filth settling on him. If there was some way he could destroy them all, even at the cost of his own life, it would be a price he felt prepared to pay. Even if he could only take down Guttmann it would be enough to salve his conscience. Already his mind was sifting through the options, though the challenge seemed daunting to the point of impossibility. Time was his enemy.

He saw the typed-up report that had been prepared and placed on top of his in-tray. He made a show of reading over it as he tried to conceive of some way out of his plight. As the morning wore on, his thoughts inevitably turned to Ruth. Just before noon, he signed the report and placed it in the out-tray, then took his hat and coat from the pegs before leaving the cubicle. He called over to Rosa.

'I should be back in an hour or so if anyone asks for me.'

'Yes, sir. Shall I say where you have gone?'

Schenke shook his head and left.

Outside in the street, the sun was shining again. Another fine day. What the party propaganda called 'Führer weather', as if the sun shone on Germany in preference to any other nation on earth. Schenke walked quickly in the opposite direction to the message drop. He stopped twice as if looking into shop windows and scanned the reflection of his surroundings in the glass. At the second shop he saw the same man pause to adjust his watch on the opposite side of the street as he had done the first time. He smiled grimly and continued along the street for a short distance before turning into an alley and breaking into a trot until he found an alcove to back into. Pressing himself against a service door, he drew his pistol, slipped off the safety and held it ready. A moment later he heard footsteps, striding fast, and the man who had been adjusting his watch came by.

'Hey . . .' Schenke called out.

Instinctively the man stopped and began to turn, and Schenke lashed out with his left fist, striking him on the bridge of the nose. The man stumbled back, his hat falling beside him, and Schenke thrust hard against his chest, forcing him off balance so that he fell onto his back, winded. Schenke stood a couple of paces away and held his Walther at waist height, pointing the muzzle at the man's chest.

'Who sent you to follow me?'

Now that the other man was helpless and hatless, Schenke

could see that he was young, little older than twenty, with cropped brown hair and brown eyes. Beneath his open coat he wore a cheap suit, and the grip of a cosh protruded from a jacket pocket.

'I don't know what you're talking about!' The man's outrage was unconvincing. 'Just taking a shortcut through this alley when you attacked me.'

'Sure you were.' Schenke plucked the cosh out and held it up. 'You always take this for a walk with you then?'

'Berlin's a dangerous city.' The man indicated the pistol. 'See what I mean.'

'Enough of the small talk. Who do you work for? Guttmann? Reitz?' There was a telltale flicker of the young man's eyes. 'You're new at this, aren't you? I wonder if that's why Reitz picked you. He wanted me to know I was being watched . . . All right, I'll use you to send a message back to him.' Schenke eased the safety on and returned the Walther to its holster as he kept his eyes on the man still lying on the ground. 'When you come round, I want you to go back to Reitz. You tell him that I don't take kindly to being tailed. You tell him that I will do what I have to for Guttmann, but that I don't appreciate being followed around by one of his errand boys. Got all that?'

The youth nodded, and Schenke held out his left hand. 'Up you get.'

As the youth sat up, Schenke swung the cosh against the side of his head, striking him hard enough to knock him cold. He sagged back onto the ground with a soft grunt of expelled breath.

'Nothing personal, kid. I just owed someone that.'

He pocketed the cosh and made his way to the end of the alley, then walked back along a parallel street to the way he had come in case Reitz's man was not alone. Ten minutes later, he was at the drop. Stepping off the street, he pretended to light a cigarette and dropped it before he could use his lighter. Letting out a curse, he ducked down, feeling a surge of relief when he saw the mark that indicated Ruth had received his message. The slip of paper had gone. So she must have read it and she should be waiting for him at the fallback meeting place.

He stood up, lit the cigarette and set off at a quick pace for fear she would not wait for him indefinitely. It would look suspicious to loiter, and an Orpo officer might ask her for her identity card. She had some fakes that she used from time to time, but close inspection risked them being seen for what they were. The bar was a good twenty minutes from the precinct. Given the time it took for the round trip and however long he spent with Ruth, it might raise eyebrows if he was away from the Kripo office for too long without a justifiable cause.

As he approached the bar, he stopped by the window of a jeweller's to repeat the precaution he had taken earlier. It was possible that Ruth had been followed, though there was no need for Guttmann to arrange for that now the jaws of the trap had closed on them. As satisfied as he could be that they were not being watched, Schenke entered the bar and made for the booths at the rear. They were divided by solid oak panels from floor to ceiling, with cushioned benches either side of heavily scored tables. The lunchtime crowd was starting to thin out, and a haze of cigarette smoke hung over those who remained.

Ruth was waiting for him in the last booth, beside a door leading to the bar's storeroom. A half-empty glass of beer sat before her, and she offered a slight smile as she saw him approaching, as any casual acquaintance or girlfriend might.

He slid in beside her so that he could look back along the bar towards the entrance.

'Thank God you got my message.'

'What's the urgency?' Ruth demanded. 'Why have I been sitting here on my own for the last two hours? I'd almost given up on you.'

Schenke held his hand up to get the attention of the waiter leaning against the bar and indicated two more beers.

'Well?' she insisted. 'I haven't got long. My shift starts at four and I have to get back across the city before then.'

'Give me a moment . . .' Schenke waited until the waiter had brought their beers, taken the money and strolled out of hearing. 'Did you make sure you weren't followed here?'

'Of course. What's happened?'

'We're in trouble, Ruth. Big trouble.'

As he explained what had happened, he could see the growing fear in her expression. When he had finished, he drank half his beer. 'I don't know how we're going to get out of this mess . . .'

She took a sip of her own drink and was silent a moment before she responded. 'There must be a way. This man Guttmann is a criminal, and you're the police. He's broken the law. He's broken so many laws. Arrest him. Blackmailing a criminal inspector is also breaking the law, isn't it?'

Schenke gave an ironic smile. 'So is a relationship between an Aryan and a Jew.'

She sighed. 'You call this a relationship? We have to communicate by a message drop and have to make sure we meet somewhere we can't be followed and where we won't be recognised. And even that has been enough to deliver us into the hands of a gangster threatening to betray us to the Nazis. I am a virtual prisoner in my own country. My family have had everything taken from them. There is no future for me, Horst. I am merely existing while I wait for the party to decide the ultimate fate of my people.'

'I haven't abandoned you,' he said, and took her hand. 'And I'm not going to.'

She half turned to look at him. 'Why not? You barely know me. A few months ago you'd have passed me on the street without a flicker of interest. You'd have read some Nazi headline in the papers about the Jews with hardly a shred of pity. Maybe you should have abandoned me. Then you wouldn't be in this mess now.'

He was stung by the coldness of her words. He wanted to offer her some hope. Some vision of a future beyond the grinding oppression of today. But there was only one thing that was in his power to give her.

'Ruth, I love you.'

She looked at him with an expression so weary and sad it nearly broke his heart. Then she touched his cheek. He pressed her hand against his jaw and kissed the palm before she withdrew it hurriedly.

'No. We cannot let ourselves be in love. It's foolish. Dangerous. Not while Hitler rules Germany. We have to be strong to survive. To deny ourselves these feelings.'

'Why? Why deny the last thing the party has not soiled?'

'Because it will get us killed,' she replied. 'Do you want to die, Horst?'

'Of course not.'

'Nor do I. And I won't die,' she added in a fierce undertone. 'I want to live. I want to survive. I want to be there to bear witness to the crimes of the Nazis and see them punished . . . and I want you to be there to see it with me. The only chance of that is if we do everything necessary to still be alive when the day comes. That means we cannot be distracted by our feelings for each other. You must see that.' Her voice was pleading.

He knew she was right. He knew that his heart would betray him if he let it. Yet he could not find it in himself to deny what he felt for her. The intensity of it was suddenly overwhelming, flaring up against the hopelessness closing in around them.

'Just tell me you share this feeling. That's all I need to know. To hold on to. Then I can face what you say we need to do.'

She squeezed his hand and her eyes gleamed. 'Of course I do.'

He felt as if he was relieved of a great burden. That there was something good to live for after all. 'Thank you.'

Both were silent before she turned the conversation back to Guttmann. 'What will you do, Horst? You can't let him become your master. Otherwise he will demand more and more from you until you are discovered, or betrayed. You have to do something. Do whatever it takes to destroy him. You understand me? Whatever it takes . . .'

'I already know that. I knew it from the moment he showed me the photographs. He has to be killed. Even if I have to do it with my bare hands.'

'Can you do that? I know you well enough to know what the law means to you. If you kill him, you will be stepping over the line, and there's no coming back from that.'

'What else can I do? If I don't kill him, and Reitz, they will destroy me. Destroy us. Not straight away. It will be like slow poison, Ruth. But as certain as a bullet to the head all the same.'

She took another sip of her beer, and Schenke did the same.

'How will you do it?' she asked. 'From what you've told me about Guttmann, he's keeping himself well guarded. How will you get to him, kill him and get away with it?'

Schenke had already begun to make his plans. 'I won't be able to do it alone. I'll need help. Someone who is also a victim of Guttmann and who has as much desire to see him dead as I do . . .'

Ruth glanced at her watch. 'I'd better be going if I'm going to make my shift. What happens now? Do we stay in touch?'

'Not until Guttmann has been dealt with. We'll need a new message drop to be safe.' Schenke searched his memory for a moment before he had the answer. The place where he had taken Ruth for safety when she was being hunted by a killer some months earlier.

'The Harsteins' house. There's a greenhouse at the rear of the garden. To one side there's a marble bench on the gravel. We can use a tobacco tin to put any messages in. I'll set it up in a few days' time. We can also meet there. The house has been closed up until the estate is settled. It's a little out of the way, but no one will suspect it.'

'All right.' She nodded. 'I'll look under the bench.'

'Don't go there for at least a week. Just do your shifts and go home. If I've dealt with Guttmann, I'll let you know. If there is no message from me when you go to look, then . . .' He shrugged. 'Then I've failed. If that's what has happened, we can only hope Guttmann is satisfied with my head. If not . . .'

'I understand. If I don't hear from you, I'll go underground. I know some Jews who have chosen that path.'

'It's dangerous.'

'What choice do I have? Guttmann does not sound like a man who tolerates loose ends.'

'True.' Schenke took her hands in his. 'I'll do my best to make sure you don't have to do that.'

'I know you will.' She glanced round the bar and saw that no one appeared to be watching them. She kissed him on the mouth, her lips lingering a moment before she drew back. 'Good luck, Horst. My love.'

He slid off the bench to let her out of the booth, and they stood facing each other for a moment before she turned and walked away, not looking back. The door into the street swung shut, and she disappeared from Schenke's view. It was tempting to go after her, to catch one last glimpse of her, but he forced himself to stay where he was while he focused his mind.

Yes, there was one person he could turn to for help in taking down Guttmann. Someone with as much to gain from the gangster's death as Schenke himself.

Chapter Twenty-Two

It was nearly two o'clock before Schenke returned to the Kripo office. Hauser was on his feet as soon as his superior came through the door, an anxious look on his face. Sitting at the next desk was a uniformed police officer in his forties. He was corpulent and looked dull-witted. He glanced at Schenke with an anxious expression as Hauser spoke up.

'Kunzler's gone.'

'What? What do you mean, gone?'

'She got away from the hospital. A hospital orderly came to take her for an X-ray, or at least that's what he told the Orpo man on duty.' He nodded towards the uniformed officer, who looked down shamefaced. 'Off they went, and the Orpo lad waited a full twenty minutes before it occurred to him to check that she really had been taken for an X-ray. Cue a frenzied search of the hospital, which yielded an abandoned orderly's jacket and cap. So nearly an hour passed between Kunzler leaving her room and our comrade here calling it in to the precinct. That was about twenty minutes after you left, sir. I didn't know where you'd gone, so I ordered him to come here to make his report to you.'

Schenke felt wretched with frustration. It had been vital for him to meet Ruth, but the price of that was the delay in getting back to the precinct, and now this latest twist. He approached the uniformed policeman, who rose to his feet, stood to attention and saluted.

'Did you get a good look at the orderly?'

The Orpo man was slow to reply, which confirmed Schenke's impression about his low intelligence. 'I saw him well enough, sir.'

'Well enough to describe?' Schenke prompted.

'Yes, sir. Like I told the sergeant. Average height and build. Thirty, maybe forty years old.'

'That's it? No beard, moustache, hair colour, distinguishing features? Think, man!'

'He was wearing a cap, sir. Couldn't see his hair. But he was clean-shaven. I noticed that.'

'Brilliant . . . What did he say when he came to Fräulein Kunzler's room?'

'Just that the doctor needed to X-ray her arm to check on how well it was healing.'

Schenke exchanged a look with Hauser, who rolled his eyes and mimed shooting himself in the head.

'Did he give a name?'

'No, sir.'

'Did he say anything else?'

'Only that he would bring her back to the room as soon as the X-ray was done . . . but that there might be a wait before her turn came,' he added quickly.

'Of course he said that.' Schenke felt like striking the fool and had to bite back on his anger before he continued. 'What about Kunzler? Did she appear to recognise the orderly?'

'I . . . I don't know, sir. I don't think so. I couldn't really say. He said that the heating was off in the wing of the hospital where the X-ray room was and he'd brought her a coat to wear. She put it on over her shoulders and they left.'

'I see. And you didn't think to find a nurse or doctor to confirm that Kunzler was being taken for an X-ray?'

'Well, no, sir. He was a hospital worker. He was wearing the overalls. I didn't see any reason to suspect him.'

'Of course not,' Hauser intervened. 'That's why you're a uniformed cop. Your orders were not to let her out of your sight and not to let her have visitors, right?'

The policeman gave a grudging nod. 'But he wasn't a visitor, sir. He looked like he worked at the hospital.'

'I've heard enough,' said Schenke. 'You're to go down to the canteen and wait there for the police artist, then give him as good a description as possible.'

'Yes, sir.'

'Go. Get out of my sight.'

The Orpo man saluted and hurried off, eager to remove himself from his superior's ire. Schenke looked round the office and pointed at Hoffer, one of the more experienced members of his section. 'Get to the hospital. See if you can find anyone else who may have seen the orderly, or anyone loitering around the place, and can give us a description.'

Hoffer nodded and went to get his coat and hat before leaving the office. Once the door had closed behind him, Schenke perched on the edge of the desk where the Orpo man had been sitting. Liebwitz joined them as Schenke thought through the significance of Kunzler's disappearance.

'She wasn't abducted. She went willingly.'

'Maybe she thought she actually was going for an X-ray,' Liebwitz suggested. 'For argument's sake.'

'No chance. She knew the man and she knew he wasn't a danger to her. Otherwise she would have asked for proof he was what he claimed to be. We'd warned her that she might be targeted as a witness to the killing of Remer. She'd have been suspicious, even if that Orpo dimwit wasn't. She knew who the orderly was and she must have known that he was there to get her away from us. She was in on it.'

'How would she have known about it in advance?' Hauser asked. 'We kept visitors away from her.'

Schenke thought a moment and shook his head in disgust at himself. 'The flowers. There was an envelope with them.'

'But why would she go on the run?' asked Hauser. 'Was she afraid that whoever shot Remer would come for her in the hospital? Does she think she'd be safer hiding out somewhere else, maybe?'

'I don't like the look of this. She may feel safer in hiding. I'm more concerned about what she's hiding from *us*. It was odd that she survived the shooting. If the killer was a professional, sent to take out Remer, he'd have made sure no witnesses survived the attack. She should be dead.'

'She *was* shot, sir,' said Hauser. 'The gunman might have thought she was done for. There was a lot of blood.'

'He made sure of Remer. Two to the chest and one to the head. So why not do the same to her? That doesn't look like the work of a pro. Someone like Reitz wouldn't have left her alive.'

'If it wasn't Reitz, then who carried out the shooting?' asked Liebwitz. 'We've been assuming Guttmann was behind it. What if he had nothing to do with it? Who are we looking for in that case?'

'It's beginning to look like Kitty Kunzler might not be quite the innocent victim she makes herself appear to be. Not abducted. Absconded.' Schenke nodded slowly. Even though he had pieced together the truth behind the forgeries and the lethal rivalry between the crime rings of Remer and Guttmann, the precise circumstances of the shooting and how it related to the struggle to control the supply of the coupons had eluded him until now. But as he went over the details once again, he began to see it all more clearly.

'Shit . . . We've been had, right from the start. The shooting didn't have anything to do with the forgeries. Nothing to do with Guttmann.'

Hauser frowned. 'How do you figure that out, sir?'

At once Schenke was alert to the danger of revealing anything about the previous night's encounter at Guttmann's house. He had to present what he knew in a way that didn't provoke any dangerous questions from his two closest subordinates.

'The key question, as Liebwitz has pointed out, is who carried out the shooting. I felt there wasn't something quite right about it from the outset. If one of Guttmann's men had done the job, he wouldn't have gone to the trouble of an ambush in a back alley. More likely it would have been a quick shot to the back of the head as Remer stepped out of the club late at night.'

'In front of witnesses?' Hauser said doubtfully. 'Better to do it out of sight. Like the alley.'

'But there *was* a witness. Kitty. And think about the extra effort involved in getting a replacement driver and employing a second man in Orpo uniform to direct the car into the alley. Why go to so much trouble unless it was necessary to lull Remer into lowering his guard? It's possible his killers

307

were afraid of him. Maybe they were amateurs who wanted it to look like the work of someone else. What if Kunzler was in on it? If she had pulled a gun on him, Remer might have disarmed her. Even if he had been killed in the street or at his apartment, she would have been in danger of being seen as a suspect by us. But presenting herself as a victim, she'd turn our attention away from her.'

'Are you seriously suggesting that she planned to get shot?' asked Hauser. 'That's a stretch.'

Liebwitz nodded. 'I agree with the sergeant, sir. It seems unlikely.'

Hauser gave the Scharführer a look. 'Well thank you.'

'Which suggests another possibility,' Liebwitz continued. 'She was in on the plot and was shot accidentally. Perhaps they panicked as a result and left her for dead. But that still doesn't explain the elaborate nature of the ambush.'

'No, it doesn't. We're missing something. Let me think . . . So Kunzler and two men arrange to get Remer into the alley to kill him, then what? The three of them were supposed to run from the scene, leaving Remer's body to be discovered. What do they hope to gain from that?'

'A fat pay-off from Guttmann for bumping off his rival,' Hauser suggested. 'That's what.'

'Except Guttmann denied it when we went to see him.'

'Well, he would.'

'I'm not so sure. He's the type who would like you to know without doubt that he was behind it but leave you without any evidence to prove it.'

'Maybe.' Hauser shrugged. 'But if Guttmann wasn't behind it, then what would Kunzler and her friends have to gain from killing Remer? If I was in her shoes, I'd need a pretty damn good reason to murder him. I don't think that being dumped by him would be enough for her to want him dead.'

'But we know that she was suspected of having a lover,' said Liebwitz. 'It is possible that they were afraid of Remer and planned to escape from him and leave Berlin.'

'They could do that easily enough without having to kill him,' Hauser replied.

'Wait a moment.' Schenke tapped his fingers agitatedly on the desk. 'Wohler said that Remer had let her get under his skin, that he had fallen for her. I doubt a man like that would be willing to see his lover walk off with another man. He'd be jealous. He'd also be very unhappy about being made to look a fool. Reputation is everything in the criminal underworld. I doubt he'd just shake hands with Kunzler and wish her well with her new partner. We know what he did to Feldwitz when he thought he'd stepped over the line.'

'Fair enough,' Hauser conceded. 'But Kitty's been used to the high life. I don't see her as the happy lover on the run, poor as a church mouse but rich in affection. She didn't strike me as that kind. Which brings me back to Guttmann. Now, if he had paid them to do in Remer, then just maybe they would take the proceeds and run.'

'Or they took Remer's money,' Schenke responded. He turned to Liebwitz. 'You remember when we found Wohler in Remer's office at the club. It looked to me like he was turning the place over. He could have been searching for something. Like a bundle of cash. And what was it Breker said? Something about reckoning up the takings against the cash in the office upstairs.'

'That's right, sir.'

'I would imagine the monthly takings of the club would

amount to a tidy sum. Enough to set up Kunzler and her new man in another city. Enough to kill Remer for. So, they plan the shooting for the night Remer takes the money back to the safe at his apartment. They kill him, split the cash with the other man and disappear. Only something goes wrong. Kunzler is wounded. They can't take her to the hospital without having someone recall their faces, even if they aren't asked any questions at the time. There's blood everywhere, she looks like she's dead or dying. So they grab the money and run. Only she doesn't die. She's taken to the hospital and is patched up and starts to recover. All very embarrassing for her partners in crime. Particularly her lover, who now has to find a way to get her out of hospital, where she is under guard, so that they can make good with the original plan and get out of Berlin . . .

'Hauser, you'd better contact the railway stations. Give the transport police a description of her. She may still have her arm in a sling. If they find her, she is to be arrested, together with any companions. If it's too late and they've already caught a train, the police are to question the station staff and see if anyone recalls seeing her.'

'Yes, sir.' Hauser picked up his phone.

'It's a shame we can't pass on the man's description as well,' Schenke said in frustration. He glanced at Liebwitz, who was staring into space, his brow slightly creased in concentration.

'It's Bachmann, sir.' Liebwitz straightened up instantly.

'What?'

'She's leaving Berlin with Bachmann.'

'How do you know that?'

'The day I went to interview him in his apartment, I saw two suitcases in his bedroom before he shut the door. There was something else. A briefcase. He seemed nervous, though at the time I put it down to the usual anxiety I encounter when I visit someone's home to question them.'

Hauser looked up from the telephone as he waited to be connected to the police office at the first of the rail stations. 'Black hat, black leather coat and Gestapo badge. Can't imagine why anyone would be anxious finding you on the doorstep.'

Liebwitz tilted his head. 'Hmm. Interesting . . . Anyway, I would suggest that the suitcases and the briefcase strongly suggest that Bachmann is our man.'

'I think so.' Schenke smiled. 'Good job, Scharführer. With any luck, they haven't left Berlin yet. They might still be at his apartment. I'll get a pool car and bring it round to the front of the precinct. Give Bachmann's description to Hauser, then get down there and join me. They might not yet realise that we're on to them, and we'll catch them with the cash.' He punched his fist into his palm. 'I think we've got them.'

Kitty Kunzler tapped the end of her cigarette to dislodge the ash into a small tray and looked across to the window of the apartment, where Bachmann stood surveying the street.

'How much longer, Otto?' She exhaled as she spoke, sending a plume of smoke across the living room. 'Where the hell is he? I thought he was supposed to meet us here.'

Bachmann replied as patiently as he could manage. 'That's what he said. Try and relax.'

'Relax?' She gave a bitter laugh and gestured towards her injured arm resting in the sling. 'I'm in pain. The police are looking for me and they think I'm a suspect, thanks to the tale you spun that Gestapo officer.'

'I had to distract him when he came to the flat. I had to point him in another direction.'

'Oh, sure . . . Anyway, I dare say they'll be looking for you as well soon.'

'There's no reason for them to suspect me of being involved in getting you out of the hospital, let alone anything to do with the shooting.' He hesitated. 'Kitty, there's no point in getting yourself worked up. He'll be here. If for no other reason than he wants to collect his share of the money.'

She followed his glance to the briefcase leaning against one of the suitcases on the floor beside the piano. She took another drag on the cigarette, and the end flared, accompanied by a sibilant hiss. 'What if we don't wait for him, Otto? What if we just keep the money? We could call a taxi, go to Anhalter station.'

'He's not the kind of man you double-cross and hope to survive.'

'You're afraid of him.'

'Why wouldn't I be? He's been Guttmann's right-hand man long enough to know where to bury the bodies. Do you really think he wouldn't be able to find us if he was determined to? It might take him months, years maybe, but one day there'd be a tap on the shoulder, or a knock on the door, and that would be the end. Besides, the police may be watching the stations. That's why we have to wait for him to come for us with a car. He can get us out of Berlin. A day's drive and we'll be in Munich. I have friends there who can put us up until we find a place of our own.'

He turned back to the window and looked down. A shrill whistle sounded from further along the street, and a minute or two later the first figures emerged from the factory gate – men in stained overalls and caps coming off the day shift and heading home. Though he tried to appear calm to Kitty,

Bachmann was starting to get worried. Six hours had passed since he had brought her back from the hospital and helped her put on some clothes from her suitcase for the journey.

'Great. A day stuck in the back of a car.'

'I'll be there to hold your hand.' He smiled. 'You can depend on me.'

'Can I? Like when that bastard shot me and you grabbed the money and ran off?'

Bachmann sighed and closed his eyes briefly. 'I thought you were dead, my darling. Anyway, he didn't shoot you deliberately. It was Remer's fault. He went for the gun and threw himself in front of you. That's what our friend said happened. And you told me so yourself when we spoke about it earlier.'

Kitty ground the cigarette out and reached for the packet on the side table to light another. It was true, she conceded. At the end, Remer had died trying to protect her. She was still surprised at that. For sure he had come to express some grudging affection for her over the time they had been together, but she had never thought him capable of loving her enough to put his life on the line for her. She had misjudged him and felt guilty about that. He had been kind to her, but he was so cautious about displaying his true feelings that it had been impossible for her to really know how he felt. It was different with Otto. He did not hide his emotions, nor his need for her, and their secret encounters over the last six months had been exciting and passionate, making her feel more alive than she had ever felt with Remer. In the end, Remer had become little more than a source of luxuries for her. A comfortable life that she paid for with her body. And she had needed more.

She sighed softly. 'I'm sorry, Otto. I know it went wrong. It wasn't your fault. I would have done the same if our positions had been reversed.'

She said it to try and ease the tension between them, even though it wasn't true. She would never have left him wounded and bloody in the back of the car. But then she was made of tougher material. As women had to be to get on in this world. She continued smoking for several minutes before she spoke again.

'Things would have been different if Guttmann had taken us up on our offer.'

'I know. I felt sure he would jump at the chance when we put it to him. I guess there is some honour among thieves after all. Or he was playing some deeper game.'

'Over the forgeries, you mean?'

'Yes. I imagine so. Perhaps he intended to deal with Remer at some point, but we just couldn't wait that long. We had to do it before Remer learned about us.'

She nodded. 'He was getting suspicious. So was Wohler. It was only a matter of time.'

Bachmann caught the sound of an engine. A moment later, a car came along the street, slowing down as it approached his apartment block. It stopped outside the entrance.

'He's here.'

The driver's door opened and a figure climbed out, crossed the pavement and disappeared from sight. 'He's on his way up.'

Kitty's hand trembled before she managed to regain control of it. 'Why do you think he's doing this? Why did he go along with us when Guttmann showed no interest?'

Bachmann turned his back on the window. 'Maybe he thought his boss was making a mistake and it would be better for Guttmann if Remer was out of the way. Maybe he just wanted a share of the money. Doesn't really matter any more. The deed is done. All that matters is that we're together and we're getting as far from Berlin as we can with enough cash to start a new life.'

She smiled at him. 'Yes. That's all that matters.'

The doorbell rang, causing both of them to start, and they exchanged a nervous smile. Their stealthy visitor had managed to reach the apartment without giving himself away on the stairs or the boards of the landing outside.

Bachmann hurried out of the living room and down the short corridor. Kitty heard the chain rattling and then the clatter of the lock before the door opened.

'We were getting worried about you,' Bachmann said.

'Are you ready to go?'

'All packed. One case each.'

She heard the sound of the door closing.

'And the money?'

'It's all there. In the briefcase.'

'Good.'

'Where's Kitty?'

'Waiting in the living room. She's been wondering where you'd got to.'

'I couldn't get away any earlier. Guttmann had us looking for someone. Anyway, that job's done and I'm free to get you out of Berlin.'

Footsteps approached along the corridor and Bachmann entered the room and grinned at her. 'See? I told you there was nothing to worry about.'

But Kitty did not return his smile. She stared past him to the man standing on the threshold. Her cigarette hand slowly dipped towards the side table as her eyes widened.

'Kitty?' Bachmann stepped towards her with a look of concern. 'What is it?'

Her gaze did not shift.

'I'm sorry it has to be this way,' their visitor said as there was a metallic click. When Bachmann turned round, he saw the silenced muzzle of an automatic pistol lined up on his forehead. 'I want the money. All of it. Hand it over.'

Chapter Twenty-Three

Schenke tapped the steering wheel impatiently as they waited to turn into the street where Bachmann lived in bohemian squalor amid the city's workers. It was late in the afternoon and shadows stretched across the façades of the shops and grimy apartment buildings. The pavements were filled with people heading home from work and housewives shopping for groceries and hunting down the more elusive of the items covered by the rationing regulations. There were carts and horses on the road, amid the cyclists, commercial vehicles and the handful of private cars exempted from the regime's order to commandeer them for military use. The Orpo man directing the traffic was holding up his hand as he waved forward the vehicles emerging from the street.

'Come on . . . come on,' Schenke muttered before glancing at Liebwitz, who was sitting bolt upright in the passenger seat, staring ahead as if in a trance.

'That was good work back at the precinct, Scharführer. The business about the suitcases.'

'I wish I had understood the significance of their baggage

earlier, sir. As well as the briefcase. That might be the same one that Remer took from the club with the takings. Although that is only conjecture. I should have considered it before.'

'Being knocked out a bit later might have caused the detail to slip your mind,' Schenke observed wryly.

'I don't consider that to be an acceptable excuse, sir.'

'Even so, good work.'

'Yes, sir.'

The last of the traffic – a cream-coloured car – cut across the junction, and the policeman raised his hand to halt the flow, then beckoned to Schenke. As he began his turn into the street, his memory was stirred.

'Did you see?' he asked Liebwitz.

'Yes, sir. The car from the printworks. The Opel. Or one identical to it. The one we were told was driven by Neger.'

Schenke considered and then quickly dismissed the idea of going after it. They had a more important task to carry out than following Reitz in the hope that he might furnish them with useful intelligence. It was vital that they check Bachmann's apartment in case he and Kunzler were there. All the same, the sight of the car in this neighbourhood was an unsettling coincidence.

'Did you see the number plate?'

'No, sir. But it was the same model. I am sure of it.'

'Too bad we can't do anything about it now,' Schenke decided. 'Which building is it?'

Liebwitz raised a gloved hand and pointed. 'The block immediately beyond the next junction, sir.'

Schenke turned off at the junction and parked at the kerb so that they would not be seen if Bachmann was watching the street. 'You've been here before; what is the layout?'

Liebwitz briefly described the entrances, the central yard and the location of the stairs.

'I'll go in the front and check with the block warden if Bachmann is in. You take the rear. He and Kunzler may have slipped in and out that way. If you come across anyone, find out if they've seen anything.'

'Yes, sir.'

'Let's go.'

They climbed out of the Adler and separated. Schenke turned the corner and paced along the front of the apartment block, passing a long queue outside a butcher's shop with hardly any meat on display in the window. He came to the entrance, where an old man in overalls was leaning against the side of the door, filling a pipe.

Schenke stopped in front of him and offered his lighter.

The man sucked on the stem until the contents of the bowl glowed, then returned the lighter with a nod of thanks.

'You live here?' Schenke indicated the door.

'Yes.'

'Then you know Herr Bachmann. Have you seen him enter or leave the building today?'

'Depends who wants to know.' The old man's eyes narrowed. 'Who are you?'

'Police.'

'Well, nobody's perfect, son. Last time I saw him was when he left first thing this morning.'

'Has he returned?'

The old man shrugged. 'If so, I didn't see him.'

Schenke was about to enter the doorway when he paused. 'Did you see another man go in or out of the block just now? A big man. Tall, broad. Around forty years old?'

'No.'

He tapped the brim of his hat and stepped into the narrow hallway of the block. The familiar stale smell of such places filled the air as he made for the stairs and climbed as quietly as he could to Bachmann's floor. As he reached the landing, he saw Liebwitz waiting at the door leading to the walkway that ran around the interior of the well in the centre of the block. Schenke took a couple of deep breaths before drawing his Walther and slipping off the safety catch. He raised it to show Liebwitz, and the Scharführer nodded and drew his own weapon. Schenke beckoned, and they approached the door of the apartment, taking up positions either side of the door. He reached up with his left hand and rapped twice.

They stood still, ears straining, but the only noises were the muffled sounds from the street and a bitter row between two women on the floor above.

Schenke pounded the door. 'Open up! Police!'

When there was still no response, he nodded to Liebwitz, who moved in front of the door, raised his foot and lashed out at the keyhole above the handle. There was a splintering crack, and a second kick sent the door flying inwards. Liebwitz ducked to one side as Schenke called out again.

'Bachmann!'

There was still no reply, no sound, and Schenke felt a surge of disappointment. It seemed they had left it too late and Bachmann and Kitty had already escaped. He raised his pistol and gestured to Liebwitz to follow him inside. The kitchen and bathroom were empty, and the door to the bedroom was ajar. Ahead lay the living room, and he could see a piano. Beside it stood two suitcases. It seemed they had not yet fled the city.

The two men entered the living room and lowered their pistols.

Bachmann was lying sprawled on his back in front of the wood burner. A bullet wound glistened on his forehead. Blood pooled underneath his head, soaking into the rug. Kitty Kunzler was behind him, slumped on an armchair, head thrown back, eyes open and jaw slack. She had been shot twice in the chest and was splattered with blood and brains from Bachmann's exit wound. The acrid smell of cordite was still hanging in the air, and it was clear that they had been shot not long before.

Schenke replaced his Walther in its holster. 'Liebwitz, keep watch on the landing. The shooter might be close by.'

'If it was Reitz, sir, then he was driving away from the scene.'

'*If* it was Reitz. Let's not take the risk, eh?'

Liebwitz left the apartment and Schenke looked at the two bodies. 'You poor fools. Double-crossed. That's what happens when you get out of your depth.'

He shifted his gaze to the cases and then swept the room looking for the briefcase that Liebwitz had described, but it was not there. Putting on his gloves, he searched the bedroom, kitchen and bathroom before returning to the living room and going over it again, looking in every cupboard and under the furniture, and even shifting the woman's body just enough to check if it was behind her. Opening the suitcases, he went through the contents but found no money. If it had been in the briefcase, the killer had taken it away.

Bachmann had obviously been paid a decent wage, enough to afford the telephone on a table in the hall. Schenke dialled the number of the precinct and asked to be put through to the Kripo office.

A woman's voice answered. 'Criminal Investigation Section . . .'

'Rosa, is Hauser there?'

'Yes, sir.'

'Get him on the line.'

Hauser's gruff voice sounded in Schenke's ear. 'Did you find them, sir?'

'We were too late.'

'They'd already gone?'

'No. Someone got to them before us. They're dead. The killer probably used a suppressor, since there was no sign any of the neighbours reacted to the sound of shots.'

'Shit . . .'

'The money's gone too. Looks like their accomplice took it after shooting them.'

'Anyone in the block see the killer?'

'I think he must have come and gone using the rear entrance. But we might have seen the cream-coloured car from the printworks driving away just before we reached the building.'

There was a moment's silence before Hauser said, 'Neger's car . . . Or, given what we know now, Reitz's.'

'I think so.' Schenke took stock before he issued his instructions. 'I want you to report this to Orpo. Get a squad up here as soon as you can, with two of our lot to take pictures and go over the scene. We'll remain here until they arrive.'

'Yes, sir. There's something else you need to know. After you left, we had a call from Darré's aide. The Reichsminister wants to know why Stoffler didn't deliver his report. The aide hasn't been able to locate him and Darré's hopping mad.'

'What did you tell him?'

'I said the last time we saw him was last night at the precinct,

322

which is true enough. Should hold them off until tomorrow. After that, we're going to have a hard time keeping his presence in the cells a secret.'

'All right. We'll speak more when we get back.'

'Yes, sir.'

'And Hauser . . .' Here was a chance to put right something that had been weighing on his conscience.

'Sir?'

'I apologise for the way I spoke to you earlier.'

'I see.' Hauser sighed. 'Very well, sir. Let's just get on with the job.'

The line went dead and Schenke replaced the handset. He took a last look at the bodies, then left the apartment and closed the door to wait for the Orpo squad and his investigators to arrive.

As night closed in over Berlin, Schenke sat in his cubicle with Liebwitz and Hauser to consider where the two latest murders left the investigation.

'I don't get it,' said Hauser. 'If Guttmann wasn't responsible for the ambush that killed Remer, then what's the connection between Reitz and Bachmann and Kunzler? He'd hardly dare to go behind his boss's back with a side project like that.' He paused before he addressed his superior directly. 'Maybe we have to rethink what you said earlier, sir. Maybe Guttmann *was* behind it all along, whatever he pretends.'

'It's possible,' Schenke conceded, even as he recalled Guttmann's denial of any involvement. If Remer's shooting had not been ordered by his rival, then he agreed with his sergeant. It would have been very dangerous for Reitz to carry out the killing independently and then take the further risk of killing his accomplices. He knew his master well enough to understand the danger if his deeds were ever discovered.

He was suddenly aware that his subordinates were watching him, waiting for further comment.

'All right, let's go with the idea that Guttmann is behind it all. The forgeries, the murders of Remer, Feldwitz, Bachmann and Kunzler, and the attack on the club. The problem is that we haven't got nearly enough evidence to arrest him, let alone hope to convict him. That lawyer of his will be straight on to his party friends to point that out. The best we can do is mount a surveillance on the printworks and catch Reitz and the others in the act of printing extra coupons to sell on the black market.'

'That'll do for a start,' said Hauser. 'At least we'll have closed that case and put a stop to the racket. It'll please Darré. Which brings us to the question of what we do with Stoffler.'

'Darré's not going to be the only one wondering what's happened to Stoffler,' Liebwitz pointed out. 'Guttmann's going to be asking questions if he isn't seen at the printworks in the next day or so.'

'Then we're going to have to set a watch on the works as soon as possible,' Schenke decided. 'Before they suspect we're on to them and stop operating during the night.'

'You could speak to Radinsky, sir,' Hauser suggested. 'Tell him we need a couple of sections from Orpo to watch the printworks and move in the moment the machines go into action.' He turned to look at the clock on the office wall. 'Ah, shit. He's probably left the precinct already. You could put the request to the duty officer.'

'Waste of time,' Schenke replied. 'He'll only push it up the chain of command and wait for Radinsky to come in tomorrow morning. I can do that myself. First thing. So it'll have to be tomorrow night. Let's hope Guttmann's greed gets the better of his caution and he continues to keep the printing going. If so, we can close that part of his crime empire down. I'll take that win for now. And we'll keep on with the murder investigations.'

'We'll be lucky if anything comes of that. You know how those gangs like to stick by their code of silence.'

'There's always a weak link,' Schenke said. 'Someone will talk eventually.'

'Not if Guttmann clears up his tracks as well as he has done so far.'

Schenke yawned. 'We've done what we can for the day. Better get home and rested. We're going to be busy tomorrow.'

Hauser and Liebwitz got up and left the cubicle. The rest of the section had already gone; only Persinger was left, waiting to relieve Baumer in the cells at eight o'clock. The sergeant and the Scharführer collected their coats and hats and nodded a farewell before they left the office. Schenke was relieved to see them go. He was finding the strain of carrying out his duties while enduring the burden of Guttmann's blackmail intolerable. He still intended to destroy Guttmann and was thinking through that when his telephone rang.

He picked up the receiver. 'Criminal Inspector Schenke.'

'Call for you, sir,' the switchboard operator said crisply. 'From Herr Stebling, Reich Ministry of Food and Agriculture.'

Schenke groaned inwardly. It was likely to be the same aide who had called earlier on behalf of Darré. He braced himself for a tirade. 'Put him through.'

'Yes, sir.'

The line clicked a couple of times and then another voice spoke. 'Is that Schenke?'

'Criminal Inspector Schenke, yes. How can I help you, Herr Stebling?'

'You can help by listening to me very carefully. I am sure you recognise my voice. I don't want you to mention my name. Do you understand? Just say yes.'

Schenke knew the hard-edged tone of the caller well enough and felt a cold tremor ripple down his spine. 'Yes.'

'Good. Listen closely and don't interrupt. I was not best pleased that you gave my new boy a beating when you caught him following you earlier. That was nothing compared to the beating he got for being spotted. It ain't going to happen again. The boss won't allow it. He's worried that you may be having second thoughts about holding up your end of the deal. So me and the lads have been out today hunting down a friend of yours. We found her easily enough, and she's a guest of the boss for the present. To make sure you behave and do as you're told.'

Schenke's heart gave a lurch. 'Ruth?'

'That's the one. Good-looking girl, for a Jew. She's being looked after. But if you try and lose any more tails or give the boss any trouble, she's not going to be looked after. You get me?'

'Yes,' Schenke said softly.

'What was that?'

'I said yes, damn you.' Schenke clung to the hope that Reitz was bluffing. 'How do I know you're telling the truth?'

'That's easy enough to prove . . . Come here, Jew. Your man wants to say hello to you.'

Schenke's grip on the handset tensed as he heard a faint commotion, and then Ruth's voice.

'Horst, I'm sorry . . . So sorry.'

'Ruth, tell me they haven't hurt you.'

'No. I'm all right, but I'm scared and—'

She was interrupted by another voice in the background. Soft and sibilant.

'That's enough, take her away,' Guttmann ordered.

'Ruth!' Schenke called out, then glanced at Persinger, but he was folding his newspaper and appeared not to have noticed his superior's anxiety.

Reitz came back on the line. 'She's safe as long as you do as you're told. We'll take good care of her.'

'I saw how you took good care of Bachmann and Kunzler, you bastard! If you harm Ruth Frankel, I swear to God I will not rest until you and Guttmann are dead.'

There was a pause before Reitz responded in a puzzled tone. 'Don't try to play games with me, Inspector. You'll never win. You know what the stakes are. No one will get hurt as long as you play your part. But if you mess us around, your pretty little Jew will be sent back to you one piece at a time until you behave.'

The line went dead, but Schenke hung on to the receiver just in case. 'Hello? Are you there?'

His hand was trembling as he lowered the receiver onto its cradle, and he tried to calm his racing mind. They had Ruth. And with that they would have complete control over him. There was no time left to him. He would have to act now if there was any hope of saving Ruth and ensuring Guttmann's destruction. Pulling himself together, he braced himself for the encounter. He would need to be persuasive, and he would need to put his life in the hands of someone he would never have trusted in other circumstances. He looked up at the clock. He had an hour to put his plan into effect. Rising from his desk, he put on his coat and hat and called out to Persinger.

'I'm off. Don't forget to relieve Baumer at eight.'

'Yes, sir.'

Schenke left the office and descended to the ground floor. Instead of making for the exit, he turned towards the steps leading down to the cells.

Chapter Twenty-Four

Baumer lowered his newspaper and stood as Schenke approached along the corridor. He looked tired and bored.

'Anything to report?' asked Schenke.

'Sauckel's out for the count and the other one has been quiet all day.'

'All right.' Schenke glanced at his watch. 'You can go now. I'll take over until Persinger turns up.'

Baumer looked pleasantly surprised. 'Are you sure, sir?'

'You've got a wife waiting for you. I haven't. Just don't let any rumours get started about me being a soft touch. Not a word, eh? Run along.'

Baumer mimed buttoning his lips before he tucked the newspaper under his arm and strode off whistling lightly. Schenke waited until he was out of sight before he approached Wohler's door and switched on the light in the cell, then slid the grille back. He saw the occupant prop himself up on his bed, squinting and shielding his eyes from the bright light that flooded the small space.

'What the hell?'

Schenke drew back the bolts and opened the door before stepping warily across the threshold.

'Oh, it's you,' Wohler grumbled as he swung his feet onto the floor and sat on the edge of the thin mattress. 'What do you want this time?'

'It's time for some plain talk,' Schenke began. 'Just between you and me. Off the record.'

Wohler shook his head. 'The only thing I have to say is fuck you and fuck that fat pig Guttmann.'

Schenke smiled. 'How would you like to say that to his face? Before you kill him? Guttmann, his sidekick Reitz and any of his dogs who get in your way.'

Wohler's eyes widened in surprise for a moment before narrowing suspiciously. 'What exactly are you talking about, Inspector?'

'A few days ago you were shouting the place down, screaming that you were going to put a bullet in Guttmann's head. What I want to know is if you actually meant it. Do you still mean it? Or have you had time to go soft while you've been left in this cell?'

'I ain't gone soft. The moment you cut me loose, that bastard's days are numbered. Fuck that. His *hours* are numbered.'

'You're going to find that something of a challenge. Have you ever been to his villa?'

Wohler shook his head.

'It's surrounded by a high wall. He has men on the gate and patrolling the grounds. At least ten of them, from what I saw. Then there's Reitz and a number of staff inside the house. You don't know the layout of the place. Like I said, it's going to be a challenge.'

'I've still got Remer's lads. I can round up enough of them

for the job. They're keen to get revenge for the hit on our boss. And we've got the hardware to do it.' He stared intently at Schenke. 'What are we discussing here?'

'A few hours ago, Reitz hit Kitty Kunzler and Otto Bachmann in the latter's apartment. With Remer and the others he's killed, it looks to me like Guttmann's cleaning up. Anyone who might stand in the way of his coupon racket is being dealt with. You've already had a lucky escape when he sent that team to the club, but he won't rest until you've joined Remer and the others. Unfortunately, from a policing point of view, Guttmann is wiping out my witnesses. I can't move against him without sufficient evidence. I don't like crime rings, or those who run them. I think they're predatory scum who should be flushed away. But as long as they don't go round shooting people and burning down nightclubs, the Reich Main Security Office is prepared to tolerate most of their activities. Guttmann has crossed the line by some way and needs to be put down.'

'And you want me and my boys to do the dirty work for you?'

'You seemed keen enough the other day.'

'Oh, I'm still keen. There will be blood, Inspector. Lots of it.'

Schenke met Wohler's gaze steadily and then nodded. 'Good. There isn't much time, so I'll come to the point. I'll get you out of here as soon as you've agreed to my conditions.'

'Conditions? What makes you think I'll agree to anything?'

'Because you'll stay in here and rot otherwise,' Schenke said. 'Until I can find a charge that will stick on you and see you sent off to the camps. Now listen. In a few minutes, I'm going to escort you out of the rear entrance of the precinct. You're going to round up your men and your weapons, and at ten tonight you are going to pick me up outside the Kreisler Theatre in Pankow. Outside the stage door at the back. I'll direct you to Guttmann's villa. I know something of the layout of the place and I'll go in with you when you attack. Once he's dead, we go our separate ways and I wipe your slate clean.'

Wohler was silent, and then he laughed. 'You're mad. Why the hell would you want to get mixed up in such a crazy scheme?'

'I told you. As things stand, Guttmann is going to get away with a number of murders. I can't allow that. And there's another reason.'

'Oh? What would that be?'

'He's holding someone at his villa. Someone who means a great deal to me. He's using her to blackmail me. When we go in, I'll find her and make sure she gets out safely.'

Wohler shook his head. 'Sweet Jesus. You're risking everything for a skirt? You're like Remer. Going soft on a woman was always going to destroy him in the end, and it'll do the same to you. Fucking knights in shining armour . . . What if it all goes wrong? My lads are good, but what if we lose the fight?'

'Then we lose. But at least we did our best to destroy Guttmann.'

'And if we win? You just carry on being a cop and pretend you play by the rules?'

'Something like that. Not so long ago I'd never have dreamed of doing anything like this. My faith in due process has taken more than a few knocks given the way things have turned out under the party. If I can't do what's right within the law, then there comes a time when the needs of justice have to take precedence.'

'I've met a few cops in my time who were willing to bend

the rules, but you take the biscuit, you really do. Leading the charge in a gang war. Now I've seen it all.'

'Believe me, I'd rather there was another way, but there isn't. Not for me.'

'What makes you think I wouldn't use it against you in the future?'

'I guess we'll have to trust one another. I wipe the slate clean for you and in exchange you keep your mouth shut about my involvement. We'll have the dirt on each other and that will be our guarantee of mutual silence after this is over. That's the deal. Now, do you want to take revenge on Guttmann for killing your boss and crippling your crime ring, or do you want to spend the rest of the war rotting away in this cell?'

Wohler ran a hand through his dishevelled hair and sighed. 'Well, shit, this'll be a tale to tell the grandchildren.'

'Only if you're raising them to go into a life of crime.'

He shot Schenke a dark look, and the two of them locked eyes before Wohler laughed and Schenke joined in.

'Life forces some strange alliances on us,' Wohler mused as his mirth subsided. 'Just like that business between Hitler and Stalin.'

'I doubt it will last.'

'It won't. Trust me, they're both gangsters. I know how it will play out.'

Schenke checked his watch again. 'Do we have a deal, then?'

Wohler extended his hand. 'We go to war.'

The handshake was quick and firm, and then Wohler gathered his coat and tie and they stepped out of the cell. Schenke closed the door quietly in order not to risk waking Stoffler, who might raise a fuss. He led Wohler upstairs and to the rear of the building, where a door gave out onto the yard. There were still a few men working in the storerooms and garages on the far side, but the blackout precautions ensured that it was dark enough to conceal the pair as they made their way to the gate giving out onto the street. As they approached the man on guard duty, Schenke called out his name and rank and the man saluted as they walked by.

A short distance down the street, he halted.

'The back of the Kreisler Theatre at ten.'

'We'll be there. Make sure you come alone, Inspector.'

'Still don't trust me?'

'Why should I? You're Kripo.'

Wohler turned away and was swallowed up by the darkness. Retracing his steps, Schenke entered the main door and went to the desk. Luck was with him. The duty sergeant was at the far end of the counter talking to a crony. He exchanged a nod with Schenke. Opening the log book, Schenke leafed back a few pages until he found the entry for Wohler being taken in for protective custody and made a fresh note in the empty space next to it. *Prisoner discharged on authority prepared by legal representative Kolbenhoff and signed off by Reich Main Security Office. 7.30 p.m. 9 May 1940.* If the night went the way he hoped, Guttmann's lawyer would soon be dead or on the run and in no position to gainsay the log. If it went the other way, Schenke would be past caring.

He turned the page to the current entries and left the precinct with his mind a raging conflict of fear, desperation and determination. Guttmann must be destroyed, along with the photos and any other evidence he had gathered for the purposes of blackmail. But most important of all, Schenke must find and rescue Ruth. If the night ended in failure, she would surely die along with him, Wohler and the others. If that was to be his end, he regretted that there would be no chance to say farewell to Hauser, Liebwitz and the rest of his team. They deserved better. And if by some miracle the attack succeeded, he would never be able to breathe a word to his comrades of the part he had played. Both prospects weighed heavily on his conscience. But as he had seen so often since the Nazis had seized power, a good conscience was a luxury, and a dangerous one. It seemed to him now that all that mattered was to survive and protect those closest to him as best he could, and silently pray for deliverance from the Führer and his followers.

The Kreisler Theatre had once been a favourite haunt of leftist playwrights and companies of actors and had been closed down within a year of the Nazis taking power. Since then, most of the windows had been broken by the party's stormtroopers and the Hitler Youth, and the entrances boarded up. The faded shreds of posters remained either side of the stage door at the rear where Schenke was waiting. There were few people abroad in the area, notorious for its petty crime. He had been propositioned by a woman shortly after he had reached the meeting place, but she had scurried off when he identified himself, and he had the narrow alley to himself while he waited for Wohler and his men to arrive.

After leaving the precinct, he had returned to his flat and changed into the plain dark clothes he used for night observations. He had put on a thick black jacket over his shoulder holster, replaced his shoes with a sturdy pair of walking boots and pocketed a torch and four spare magazines for his pistol. Finally he had pulled on a dark woollen cap. Although he felt no hunger or thirst, he made himself a quick meal of dark bread and cured sausage and a mug of ersatz coffee. It was better to go into action with a full stomach.

Leaving his apartment at nine, he had hurried through the dark streets until he reached the theatre some twenty minutes before ten. The sky was clear and, thanks to the blackout, the stars shone brightly high above. It was cold, and he was grateful for the jacket and cap. And yet he still trembled, though not because of the cold. The imminence of danger had often had that effect on him, from the time he had taken up motor racing many years before. It passed the instant he had to focus on the task, but he still felt a small degree of shame over it and so rubbed his gloved hands together vigorously in an effort to dispel his nerves.

Ten o'clock came and passed and he examined the luminous marks on his watch and saw that Wohler was fifteen minutes late. The possibility that Remer's lieutenant had no intention of honouring the deal was a calculated risk, and Schenke desperately hoped that he had accurately gauged the man's hatred of Guttmann and his thirst for revenge. If not, he had resolved to try and infiltrate Guttmann's villa by himself to find and free Ruth, whatever the odds against him. There was no option to abandon the task and accept servitude to the crime boss. That prospect was something he would not live with.

He was about to check his watch again when he heard the rumble of an approaching vehicle and saw the thin beams of masked headlights judder across the alley before a covered lorry turned the corner and drew up beside the stage door. He approached the driver's side as the window wound down and the dim dashboard lights illuminated the features of the man at the wheel. Schenke hesitated and shifted his right hand towards the opening he had left between the buttons of the jacket.

'Where's Wohler?'

'Waiting for you in the back, with the others. He said you'd tell me where we're going.'

'Berbuerstrasse in Mitte. You know it?'

'Yes . . . Get in.'

Schenke could hear movement inside the vehicle and some muttering, and he eased his fingers around the butt of his Walther. The rear canvas cover was thrown back and he saw that the interior of the truck was lit by a torch. There were four men in there besides Wohler, who beckoned to him. Schenke climbed in and sat on the wooden bench opposite as Wohler let the canvas flap drop back into place.

'You're late,' said Schenke.

'Had to wait until one of my boys turned up and fitted this.' Wohler patted the canvas. 'Nicked it from one of the fire warden trucks a few months back. Gives us the cover we need to move about the city at night. Especially if the air raid sirens go off.' He turned to one of the men behind the cab. 'All right. Give Dieter a rap.'

The man knocked on the rear of the cab and the vehicle lurched into motion. The torch, which was fixed to the metal frame that held up the cover, revealed that the other men were dressed much like Schenke. 'Time for some introductions,' said Wohler. 'Lads, this is the Kripo inspector I told you about.'

They looked at Schenke without expression. All but one of them were hard-faced men in their late thirties or early forties. The exception was a youth who looked to be barely in his twenties but was tall and heavily built. Wohler pointed to them in turn.

'No surnames for you to remember if we get out alive. So,

this one's Karl, then Mathias, Willi, and the lad is Willi's boy Walter.'

'Keeping criminality in the family then,' Schenke commented. 'Nice.'

Willi glowered back and there was a strained atmosphere for a few seconds before he roared with laughter and reached over to slap Schenke's knee. 'He's all right, this one! For a copper, that is.'

The tension vanished and the other men took turns to shake Schenke's hand while he concentrated on making sure he could recall their names. Their lives might depend on correct identification that night.

Wohler spoke above the rattle of the vehicle. 'Time to tool up, boys.'

On the floor between the benches lay some wooden boxes with rope handles at each end. Wohler opened the one at his feet and Schenke saw the dull gleam of metal as he pulled out a sub-machine gun with a wooden stock.

'MP35,' he explained. 'Have you used one before?'

'No. But I've seen them in the precinct armoury. It seems the police aren't the only customers of the Bergmann company.'

'True, but the difference is ours were rather more difficult to get hold of. Now look here.' Wohler raised the weapon so that Schenke could see it more clearly. 'Magazine goes into the right side and ejects cases to the left. You cock it like a rifle, so.' He pulled back the lever and locked it up before pressing the trigger to release the spring, which made a sharp clack. He tilted it to the side so that Schenke could see the two triggers in the guard. 'It's got a progressive trigger. First one for single shots, pull it back with the second trigger and you get a burst. Here.'

Schenke took the gun and tested its weight, finding it to be about what he expected. Wohler handed out the rest of the weapons to his men and took the last one for himself. The other chests were already open, and Willi was handing out webbing and ammunition pouches.

'Six magazines each should do the job, provided we don't piss the bullets away like raw recruits, eh, Mathias? You remember those Bavarian replacements back in '18? Just spraying away at the Tommies without even opening their eyes! Fucking useless. Better not be like them, Inspector.'

It was half jibe, half warning, and Schenke could understand his concern.

'I can handle it with my eyes open, thanks.'

The last crate contained grenades, and Wohler and his men passed them round, tucking the long wooden handles into their webbing.

'What about me?' asked Schenke.

Wohler shook his head. 'These lads served with me on the Western Front and later in the Steel Helmets, like your Sergeant Hauser. We were trained to use grenades. They're straightforward enough, but I ain't going to risk some flat-foot not counting down the fuse right, or fumbling one of the bastards and wiping us out.'

'What about Walter?'

'Willi started training him as soon as he was old enough to hold a gun. Walter knows what he's doing.'

'Fair enough,' Schenke conceded. He looked round at his heavily armed comrades and shook his head. 'How the hell did you get hold of all this kit? You could fight a small war with it.'

Wohler grinned and tapped his nose. 'Secrets of the trade, Inspector. We may be on the same side tonight, but once this is over the truce between us ends. I don't want you fucking up my organisation when I get it running again. So don't ask questions and I'll tell you no lies. We're in this to kill Guttmann and get your woman out of his clutches. Clear?'

'Perfectly.'

'Good. Now tell me about the layout of the villa.'

Schenke described what he could recall from his two visits.

'What about the rear of the property?'

'There's a lawn at the back and then trees, and then I imagine the wall that surrounds the gardens, though I couldn't see that.'

'How high is the wall?'

'Well over two metres, I'd say.'

Wohler lowered his gaze before he looked round at the others. 'Listen, boys, this is how we're going to play it. Dieter will remain with the truck to guard it. The rest of us will be in two groups. I'll lead the first with Karl and Mathias. We'll take the front, light the place up and pour fire on Guttmann's lads. Willi, you take Walter and the inspector and work your way round the back. I'll give you ten minutes before the show begins. While the other side are responding to the diversion, you get over the wall and make for the rear of the house. Take down anyone who looks dangerous. The only ones I don't want you shooting are the inspector's woman and Guttmann. You save Guttmann for me.'

'What's your woman look like, Inspector?' asked Walter.

Schenke described Ruth as well as he could, and Walter nodded. 'Sounds like quite a piece, even if she is a Jew.'

'Once you reach the house,' Wohler continued, 'you can open up on those still facing us at the front. My guess is they'll fold the moment they're taking fire from front and rear. I expect them to run, but if they don't, we're not taking any prisoners. If they try to surrender, kill them. The only living people coming out of the villa are those of us that survive and the woman.'

His words had a sobering effect, and for the rest of the short journey the men quietly adjusted their webbing and applied black shoe polish to their faces and hands before sitting in silence cradling their weapons. A few minutes later, the lorry slowed and the driver banged three times on the rear of the cab before turning into Berbuerstrasse. After a short distance, he drew up. The engine was switched off and Wohler turned off the torch and drew back the flaps at the rear of the truck.

'We're here, boys. Out you get.'

Chapter Twenty-Five

They climbed quickly out of the truck as the driver killed the lights and darkness swallowed up the street. The only illumination came from the stars and the feathery sliver of the moon. Just enough to make out the trees lining the road and the dark bulk of the nearest building. It was quiet, apart from the whistle of a distant train and some light music coming from further along the street.

Wohler paused by the driver's window. 'As soon as the fireworks start, bring the truck up. Thirty metres from the gate should do it. If all goes well, we should have completed the job before Orpo turn up mob-handed. If they arrive before we can get out, go back to the end of the street and wait there. If we're not with you after ten minutes, it means we're not coming and you get out of here.'

'Boss, I—'

'Those are your orders, Dieter. You do as you're told just as you did when I was your squad leader back on the front.'

'Yes, sir.'

'Good man.' Wohler beckoned to the others. 'Load magazines.'

The men reached for the nearest of their pouches and fitted the magazines to their sub-machine guns with metallic clicks.

'Check safety and cock your weapons.'

Schenke, unfamiliar with the MP35, took longer to complete the procedure, and there was a disapproving grunt from one of the dark figures. 'Any time tonight would be good, Inspector.'

With the lever pulled back and up, he announced he was ready.

'Let's move,' Wohler ordered. 'Single file. Keep watch on both sides and ears open.'

The six men moved off at a trot, keeping to the grass along the side of the kerb to minimise the sound of their footfall. Schenke brought up the rear, anxious not to lose contact with the others as he favoured his weaker leg. He estimated that it was another four hundred metres to the gate of Guttmann's villa. An easy enough distance to cover, but the peril at this stage was being spotted and reported to the police by one of the locals.

Halfway to the gate, Wohler raised his left hand and hissed, 'Cover.'

His men peeled off the grass and crouched against the ivy-covered wall. Schenke squinted into the darkness to try and make out what had caused Wohler to halt them. Then he saw the outline of a couple walking four or five small dogs, dachshunds, on the other side of the street. He could hear their muted conversation and kept still as they slowly passed by. They did not pause and there was no shift in the tone of their voices to indicate they had seen the men crouching opposite. Wohler waited a moment longer before he rose cautiously and stepped away from the wall.

'Move on.'

They continued until they could make out two men outside the gate, their presence given away by the glowing red tips of their cigarettes.

Wohler halted his party and crept back to Schenke. The corner of the wall that surrounded the villa was close by.

'This is where we part company. Willi?'

'Boss?'

'Take your lot down along the wall and round to the back. Keep it quiet and keep your ears open for anyone patrolling the other side of the wall.'

'Just like trench raids.' Willi gave a dry chuckle.

Wohler patted him on the shoulder. 'Try not to enjoy yourself too much, old man. We'll open fire ten minutes from now.'

He turned to move to the position at the head of the file as Willi stood up.

'On me.'

He led the way along the path between the wall and the high hedge that formed the boundary of the neighbouring property. It was even harder to see in the narrow space, and Schenke found it difficult to gauge the distance between himself and Walter ahead of him. For most of the way the ground was soft earth with frequent stretches of puddles and mud, and he had to be careful not to slip and fall. Every so often he checked his watch and saw the minutes ticking away. They reached the corner at the end of the wall with barely three minutes to spare. The rear of the villa's grounds gave way to a strip of woodland. Willi crept along the wall until they came to a section where the top had crumbled away, leaving an easily scalable height of less than two metres.

'We go over here,' he whispered. 'Me first, then the inspector. Give me a boost, son.'

Walter carefully leaned his MP35 against the masonry, then cupped his hands and heaved his father up. Willi dropped down on the far side and moved two paces forward before crouching and listening to make sure that he had not been spotted. Then he glanced back.

'Next.'

Schenke stepped up, placing his boot on the youth's hands, and was lifted effortlessly so that he could clamber over using his free hand. He jumped down, legs braced to absorb the impact, and took his place at Willi's shoulder while Walter picked up his weapon and hauled himself up and over the wall to join them.

Ahead of them lay a thin screen of bare trees, then the broad sweep of the lawn and on the far side the looming bulk of the villa. A pair of Guttmann's men were keeping watch from the terrace outside the dining room, barely visible against the sheen of the windows in the moonlight. Willi checked his watch and whispered, 'One minute to go.'

Wohler mentally read off the seconds as his gaze shifted between his watch and the two men guarding the gate. His right hand tightened around the stock of his MP35, and he curled his finger into the trigger guard before easing the safety off with his left and pushing it forward to support the forward grip.

'Safety off,' he whispered. 'We go in open order in five . . . four . . . three . . . two . . . one . . . Now.'

He rose up and stepped onto the pavement, Karl moving out to his left on the road and Mathias on the grass fringe to his right. Raising the MP35, he walked forward at an easy pace. Ahead, Guttmann's men were not yet aware of them and were talking in relaxed tones before one of them laughed and took a deep drag on his cigarette. The tip flared, revealing his features beneath the brim of his hat, and at that instant he turned towards Wohler.

'Who's there?'

At a distance of twenty metres, Wohler had him squarely in his sights and squeezed enough to fire a single shot. There was a brilliant fiery flash from the muzzle as the shot crashed out, shattering the silence of the affluent neighbourhood. Guttmann's man spun round and dropped to one knee. A second shot struck him in the head, and he tumbled onto his back in front of the gate. Wohler was already lining up on the man's companion, whose momentary shock and hesitation sealed his fate. As he drew out a pistol, Wohler tightened his trigger finger, and a burst of 9mm bullets struck the man in the chest, driving him back two paces before he crashed to the ground, his pistol clattering onto the pavement behind him.

Approaching the gate, Wohler saw that it was bolted from inside. He was about to reach through the bars to work the bolt loose when he saw a third man on the other side, pistol raised. He threw himself back as three shots were fired, one striking the gate and sending sparks bursting into the air. There were shouts as Guttmann's men called for help. Wohler turned to his own men and gave the order. 'Grenades.'

Lowering the muzzle of his sub-machine gun, he pulled a grenade out of his webbing and unscrewed the cap on its base. The fuse string tumbled out, weighted by a small ceramic plug. Looping the end over a finger of his left hand, he turned to the others. 'Short range, over the wall. Ready? Now!'

They pulled the strings, counted to two and lobbed the grenades over the wall. Wohler heard them land on the gravel, but Guttmann's men had no time to react before the three explosions roared almost together and a brilliant flash lit up the night. At once he rushed to the gate and put his hand through to loosen and draw back the bolt as his men took up position on the stone pillars on each side, aiming through the iron bars. With a clank the bolt came free and he heaved one of the gates open, running through and taking cover behind a car parked on the drive just beyond. Around him he could see two of Guttmann's men on the ground. One was still, while the other lay on his back gasping, what was left of his left leg in shreds. Mathias and Karl scurried through the opening and ducked down beside Wohler.

Already he could hear the shouts from several directions as more of Guttmann's men hurried towards the gate. Against superior odds, it would be suicide to risk a frontal charge up the drive, so he pointed along the wall. 'That way. Let's go.'

Keeping low, they ran along the inside of the villa wall for twenty metres before Wohler saw two dark shapes coming the other way.

'We're under attack!' he called out. 'They're right behind me!'

The two men hesitated, and one called back, 'Who's that?'

He was answered by a burst from Wohler's MP35 that caught him and his companions and cut them down.

'Keep going!' Wohler called back to his comrades. He knew that the muzzle flash of his weapon gave away their position. That was one of the main dangers of firefights at night, and it was vital to keep changing position between engaging the enemy. They ran on for another ten metres towards a row of shrubs on the gentle slope towards the villa, then veered behind them until they came to a paved area with raised flower beds. Wohler ordered his companions to take up position on either side, and they raised their weapons as he made a rough calculation of the rounds he had expended. He was satisfied that enough remained for a few aimed shots or one final burst.

Flashes from a short distance in front of the villa revealed the presence of their opponents as they eased up on firing at the last place they had seen Wohler shooting from. Then there was a shouted warning, and a moment later a grenade thrown by one of Guttmann's men went off by the wall, and two more by the car parked inside the gate. The second ignited the petrol tank and the vehicle was engulfed by a fireball that lit up the surroundings and exposed three more of Guttmann's men, two of them armed with rifles, some fifty metres away.

'Ten men, that copper said,' Karl snarled. 'Fucking liar. There's got to be twice that. And they're armed to the teeth!'

'Save it for later,' Wohler snapped. 'Shoot 'em down!'

He took aim and squeezed off the rest of the magazine in a single burst, striking one of the riflemen. Karl and Mathias joined in as he ejected the spent magazine and loaded another. This time their enemies were quicker to react and darted out of the light to return fire. Bullets zipped overhead, crashing into the bricks of the raised flower beds and cutting through the bare stems of the pruned rose bushes.

There was a sudden cry from Mathias, to Wohler's left, and he went down. Wohler crawled towards him, calling out urgently, 'You hit?'

The veteran was clutching the side of his face. 'Just a splinter or a stone. I'll live.'

'Good.' Wohler turned to Karl. 'Covering fire!'

As his companion fired a rapid succession of shots towards the enemy muzzle flashes, Wohler pulled Mathias's sleeve. 'Move.'

They scurried behind the flower beds, Wohler scanning the ground ahead for another fire position. Behind them, Karl emptied his magazine with a burst and set off after them.

At the rear of the villa, Schenke flinched as he heard the first shots and the explosion of the grenades. He began to rise before Willi pulled him back down.

'Wait a moment.'

The men on the terrace were on the move, hurrying around to the left of the villa. There was more movement as four men emerged from the gloom around the garden and ran towards the building. A deep voice that Schenke recognised as belonging to Reitz bellowed across the lawn.

'Alarm! To the front!'

Willi gave Schenke a gentle shove. 'All right, now we move. You stay out to my left, Walter to the right. Keep your finger off the trigger until I shoot. After that, you're free to shoot anything that isn't us.'

They set off across the lawn, spreading out as Willi had ordered. Schenke felt his heart pounding with anxious excitement as he raised his weapon and trotted forward, keeping up with the others as they made for the steps leading to the terrace. The sound of gunfire from the other side of the villa was almost continuous now, loud as a battle, and he knew that the police would be alerted within moments and the order would be given to send armed squads racing to the scene. There was perhaps ten to fifteen minutes before they arrived.

The small group closed up as they reached the steps, and Willi led the way up to the terrace. There was no sign of the men who had been on duty there, and Schenke started towards the doors of the dining room before a curt order from Willi halted him.

'We go round to the right and take the bastards from behind. That's the plan. We clear the house after we've dealt with the men outside. Come.'

He continued at a slow trot around the corner of the dining room and down another set of steps onto a gravel path leading to the front of the villa. Some more grenades detonated, and there was a burst of bright orange light that silhouetted several figures briefly before the glow was swallowed up by the night. Schenke could hear the roar of flames amid the gunfire. As well as the rattle of the sub-machine guns there was the bark of rifles and the dull crack of pistols. Willi led them off to the wall on the right and they moved up to the rear of the men defending the villa, stopping when they reached a woodpile beside a long, low toolshed. He indicated the end of the logs.

'You stay here and cover our flank. The boy and I will deal with the lot facing Wohler. Just take down anyone you see coming round the side of the villa. Clear?'

'Yes.' Schenke kneeled down and braced his elbows against the logs to steady his aim.

Willi and his son continued along the rear of the toolshed and then moved apart before they dropped to the ground and took aim at the men facing Wohler and his companions.

As they ran to find another position to resume the attack, Wohler saw figures emerging from the shadows at the side of the villa.

'Down!' He threw himself onto the grass and shoved Mathias to the side so that there was a gap between them. Karl dropped behind them as Wohler sprayed the area to the side of the house. He could not tell if any of his bullets had struck home, as Guttmann's men had also gone to ground and now blocked any further movement in that direction. More fire was coming in from their left from the men they had engaged earlier, with rounds tearing up the grass and cutting through the air just above their heads. A light machine gun opened up from the balustrade around the porch.

'Bollocks,' Wohler muttered. 'Looks like they're as well tooled up as we are. And there are more of them. Karl!'

'Boss?'

'Lay some fire down to the left. Try and keep the machine gunner's head down!'

A moment later, Karl's MP35 opened fire, a mixture of single shots and bursts. They were dangerously exposed, Wohler realised. Caught in crossfire, they were pinned down and in danger of being picked off as their enemies moved in around them.

'Where the hell are Willi and the others?' Mathias called out as he reloaded. 'They should be in position by now, dammit.'

Wohler did not answer. There was no point wasting breath. Willi knew his job. He'd learned his battlefield skills in the quagmire of trench warfare and could be relied on. There had been no sound of gunfire from the rear of the villa, and Wohler forced himself to believe that his man would enter the battle at any moment. He saw a figure rise and make a dash from the side of the building and then pause to throw a grenade. He hit the man with a single shot before he heard something strike the ground a few metres to his front. Before he could shout a warning, there was a blinding flash and a roar and he was showered with soil and clumps of grass. It was only a matter of moments now before more of the enemy were close enough to use grenades. Seconds later, another one thudded between him and Mathias.

'Shit . . .' Mathias lurched towards the grenade and threw himself on top of it. It went off, thrusting him up with the blast before his body fell back limply.

'No!' Wohler yelled. 'Mathias . . .'

Then he opened up again on the men at the side of the house.

Suddenly there was another grenade explosion off towards the drive, then another. A third landed inside the porch and silenced the machine gun with a roar. Bursts of fire lit up the other side of the garden as Willi and his group joined the attack. The enemy fire slackened as they turned to face the new danger. Some tried to flee and were caught in the glow of the flames licking up from the wrecked car and shot down. The men at the side of the house had stopped firing as their attention was distracted, and Wohler lowered his gun, pulled out his remaining grenades and hurled them in quick succession. They went off in a deafening sequence, each blast briefly illuminating the handful of men spread out across the grass there. As soon as the last one had detonated, he jumped to his feet, MP35 raised, and charged forward with an angry roar, shooting at anyone who still moved. Karl chased after him, also shouting as he fired into the prone bodies of the enemy and the two men who stood and tried to flee.

Reaching the corner of the building, Wohler backed against the brickwork and changed the magazine. There would be only two more left in his pouches. Karl came rushing up and joined him, breathing hard.

'I think we got 'em all on this side. What about Mathias?'

'He's had it. Took the full force of the grenade.'

The fire at the front of the house was slackening and Wohler glanced round. He could see five men by the light of the flames returning the fire of Willi's group and he gave Karl a low whistle to attract his attention and point out the enemy. Now the position was reversed and they could lay down a punishing crossfire.

'Ready?' They raised their MP35s and took aim. 'Let 'em have it.'

Single shots and bursts tore into the men, toppling the first two before the rest jumped up and ran towards the gate. They never made it, caught by a burst from the other side of the garden. There was no further movement, and the sudden cessation of shooting made the sound of the flames and the groans of injured men sound eerily loud.

'Think we got them all,' said Karl. He was about to step out when Wohler pushed him back.

'Wait, you fool. You want to be shot by our own side?'

He drew a breath and called out, 'Willi! You there?'

There was a pause before the other man's voice, unmistakable, called back. 'Here, boss!'

'We'll come towards you! Keep us covered!'

'Soon as you're ready!'

Wohler lowered himself into a crouch as he scurried around the corner and made his way along the front of the building. He stopped as he reached a large ornamental planter and raised his weapon, calling back to Karl, 'Move!'

Karl ran past him to the porch balustrade and squatted as he took aim and called out for Wohler to move, and in this way they leapfrogged their way over towards their comrades. As Wohler reached the porch, the bodies of the machine gunner and his companion, faces bloody and torn by shrapnel, were just visible in the moonlight. He took cover and called to Willi. 'You come to us.'

Moments later, the five remaining men were crouched by the bullet-scarred front door, facing outwards.

'Where's Mathias?' Willi asked.

'Took a grenade.'

'Dead?'

'Quite.' Wohler scrutinised the grounds in front of the house, the bodies and the burning car, but there was no sign of any further resistance from the men outside the villa. The most dangerous part of the attack was yet to come.

Chapter Twenty-Six

'Karl, you cover the rear of the house. Shoot anyone who makes a break for it. If you see Guttmann, shoot him in the legs.'

'Yes, boss.'

Karl hurried off the way he had come and disappeared round the corner. Wohler turned to the others. 'We go through the front door and sweep the ground floor. Once it's clear, we move up, one floor at a time. Schenke, you're with me. Willi, I'll let you have the honour of announcing our arrival.'

The older man grinned and took out a grenade, undoing the cap and grasping the string as he approached the door. Walter reached for the handle and opened the door fractionally. A shaft of light lanced out across the bodies on the porch. The moment the gap was wide enough, Willi pulled the fuse string and tossed the grenade into the entrance hall. There was a flash and a roar as glass shattered in the windows on either side of the porch. Light poured out of the torn blackout curtains. Walter thrust the door wide, and he and his father ran in and went to the right as Wohler and Schenke went to the left. Their sub-machine guns were raised to cover the interior, the stairs and the corridors on either side, but nothing moved. The chandelier had taken the force of the blast and hung in glittering tatters, the few remaining light bulbs casting a dim, wavering glow across the hall. Broken crystals crunched underfoot.

'Guttmann's study is this way.' Schenke motioned towards the corridor. 'Best place to start looking for him.'

Wohler nodded, and they moved forward, one to each side, covering the doors as they advanced. When they reached the door of the study, Schenke saw that it was slightly ajar and the light was on inside. He listened for a moment, but there was no sound from within. Kicking it open, he waited for any response, just in case. There was nothing, only silence, and he cautiously stepped over the threshold, MP35 raised. The study was empty.

'Where next?' asked Wohler.

'Just a moment.' Schenke lowered the gun, hurried round the desk and tested the drawer. It was locked. Stepping back, he took aim and fired two shots to smash the lock, then pulled open the splintered front of the drawer. There were several folders inside. He took out the first and flipped it open. There were the incriminating pictures of himself and Ruth. The second folder had Stoffler's name written on it. He took that too, stuffing both into his jacket, and was about to leave when he noticed a folder at the rear of the drawer with the word 'Party' on the cover. He pulled it closer and opened the cover, and his eyes widened in astonishment and disgust as he saw a slightly blurry picture of a naked man on a bed with two women. There was no mistaking the identity. Goebbels. There were other photos beneath, faces from the regime that he recognised and some he didn't.

'For fuck's sake!' Wohler snapped. 'What are you doing? The Orpo will be here soon. We have to find Guttmann. Move!'

Schenke considered seizing the third file, then almost at once decided against it. Possession of such images was too dangerous. He left the drawer open and hurried after Wohler as they made for the dining room. There was no one there either, nor in the other rooms they searched before returning to the hall.

'We'll try the kitchen,' Wohler decided, moving around the end of the hall as he covered the stairs and landing with his sub-machine gun. They passed through the door behind the stairs and entered a short tiled corridor with pantries and stores on either side. Schenke saw shelves filled with jars, tins and black-market luxuries as well as lamps, kerosene tins and spare tablecloths and napkins, neatly folded. There was a closed door at the end, and Wohler held up his hand. They could hear voices from the far side. Muted words. As he turned the handle, the sound died instantly. He thrust the door open and leaped into the room, gun raised. Schenke followed him in and saw three women and a man shrinking back against the counter on the far side of the kitchen.

'Who are you?' Wohler demanded.

'We . . . we're the staff, sir,' the man volunteered, and gestured at his companions. 'I'm Herr Guttmann's butler.'

'Where's Guttmann?'

'I don't know, sir. I just gathered the others in here when the shooting started.'

Wohler aimed his gun. 'I won't ask again. Where is he?'

The butler winced and raised his hands pleadingly. 'I swear it. I don't know!'

Schenke saw Wohler's finger begin to tighten, and he thrust the muzzle aside. 'No!'

'What the hell are you doing?'

'I'm not going to let you shoot them.'

'Fuck that. They're Guttmann's people.'

'I don't care. We don't shoot them,' Schenke said firmly.

Wohler stared at him, and then gave a snort of disgust as he lowered his weapon. 'Please yourself.'

Schenke turned to the others. 'Have you seen a dark-haired woman? She was brought to the house earlier on.'

One of the maids raised a trembling hand and pointed to the ceiling. 'They took her upstairs, sir. Locked her in the attic.'

Schenke indicated the large table in the centre of the kitchen. 'Under there. All of you!'

They scrambled beneath it, and he crossed to the back door leading to the garden, locking it and pocketing the key. Moving back to the door he and Wohler had entered by, he paused. 'You'll be locked in here. When the police come, make sure you let them know you are unarmed.'

He stepped into the corridor, closed the door and locked it, leaving the key half turned in the slot. Wohler led the way back to the foot of the stairs and beckoned to Willi and his son. 'We're going up. Keep your eyes and ears open. There may be more of them.'

With Wohler leading, they climbed the wide staircase, keeping the landing above covered with their weapons. Reaching the top, Wohler took a quick glance along the corridor that ran the length of the villa, with bedrooms and bathrooms on either side. Most of the doors were open. The one at the end of the corridor to the left was closed.

'The room at the end looks like the best bet, but we'll check the rooms on each side as we go. Schenke, you cover the rear, in case there's any more of the bastards at the other end. Let's go.'

Wohler took the left-hand side while his comrades moved

along the right. Schenke followed, covering the corridor stretching along the other wing of the villa. The rooms on either side proved to be empty, and they closed each door as they moved along. At the end, Wohler pressed himself against the wall next to the imposing door frame topped by a gilded plaster cornice. Schenke closed up beside him while the other two made ready on the opposite side of the door. Wohler reached out and rapped before snatching his hand back.

'Guttmann! We're coming for you!'

When there was no response, he quietly gave the order. 'Grenade.'

Willi handed his MP35 to his son before he unscrewed the grenade's cover and gripped the string. Wohler reached for the door handle and gave it a turn, but the door was locked. At once splinters exploded from the surface as a burst of automatic fire worked its way across, showering those outside with fragments of wood. Wohler gasped as they pressed back against the wall, and Schenke saw that his left hand was a mangled mess of bloody flesh.

'Boss!' Willi called out.

'Stay back!' Wohler ordered, as another burst smashed through the door. Resting the barrel on his left wrist, he angled the sub-machine gun's muzzle at the door and fired a burst in return. Then he nodded to the nearest of the empty bedrooms. 'Take cover in there. Willi, the moment the door's open, you give them your grenade.' He turned to Schenke. 'Here, take my gun and get into cover in the room opposite the others.'

'What are you going to do? You're injured.'

'I'll live. Just do as I say.'

Schenke fell back, opening the door and ducking inside. He saw Wohler take his last grenade and make it ready, then he pulled the string, wedged the shaft into the door handle and sprinted towards Schenke, diving through the doorway. There was a deafening blast and a flash. As acrid smoke billowed in the corridor, Willi darted out and tossed his own grenade through the shattered door, and there was another explosion. Then before Wohler could stop him, he raised his gun and charged in, closely followed by his son.

Schenke raced to the door at Wohler's shoulder as the latter held out his hand to retrieve the MP35. Walter was staggering back, arms hanging limply, his gun lying on the rug. Willi was on the floor, crawling for the cover of a sofa that had been positioned to face the door. Over by the bed, Schenke saw Reitz kneeling as he shifted his aim towards the new targets at the doorway. Wohler raised his weapon with his good hand and let rip with a wild burst that stitched across the panelling behind Reitz.

Schenke had only an instant to react. He swung his muzzle round and loosed off a burst as soon as the sights fixed on Reitz. The bedclothes leaped up and mattress filling burst out before the last two rounds caught Reitz in the shoulder and he dropped out of sight. Rushing across to the side of the bed, Schenke took aim as he saw Reitz struggling to get up, blood dribbling from his mouth. His weapon, an MP38, was just out of his reach, and Schenke snatched it up and tossed it over the bed.

Beaten, Reitz shifted onto his elbows and looked up at him with a sour expression. 'I told the boss it was a bad idea to try and turn you.'

'He should have listened,' Schenke replied coldly. 'And now you're going to pay for killing Remer, Feldwitz, Bachmann . . . Kunzler.'

He took aim at the man's throat, then paused as he saw the frown on Reitz's face. The gangster shook his head. 'I did Feldwitz . . . The others? You got the wrong man . . . So much for the Kripo's detective expertise.' He made to chuckle, but coughed up blood instead and grimaced.

'What do you mean?' Schenke demanded, kicking him in the leg. 'Tell me.'

Reitz sneered. 'I didn't kill them. So fuck you.'

There was a howl of rage and grief from behind Schenke as Willi stood up and saw his son slumped against a wardrobe, head lolling on his chest. 'Walter!' He bent to raise the lad's chin and saw that he was already dead. 'No!'

Before Schenke could react, the veteran strode across, raised his weapon with an agonised roar and loosed off the rest of the magazine into Reitz's torso. Reitz's large body jerked and convulsed under the impact, and blood spattered Schenke and Willi. Even after the magazine was exhausted, Willi kept his finger on the trigger as if willing more bullets to appear.

Wohler approached him and set his weapon down on the bed, then turned his comrade towards him. 'Corporal! Get a grip on yourself, man!'

The veteran instinctively stiffened, although his eyes were filled with the despair of loss.

Wohler softened his tone. 'Now give me a hand. Schenke, cover the door.'

Schenke returned to the shattered and scorched timbers of the door frame and held his weapon ready. Behind him, Wohler and Willi laid out Walter's body. While Wohler took the remaining magazines and grenades from the young man's webbing, the veteran went down on his knees and cradled his son's head, before setting it down gently, brushing a strand of hair from his forehead and bending to kiss him on the cheek. Then he closed Walter's eyes, took a deep breath and stood to fetch the guns from the bed.

'There's still Guttmann to find. He's up here somewhere, boss.'

'Then let's get to it.'

Wohler had torn a strip from the pillowcase on the bed to bandage his hand and now tied it off securely with his clenched teeth before he took his MP35 from Willi and they both loaded a fresh magazine.

'We must hurry,' Schenke urged. 'I think I know where he must be. Look for the door to the attic.'

They made their way back along the corridor and crossed the landing to the other wing. The first door along opened onto stairs leading into the gloom above. Taking out his torch, Schenke turned it on and shone it upwards. There was a landing halfway up before the stairs doubled back over their heads. If Ruth was up there, as he had been told, and Guttmann had hidden there with her, then she was in danger, and he did not want the others to repeat their room-clearing tactic of a moment ago.

'I'll go first.'

Wohler made to shove him out of the way, but Schenke stood his ground. 'No. I'll lead this time. I have to save her.'

Wohler shook his head. 'You're just like Remer . . .'

Schenke turned and began to climb the steps, clutching the torch in his left hand. The line of his gun barrel followed the beam of light. Beneath him the stairs creaked under the weight of the three men climbing towards the attic. He paused at the landing and shone the torch around the corner. The steps ended with another closed door, and knowing there was little time to waste, he smashed the lock with two aimed shots. The door swung inwards with a protest from the hinges. The lights in the attic were on, and as he continued to climb, he called ahead of him.

'Guttmann! This is Inspector Schenke.'

'Horst!' Ruth called. She made to say something more, but was cut off by the sound of a slap as Guttmann snarled at her to be quiet.

'This is a police raid!' Schenke continued. 'Throw down any weapon you have and surrender.'

'Bullshit!' a different voice responded. 'I don't see any police outside.'

Schenke hesitated. There were two of them up there with Ruth, but who was the other man? The voice was familiar.

He continued up the steps, maintaining the bluff. 'I'm entering the attic. Sergeant Hauser, if I come to any harm, make sure that neither of those men come out of there alive.'

Wohler grinned and gave a mock salute. 'Yes, sir! No prisoners.'

Schenke held his MP35 out to the side and raised his other hand as he entered the attic. On either side were storage boxes, and some five metres away was a metal-framed bed with a thin mattress. Ruth was on her knees at the end of the bed and Guttmann sat beside her holding a pistol, the muzzle pressed under her chin. He was dressed in a dinner suit once again. A short distance away stood his lawyer, Kolbenhoff, holding a revolver aimed at Schenke.

'Put that formidable-looking weapon down,' Guttmann said calmly. 'Or I shall blow the Fräulein's brains out of her pretty little head.'

'All right,' Schenke lowered the MP35 to the floor.

'Kick it away from the door and step forward.'

He did as he was told and took two steps towards the bed, anxiously watching as Guttmann pressed the muzzle into Ruth's throat. She winced and let out a cry.

'That's close enough,' said Guttmann. 'As you can see, we have a hostage and she's going to be our ticket out of here.'

'She's a Jew,' Schenke responded. 'I don't think my men will be too worried about her being caught in any crossfire.'

Guttmann smiled slightly. 'But this particular Jew means rather a lot to you, Inspector. So you'll ensure that those men with you, whoever they are, hold their fire until we are away from the villa. One of your vehicles will serve such a purpose very nicely.'

Schenke's gaze shifted to Kolbenhoff, and a sudden connection snapped into place in his mind. The surprise in Reitz's voice over the telephone when Schenke had accused him of killing Remer. And again just now before he died in a hail of bullets in the bedroom.

'This is all on you, isn't it? You're the one who was behind the ambush in the alley. You were the replacement driver . . . You cut a deal with Kunzler and Bachmann to kill Remer and share the takings from the club. Only you took it all.'

'Shut up!' Kolbenhoff shouted. 'Keep your mouth shut or I'll shoot!'

Schenke saw Guttmann turn towards his subordinate. 'Is this true?'

'Of course it isn't. The cop's lying.'

'I wonder . . .'

Schenke's heart was pounding, but he continued. 'He did it all right. He's the reason why your men are dead. Why Reitz is dead.'

Kolbenhoff brandished his pistol. 'Quiet! One more word and I swear I'll kill you!'

Guttmann lowered his own weapon. He shook his head and spoke in a sad tone. 'No . . . no, I think the inspector is telling the truth. It makes sense of things . . .'

'He's lying! Why would I be stupid enough to try something like that behind your back, boss?'

'Why indeed? Was I not paying you enough, Kolbenhoff? Did you have more ambitious plans in mind, perhaps? Either way, I am disappointed in you . . . Very disappointed.'

'What—' Kolbenhoff turned to look at his employer just as Guttmann fired three times. The range was close and all three bullets struck Kolbenhoff in the chest. He tumbled amid the boxes stacked along the side of the attic, writhed a moment and then lay there bleeding out. Guttmann turned his pistol and held the muzzle against the side of Ruth's head.

'I despise those who let me down, Inspector. You could have earned a small fortune if you had let our arrangement play out.'

'That was never on the cards,' Schenke replied. 'Lower the gun and surrender.'

'I think not. Nothing has changed.' Guttmann eased himself off the bed and pulled Ruth up in front of him. 'This woman is my means of escaping you and your friends. Tell them to get out of my house, and have one of your cars made ready for me and this lady of yours.'

Schenke's guts tightened. There was no way Wohler would permit Guttmann to escape, and that would mean Ruth was likely to be killed. There was no police car for Guttmann to flee in. He would surely realise that his villa had not been attacked by a force of policemen the moment he saw Wohler rather than Hauser. There was only one chance to save Ruth now.

Schenke tensed his muscles, ready to spring, and spoke clearly, gambling everything on Wohler's desire to finish Guttmann off in person; up close and personal. 'Grenade.'

Guttmann frowned. 'What?'

A second later, Wohler's arm swung round the door frame. The grenade dropped a short distance in front of Guttmann and Ruth and rolled to the side.

Guttmann's jaw dropped open in terror, and he stumbled back, releasing Ruth as he did so. As Schenke had anticipated, the fuse was still capped. He sprang forward, thrust Ruth aside and hurled himself at the gangster. He caught his wrist and twisted his pistol hand up as Guttmann pulled the trigger and fired into the ceiling. Schenke's body was pressed against the soft flesh of the larger man, and the smell of his scent was cloying as they struggled. Guttmann's other hand came up and his fingers clenched around Schenke's throat. Behind them, footsteps pounded across the floorboards as Wohler and Willi rushed to Schenke's aid. A flurry of blows to Guttmann's head drove him back, and he lost his grip on the pistol and on Schenke, and slumped to his knees.

Schenke rushed to Ruth's side as she stood up, trembling. He took her arms. 'Are you injured? Are you hurt?'

She shook her head and buried her face in his chest. 'Oh God, I was so scared . . .'

'I know.' Schenke held her briefly, then drew back to address Wohler. 'We have to get out of here. The police will arrive any moment.'

Wohler was standing over Guttmann. 'I don't care if your lawyer was the one behind Remer's death. You were the one who sent men to the club to kill me and burn the place down. That's good enough for me.'

Guttmann looked up, blood oozing from a cut on his brow as his fleshy face twisted into a sneer. 'If Kolbenhoff hadn't killed Remer, then I would have done eventually. And you along with him. As slowly as possible.'

'I don't doubt it.' Wohler bent down to retrieve the grenade, which still had the cover screwed on its base. 'The rest of you, get out of here. Find Karl and get to the truck as quick as you can.'

Willi hesitated. 'What are you going to do, boss?'

'Just go,' Wohler ordered as he unscrewed the cap.

Schenke needed no further encouragement, and he bundled Ruth out of the attic and down the stairs.

When the others were a safe distance away, Wohler stepped round Guttmann and savagely pulled his dinner jacket down from his shoulders, far enough to insert the grenade and thrust it down. He leaned in so that his clips were close to Guttmann's ear.

'I wanted to tell you in person. This is for Remer and my boys . . .'

He pulled the string, turned and ran for the door as Guttmann desperately attempted to reach around his corpulent body to grab the grenade. Wohler was halfway down the first flight of stairs when he was deafened by the roar of the explosion.

In the hall, Schenke paused and spoke to Ruth. 'Go with Willi. I'll catch you up.'

He tore free of her grasp and rushed towards the kitchen. Unlocking the door, he flung it open to see the four staff still huddled under the table. He took the key to the rear door from his pocket and tossed it to the butler. 'Here. Go out the back and get away from the house. Now!'

As they rushed to obey his order, he turned back to one of the storerooms and grabbed two tins of kerosene, then trotted back to the hall. Wohler was coming down the stairs and saw him.

'What are you doing?'

'You go. I've one last thing to take care of.'

Wohler shrugged and ran towards the door while Schenke made his way to the study. He placed the cans on the desk and retreated to the door before drawing his pistol and emptying the clip, puncturing the cans, which sprayed their contents across the desk and floor. Reaching for his lighter, he picked up a newspaper from a rack beside the fireplace and lit the end of it, then tossed it onto the desk. There was a *whoomph* as the kerosene ignited. He turned and ran after the others, rushing out of the shattered front door and down the drive.

In the distance, he could hear several lorries approaching. Dieter had brought the truck up to the gate and Schenke went to the rear, where Wohler was holding the flap open with his injured hand. He held the other out to Schenke and hauled him inside, then Karl banged the rear of the cab and the truck lurched into motion. A moment later, he turned on the torch. Schenke saw that Wohler, Willi and Karl were on the bench opposite, while Ruth was next to him. He put his arm round her and drew her close as she clung to him.

Willi's hand was covering his eyes as tears trickled down his cheeks. Karl removed his magazine and checked his weapon was safe before he laid it on the floor. At the rear of the truck, Wohler looked out of a gap between the flaps at the glow of flames consuming the house, and muttered, 'Rest in pieces, Guttmann, you bastard.'

Chapter Twenty-Seven

10 May

'So what happens now?' Ruth asked as she propped herself up in the bed and pulled the quilt up to cover her bare chest.

Schenke handed her one of the mugs of coffee he had made in the kitchen and sat next to her. *What happens now?* It had been the question that had kept him awake most of the night, and he still had no clear answer. He had been too physically and emotionally drained to think much at all on the journey back from Guttmann's villa. They had passed the small convoy of Orpo lorries heading the other way, and for a few nervous moments he had feared that one would turn round and come after them, but they were fortunate not to be challenged. Dieter drove back to the theatre and drew up at the place where Schenke had waited earlier that night.

'This is where we part company, Inspector Schenke,' said Wohler as he held out his good hand. 'It's been an . . . interesting experience fighting on the same side for once.'

Schenke hesitated before extending his own hand, and they shook firmly before he smiled self-consciously. 'Trust me, I won't be making a habit of it. If our paths cross again, we won't be allies. You understand that?'

'I wouldn't expect anything else. It was a case of my enemy's enemy, and so . . . Frankly, I would feel more comfortable if we put tonight behind us and never had cause to mention it again. I have a reputation to build. It would not be helped if word got out that I had been helped by a cop in taking Guttmann and his ring down.'

'It wouldn't do my reputation much good either.'

Wohler fixed him with a firm stare. 'Then we have an understanding. A shared secret that stays that way until we die.'

'Yes.'

'Good.' He withdrew his hand, then looked at Ruth, who had barely spoken during the journey. 'I hope she's worth it.'

She gave him a frosty look, and Schenke took her arm. 'Come on. We have to go, before we attract any attention.'

He jumped down from the bed of the truck and helped her out. It was a cool night, and he put his jacket around her to keep her warm. Wohler closed the flaps, and the truck moved off. It was quickly swallowed up in the darkness, the tiny glimmer of the rear lights all that was visible before it turned the corner and disappeared.

As they walked back to his apartment, Schenke placed one arm around Ruth while he kept the two files he had taken from Guttmann's study firmly grasped in his left hand. They crept into the building and climbed the stairs carefully so as not to wake the block warden, who might come out and ask some difficult questions. It was only when they were safely in the apartment with Ruth nursing a glass of brandy that she began to emerge from the trauma of the day's events.

'They said they were from the Gestapo when they came for me. I thought I was as good as dead when they bundled me into a car and put a hood over my head.'

She was trembling, and Schenke took the glass from her and held her hand to comfort her as she continued. 'It was when they took me up to the attic and removed the hood that I realised they weren't Gestapo. The big man, Guttmann, told me that I was to be their insurance policy to make sure you behaved. That's when I began to feel guilty, Horst. Without me, you would never have been put in that position. And you would not have had to risk your life to come and find me.'

He shrugged. 'I've long since learned that regret changes nothing. Events will play out and you do what you need to accordingly. There was nothing else I could have done but get you out of his hands. It was the least dangerous option.'

'Other than choosing to work for him.'

'That was never going to happen.' He picked up the folder containing their photographs from the table where he had set it down along with Stoffler's. Crossing to the wood burner, he opened it and placed the file inside, then took out his lighter and set it alight. Yellow flames licked over the glossy surface, which began to bubble and buckle before being consumed by the blaze and turned to ash.

'It's not in my nature to be blackmailed. At first I thought I might have to go along with it. When I realised I could not, that meant I had to rescue you.'

'And risk dying in the attempt.' She smiled sadly. 'My knight in shining armour . . . What happens now?'

Now, with Ruth's question, his thoughts returned to their predicament. 'What happens now is that I have to go to work and pretend that last night did not happen. Meanwhile, you stay here and rest. There's plenty of food in the pantry. Help yourself. I need to get dressed.'

He washed and shaved before putting on a fresh shirt and

suit and combing his hair. Then he made a last inspection of his hands and face to ensure there were no scratches or smears of boot polish or any other residual traces of the night's action. Putting his coat on, he returned to the bedroom door. 'I'll be back by six. Try not to make any noise in case anyone comes to see who is loitering in my apartment. We can talk then about what will happen. You should be able to return to your lodgings and your job for now. But we need to make plans for your safety if the authorities make any further moves against Jews . . .'

'This will be the second time you've saved me. Why?'

He regarded her for a moment. 'You must know. You said you loved me.'

'I did? When?'

'When we met at the café the other day.'

'Ah . . .' She looked embarrassed at giving herself away.

'And I feel the same,' said Schenke. 'God knows that's foolish, dangerous. But I do and I can't deny it, so there we are.'

She shook her head and replied sadly, 'There we are.'

'I'll see you later.' He turned away, took his hat from the peg in the hall and left the apartment.

It was nearly eight o'clock when he entered the precinct, after having stopped at a kiosk to buy some cigarettes. He was immediately aware that something was in the air. There was no duty sergeant at his station, and as he passed the canteen door, he saw a large group of uniformed policemen gathered round the radio in the far corner as a voice concluded, 'Further bulletins will be delivered during the day . . . Hail Sacred Germany! Heil Hitler!' At once martial music cut in and filled the room, and there was an instant hubbub of anxious exchanges.

When he reached the Kripo office, he found all his subordinates gathered around Hauser's desk. They looked round as he took off his hat and approached them.

'You've heard the news?' Hauser queried.

'I heard the commotion down in the canteen just now. What's up?'

'It's begun,' Hauser replied simply.

'What has?'

'The Führer's great offensive against the Allies. The first wave went in this morning: Germany has invaded Holland, Belgium and France. We're in for it now. Poland was merely the beginning. He means to defeat France and Britain as well . . . It will be just like before.' Hauser's ashen expression of despair told of the memories of trench warfare that haunted much of his generation.

'Let's hope it's different this time,' said Rosa. 'The Führer is a man of peace. He has been forced into this war. No one wants to repeat what happened before. Not even our enemies. They'll come to their senses and put a stop to the fighting.'

Schenke forced himself to smile encouragingly. 'Let's hope so.'

But he could see that Hauser was not convinced and was badly shaken by the news.

'It *will* be different,' Liebwitz insisted. 'The war in Poland demonstrated as much. Tanks and aircraft have changed things. Wars are fought far more quickly in this modern era. And Germany has the best men and equipment in the world.'

Hauser looked at him bleakly. 'You have no idea what you are talking about. You were barely born when the last war ended.'

'I have read articles about military affairs in the *Black Corps* journal, Sergeant. I believe I am well informed enough to comment.'

Hauser stared at him a moment and then looked down at his folded hands. 'God help us . . .'

Liebwitz arched an eyebrow as he considered the impact of divine intervention, and then shrugged as he discounted the notion. History was singularly lacking in proof that anyone's God determined the outcome of a war. He turned to Schenke.

'There's some other news, sir. An important development that affects us.'

'Oh?'

'There was a gunfight at Guttmann's villa last night.'

'A gunfight?' Schenke asked, as innocently as he was able. 'Explain.'

'First reports indicate that it was likely the work of a rival gang. Most of the villa was destroyed by fire and several bodies were discovered outside the building. Orpo discovered the villa's staff hiding in the grounds, but they didn't have much to tell the police about what took place.'

Schenke listened with a neutral expression. 'What about Guttmann?'

'No sign of his body in the grounds, sir. They haven't been able to search the ruins yet.'

He nodded thoughtfully before he responded. 'If he is dead and most of his men with him, then that simplifies matters for us. It will put an end to the coupon forgeries racket. Same goes for the murder investigations.'

'*If* he is dead,' Liebwitz observed.

'Yes. We'll know once the ruins have been searched. We can check any human remains against dental records.'

'Yes, sir.' Liebwitz looked disappointed. 'It's a pity. We were very close to making arrests. Now it seems that none of the men responsible for the crimes will face justice in our courts.'

'Maybe. But sometimes justice is served up outside of the courts, Scharführer. If Guttmann is dead, good riddance. I doubt many will mourn him.'

'All the same, sir, I consider it an unsatisfactory outcome from a legal point of view.'

'We can't always have things resolved the way we would wish them to be. In our line of work that is the exception rather than the rule.'

'I find that . . . discomforting, sir.'

'Better get used to it, Liebwitz. If you want to continue being a member of Kripo.'

A fleeting look of concern crossed the Scharführer's face. 'It occurs to me that since the scope of the war has widened considerably, Germany will require every able-bodied man to serve at the front, and I—'

'Don't even consider it,' Schenke said firmly. The idea of Liebwitz in uniform being bullied by NCOs and his comrades because of his peculiar personality disturbed him greatly. 'One more man in uniform amongst millions will make next to no difference in terms of the outcome of the war. But one man with your ability and integrity can make a big difference to fighting crime in Berlin. You are needed here, Liebwitz. That is your duty. That is how you serve the Reich best.'

Liebwitz considered his superior's words. 'Very well, sir. You make a compelling argument. I shall serve Germany here.'

'I am glad to hear it.'

Schenke saw that Baumer was present, and he turned to him. 'Aren't you supposed to be on duty in the cells?'

Baumer straightened up with a guilty look. 'Sorry, sir. With all the excitement about the war announcement, I forgot. I'll relieve Persinger now.'

'No need. I'll relieve Persinger. I have to go down there and release Stoffler in any case.'

He turned away from Baumer and steeled himself before he addressed Rosa. 'I'd like a word in my office.'

'Yes, sir.'

He crossed to his cubicle and sat behind his desk. Rosa followed him in.

'Close the door, Rosa, and sit down.'

She did as instructed and waited for him to begin. Schenke reached into his pocket to take out the packet of cigarettes he had bought earlier. He broke the seal and plucked one out. 'After all that's happened in recent days, I need a smoke. How about you?'

She nodded and took a cigarette.

'Neue Front,' he said. 'That's the brand you like, isn't it?'

Rosa froze momentarily and sat back with the unlit cigarette between her fingers. 'Why, yes, sir. It is.'

Schenke lit up, all the while watching her closely. He exhaled to the side before he spoke. 'I'm disappointed, Rosa. I thought you were one of us.'

'Sir?' She affected a look of incomprehension.

'Don't waste my time pretending that you don't know what I'm talking about. How long have you been taking money from Guttmann?'

'I don't know what you're talking about, sir,' she protested.

'Rosa, Guttmann told me he had got his hooks into someone in the section. It didn't take me long to work out who. So let's not play games, eh? If you deny it now, I can have you placed under formal investigation. You're going to have to explain how you can afford the expensive clothes and perfumes you are so fond of. Who knows what else will be uncovered? Once it's out in the open, you'll be tried and sent to jail, and you know how the other prisoners treat bent police officers. So spare me the denials and admit the truth.'

She stared at him for a few seconds before she looked down. 'What happens if I do?'

'I want you out of the precinct just as soon as you've handed me your resignation. I want you to walk away and never enter this place again or contact me or any of the section. I want you to disappear from our lives, frankly.'

'I see.' She looked at him suspiciously. 'And you won't have me investigated.'

'That's the deal.'

'Why?'

'You've served over ten years in Kripo. You've done plenty of good work for us. I don't imagine you have been on the take all that time. How long have you been in Guttmann's pocket? The truth.'

She bit her lip. 'Since the start of the year. I swear it.'

Schenke took another drag on his cigarette. 'All right. I'll take your word for it. With Guttmann dead, that's over for you. I don't know if you approached him or he ensnared you. I'd like to think it was the latter. Either way, you can't stay in the section. Go and write your resignation and leave it on my desk. I've got some other business to attend to in the precinct. I want you gone before I return.' He nodded towards the door.

She rose and hesitated. 'I'm sorry, sir. I didn't have any choice. I—'

'Just go.'

She made to speak, then paused, closed her mouth and

nodded sadly. Schenke watched her return to her desk and reach for a sheet of paper from her drawer. He took a last drag before he stubbed the cigarette out in the metal tray. Then he left the office and made his way down to the cells.

Persinger was waiting at the end of the basement corridor. He hesitated and indicated Wohler's empty cell. 'What happened to the other one, sir? He was gone by the time I arrived last night.'

'I know. I had a few questions to ask him before I left the precinct. I figured you would be down before I was finished so I sent Baumer home. Five minutes later Wohler's lawyer turned up, waving a release order under my nose. So I had to take him up to the front desk to sign him out. By the time that was done it was past eight and I knew you'd be on duty down here. I should have come down to let you know what was going on. But it was late and I was tired. I'm sorry.'

Persinger shrugged. 'Lawyers, eh? Sometimes wonder whose side they are on.'

'Quite.' Schenke indicated the next cell. 'We don't need to hold this one any longer. I'll deal with him. You can go.'

As the man strode off, Schenke rubbed out the cover name chalked on the board and opened Stoffler's cell. The prisoner was on his bed and sat up. Stubble darkened his cheeks and made his complexion look even more sallow. He regarded Schenke with undisguised antipathy.

'I doubt you have heard the news yet,' Schenke began.

Stoffler indicated the barred window above the bed that admitted light from the street through a grating. 'I heard a loudspeaker car pass the precinct a while back, telling people to listen to the radio. What's happened? Is the war over?'

'No . . . Far from it. But that's not the news I'm talking

about. Guttmann's dead. So are Kolbenhoff, Reitz and the rest of his crime ring.'

Stoffler looked shocked. 'But . . . but how?'

'One of his rivals decided to settle matters with him. There was a shootout at Guttmann's villa before a fire burned the place down. He's dead. Which is good news for you at least.'

'It is?'

Schenke nodded. 'You are no longer being blackmailed by either of those gangsters. You'd be well advised to keep that as closely guarded a secret as you can if you don't want to fall into the clutches of men like Guttmann, or slip up and find Himmler's thugs at your door.'

Stoffler winced.

'You've been given a reprieve,' said Schenke. He reached into his coat and took out the folder he had taken from Guttmann's desk. He tossed it onto the bed and two of the photos slid out. Stoffler recoiled from them. Then he looked up at Schenke suspiciously.

'Is it your turn to blackmail me?'

'No. I'm giving you those photos. I suggest you destroy them as soon as you get out of here.'

'Why? Why are you doing this?'

'You don't strike me as the kind of man who would have willingly helped with the ration coupon racket. You had to be forced into it. You had no choice. I don't like blackmail. Neither do my men. I know what it's like to be the victim of someone like Guttmann. You're lucky that he's dead and I was able to retrieve these photos before anyone else could. Now I want you to take them and get out of here. Go back to Darré and explain that I placed you in protective custody because I feared for your safety. You can tell him Guttmann was behind the racket and you suspected he was getting the coupons from the printworks. Say that Guttmann found out that you knew, and threatened to kill you if you spoke up, and that you came to me for protection.'

Stoffler digested this before he responded. 'What if Darré doesn't believe it?'

'It's up to you to make sure that he does. I've done what I can to get you off the hook, Stoffler. The case is closed as far as me and my men are concerned. The rest is up to you. I'd be very careful who you trust in future. Who you associate with. Understand?'

Stoffler nodded as he gathered up the photos and slid them back into the folder. Then he paused and sniffed the file. 'A fire, you say?'

Schenke gave him a long, hard stare and injected a measure of threat into his voice when he addressed the other man. 'Don't ask questions that might cause me to change my mind . . . Now get your things and I'll walk you out of the precinct.'

Stoffler hurriedly put on his jacket and coat and placed the file out of sight in his jacket pocket. Then he picked up his hat. 'I'm ready.'

'Before we go, there's something that's been puzzling me. Why did you give us the information about the Vogler printer so readily? You could have gone along with Hauser's line and pinned the blame on the press at Remer's club. That might have distracted us from what was going on at the printworks.'

'Like I said, anyone who knew anything about printing would have told you the Vogler wasn't up to the job. If I hadn't pointed that out, you'd have been suspicious when you did find out.'

'Fair enough.'

They left the cell, walked to the stairs and climbed to the hall. The sound of martial music was still playing from the radio in the canteen, and more uniformed men were crowded about it, smoking as they waited for the next bulletin.

Schenke signed 'Sauckel' out of the log book and walked with him to the entrance of the building. Outside it was a fine spring day and the sun was shining from a clear sky, smiling kindly on the people of Berlin. The street was almost deserted, almost peaceful.

Stoffler turned and held out his hand. 'Thank you, Inspector. I shan't forget this.'

'I'd rather you did. For both our sakes,' Schenke replied, not lifting a hand in response. 'I never want to have any cause to see you again. Just go.'

Stoffler nodded and made his way down the empty street in the direction of the nearest U-Bahn station. Schenke watched him before his gaze was distracted by a vehicle coming in the other direction. A van with two large loudspeakers fixed to its roof. As it approached, there was a crackle before a voice announced, 'People of Germany! People of Germany! This morning the Führer announced the invasion of our enemies' lands. The hour of our deliverance has come! The time to avenge the national humiliation of Versailles is upon us! Germany is rising up to avenge the great wrong that was done to her by the warmongers of France and Britain! The great challenge of our age lies before us. We will meet that challenge and crush all those who dare to stand in our way! Long live sacred Germany! Heil Hitler!'

The van continued a short distance before it blared out a repeat of the message. Schenke lit a cigarette and took a last glance at the serene blue sky before turning to enter the precinct and climb the stairs to the Kripo office.

Historical Note

The Nazi party liked to present itself as morally robust, demanding the highest standards of discipline and virtue from its members, while decrying the integrity of its political opponents and victims in the most robust terms. In reality, the Nazis were venal and violent, with scant regard for the rule of law, and their cult-like status allowed their followers to excuse them of crimes large and small. Sadly, this is common in reactionary populist political movements to the present day.

On seizing power in 1933 the Nazi party cracked down hard on those it defined as criminals. They mainly focused on petty offenders such as pickpockets, prostitutes and vagrants, who were labelled as 'un-German'. Repeat offenders were often sent to the camps for 're-education'. Other 'criminals' included any and all political opponents of the Party, trade unionists, homosexuals and those who failed to subscribe to the ideology and doctrines of the Nazi movement. In contrast, the criminality of Nazi party members was either covered up or treated far more leniently. The reactionary nature of those who ran the German courts and the far-right politics of many in the police force enabled the criminality of the Nazis, even before they came to power. Those found guilty of violence towards and even murder of political opponents were given farcically light sentences or were exonerated altogether. When Hitler and his cronies attempted a coup in 1923, resulting in a number of deaths as they marched on the seat of power in Munich, the ringleaders were presented as 'patriots' and suffered the lightest of prison sentences for their actions. Those who recognised the danger of treating the Nazis leniently and warned of the consequences were treated as fear-mongers, particularly by the right-wing press and the oligarchs who sought to use the Nazis to protect their wealth.

There were many other law-breakers in Berlin at this time. The kinds of crime gangs depicted in *A Death in Berlin* thrived during the heady Weimar years and continued to do so under the Nazi regime. Like the Mafia, they developed extensive networks of underworld contacts and were run in a hierarchical fashion by mob bosses who insisted on strict codes of conduct, with harsh penalties for those who broke their rules or ran up against them. The gangs of Remer and Guttmann are based on the so called 'ring clubs' whose members originally wore distinctive rings to identify themselves. After the Nazis came to power, greater discretion was required to conceal their identities. Most of these men were hardened criminals who had served time in prison, and they provided a ready supply of recruits for the gangs when they were released.

Although the Nazi leadership promised to crack down on the gangs, they were hampered by the high degree of loyalty in the gang members, who adhered to the 'omerta' demanded by their bosses. The gangs therefore continued to thrive, and the regime often turned a blind eye to some of their activities, particularly their dealings in the black market. Besides their established influence and codes of loyalty, the gangs were also helped by the straightforward corruption of those now in power. Senior Nazi officials were fond of their luxuries, and many were more than willing to overlook the illicit activities of those who could keep them supplied with the kind of goods that became scarce as the war progressed. Given the need to demonstrate the rectitude of the government to the public, an occasional seedy character was thrown to the wolves. Those at the very top, no matter how corrupt, were immune, however. Then, as now.

As a consequence, policemen like Criminal Inspector Schenke, and those on his team, had to tread very carefully when dealing with gang members, who might have powerful political connections. This was an additional burden when working within a regime that was, to all intents and purposes, a ruthless criminal kleptocracy that tolerated no opposition to its extreme political ideology.